Praise for

Time Rovers – Book 1

Award-winning!

Winner 2006 ForeWord Magazine's Book of the Year Award~Editor's Choice for Fiction

Winner Independent Publisher Book Award 2006~Gold Medal Science Fiction & Fantasy

Winner 2006 Golden Quill Award Paranormal Category

Winner 2006 Bookseller's Best Award Paranormal Category

Winner 2006 Daphne du Maurier Award Paranormal Catagory

Winner 2006 Prism Award Time Travel Category

Compton Crook Award Finalist

National Readers' Choice Award Finalist

Pluto Award Winner

‡

"A rousing mystery-adventure..."
~ Baryon Magazine

‡

"Sojourn is a rare, well-researched and entertaining tale of time travel set against the backdrop of Victorian England and the Whitechapel Murders."
~ Casebook: Jack the Ripper

‡

"This is a brilliant novel... Put this one on your list of absolute must-reads."
~ Coffee Time Romance (5 Coffee Cups)

‡

SOJOURN

JANA G. OLIVER

WWW.DRAGONMOONPRESS.COM

Sojourn: Time Rovers~Book 1

ISBN 10: 1-896944-30-2 Print Edition
ISBN 13: 978-1-896944-302

ISBN 10: 1-896944-41-8 Electronic Edition

CIP Data on file with the National Library of Canada

Dragon Moon Press is an Imprint of Hades Publications Inc.
P.O. Box 1714, Calgary, Alberta, T2P 2L7, Canada

www.dragonmoonpress.com

Dragon Moon Press and Hades Publications, Inc. acknowledges the ongoing support of the Canada Council for the Arts and the Alberta Foundation for the Arts for our publishing programme.

The Alberta Foundation for the Arts
COMMITTED TO THE DEVELOPMENT OF CULTURE AND THE ARTS

Alberta
COMMUNITY DEVELOPMENT

Canada Council for the Arts   Conseil des Arts du Canada

Printed and bound in the United States.

S⊕JOURN

JANA G. OLIVER

WWW.TIMEROVERS.COM

To those who pursue
'The Great Victorian Mystery'

&

To the women of the East End
Requiescat in Pace

Acknowledgements

Just like time travel, there are many people behind the scenes who make the magic happen. Without their support, Jacynda, Alastair and Jonathon would just be rattling around in my head instead of yours.

* It all began with the infamous Tee Morris, fellow author and force of nature. He 'paid it forward' so far that my heroine will still owe him in 2057. Liberal rations of rum don't begin to even the debt, my friend.

* Gwen Gades, publisher of Dragon Moon Press, took a gamble with my odd notions of time travelers, shape-shifters and Jack the Ripper.

* Editor Adrienne deNoyelles gently prodded me toward a better story while teaching me the finer points of punctuation, all in record time. Her insight into the characters was uncanny and her humor decidedly wicked. Bless you!

Others who contributed include:

* The delightful J.R. Fisher, whose generous contribution to the Wake Co. Literacy Council during the Trinoc*coN Charity Auction earned him the plum role of Chief Inspector J.R. Fisher.

* Ripperologists Ally Reineke and Judith Stock (a noted collector of the weird and arcane) vetted my manuscript so my Victorian and Ripper facts were correct and my fiction plausible.

* Thanks to: Aarti, Christine, Dwain, Eva, Fredda, Nanette, Ron, Teresa and Vally, the writers group that held my toes to fire. Thanks guys!

* Many thanks to Nanette Littlestone and Tyra Mitchell for their extensive input on the rough manuscript.

* Cover art is, well, an art. I am blessed by the creative genius of two professional artists: L.W. (Lynn) Perkins who created Jacynda's image and Christina Yoder who designed the cover. They're an awesome team.

* Research is the lifeblood of a good plot. Doubly so when writing historical fiction. My infinite respect and gratitude goes to Stephen Ryder for his magnificent website, Casebook: Jack the Ripper. (www.casebook.org). It is a priceless resource. In addition, my thanks to all those who answered my curious questions about the crimes and the times.

* My regards to Lee Jackson, purveyor of The Victorian Dictionary website (www.victorianlondon.org) for his incredible collection of Victorian articles and minutiae.

* A tip of my hat to Hywel Williams for assistance regarding the London Underground in 1888. His excellent website may be found at: (http://underground-history.co.uk/front.php)

* To Linda Craigg (CMT/NMT) and Dr. Ross Jacobson for keeping my body healthy as I spent long hours at the keyboard.

* A thanks to Melody and Steve Black who allowed me to use Casa Black in Las Vegas for a writer's sabbatical. The Elf cookies were deliciously fattening!

* Fellow authors Michelle Roper and P.C. Cast were always there to commiserate when things weren't going right and to celebrate when they were.

* To Harold, the ever-patient husband, who valiantly offers plot advice while soaking in the hot tub, edits my verbose prose and knows when it's best to be very, very quiet so I can work.

* And finally, Midnight the cat: GET OFF MY KEYBOARD!

Author's Notes

What was I thinking? Why would anyone try to weave a story around one of the most widely known crime sprees in history? And, to add to the stress, include time travel and a new kind of shape-shifter? I have to admit this book has been one of the most challenging projects I've undertaken. I wanted the 1888 bits to be accurate, the 2057 bits to be unnerving, the shape-shifters completely different and still manage to tell a good story.

The mistakes are mine. I embrace them. None of us is perfect, especially those who poke our noses into history. No matter how many little pushpins you jam into maps and how many books you scour, you're going to miss something.

How much is real, you ask? When I wrote about the two constables hauling an inebriated Kate Eddowes off to Bishopsgate Police Station to sober up on the night she met her end, that actually happened. When I mention street names, they existed in 1888. I tried very hard to ensure that all the facts relating to the Whitechapel murders were spot on. The mob's attempt to hang Alastair was based on more than one incident where Whitechapel's skittish citizens grew a little too zealous. The cost of an East End prostitute was a pittance, their lives brutal and short. Who was Jack the Ripper? I leave that to history and to the 'Ripperologists'.

For those of you wanting to know more about the Whitechapel murders and Late Victorian England, visit my website (www.janaoliver.com). You can view my extensive bibliography, pour over maps and learn a few Victorian tidbits in the process.

"Time is an illusion, lunchtime doubly so." Douglas Adams

Jana Oliver
Atlanta, GA
December 2005

"The greatness of Evil lies in its awful accuracy. Without that deadly talent for being in the right place at the right time, Evil must suffer defeat. For unlike its opposite, Good, Evil is allowed no human failings, no miscalculations. Evil must be perfect...or depend upon the imperfections of others."

—*The Outer Limits*

1

Pompeii, August, 79 A.D.

The sky was falling.

Pumice stones rained in a dissonant curtain, shattering roof tiles and clattering in the courtyards. An amphora near Jacynda Lassiter's feet exploded. Crimson wine splashed her pure-white stola, cascading onto the ornate tiles. She braced herself in the doorway as an earth tremor rocked the walls of the villa, her eyes flooding from the scorching stench of sulfur.

She wiped away tears with the back of her hand. "Alfred Bartlesby?" The academic didn't acknowledge her, his pale, bald head bent over a table illuminated by the anemic light of a half-dozen oil lamps. He huddled over a mound of papyrus scrolls, seemingly oblivious to Vesuvius' rage.

"Bartlesby?" she called again.

Cynda turned at the sound of a choked sob. A terrified girl, infant in arms, fled along the street.

Cynda shivered at the sight. They were racing toward their graves. There was no sanctuary to be found here. The once-thriving metropolis of Pompeii, the jewel of Campania, was about to become an ashy footprint in history.

Her distraction had cost valuable time. "Bartlesby?" she called again, taking a few steps forward. The academic still ignored her, murmuring to himself as he furiously inscribed notes. One of the lamps guttered and died, but he didn't notice.

"Hey!" she shouted. "The bus is leaving!"

Bartlesby glanced up, surprised to see her. "Ah, well, actually, I would like to stay a while longer." He pointed at the papers in front of him. "I have a bit more work to do."

"Not an option," she called over the sound of the pounding stones on the roof. Ash filtered downward from the ceiling, from every crack and crevice, cloaking them in a fine layer.

"I paid extra to stay until the last moment," Bartlesby protested.

Cynda swore under her breath. This one was a linguist. He'd be hard to budge. She opened the case of the golden pocket watch nestled in her palm. The time interface's digital display hovered in the murky air above the watch.

"It is the last minute, Mr. Bartlesby. You are about to become a permanent fixture of the Pompeian landscape."

His eyes widened. "So soon?" Still he made no effort to rise.

Exasperated, she grabbed the academic's pudgy arm, hauling him off the low stool. He juggled his scrolls, grasping them to his chest while stammering protests. A parchment tumbled out of his fingers as they reached the door. He bent to collect it.

The digital display flashed bright red.

Time Incursion Warning!

Cynda leaned out into the street and stared up at the boiling mountain. An unearthly roar split the air, nearly deafening her. Death surged toward them—an impenetrable wall of superheated material, the pyroclastic flow that would entomb the city for sixteen hundred years.

"Oh, my God." Cynda's hand shook so violently, it took her two attempts to perform the required maneuver to initiate the transfer—wind the watch stem four times forward, two back, three forward, one back. A hum emanated from the device, barely audible over the cacophony of destruction.

The holographic clock wavered in the murky air, counting the seconds until the transfer.

3...2...1...

Cynda closed her eyes and prayed as the characteristic halo encompassed them. A moment before they shifted into the future, blistering heat shrouded them. In the distance, she heard the agonized screams of those who had no means of escape.

‡

2057 A.D.

Time Immersion Corporation

Cynda bit her lip in frustration, waiting in the penitent posture until the disorientation lessened. Apparently, Bartlesby forgot that part of his pre-transfer briefing as he struggled to his sandaled feet. He was back on his knees in an instant, retching.

When she finally stood, the 'tourist', as the customers were euphemistically called, was out of the time pod and teetering toward the Arrivals Lounge, flanked by two customer service reps. One toted his stack of papyrus, nodding her head in agreement while Bartlesby babbled incoherently, windmilling his arms to indicate explosions. A trail of ash cascaded from his stola. In his wake, one of the DomoBots tidied up the mess with electronic expertise.

Cynda was in no hurry to climb out of the time pod. Every Time Rover had a personal ritual to reorient to the Now. Some recited off-color nursery rhymes, others counted back from one hundred until they felt their brain cells stabilize. Cynda's trick involved wedging herself in the door of the garlic-shaped time pod and inventorying the chronsole room: the 'Reorientation to Place' technique.

She began her mental checklist. *Corporate cobalt decor—check. High ceilings—check. Ergo chairs and desks—check. Bored employees—check. Low thrum of technology just one notch above my tolerance level—check.*

Concerned eyes peered over the top of the chronsole counter.

"Hey!" Ralph called in greeting. That's why she'd gotten out of Pompeii alive—Ralph had been the chronsole operator. He was known for swift extractions.

"Hey," she responded in a dry whisper. Clearing her throat made no difference—most of Vesuvius still seemed lodged there.

Her first few steps out of the pod would have made a drunk proud. Until she put chocolate into her system, her equilibrium would be on the fritz, along with her sense of humor. PTS—Post Transfer Syndrome. It beat PMS hands down.

Behind her, the pod door closed and went into what they jokingly called 'Spin Dry': a maintenance cycle that reminded her of one of those old front-loading washing machines.

She halted at the chronsole desk and leaned on the nano-laminate top. It was currently a fetching shade of blue. At the beginning of each hour, it shifted color to add visual excitement to the work environment. In Cynda's opinion, it failed miserably.

"Hey," Ralph repeated, his glasses reflecting the overhead lights. Most folks had their eyesight corrected by an OpticBot, but not Ralph. He said the glasses made a statement.

Without prompting, he pushed a candy bar across the counter, one of the vintage kind with loads of sugar and preservatives. No high-protein, high-energy wallpaper bricks for her. Peeling off the wrapper with all the finesse of a gorilla, she demolished the first bar. Her hands continued to shake. He thoughtfully liberated the second candy bar, eyes blinking rapidly to overcome the stench of sulfur that seemed to envelope her. Wisely, he didn't comment.

Her mouth half-full of chocolate, she demanded, "Why in the hell are we cutting these so close? Why couldn't I have snagged him a couple days earlier? If the transfer hadn't worked..." She trailed off, attempting to short-circuit the profound tremor running the length of her body. The jump from Pompeii had been suicidal, even for a Senior Time Rover. Neither she nor Bartlesby were meant to be entombed with the city. The discovery of their bodies during the excavations in the Eighteenth Century would have required a lot of 'fixing'. Either way, she and the tourist would be dead.

Ralph looked genuinely chagrined. "I guess marketing is trying to make up last quarter's shortfall. The longer the tourist is on site, the more money. It's all a matter of economics—at least from TIC's point of view."

"Economics? Do they have any idea how those people died?" she demanded, the image of the young girl cradling the child replaying in her mind.

"No, they probably don't. Marketing's never been real strong on reality." Ralph lowered his voice. "I'm really sorry, Cyn. I wouldn't have made you go that close to the end. I'd have fudged the time."

Her anger melted. It wasn't right for her to chew on him. Ralph always looked out for her. They'd been buddies ever since he'd beaned her over the head with an alphabet block in pre-school and she'd promptly retaliated with a toy truck. They'd both been sent home with notes to their respective parents. From that moment on, they were joined at the hip. Lovers came and went, but Ralph was a constant.

"All we need is for one of these guys to croak and—"

He touched her arm, and she fell silent. A statuesque blonde customer rep was exiting the Departures Lounge, guiding a middle-aged couple toward one of the time pods.

"You'll see, Marjorie, it'll be fun," the man said, tucking a hip flask into the pocket of his voluminous raccoon coat. The woman shook her head in dismay, apparently not as keen about the upcoming adventure as her husband. The rep ushered them inside the pod and encouraged them to relax.

"You'll be at your destination shortly," the rep said with practiced ease.

"I have motion sickness," the woman warned.

"Not a problem. No motion involved."

Ralph and Cynda traded looks. This lady was in for a helluva surprise. "A forty-story plunge down a drainpipe" was how one Rover described it. Oddly enough, the length of the drop didn't seem to change no matter how much time you covered; just one long drop, followed by a very sudden stop.

The rep tapped her high heels over to deliver the Time Order and a warm smile to Ralph. She leaned against the chronsole, her well-rounded bottom jutting in the air. It was too perfect—no doubt the latest in posterior implants. Perky one day, sultry the next. You decided what you wanted your butt to look like, and the implant changed to match your expectations. From what Cynda heard, they cost a fortune. Apparently, customer reps made more than Rovers.

"Hi, Ralph," the blonde said, her voice low and full of promise.

His eyes twinkled. "Hi there. Are we still on for dinner?"

She beamed. "Sure are. And dessert, I hope."

"Always dessert," Ralph replied.

Cynda noshed her way through another candy bar, watching the pair with amusement. For some reason, Ralph's silver-streaked ponytail and oval, Teddy Roosevelt glasses simply mesmerized young women. It never made sense, but the beneficiary accepted he was a skirt magnet. Last week, it had been a brunette in accounting. Today, it was Miss Well-Rounded Caboose in the nostalgia heels.

The blonde threw Cynda a sidelong glance. With a decided sniff, she returned to business. "The Hartmans are scheduled for 1925 Chicago. Mr. Hartman wants to get a glimpse of Al Capone."

"Roaring Twenties Chicago," Ralph said, inserting the nano-drive containing the Time Order into his terminal. His fingers flew over the touchscreen as the entries scrolled in the air. Studying the order, he observed, "A seven-dayer. Big bucks for that."

"It's their thirty-fifth wedding anniversary," the rep replied. "Mr. Hartman wants to give his wife something special and then write a few 'man on the scene' articles for *Roaring '20s Retro Magazine*."

Ralph raised an eyebrow, double-checked his entries and announced, "Ready."

The rep nodded her approval. "Go for it." He hesitated, looking around. "Which Rover's handling the Outbound?"

"No one."

Ralph shot Cynda a quick look. "They're flying solo?"

"New policy," the rep replied. "Unless it's a dangerous locale, no need for an Insertion Escort."

"Chicago in the middle of a gang war? Nah, no danger there," Ralph grumbled.

A noncommittal shrug from the rep. "You know Corporate."

Ralph muttered under his breath as he keyed in the approval code. The pod door closed automatically. A few seconds later, the couple haloed their way into the past. The vid-monitor didn't transmit Mrs. Hartman's final words, but her wide eyes and quaking hand at her mouth delivered the message effectively enough.

"Incoming," Ralph said, waggling an eyebrow. A moment later, a reassuring "Chron Transfer Complete" emanated from the computer speaker. The blonde tromped off, her heels making a racket. Her fanny wiggled unnaturally in time with her strides.

"No Outbound Rover?" Cynda muttered. "This isn't a good sign, Ralph."

"Time to polish the old vid-résumé, I think."

Cynda bent over the chronsole and smirked. "I see you're working your way through the customer *rep-tile* pool," she chided, indicating the retreating blonde.

"Be nice. She's a blast."

"Oh, I bet. You just like her designa-tush."

"Hey, you're not the only one to get time lag, you know," Ralph protested. "Since I don't like chocolate, sex is the best way to cure it."

"Nonsense. All you chron-ops get are hangnails."

Ralph frowned and promptly retaliated. "You have another assignment."

"What? You've gotta to be kidding me!" Cynda's eyes danced around the room, hunting for the boss. "Where is that moron?"

"Referring to our fearless leader as a moron, though technically correct, is probably not a good career move," Ralph advised. He conscientiously opened another candy wrapper and handed over the contents.

She shook her head, waving the candy bar in her agitation. "I'm not going anywhere. TIC owes me eight days off. I've just set a new world's record for time leaps."

"Actually, not. I believe that Harter Defoe did that in—"

"I don't need a walking encyclopedia. I'm going to get this settled and go home. I need some...down time." She blinked, but it did no good. It looked as if someone had stuck a crimson filter in front of her eyes. The chocolate wasn't having the desired effect against the time lag.

Ralph's mouth twitched into a slow, libidinous grin. "Down time?"

She refused to be baited. "Where is our fearless leader?"

"Thad's gone for the day. Meeting at Corporate." Ralph pushed a pulsating hot pink nano-drive across the counter and pointed toward the Rover's locker room. "Hie thee hence. I don't want you busting my eardrums when you find out where you're going."

Hot pink? "An Overdue? Where?"

Instead of answering her, he logged himself out and rose from his chair. A young man stood nearby, digital clipboard in hand. The next shift had arrived.

"Where?" Cynda demanded, reluctant to claim the nano-drive and obligate herself.

Ralph pointedly ignored her. Addressing his replacement, he said, "Five out today. One Overdue. Cynda's handling that." Before she could complain, he pushed the hot pink time bomb closer toward her and commanded, "Away, loud strumpet."

Her eyes narrowed. "I could refuse this, you know. I have enough seniority."

"You could," Ralph said. They both knew she wouldn't.

He donned a set of vintage headphones, adjusting them on his ears. Classic Led Zeppelin wafted around him. Waving, he hiked toward the double doors at the far end of the Chronsole Bay.

"Be sure to say hello to Oscar for me," he called right before the doors thudded behind him.

"Oscar?" Cynda repeated. "Oscar who?"

The next shift's chron-op plopped in the chair, executing a sunny smile in her direction. He looked all of twelve. Her mind rummaged for his name. *Irving? No, that's not right.* She conjured up the mnemonic. *Ivan the Infant.* That was it. Ivan. *What had his parents been thinking?*

Bewildered, she scooped up the drive and headed for the closest empty desk. Jamming the drive into a port, she fidgeted as the information materialized at eye level.

Retrieval Order—Overdue Tourist
Location: London, East End
Date: August 25, 1888 A.D.
Time Grid: Late Victorian
Wardrobe Code: LVL1888F—Class 4
Due: August 21, 1888 A.D.

"1888? Oscar...Wilde." *Oh, damn.*

"Thad, you son of a..." Cynda let the oath trail off, realizing it was wasted. He knew she loathed Victorian London, rated it right up there with Europe in the throes of the Black Death. She scanned the rest of the order.

Tourist Name: Michael A. Turner
Profession: Professor of Sociology
Age: 57
Last Known Location: A. Phillip's Boarding House
Address: New Castle Street, Whitechapel
Special Instructions: Insert Rover on 8/24/88 for retrieval.

She checked the time date again. TIC was cutting it close—no one was allowed in London after August 26. Company policy.

"Just like having four days off between leaps," she muttered. She studied the digital image of the missing academic; he looked like someone's granddad. Maybe this trip wouldn't be that hard, after all.

To escape the smiling child at the chronsole, Cynda carried the nano-drive to the locker room. Flipping the drive into her locker, she peeled off the stola. As she prepared to toss it in the recycling basket, she spied the scorch marks. A shudder coursed through her.

"Too damned close." To get her mind off the near-fatal encounter, she selected her favorite peach body wash. After a moment's thought, she slung it back in the locker. Given where she was headed, a shower was a complete waste of time. After a moment, she picked it up again. There was one more stop to make before she headed to London, and for that, she shouldn't smell like a lab experiment gone awry.

‡

The door chimed as Cynda entered the deli, a quaint holdover from when restaurant owners actually welcomed each customer in person. She loved Eli's Deli for many reasons, all of them having to do with lack of technology. At other delis, you placed your order using your Personal Security Interface (PSI) as the link. The order was ready when you walked inside the door, the cost auto-debited from your bank account, and the caloric intake added to your nutritional database. No need to talk a real person.

Which is why she adored Eli's; they still relied on the personal touch. Cynda savored the ability to order her food from a human being, not the PSI on her wrist or a gleaming Server-Bot with a false smile and a paper hat.

"Hello, beautiful!" Eli called from behind the counter.

Another reason she loved this place. Eli was in his mid-sixties and learned the business from his father and grandfather, both named Eli Greenwald. She'd dubbed him E3, and he liked it.

"The usual?" he asked, eyeing her closely.

"No, I think I'll have the…" She stared up at the chalkboard listing the day's special. "I'll have the tuna salad on whole wheat, please. And a couple extra kosher pickle spears." She pushed her auto-cooled lunch tote across the counter and they traded looks.

"Fish on wheat, hold mayo, extra mustard and lettuce, two spears, coming up," he intoned, giving her a wink. Scooping up her lunch tote, he vanished into the kitchen to collect the pickles while his daughter made the sandwich at a nearby worktable. Every sandwich was made by hand. Eli swore he could tell if a Bot made his food, though she thought that might be a bit of an exaggeration.

Cynda waved her left hand near the register interface. The cost of the meal vanished from her bank account while the calories were added to her Daily Intake Record for insurance purposes. The register interface beeped.

"Recommend extra mayo and cheese to increase overall body mass," it said.

"Deny," she said.

"Recommend double chocolate milkshake to increase caloric—"

"Deny," she said, frowning.

"Recommend—"

"Override."

The thing beeped and stopped bugging her. Thin was her thing; it was just what the parental DNA had provided. Perfect for being a Rover. Less weight reduced the time lag and the cost of transfers. Unfortunately, the insurance companies didn't see it that way.

Leaning against the counter, Cynda resisted the urge to drum her fingers. Other customers picked up their sandwiches and left. She made sure to look nonchalant, or at least as mellow as one could when committing a criminal act. Word was you got five years for the first conviction, and the numbers piled up with each subsequent brush with the law. She was courting a jail sentence because of the tomato seeds she'd hidden in the bottom of her lunch tote.

It was Blair's fault. Her wild-haired brother had somehow talked their parents into jumping ship—going Off-Grid, as it was called. Now they were stuck *out there*. Because of him they had no health insurance, no guarantee that next year's crop would thrive and they'd have enough to eat, no PSI units, none of the supposed perks of being part of society. They were now *persona non grata*. Because of Blair's boneheaded defiance, she risked everything to smuggle seeds to her parents.

Seeds were money to an Off-Gridder. The non-genetically modified varieties were rare, and easily a quarter of Cynda's paycheck went into each packet. Once her parents had their own supply, her father would be able to establish his medical practice, no matter how rudimentary it might be, and that would generate income. Until that day, she would break the law. If it all fell apart, she'd be the one doing the jail time while Blair played farmer and ranted against the evils of society.

"Creep," she muttered. "I should have drowned you when I had the chance."

Her eyes slipped over the few patrons dining in. Nobody seemed out of place, but then a Gov agent wouldn't. She had to figure her PSI interface would be mum about that, as well. The security geeks would know how to block that information. The PSI was great for scoping out your fellow citizens, but it seemed mute when it came to the Powers That Be.

She heard the double doors open behind her and Eli reappeared, lunch tote in hand. He placed the wrapped sandwich inside and handed over the tote with a smile.

"I picked the crispest pickles for you," Eli said.

"Thanks, E3. I appreciate it. Yours are always the best."

Turning, she caught sight of a man paying a bit too much attention. She knew it wasn't her figure. Ralph had once described her as a pipe cleaner with boobs.

Bluffing, Cynda took her sandwich to a nearby Designated Green Space. The ordinances allowed you to eat in a DGS, providing you weren't there longer than thirty minutes: a rule designed to prevent vagrancy. Stay over the half-an-hour limit, and one of the black and white CopBots would order you to move on.

Settling on one of the ergo benches, she unwrapped the sandwich and took a bite. A satisfied sigh came unbidden; Eli's creations were always heaven. A few benches away, the man who'd been watching her in the deli took a seat, licking a vanilla ice cream cone. A check of the PSI unit on her wrist told Cynda he was 37, single and worked for a mortgage company. On the Social Compatibility Scale, he rated 8.7 out of 10.

Not likely. The chickens were coming home to roost sooner than she'd hoped. The trip to Victorian London took on a new urgency. Maybe the heat would die down while she was gone. If not, she and Eli would be sharing the same cellblock at the Correction Facility. She wondered if E3's wife would be able to smuggle in some dill pickles every now and then.

2

Monday, 24 September, 1888
London

Pressing the coins into the hansom driver's rough hand, Alastair shook his head at the question. "No, you do not need to wait."

"As you wish, sir," the jarvey replied, touching his battered cap in respect. He jiggled the reins, and the cab clattered down the street. Alastair watched it turn the corner as he dropped the remaining coins into his pocket. He regretted spending the money, but he'd run late at the hospital, forcing him to secure a ride to Marylebone. Flipping open his pocket watch revealed it was three minutes until five. He would be on time.

Alastair released a deep sigh as he mounted the stairs to the house. It was a three-story, white stone affair with a glowing gas lamp at the front door. It spoke of money, but then Lord Wescomb was a well-regarded barrister and came from landed gentry. He could easily have afforded a house in Knightsbridge or Mayfair, but preferred to be close to the law courts.

Alastair turned toward the clean and well-lit street. He'd once lived in a place like this, free of worry, free to spend a few coins on a cab journey. All that lay in the past now.

After another deep breath, he knocked on the carved oak door. The maid promptly answered.

"Doctor Alastair Montrose to see Lord and Lady Wescomb, at their request," he said politely. *Summoned to their presence was more like it.* The note he'd received, while cordial, did not allow him the option to decline.

"This way, Doctor," the maid replied.

Alastair stepped inside, glancing about as inconspicuously as possible. The carpets proved richly hued and the walls were of the finest hardwood. The delicate scent of flowers caught his nose. He found the source; an elegant lead crystal vase filled with an abundance of colorful blooms.

Chagrined, he realized the maid waited. He removed his coat and hat, passing them to her. She hung them on a hall tree, exhibiting a calm demeanor he wished he could borrow.

Perhaps the Wescombs wish to donate to the clinic. His mind immediately discarded that fanciful notion. This summons was something else altogether.

Alastair took time to straighten his tie and jacket in the hall mirror, smoothing his hair and moustache. He looked as presentable as a young physician might, given his reduced circumstances. He'd made a point of wearing his best suit and polishing his shoes. A downward glance revealed they'd survived the journey in tolerable shape.

"They're in his lordship's study," the maid advised, gesturing down the long hall.

When they reached their destination, Alastair hesitated at the study door, as if retreat remained an option. Inside, he heard the reassuring sounds of a crackling fire and low voices. The maid gave him an inquisitive look. He nodded for her to proceed. She knocked and was readily granted entrance.

The room proved surprisingly intimate, with tall bookshelves on three walls and a massive hearth on the fourth. Lady Sephora Wescomb sat in a brocade chair near the stone fireplace, her intelligent eyes observing him with a hawk's intensity. Her silvered hair glinted in the gaslight in contrast to her deep-purple gown. It was cut in the latest fashion, with black lace at the bosom and at the cuffs. Her husband, Lord Wescomb, leaned back in a heavily padded chair with a faint look of amusement, adjusting his embroidered waistcoat over a slight paunch. Alastair delivered a nod in his lordship's direction and it was returned. He followed suit with the lady of the house.

"Come in, Doctor," Lady Sephora commanded, executing a graceful gesture toward a chair set equidistant between herself and her husband.

"Thank you, Lady Wescomb," Alastair replied as the maid closed the door behind him.

"You haven't changed a bit, young man," Lord Wescomb observed with a bemused chuckle.

"Thank you, my lord." Alastair settled into the chair, ill at ease.

A glass of sherry rested on a walnut table near his elbow. He reached for the liquor and sipped, waiting for his hosts to open the conversation.

Lady Sephora's form abruptly shifted, strawberry-blonde tresses replacing the silver, her matronly figure exchanged for a girlish shape. Wescomb altered as well, his hair now dark and his face thin. Indeed, the pair now appeared as they might have two decades earlier.

"Are you not going *en mirage?*" Lady Sephora's voice matched her youthful appearance.

Alastair shook his head. "No, thank you. I have no need to do so." The moment after he spoke, he inwardly grimaced. He'd foolishly reminded his hosts of his aberrant behavior.

"Surely you go *en mirage* on occasion," she said.

"No, I don't."

The Wescombs traded looks. "Not at all?" Lady Sephora pressed, adopting a puzzled tone.

Alastair felt the trap closing. "No."

The low sigh from his hostess sounded like a reproof. In contrast, Lord Wescomb's face gained a slight smile.

"You always were a maverick," he said. From his lordship's mouth, it sounded like a blessing.

"I am not like the others, my lord."

"In that you are wrong," Wescomb retorted, his voice changing timbre in an instant. "You are more one of us than you wish to believe."

Alastair drained the liquor, set the delicate crystal glass on the table and rose, knowing he risked angering his hosts with such an abrupt departure.

"Thank you for the sherry. If that is all, I must—"

"Please, Doctor," Lady Sephora urged, gesturing toward the empty chair. "Don't make a scene. We are merely concerned for your health."

"I appreciate your concern; however, I cannot live as you prescribe. I do not wish to embrace this...*transitory* existence you so readily cultivate."

An awkward moment ensued; the urge to flee barely held in check by the social graces. Alastair stared into the fire, debating his next move. The gaslights on either side of the mantel hissed into the silence.

"I understand you no longer practice with Dr. Hanson in Mayfair," Lord Wescomb said.

Sensing a merciful shift of topic, Alastair returned to his seat.

He elected not to ask how his host knew about his change of venue. Apparently, the Transitive community paid more attention to him than he cared to admit.

"Yes, there have been changes in my professional life. I now practice at the London Hospital and a small clinic in Whitechapel."

"I see. Do you enjoy your work at the clinic?" Wescomb asked, leaning forward in his chair.

Alastair gave a faint smile. "Infinitely so. The conditions are of the most primitive nature, and the people of the lowest sort, but they are grateful for any help they receive. They have so little."

"Indeed."

"When did you begin your work in Whitechapel?" Lady Sephora asked.

The relevance of the question puzzled Alastair. "In mid-July."

"I understand that Dr. Hanson was quite displeased with you," Wescomb said.

"We disagreed as to which patients I should treat."

"What I heard about that young boy was true, then?" Wescomb asked.

Alastair shifted uncomfortably, adjusting his jacket. *What was the purpose of this close questioning?* "Dr. Hanson refused to allow me to treat the injured boy in the surgery. He didn't want our patients to think we attended those of the *lesser classes,* as he put it." Alastair's jaw tightened at the memory of their argument.

"We have been to the East End, *en mirage.* It was most disheartening," Lady Sephora observed with a distant expression on her face, as if she could still see the filthy streets and the ragged ghosts that inhabited them.

"They want for the most basic necessities," Alastair said.

"What of Hanson's daughter, Evelyn? Are you still engaged?" Wescomb asked out of the blue.

The query snapped Alastair back to the moment. He noted the pair switched back and forth, as if this had been rehearsed.

"We have broken our engagement. Evelyn has requested that I no longer see her. She cannot fathom why I wish to treat the poor. She deems it a waste of my talent."

"Not surprising," Wescomb huffed. "Evelyn always struck me as quite shallow. I said the same to Sephora after the first time I met her."

Lady Sephora nodded. "Which I believe was the first time we met you, Doctor. At the Endicotts' party. You and Evelyn never seemed to be a matched set, if you follow my meaning."

Alastair opened his mouth to protest, then abandoned the effort. They were correct, though it stung to admit it. Evelyn heeded her father in all things, even the matter of a potential husband.

Alastair's eyes drifted to his hostess. Sephora Wescomb was the converse of young Evelyn; she valued her independence and exercised her brilliant mind regularly, much to the annoyance of most males. Lord Wescomb seemed to comprehend that his wife was as rare as a clear day in London and should be cherished as such.

"Are you courting someone at present?" the lady asked after a diminutive sip of sherry.

That was over the mark. "Is there some reason I'm here?" Alastair asked, chafing to be away from the probing questions.

Wescomb replied, "We've been instructed to make these inquiries, Doctor."

"By The Conclave?"

A brusque nod. "There are rare few of our kind that do not go *en mirage,* and The Conclave wishes to ascertain your mental health. It is not regarded as wholesome to avoid our true natures."

"I am not unbalanced, if that is your concern."

"Perhaps not yet. Still, you live outside the rules, and especially during this time it is dangerous to do so," Wescomb advised.

"I remain circumspect. I don't flaunt myself like Keats."

Wescomb quickly nodded in agreement. "Keats does have his fun, but be assured that at present, all are under orders to appear as pedestrian as our fellow citizens. What with these unseemly murders in the East End, it is vital that we remain out of public scrutiny."

"Then how does my behavior present a problem?"

"Our particular endowment must be exercised or it will run amok," the lady cautioned.

Alastair shook his head. "It never has with me. I have control of it."

Lady Sephora's expression grew stern. "So you have said in the past, and I must admit you have mastered your need to go *en mirage* quite well. However, even the best of us will eventually succumb—"

Alastair rose abruptly. "I resent the implication that I cannot keep myself in check."

Wescomb rose as well, and his voice took on a hard edge. "If my good lady and I are unable to overcome this...predilection, then why do you believe *you* are so invincible?"

"With all due respect, Lord Wescomb, I just am. May I now be excused?"

His hosts studied each other until Lady Sephora gave a resigned nod.

"Please be cautious, Doctor. Many eyes are upon you," she said.

"As always, my lady," he replied with open discontent.

Without further pleasantries, he departed the room at a brisk march. Brushing aside the maid's assistance at the front door, Alastair collected his coat and hat and exited onto the street. Twilight hung in the air. The street's deepening shadows matched his mood.

Inside the study, Wescomb sank into his chair with a long exhalation. "The boy is riding for a fall, I think. No one is capable of denying our legacy. He is a fool to think he can."

His wife rose and closed the door in a rustle of silk. "He'll learn it soon enough."

"What will The Conclave do?" Wescomb asked.

"I am not sure," she said. "They are so skittish at present. Knowing they have a rogue, even one as well mannered as Alastair, may cause them to react irrationally. They are most adamant that our young doctor be held accountable for his unhealthy behavior."

"Let us hope this East End lunatic ceases his reign of terror and normalcy returns."

The lady's face grew thoughtful as she returned to her chair. "And that the fiend is not one of ours."

Wescomb shook his head vigorously. "Good God, Sephora, I really can't believe—"

"It does not matter what either of us believes, John! It's what The Conclave presumes. If they are convinced that Alastair is behind this butchery..."

Silence descended as each mulled the implications. Wescomb poured himself another glass of sherry. His wife held out hers, and he performed the honors.

She studied the amber liquor. "We must pray for Alastair's future...and his sanity," she said softly.

Wescomb nodded solemnly. They drained their drinks. After only a moment's hesitation, both hurled the crystal into the blazing fireplace. The remnants of the alcohol flared brilliantly, and then vanished in the flames.

✝

It took many blocks before Alastair's temper cooled, his anger replaced by gnawing unease. A sensible man wouldn't have lost his temper. The Wescombs had shrewdly attacked his weakest point: the urge to go *en mirage*. By resisting it, the urge only grew stronger. Though the Wescombs were circumspect in their practices, others of his kind regularly adopted bizarre forms and saw it as a grand charade.

"It's still a dangerous game," he muttered, "and I shall not play it."

When he became aware of his surroundings, he found himself on Threadneedle Street near the Bank of England. Pausing at an intersection, on a whim Alastair cut south toward the Thames, keen to judge how the new bridge was progressing. Something about the nascent structure always brightened his spirits, gave him hope.

As he stood along the riverside near the Tower of London, a slight breeze danced over the Thames. In the distance, he could see the massive concrete piers breaking the surface like two continents rising from the depths. Fascinated at this marvel of engineering, he'd eagerly followed the news articles, relishing every minor detail. He could hardly wait until the first time the structure's twin spans rose heavenward to allow a ship to pass beneath.

"Amazing," he murmured.

Shifting his gaze toward the East End, he felt his melancholy return, descending on him like a thick London 'particular'.

"Such deprivation within sight of such a marvel. How can it be like that?" he mused.

The Tower of London's high gray walls loomed in the darkness as he hiked the Minories and then north toward St. Botolph's Church. As always, he was transfixed by the women trolling the exterior, circumnavigating the church like fallen angels in search of holy redemption. They'd learned that if they kept moving, they wouldn't be arrested for prostitution.

Various offers came his way, but he ignored them as he made his trek along Whitechapel High Street and then onto Commercial Street. The thoroughfare bustled with bodies; costermongers hawked their fruits and vegetables in strident voices. A newsboy chanted the latest scandal while a potman dished out pints of porter and stout to waiting customers. A lamplighter descended to the street, his task complete. Above him, the gas lamp spread its limited glow. "All-a-bloomin'," a flower merchant called as a young man chose a red rose for his sweetheart. The grating squeak of a wheelbarrow announced a scrap iron merchant wending his way through the teeming throng.

"Sir, spare a tuppence? I can get a bed if you do that, sir," a tattered woman wearing a threadbare shawl called from her place on the street. Before her sat a battered wooden bowl inhabited by a solitary copper coin. Alastair knelt and placed two pence in the woman's hand, rolling her dirty fingers over the disks. She blinked in surprise at his touch.

"Bless you, sir," she said. "I'll not use it for drink. I swear it."

"I know." He could ill afford to give away even a few pence, but something about the woman struck his heart. "May God bless you," he said as he rose.

Partially obscured in the shadows of a doorway, a young woman asked in a husky voice, "Fancy some company, luv?"

Alastair ignored her. She persisted, catching up with him as he navigated his way through the dense crowd.

"Come now, luv, don't be that way."

He gave her a sharp look. Something felt odd, though her appearance gave no doubt as to her station in life: a plain, lower-class girl wearing a cheap straw hat, mismatched clothes and carrying a worn umbrella. Grabbing his arm, she forced him to match her pace. A strange tingle flooded through him, heralding the presence of one of his kind *en mirage*. Only one person would be so bold as to approach him in this manner.

Alastair glared and whispered, "By the devil, Keats, is that you?"

The young woman tittered. "Why do you think that?"

Indeed, it was Jonathon Keats, the rascal who claimed to be his friend. Alastair tried to shake himself free, but his companion clutched his arm like a beggar would a gold sovereign.

"Stop squirming," the *girl* whispered, and then flashed a smile at a passing tradesman. "You'll attract attention."

That was rich. "What are you doing?"

"Hunting the killer, you see," Keats replied in a conspiratorial whisper, revealing no hint of the man underneath.

"Do you not realize the danger your stunt poses?"

"I'm not the one who was summoned to our lordship's house tonight." Leaning in closer, pressing against his forearm, Keats asked, "Just how did that go? Did they give you twenty whacks on the bum and make you stand in the corner?"

This time, Alastair did manage to shake the nuisance free, and none too gently. In a swift gesture, he propelled them down an alley. Jamming *her* up against the sooty brickwork, he snarled, "How did you know I was with the Wescombs?" *Is Keats spying on me for The Conclave?*

"Oh, really, Alastair. Your name is on quite a few lips, old boy. Word is that you've gone *Opaque* on us."

Alastair's mouth twitched. "I prefer not to play around like you do," he retorted.

"I don't play; I conduct experiments," Keats announced in a grand tone. "Just like any great scientist."

"Just like any proper madman, you mean."

A couple entered the alley: a tradesman and a prostitute by the looks of them. After a quick glance in their direction, the woman hiked her skirts and leaned back against the brick wall as the man undid his pants, seemingly unconcerned that they were not alone.

"Oh, God," Alastair said, averting his eyes. With a smirk, his companion did the same.

"Just a knee-trembler," Keats said, employing the vernacular. "Nothing to be alarmed about. In fact, if you want to blend in," *she* said, mischievously reaching for her skirts.

Alastair shoved the irritant further along the dark alley. "Why does The Conclave care what I'm doing?" he whispered, mindful of the couple behind them.

That earned him an amused look. "You confound them. You don't play by the rules. They're uneasy with anyone who doesn't blindly follow their lead."

"I am minding my own business. Can't they see that?" Alastair insisted

"No, they can't. Besides, this isn't all fun and frolic," Keats said, his voice less gleeful than before. "It's what we need to do to survive. Fortunately, it harms no one...unlike some vices."

Alastair glared. "I will debate that last statement until my dying day."

"Which might not be too far away if you keep denying your heritage, my friend," Keats remarked. "You know what that can cause."

"I shall not become...unstable."

Keats shrugged. "Old Roger Diamond said the same thing. I've heard he's confined in a straitjacket now, thumping his brains against the walls of his family's manor house in Dorset."

"I am not so inclined," Alastair persisted.

"Maybe not, but *they* prefer predictability."

"I'm quite predictable," Alastair protested, his voice rising higher than he intended.

"Nonsense. Predictable people don't toss away their future over some street waif. Predictable people..." Keats paused and then continued in a lowered voice, "go about *en mirage* on occasion. You, however, are as opaque as..." *She* gestured toward the pair at the other end of the alley.

At that, the tradesman gave a short grunt and then stepped back, buttoning his trousers. The prostitute dropped her skirts.

"Bless ya, luv," she said, humming to herself as they left the alley. They parted at the street, the act of dispassionate commerce complete.

Keats shook his head in dismay. "Despite the killer, they still go off with strangers. I just don't understand."

Alastair grasped the illusion's arm and marched toward the street. "I've had quite enough of you for one evening."

"Treat me nice," Keats teased. "If I give a shout, the crowd will be on you like a pack of hounds. From what I hear, you're about the killer's height and your hair is nearly the same color. Might take a bit of time for the mob to realize they've got the wrong fellow."

Alastair released *her,* unsure if the crank might pull such a stunt. He straightened his jacket, then strode toward the street, hoping Keats wouldn't rejoin him.

The pest appeared at his side, eyeing passing gentlemen with stealthy glances.

"Mindless twit," Alastair grumbled. "Don't you have someone else to torment?"

His companion turned serious in a flash. He latched onto Alastair's arm again, leaning close. "Be careful," Keats whispered. "On all accounts. I would miss your gloomy person more than you might realize."

After disengaging herself, Keats adopted a saucy walk, veering toward the mangle of bodies loitering outside the Princess Alice. The moment before crossing the threshold into the pub, *she* executed a short wave.

"Bloody lunatic," Alastair muttered. "He's the one they should be worrying about, not me."

In time, the doctor reached the ramshackle building on Church Street that housed the clinic, a tailor's shop, a saddle maker and ten families squashed into tiny, airless rooms. Situated on the ground floor in a space no more than fifteen by fifteen in size, the clinic consisted of two wooden tables, a few benches and an endless supply of the sick and injured.

Tonight was no exception; all the benches were full. Some of the patients held their heads, while others had barking coughs. One man cradled his injured arm, a thick line of blood congealing on his shirt. Alastair's fellow physician, Daniel Cohen, was attempting to place a stethoscope on a sobbing toddler's chest. He glanced up, spied Alastair, and then shook his head in disapproval.

"I won't bother arguing with you," Daniel called over the noise. "You won't listen to me anyway."

"You need help tonight," Alastair replied, removing his hat, coat and jacket.

"You require a night at leisure," Daniel replied. The recalcitrant child grasped the stethoscope and tugged on it playfully. Daniel obliged by placing it on the youngster's chest.

"I'll take tomorrow night off," Alastair said, rolling up his sleeves.

"So you always say," was the curt reply.

Alastair crossed to a cabinet and tucked his garments inside to prevent them from being stolen and pawned for ready money. He gestured for the next patient to come forward: an older man spitting blood into a dingy grey handkerchief.

At least here no one questioned his sanity.

3

No doubt they made a curious pair to any onlooker: the somber physician and the gregarious bootblack. Davy Butler had spied him the moment he left the clinic and now tagged along at his side, whistling a tune. As usual, the boy's face begged for soap and water.

"How's your leg this evening?" Alastair asked, noting Davy wasn't limping as much as usual.

"Right as rain," the lad chirped.

Alastair delivered a skeptical look. Davy would say anything to mollify him; it was the child's nature. His mind skipped back to their first meeting—the twist of fate that had cost Alastair his future in Mayfair—Davy lying in the rain-soaked street, his right leg bent at an impossible angle while a carriage driver bellowed a torrent of abuse. Fighting back tears, the boy had insisted he couldn't be hurt, that he had to work to feed his mum.

In the end, Alastair ensured Davy's widowed mother was fed and the rent paid. After a fortnight's convalescence, the boy was on the streets again, hawking papers while leaning against a crutch. Once his leg healed, he returned to sweeping the streets, polishing boots and scavenging along the Thames during low tide for discarded items he could sell. To his credit, and Alastair's supreme annoyance, he'd insisted on repaying every penny of the doctor's generosity.

"You sure your leg's not troubling you?" Alastair probed.

"It pains sometimes, but it's not bad. Not like some I've seen. You did right by me, doc."

"Well, that's good, then. How much did you make today?"

"'Nuff for two days' food," Davy announced proudly.

"Good job." Alastair clapped the lad on the back. "How is your mother?"

"Her cough's worse," Davy admitted. "She works too hard."

"Yes, she does. Have her come to the clinic tomorrow night."

"I'll try, doc. You know how she is."

"Yes, I know." *Stubborn, like you.*

A smile bloomed on the boy's face. "I'd best be goin'." He tapped his cap. "G'night!"

"See you tomorrow, Davy. My regards to your mother."

"Right, doc." The boy scampered across the street and into an alley like a gazelle.

The sight made Alastair smile. A success in a sea of failures.

He paused to purchase a paper and then immediately thought better of it. Every penny counted. The clinic accepted what a patient could afford to pay, which was typically nothing. The cost of medicines, bandages and other supplies came from the pockets of the physicians and what pitifully few charitable donations they could raise. That evening, one of the children offered her dolly in recompense. Alastair had declined, a thick lump forming in his throat. It was clear the doll was all the child had to her name, other than a case of consumption that would carry her to the grave within the month.

"Sir?" the newsboy asked. Alastair realized he'd been woolgathering.

"No, I've changed my mind. Thank you." He continued toward home, recalling when the cost of a paper was a trivial expense.

Pausing outside the boarding house, he stared upward at the window of his room. A world away from his accommodations in Mayfair.

"At least I'll go to my grave knowing I made a difference," he murmured.

Knees and back complained as Alastair hiked the stairs to the second floor. The Wescombs' interrogation still raged through his mind like a squall.

Maybe now they've issued their warning, they'll leave me alone. He unlocked his door and pushed it open with a faint creak. The room looked untouched, with his medical books and diary on the rickety table and his spare suit hanging on a hook near the door, airing.

Delusions of persecution: one of the first indications that a Transitive was losing control.

"Nonsense. He shut the door and stripped off his coat. "Utter nonsense."

✝

He was too weary. The words would not come tonight, no matter how long he stared at the blank page. Sighing, he leafed back in the diary, savoring earlier entries.

Friday, 31 August, 1888
   Tonight, I tasted glory.
   It happened with minimal commotion, as if she knew her fate and was willing to grant my quest without struggle. When it was done, so aflame was I that I rushed headlong into the streets to proclaim my triumph. None understood.
   All things have a beginning. Tonight was mine.

Flipping forward in the diary with a gloved hand, he read further.

Thursday, 6 September, 1888
   I detest funerals. They speak only to the living. Why would we, those who still draw breath, care of such things? I note the polished elm coffin was well regarded. Pity I could not claim credit for placing her within.
   My search continues.

He closed the book and wrapped it in the fabric shroud, hiding it at the bottom of the wardrobe. Another time, the words would be there.

‡

Cynda blinked her eyes, allowing them time to adjust. There was nothing quite like the darkness of a Victorian back alley. The pitch-blackness was augmented by the potent stench of far too many unwashed people and too few toilets, intermingled with the rank bouquet of rotting garbage.

She fidgeted under the weight of her clothes. Though she'd opted for fewer petticoats than the Victorian norm to keep the burden under an oppressive twenty pounds, it was still a far cry from the feather-light stola she'd worn a short time before. As Ralph had once astutely observed, "Clothes are the measure of the time." At the height of its glory, Pompeii was an exquisite city boasting ideal weather and three crops a year. At the height of the British Empire, London, at least the East End, was a festering dump.

"Rule Britannia," Cynda muttered, trudging down the alley. She carried a black Gladstone bag with a spare dress, toilet items and a substantial stock of chocolate packaged in appropriate Victorian-style wrappers. She didn't plan on staying that long, but Overdues could be tricky. They tended to wander. Even though Whitechapel wasn't that big—only about a square mile—there were a lot of holes to hide in if a tourist didn't want to be found.

She squeamishly gave a dead rat a wide berth. Those were never mentioned in TIC's sales literature. Neither was the stark poverty of the East End, or the lack of adequate sanitation. Instead, the vid-brochures waxed poetic about the virtues of time travel. *'Imagine standing in the cheering crowds as Queen Victoria celebrates her Golden Jubilee (1887) or conducting research elbow-to-elbow with Lenin in the British Library (1902). Be there as history happens!'*

"What a crock." Despite her misgivings, academic chrono-research was here to stay. One trip could deliver fodder for a decade's worth of professional articles and Vid-Net interviews—exposure that led to tenure and fatter salaries. As the leader in time immersion technology, TIC was always eager to exploit history and make an unholy profit in the bargain.

Until the last buyout. TIC had yet to regain its footing. Wage cuts ensued, then layoffs. Even Victorian London looked rosier than her employer's future.

Cynda paused at the entrance to the street to get her bearings. Despite all the chocolate she'd consumed before her departure, the mental fog remained. She blinked again, which only resulted in making the gas lamps appear multi-colored, like giant roman candles blazing into the grimy night. Every now and then, a bolt of lag-induced lightning would seem to strike the street in front of her, exploding in a burst of brilliant colors. The resulting thunderclap echoed like a thousand badly tuned cymbals. Her skin danced a two-step across her bones—all classic signs of advanced time lag. She was nearing the end of her reign as a Time Rover. Desk duty beckoned.

"Not a chance," she said, shaking her head vigorously. She resisted the temptation to rummage in the Gladstone bag for more chocolate. If Ivan the Infant were on the ball, she'd be near the boarding house. Once she'd checked in, she'd track the missing academic and line him up to go home. Finding Professor Turner shouldn't be difficult; Cynda was one of the best trackers in the business. She'd start with the closest pubs, and if that failed, then the brothels. Protected for a time from the local diseases and safely beyond the scrutiny of their spouses, the academics ran wild. If Turner wasn't conducting research of a horizontal nature or drinking his weight in cheap booze, she'd head for the British Library. That was always her last resort.

A couple stumbled along, their off-key singing augmented by the level of cheap gin in their bellies. A bobby watched from the other side of the street with a benign expression. That puzzled her; she couldn't remember a cop there in the past.

Navigating around piles of trampled horse manure, she hiked toward the boarding house. As men passed, a few politely tipped their hats in respect. She found that unnecessarily quaint. A carriage sailed by, the clip-clop of the horse's hooves echoing in the narrow street. She passed a stable and then, a bit further on, a pub going full tilt. Frowsy, middle-aged women stood outside, gossiping. When an unaccompanied male wandered within range, their antennae went up like a praying mantis scouting its next meal.

"Hello, luv," one of them called. The man sped up, his work boots slapping against the cobblestones as he hurried by. Apparently, he wasn't interested in what she was offering.

Cynda trudged on until she reached her destination: a nondescript structure on New Castle Street.

A. Phillip's Boarding House. A Warm Welcome and a Soft Bed, the sign read. The bed sounded good.

Maybe I'll sleep for a week and then find Turner. She mulled the idea and then shook her head. *Not here. Anywhere but here.*

Sweating from the exertion and the weighty clothes, Cynda hauled herself up the stairs and gave a quick knock. A twinge of unease caused her to glance over her shoulder. In the dim gaslight, she thought she saw a man watching her from the other side of the street.

When the door opened, Cynda swung around. Her balance faltered and she steadied herself on the door jam, the Gladstone banging into her knee.

"Yes, miss?" a woman asked in a less-than-friendly tone. She appeared to be about fifty years of age, with graying hair and a doughy complexion. Her breasts were a continent all their own. She wasn't Annabelle, the boarding house's owner.

Momentarily disconcerted, Cynda blurted, "I'm looking for a room."

The woman gave her the once-over and then frowned, hands moving to her hips. "Mind you, we don't rent to those who ply the trade...or those who drink too much."

It took a moment for Cynda to understand what she meant. "Oh, no, I'm not...I've stayed here before. Miss Annabelle knows me. I'm Jacynda Lassiter."

A look of chagrin. "Oh, I'm sorry, Miss. Annabelle's spoken of you. Come in, come in. You walked here alone?" the woman asked, surveying the street. Before Cynda could reply, she added, "Not safe for a young lady anymore. Come on, I'll take you to my sister."

What's up with Annabelle? Cynda took another look over her shoulder. The man was gone. Probably another lag-induced hallucination. She heaved a sigh of relief and hoisted herself over the threshold. The door closed behind her with a reassuring thud. The nearest wall provided needed support as she followed the heavyset woman toward the back of the building.

"I'm Mildred, by the way. Annabelle's had a bit of an accident. Hurt her foot a few days back. I'm here to help her."

"Good to hear it," Cynda said, and then winced. That sounded less than sympathetic. Fortunately, Mildred didn't appear to notice.

Annabelle Phillips sat close to the warm stove, one leg propped on the seat of a chair. She always had a reedy look to her, as if she were hollow and with a slight draft of wind might play a tune. Kneeling next to her, examining the swollen ankle, was a young man with rolled-up shirtsleeves. He glanced upward at Cynda, his eyes an exhausted brown. A frown creased his face and she returned it. He wasn't Professor Turner, the wayward academic. *That would have been too easy.*

As Cynda opened her mouth to ask about accommodations, four scintillating lightning bolts set the kitchen in motion like a child's toy. Sparkly-blue dots morphed into steel-gray ones. Right before the gray faded into black oblivion, Cynda staggered into the young man, her knees giving way.

"Need chocolate..." she whispered, and then fainted at the startled man's feet.

4

Cynda clearly remembered the pressure of cold metal on her chest and a reassuring voice near her ear. She also remembered opening her eyes and seeing the hideous blue spider hanging in front of her. Easily the size of a five-foot solar panel, each of its eight hairy feet sported a pink ballet shoe. Compound eyes leered at her with menacing intent.

"Get away!" she shouted, batting at the arachnid. It stuck out its bright purple tongue. "I hate spiders. Get away, get away!" She swung and connected. The thing spouted an oath and then disappeared.

When she finally regained her senses, the scene had changed. She was in a bedroom. Sitting a discreet distance away was the guy from the kitchen. He pressed a cloth to his cheek, and his eyes held no warmth. Fussing nearby was the woman who had met her at the front door.

"I really don't know why she's this way, Dr. Montrose. Annabelle says she's been quite sensible in the past."

The physician didn't reply, but allowed her to refresh the cloth in the basin. He replaced it over the injury.

Oops. In her zeal to nail the planet-sized spider, Cynda had cold-cocked a doctor. She suspected her bill had just doubled.

He noted she was awake. "Are you normally in the habit of striking people, Miss...Lassiter?" he asked coolly. When he removed the cloth, she realized why he was so pissed. A sizeable crimson blotch sat just below his left cheekbone, one that would probably degrade into a bruise by morning.

She shook her head at the question, contrite.

"Are you given to drink?"

"No. Why?"

"You claimed there was a spider in the room, the size of an omnibus."

"Oh."

"Have you been treated for mental instability?"

"No. You just startled me."

"I see. Well, you appear to have recovered. If you need anything, ask Mildred. I've had quite enough of a day as it is." He rose, dropped the cloth into the basin with a noisy splash, and left the room.

"Oh, dear," Cynda moaned. *So much for being discreet.*

Mildred looked chagrined. "He's usually very polite. I think he's quite tired."

"Makes two of us." Her brain jostled her. "Ah, is there a Professor Turner staying here at present?"

"No, miss."

"Has he been here recently?"

"Don't know, miss. I've only been here since Thursday last. You'd have to ask Annabelle about him."

"I will. My...uncle...said I should say hello to him while I was here."

Mildred nodded. "Do you need anything to eat, miss?"

"No, thank you. I just want to sleep."

"I put all your things in the wardrobe. Oh, and I'd lock your door, you being alone and all. Our lodgers are good people, but you can never be too careful."

"I'll do it. Good night...Mildred."

Once the woman was out the door, Cynda slid her feet from under the covers and sat on the side of the bed, wiggling her toes to regain feeling. Her boots just weren't right. Luckily, she'd not have to wear them very long. She stared at her underwear, if you could call it that. The "onesie," a combination chemise and drawers, would have amused the folks in '057. It lacked a crotch, more for ease of personal necessity than for anything remotely fun. Edged in lace, it did nothing for her figure.

As she stood, lightning erupted like her own personal fireworks show. Cynda bent over and clutched her stomach to keep from heaving. After a series of deep breaths, things seemed to stabilize. With tentative steps, she made her way to the door, locked it with the skeleton key, and then headed to the wardrobe.

Her black and navy dresses hung neatly inside. Cynda hunted for the time interface. The pocket watch wasn't where it should be—tucked under the ruffle in the false bodice panel of the black dress.

She checked the other dress. Nothing.

Cynda dug around the floor of the wardrobe, in case the watch had fallen out. Panic broke a sweat on her forehead as she pawed through her luggage. She found the watch wrapped inside a stocking and tucked into a boot. Mildred's handiwork, no doubt.

"Thank God." She kissed it like it was a religious icon. No interface, no way home. Not long ago, she'd have trusted TIC to retrieve her. That trust was growing as thin as Annabelle's physique.

To celebrate her safe arrival, Cynda ate two pieces of chocolate without actually tasting them. Edging her way back to the bed, she tucked the watch under the pillow and then turned the bed covers back, checking for bugs. Thankfully, there were none; Annabelle kept a clean place by Victorian standards. That was the primary reason it was used as the 'safe house' for 1888. And the landlady wasn't inclined to ask awkward questions. Cynda blew out the candle and snuggled under the covers. As she drifted to sleep, she wondered if spiders really did have tongues.

‡

Though he'd tried to make himself as nondescript as possible at the Princess Alice, Jonathon Keats earned a few propositions he didn't dare accept. After trading jokes with a saddler and sipping a pint of beer, he set off for the next pub.

He'd lied to Alastair and regretted it. He wasn't looking for the Whitechapel killer, though if he fell over him he'd be happy to tote the fiend to the nearest police station. On the contrary. Detective-Sergeant Jonathon Keats was on the trail of bigger quarry: anarchists.

From the very first, Alastair had tagged him as an erratic fop. Keats had to admit his performance was spot-on; his father had been an ideal role model in that regard. As Alastair had occasionally made remarks sympathetic to the Irish separatist cause, Keats had allowed the delusion to stand. At present, it was best that his friend not know he was a cop. Just when Keats would reveal his true vocation remained an issue. The longer the deception, the greater the damage would be when his friend finally learned the truth.

"Not yet," he said under his breath. The doctor wasn't the kind to plant bombs, but still, caution ruled. If the wrong person learned Keats worked for Special Branch and was nosing about Whitechapel, his next assignment might involve floating face down in the Thames after a "misadventure."

From his location in front of the Ten Bells, he saw a man

loitering near the entrance to Spitalfields Market. The fellow was a copper. Keats couldn't determine precisely what betrayed the fellow: He just didn't fit the street. Because of the murders, there were a lot of cops wandering around now, but any seasoned veteran of the East End could spot them with little difficulty.

Keats knew the streets intimately. Every few pubs he would shift forms, working through the three he preferred: the plain streetwalker, an Irish match girl and a sailor. Each had their own story, and it was dicey to keep them straight. He had to remember whom he'd talked to and in what form, lest they'd met at another pub. It was an immense challenge, and one Keats relished.

Making his rounds, he kept an eye out for one man in particular—Desmond Flaherty. Sometime in the last fortnight Flaherty had gone to ground. Keats was sure his absence meant something. The Fenians were growing restive. Of the lot, Flaherty was one of their most rabid, with a penchant toward explosions—the more spectacular, the better. If he hadn't been in jail at the time, Flaherty most certainly would have been involved in the attempt to dynamite London Bridge in '84, or the Houses of Parliament the following year. It was said in low whispers in smoky pubs that Flaherty wanted to make his own mark in just such a dramatic fashion.

Whatever the Fenian was planning would be big. Fortunately, Keats' superior at Special Branch felt the same, and allowed him the liberty to scramble around the streets of Whitechapel at all hours in addition to his other duties. There was one liability: Chief Inspector Fisher was an Opaque with no knowledge of the Transitives. Keats walked a thin line between duty and discovery.

He hiked in troubled silence toward Dorset Street and The Britannia, currently *en mirage* as the sailor. The pub was chock-a-block, but Flaherty wasn't jostling elbows with the other drunks. Seven more pubs gave Keats sore feet and a dull headache, but no news as to the Fenian agitator's whereabouts. His usual contacts were as mystified as he was. To the person, they felt uneasy. That told Keats reams.

After shifting back to his usual form in a darkened side yard, he caught a hansom cab near Aldgate Station and instructed the driver to take him to his lodgings in Little Russell Street. As the cabbie headed west, Keats fought the urge to fall asleep. By the time he trudged up the stairs to his rooms on the second floor, it was nearing three in the morning. He tossed aside his bowler hat and coat. Despite the late hour, his landlady ensured that there was a bit of fire left for him when he returned. To foster her good humor, he always paid his rent on time and brought her flowers whenever the mood struck him.

With a bit more coal and the liberal use of the bellows, the fire reignited. Too tired to fill the kettle, he propped his feet on the ottoman and sighed into the comfort of his favorite chair. Opening a book, he read until the welcome warmth of the fire caused him to doze.

A knock on the door roused him. He squinted at the mantel clock—just after four.

"Who the dickens is this?" Keats propelled himself upright. Reaching to throw the bolt, he hesitated. He dug in the brass umbrella stand and extracted a truncheon, hiding it behind his back.

Cautiously cracking the door, his eyes widened in surprise.

"Keats?" a voice inquired. "Umm...pardon for the early hour."

"Sir?" Keats opened the door immediately. "Come in!"

Chief Inspector J.R. Fisher strode into the room and then abruptly halted, as if unsure of what to do next. Keats' mind raged as he locked the door and replaced the truncheon in its hiding place.

"What is wrong, sir?"

In lieu of an answer, the Chief Inspector knelt and jabbed at the coals in the fireplace with the poker. As usual, he was dressed in a black suit, his brown hair, moustache and beard immaculate. Faint strands of gray could be discerned at his temples, and it seemed to Keats the amount increased with each passing week. Fisher's eyes held a sharpness, though at present they seemed wary. He carried himself with more grace than most cops, or gentlemen, for that matter.

Why is he here?

The sigh that escaped Keats' lips broke his superior's trance.

"Oh, I apologize," Fisher said, rising. He immediately sank into Keats' chair. Noting the opened book on the ottoman, he studied the cover. "Ah, *Beeton's Christmas Annual*." He leafed through it until he reached the bookmark. "*A Study in Scarlet* by Mr. Conan Doyle," he said, looking up with an amused expression. "What do you think of it?"

"Holmes is quite an amazing detective. A bit of a misanthrope, but utterly unique."

Fisher nodded and returned the book where he found it. "There are those who say it is a bunch of twaddle."

Keats frowned. "Holmes' method may be as viable as any other in the right circumstances."

"Indeed."

Keats blurted, "Sir, why are you here?"

Fisher studied him. "First, give me a report of your night's activities."

He's buying time. "Flaherty is not to be found. I made a round of the pubs and spoke with my contacts. He's vanished as surely as if the devil had personally carted him off to purgatory, which is too much to hope for," Keats grumbled.

"Which pubs?" Fisher asked. Of course, he'd want the details. The man was so thorough he could probably tell you precisely how many coins he had in his pocket and their exact denominations.

Keats ticked the establishments off with his fingers. "Paul's Head, Horn of Plenty, Blue Coat Boy, Britannia, Queen's Head, Princess Alice, Kings Stores, Ten Bells and the Alma. I wanted to go to the White Hart and the Frying Pan, but it grew too late."

"Good heavens, you have made the rounds, Sergeant."

Keats nodded.

"Yet, no sign of the man. Blast, what mischief is he up to?"

"Nothing good, sir. You can lay odds on that."

"Do you have anything to drink?"

Keats jarred at the change of subject. "I can make tea."

"We are not on duty at present. Perhaps something more robust?"

"I have whiskey, sir."

"Irish?"

"Indeed."

"That'll do."

Keats unstopped the bottle and poured the liquor. His superior took the glass and sniffed at it. A faint smile played across his face. "We're told the Irish are ignorant, lazy and not worth the powder to blow to Hell, and yet..." He took a sip of the liquor. "I think we misjudge them, to our loss."

Keats nodded in agreement. "To a restful retirement in Bournemouth."

"Amen," Fisher replied and took a heavy gulp.

Keats savored the whiskey. "My report could have waited until morning," he observed.

The Chief Inspector's eyes rose from his glass. A short nod signaled the barrier was about to be breached. "I have had the most...remarkable experience, and I'm not sure how to proceed." Fisher paused and then continued, "You are a sensible fellow and a discreet one."

Keats' anxiety overrode his sense of pride at the compliment. "I try to be, sir."

"What I am about to relate to you could...ruin my career."

Good Lord. "Well, then," he said, gesturing around him, "consider our conversation as going no further than these four walls."

A solemn nod. Fisher set his glass aside and then knelt by the hearth again, prodding the coals with the poker as if trying to find the proper words inside the flames.

"I was in Rotherhithe tonight, tracking an informant on Swan Road. I thought he might supply useful information regarding that kidnapping last week. Finding a hansom for the return journey proved impossible, so I walked. Along the way I was accosted by a hysterical family who were forced to flee their lodgings because of an invasion."

"Invasion?"

"A lunatic burst in upon them, frightening them senseless. They escaped, but unfortunately their small daughter was trapped with the intruder."

"Good heavens," Keats said.

"I sent the father in search of a constable and went to see what I might do." Fisher abruptly dropped the poker onto the hearth and rose. "Perhaps I'm being overwrought. Maybe after a good night's sleep..."

Their eyes met. Keats saw uncertainty, a hint of fear. "Go on, sir. I want to hear what happened."

Fisher took an immense breath and let it out so slowly Keats thought it would be dawn before he finished. The man returned to the chair and clasped the glass, tilting it slightly to let the amber liquid gently roll from one side to the other. Keats couldn't help but notice the fine tremor in his hands.

"I found the man gibbering in a corner of the room. The little girl was petrified, but he hadn't harmed her. I coaxed her away, and she rejoined her family."

Keats let out a whoosh of air in relief. "Thank God."

Fisher's eyes grew solemn. "The man was ill, shaking with a fever. I knelt beside him and asked if I could help him, and, by God...he...changed."

"What?"

"Changed...altered form."

He cannot mean... "In what way, sir?"

"One moment, his face was dirty white and sweaty, and then it became as black as Newgate's knocker. Even his eyes and hair altered color. It was as if another man had taken his place for an instant."

Oh, God. Keats struggled to keep his voice level. "Did he say anything?"

"Only nonsense. He was out of his mind with fever."

"Then what happened?"

"I had thought perhaps my eyes were playing false with me, but he changed again. I would have sworn I was looking at a charwoman, old and gnarled with knobby hands and soot under her broken fingernails. Then he shifted into a young girl with fine rings on pale hands, flaxen hair and clear, sea-blue eyes." Fisher rose and paced the room. "I shook myself severely, certain my senses were befuddled. The illusion vanished and he slumped to the floor."

He's seen one of us, someone too ill to control their ability. How the hell do I explain this?

Before he could formulate a strategy, Fisher rubbed his hands over his face and murmured, "Then he died."

Keats' eyes jumped to his superior. "Did you touch him?" he demanded, springing to his feet.

"No. Why?"

Sensing his error, Keats sputtered, "Ah...I thought perhaps there might be some sort of...contagion."

Fisher gave him an odd look, then polished off the remainder of the whiskey. He continued, "The constable arrived, and the body was transported to the morgue. I demanded an immediate autopsy."

"And?"

"There was nothing unique about the fellow; he had a lung abscess. It was what killed him."

"You've filed a report?"

"Not yet."

Perhaps he still had a chance to mitigate the damage. "What is your dilemma, sir?" he asked, more in control.

"I know what I saw, Keats. I am not a man given to excess drink, nor one who frequents the opium dens. I am a stable man, free of delusions. And yet..."

Keats refilled their glasses, waiting him out.

"I feel I cannot trust my judgment. I saw the most extraordinary thing, and I cannot explain it. There is only one logical conclusion: The stress of my position has worn my mental state to the point where it cannot be trusted. I feel I should resign."

"You cannot!" Keats snapped, causing his guest to start at his vehemence.

"I appreciate your ardor on the subject, Sergeant, but it is my choice. I have money laid aside. My wife would readily welcome a new start. We could find a place in the country and raise horses. I would rather like that." His voice sounded raw.

"You might like it, but I wouldn't," Keats said sourly. Unlike most of the officers he'd worked with, Fisher took the effort to analyze a situation. A man ahead of his time, he studied the criminal mind and kept abreast of the latest investigative techniques. Others would jump to a conclusion and then bend the facts to fit their suspect. If Fisher left the force...

Keats' future flared in front of him like a bolt of summer lightning. Inspector Ramsey would become his superior, elevated to Chief Inspector the moment Fisher resigned. "The Ram" was well named. A bull-headed man with a mind as firmly closed as a spinster's knees, he detested Keats, viewing him as Fisher's pampered acolyte. The moment his mentor left, Keats' head would be on the block. Then he would become a wastrel, just like his father.

Fisher watched him intently. "Ramsey's a good man," he offered.

"Maybe he's a good man, sir, but I'll argue about his skills as a copper."

Fisher's eyes narrowed. "You would do well not to say such things outside of this room, Sergeant."

"I won't, sir. But I thought we were being candid."

A short grunt of acknowledgement came from his visitor.

After another sip of whiskey, Keats asked, "Are you sure this is what you must do?"

Fisher leaned forward, a strange light in his eyes. "I came to hear your advice. You know me as well as most. Have you witnessed any signs that my brain is edging into dementia?"

There it was—the dilemma. The Conclave's ironclad rule stated that the Opaques were not to know of the Transitives. There were exceptions—family members and such—but in general, The Conclave took steps to hide the truth. A lesser person might meet with an accident, a tumble off a train perhaps. A man as important as Fisher they would seek to discredit, banish into retirement. If that tactic failed, his life was forfeit. Fisher's future was as dismal as his own if Keats didn't handle this properly.

He took a deep breath and then plunged in. "You must stay, sir."

Fisher eyed him with what appeared to be desperate hope. "You think me sane?"

"Yes, I do."

"Why do you say that?" he challenged. Keats' averted gaze supplied the answer. "Good God, you've heard of this sort of thing before, haven't you?"

I don't dare... "Not as such, sir. Nevertheless, I do know there are many unexplained events in the world, and you may have indeed witnessed one. There are strange men in India who, in trance-like states, tread across glowing coals without any apparent injury. The rational mind cannot explain that, yet it is documented fact. Perhaps you have witnessed such a unique phenomenon."

Fisher leaned back in the chair and stared at the fire. His brows furrowed. The mantel clock chimed half past the hour. As the sound died away, he set his glass on the hearth, rose and straightened his jacket.

"I shall stay at my post for the time being. I wish to keep this event to ourselves. However, if you see anything in my behavior that indicates a softening of the mind, you are to tell me instantly, do you understand?"

Keats nodded and rose from the chair. "I doubt I will see such a thing, sir."

"When we are less weary and I've had time to think, we shall find a private moment to speak further on this matter."

He paused at the door, placing a hand on Keats' shoulder. With a thick voice, he said, "Thank you, Jonathon. I appreciate your candor."

"You're welcome, sir. I'll see you in the morning."

A wry chuckle. "It's already morning, Sergeant."

"So it appears, sir."

Once his visitor had departed, Keats bolted the door and slumped into his chair near the hearth. Rubbing his face, he sighed heavily. Keeping Fisher as his superior meant the world to him. Having the man one step closer to the Transitives was Keats' worst nightmare.

5

Tuesday, 25 September, 1888

Jacynda woke with a start. She'd been dreaming about a gaggle of flamingos that had sailed across time to teach her the *pas de deux*. No matter how hard they tried, she kept falling on her face.

A loud knock at the door.

"What?" She grimaced. That had been too blunt. She'd have to be more careful.

"Breakfast, Miss Lassiter," Mildred's voice called.

"Thank you." The sound of retreating footsteps. Was Mildred aware that Cynda wasn't quite like her sister's other guests?

It took three attempts to crawl out of bed. Much to her annoyance, she found the spider lurking in the washbasin. Smaller now, it wore a shower cap and was scrubbing under one of its many armpits, whistling a tune.

She stifled a shriek and downed more chocolate. When her head stopped spinning, the washbasin was empty.

It's never been this bad. Cynda splashed cold water on her face and then rummaged through the wardrobe for the black dress. It seemed to weigh even more this morning. She finally wiggled into it, did a passing job on her hair and brushed her teeth with the tooth powder.

"Yuck." She spit the stuff into the washbasin.

Lacing the boots took an eternity, interspersed with head-spinning vertigo. As she rested between bouts of lacing, she heard a newsboy crying out the headlines on the street below. The clock was running.

TIC allowed three time insertion points in 1888 London, all

well before the murders began on the last day of August. After that, London was a no-go zone until 1889. Too many would-be fortune hunters sought to uncover the identity of the Whitechapel killer and, in the process, royally screw history. "Jack the Ripper," as he would soon be dubbed by the salacious Victorian press, had method in his madness, and far be it from TIC or any other time broker to mess with his legacy.

Cynda had just a few days to round up the missing tourist and leave the city before the first prostitute would be found dead in Buck's Row. Once the murders began, every suspicious gentleman came under intense police scrutiny. TIC's tourists were prime targets.

With a heavy sigh, she finished the lacing, making a mental note to put on the boots before the dress the next time.

A flitter under the curtain caught her notice. A moth ruffled its wings on the windowsill. Cynda shooed it outside and shut the window with a noisy thump. Her hands came away dark with coal dust. She brushed them on her skirt rather than tempting fate at the washbasin again.

The boots continued to pinch as she made her way to the stairwell. And there it was…fifteen steps to the first floor. The night before, she'd been unconscious on the way up. *Who had carried me?* Probably the doctor.

"How Gothic," she said, shaking her head.

Cynda grasped the banister and made the first step, then the next, heavy skirts dragging behind her like Jacob Marley's chains. A bolt of lag lightning crashed into the newel post at the bottom, shattering into a burst of brilliant pinwheels. She ignored it and kept moving downward, one step at a time. She doubted the doctor would be that sympathetic if she cracked an ankle.

"Four more…three…two…" She heaved a long sigh of relief when she reached the bottom step. A quick look around proved no one had seen her performance. "Perfect."

The sound of amiable conversation and the smell of food lured her toward the dining room. It was moderate-sized, with bright gold floral wallpaper and oppressively heavy drapes in the style of the time. A fire burned in the hearth. China dishes mounded with food covered the top of a large buffet. Annabelle's was a favorite stop for Victorian travelers; her scones were legendary.

Five guests were already at the table. Cynda let her eyes hopscotch over the four male faces. None of them was the missing academic, but then that matched Mildred's report.

Stifling a choice swear word, she entered the room as quietly as possible. Two of the men were discussing the prime minister in less-than-flattering terms.

"He's got his nephew at the trough, doesn't he?" one observed.

"That says it all."

"Balfour's not that bad of a chap," the other man retorted.

"Well, that remains to be seen."

Belatedly, they looked up. Cynda made her apologies and headed for the buffet table to gather a plate and inventory the selection—gammon, eggs, crusty bread and cheese. Not a fruit in sight. Heavy on protein, heavy on starch. She kept the groan to herself. The mantra of the moment was to blend in as best as possible. Unless one of her fellow diners was an American, she should do fairly well. Eccentricities of speech and mannerisms could be fobbed off as a Colonial defect.

Managing the heavy skirts and the plate took some doing, but she arrived at the table without tripping—a major faux pas for someone supposedly accustomed to the garments. As she settled into the chair, three of the men rose out of respect. She gave a polite nod. The fourth gentleman pointedly ignored her; head bent, working a crossword puzzle with religious fervor. Quite unusual during a meal. He received a stern look from Dr. Montrose, but didn't notice.

Cynda arranged her cutlery. As expected, almost all eyes were on her.

"Good morning, Miss Lassiter," the doctor said, tucking a napkin in his lap. The dark circles under his eyes were a shade lighter this morning. True to her prediction, his cheek sported a magnificent bruise. "I trust you are...improved."

Not really. "Much better, thank you, Dr. Montrose," she fibbed.

"No further...incidents?" he asked, eyes narrowing.

She ground her teeth. "No, I'm fine. I appreciate your concern." *Just pad your bill and leave me be.*

As if on cue, another gentleman chimed in. "Horatio Bottom, and this is my wife, Millicent," he said, indicating the plump woman setting next to him. "We're from Dover."

"I am pleased to make your acquaintance," Cynda replied. Her stomach growled in response to the food. A quick glance at the doctor indicated he'd heard. He dabbed at his mouth with a napkin in an attempt to hide his smile.

"Lucius Everson, miss," the gentleman next to her announced.

"Good morning, sir. Are you perhaps a wool merchant?" That was fairly easy to guess since he had stray bits of the stuff on his coat sleeve. Still, it made for a nice opening gambit.

"Why, yes, I am." He traded glances with the doctor and then sighed. Apparently, the puzzle jockey wasn't going to be polite. Everson performed the introduction. "And that is Mr. Hix," gesturing toward the man fixated on the newspaper. No response from the miscreant as he tapped a pencil on the paper in thought, smoke-colored glasses perched on the end of his nose. Odder still, he wore black gloves at the table.

Whoa, this one's eccentric.

Embarrassed at the man's lack of manners, Everson explained, "My apologies. He's a bit caught up right now."

"Humpff?" the fellow said, but he didn't look up.

"Is Mr. Hix a wool merchant as well?" she asked.

"No, he's an accountant. Probably a good one, I would gather, given his degree of *single-mindedness*," Everson replied.

"I understand," she said politely. Now that the formalities were over, she dug into her breakfast. Resisting the temptation to pick the ham up with her fingers and stuff it in her mouth, she methodically cut and ate the fatty meat in manageable bites.

"Are you from America?" Mr. Bottom asked, applying marmalade to a piece of bread he'd plucked from a silver toast rack.

"Yes, I am."

"Is this your first trip to London?"

"No, I come here fairly often. My uncle is unable to travel, and so I come here in his stead." Her brain gave her a thumbs-up on speech complexity. Now if she didn't blurt something stupid, she'd carry it off.

"In his stead?" Mr. Bottom asked with a puzzled look.

"I conduct research for him."

"Research?" the doctor jumped in.

"My uncle is an historian." *Good old Uncle TIC.* "I was to meet a gentleman here at the boarding house—a Professor Turner."

"We don't know anything about him. We just arrived yesterday," Mr. Bottom said.

"Unfortunately, Professor Turner departed last week," Everson explained. "You should check with Annabelle. Perhaps he left a forwarding address."

"I shall. Did he mention where he might be headed?"

A shake of the head.

"What time period is your uncle researching?" the doctor asked.

"He is most fascinated with the reign of Queen Elizabeth the…" She dabbed at her mouth to conceal her near blunder. At this point in history, there was only *one* Queen Elizabeth. "I am his research assistant."

The doctor's eyebrow rose. It helped erase the lines underneath his eyes. She wondered what he looked like when he was truly rested.

"An unusual occupation for a young lady," he remarked.

Was that a note of sarcasm? "Yes, it is."

"You travel alone?" That was from Mrs. Bottom.

"Yes," Cynda replied.

Mr. Bottom shook his head. "Not to alarm you, miss, but London has become quite...unhealthy for a young lady on her own."

Wait a few days. "I am careful, Mr. Bottom. I will engage an escort before I venture too far, have no fear."

"Oh, excellent." That seemed to put the man at ease, though it was a complete fabrication. The doctor watched her intently, as if he discerned the falsehood. Now that she gave him a second look, she realized he was tall by Victorian standards, handsome with brown hair, intelligent eyes, and a neatly trimmed moustache.

Not worth my job. She concentrated on one of the pieces of dark bread instead. Dalliances with the locals were listed in the TIC Employee Manual under "Reasons for Immediate Dismissal." They still happened, but not very often. A Senior Time Rover was paid quite handsomely, including a company apartment. To sacrifice all that for a little horizontal time didn't make much sense.

Besides, Chris will be waiting for me when I get home.

That thought made her smile and seemed to encourage the doctor.

"What is your opinion of the Virgin Queen?" he asked out of left field.

A slight choked sound came from Mrs. Bottom. Apparently, one didn't use the 'V' word over breakfast.

Why not go for it? "I've found Elizabeth a study in contrasts. She desired a man in her life, but feared for her throne, and her country, if she wed. So she remained unmarried."

"Do you think that wise? Would not the country have been stronger with a king?" the physician asked. He sipped from a teacup held with a steady hand.

"I believe a consort would have proved a distraction, and would have in effect relegated her to second-class status. Watching her father's..." She hesitated. *Wheel of wives* wasn't a good choice of words. "Watching her father's frequent marital...forays, two of which were abruptly severed at the Tower, no doubt taught her that she was the ship of state's best captain."

"Do you agree with her?"

Again, the challenge. Except for Hix, all the guests were riveted on the verbal fencing match.

"Yes, actually, I do."

"Do you feel she was less of a woman for that decision?"

She barely kept the frown off her face. "I feel it made her stronger. She knew what she wanted and was willing to sacrifice to get it. In the end, England was her lover."

The doctor raised his teacup in a slight salute. "Well said."

As if I needed your approval.

"I just can't imagine trying to manage a country," Mrs. Bottom replied, shaking her head. "Quite impossible."

Cynda shrugged. "Bess was an extraordinary woman." Feeling that put the cap on it, she dusted her hands on the napkin and stood. Only the doctor caught her intention and rose with her, Everson and Bottom following belatedly. Hix was still murmuring to himself, oblivious.

"Good morning, all," Cynda said, feeling magnanimous. She'd held her own and hadn't made a complete ass of herself. It'd been fun. As she reached the door, she heard Mr. Bottom say under his breath, "American women are very independent thinkers."

You don't know the half of it.

Annabelle's leg appeared considerably less swollen than the night before, which she roundly attributed to Dr. Montrose's expert care.

"A fine physician. I don't understand why he's here in Whitechapel. He could practice anywhere he wanted," she said. Before Cynda could jump in, she asked, "Are you feeling better, dear?"

"Yes, much. I was just tired. Now, back to my question. When was the last time you saw Professor Turner?" Annabelle set the mending in her lap, tapping a thin finger on her chin. "A week ago. Said he had more research to do. He made sure I was paid in full."

"Did he leave a forwarding address?"

"No."

"Any idea where I should look for him?" Cynda asked quietly. "My...uncle is keen to find him."

"Professor Turner was fond of his ale...and those kind of women. You know what I mean."

Surprise. "Then I'll start with the pubs." If she were lucky, he hadn't wandered too far.

Annabelle picked up her mending and inserted a tiny stitch in a shirt collar. "What you do is most peculiar, Miss Lassiter."

Cynda patted the woman's shoulder as she stood. "Yes it is."

She found the doorway blocked by Dr. Montrose. *How much had he heard?*

"Just checking on Miss Annabelle," she said politely.

"I see," was the cool reply. He stepped backward and she scooted around him.

She could feel his eyes on her as she headed for the stairway. The doc was far too observant for her liking.

6

The sound of an opening door roused Keats mid-snore. The bemused expression on his superior's face told him he'd been caught red-handed.

"I apologize, Chief Inspector," Keats said, shifting upright. It was a measure of his exhaustion that he could doze off in a hard chair.

Fisher closed the office door and maneuvered his way behind his tidy desk. Though the room was pathetically small, he kept it organized with military precision, unlike most of his fellow inspectors at Great Scotland Yard.

Eyeing Keats, he observed, "You look knackered, Sergeant. Did my...revelation disturb your sleep?"

His subtle hesitation was a warning to keep their conversation indistinct. The walls weren't that thick.

"Actually, I got to thinking of a whore I know, and how long it had been since I'd last seen her."

"Sergeant?" Fisher asked with more than a hint of disapproval.

Keats backtracked. "Oh, not like that, sir. She's a fountain of information, if you pay her price. It took time to track her down— she's in a brothel on Flower and Dean now. Looking the worse for wear, as well."

Fisher settled into his chair. "What did this *fountain of information* tell you, Sergeant?"

"Her regulars include a variety of Irish sailors and dockworkers. One of them, a fellow named Lynch, has worked with Flaherty in the past. I thought she might have heard something from the fellow."

"And?" Fisher prodded.

"Lynch availed himself of her services about a week ago. After she set him to rights, he started bragging about how he and his mates were going to do something quite spectacular."

Fisher leaned forward. "How so?"

"He told her that what they had planned would make the Clerkenwell blast look like a church social. He didn't relate particulars. She says he's always bragging, talking big, but this time, it seemed different."

Fisher tented his fingers. "What is grander than destroying a prison?"

"Guy Fawkes Day is approaching, sir. Maybe they intend to have another go at the House of Lords."

"Intriguing thought. I dare say there are a few we might not miss."

Keats struggled not to smile. Fisher had an intolerant view of useless nobility.

"Issue inquiries if any dynamite or gunpowder has gone missing in the last few weeks," Fisher instructed.

"Yes, sir. Is that all, sir?" Keats asked, hoping it was.

His superior tapped a folder on the right side of his desk. New cases always went on the right. "One more thing." He riffled through it, extracting a single sheet of paper. "We are to conduct a discreet inquiry into certain citizens who reside or occasionally stray into the East End."

"Sons of the realm making the rounds of the brothels again?" Keats asked wearily.

"Indeed. No doubt those who have submitted these names are rivals bent on a little mischief."

"Tantamount to wasting our time," Keats grumbled. "Couldn't one of the local inspectors handle this?"

"Yes, but it's been handed to us." Fisher pushed the list across the desk. "I doubt that any of these fellows is the East End killer, but we do what we are told."

"I'll look into the matter." *Along with all my other cases.* Keats retrieved the list from the desk but didn't bother to examine it, tucking it inside his coat. "How soon do you need my report?"

"As soon as you can manage. Frankly, Flaherty is more important to me than those names."

"Sir?" Keats asked, surprised. The anarchist was a long shot at best.

"The Whitechapel killer slays one at a time. A crazy Irishman with explosives can kill hundreds. With our luck, the deaths would include someone important, at least to the Crown. We don't need that kind of censure."

Keats nodded. "Still, it would be a feather in our cap if we found the East End butcher."

"It would, but I'm not counting on that. Abberline is no fool. If he hasn't flushed the fellow out, it's unlikely we'll encounter him."

"Unless he's an anarchist," Keats observed, pausing by the door.

"Not likely. Madmen tend to confine their lunacy to one track. Flaherty prefers explosions. Killing one whore at a time would be a waste of his talents—at least in his mind."

Keats pondered the observation. "I shall be back with the information as soon as I can."

"Thank you, Sergeant."

After he ate breakfast at a dining room, Keats studied the names on the list, taking note of their addresses, occupations and political connections.

A barrister's son, the nephew of a Conservative Lord, a chemist and a dentist. All a waste of time, I'm willing to wager. He returned the list to his pocket and poured more tea, savoring the moment of relative quiet. It was going to be another long day. He was in no hurry to dive into it.

"First, Marylebone," he murmured. This time, the Wescombs might not welcome him quite so warmly.

‡

Lord Wescomb smoothed his moustache with his thumb, brows furrowed in deep thought. "I can't say this is good news, Keats."

"No, my lord." Keats attempted to balance a delicate china cup and saucer on his knee, fearful of upending the contents on the expensive furniture. Usually he did not have such difficulty, but his nerves were taut at present.

Lady Sephora noticed his discomfort. "Set your tea aside if you feel the need, Sergeant."

"Thank you, my lady," Keats replied gratefully. He selected a biscuit and nibbled on it, pointedly catching the crumbs before they tumbled onto the floor in Lord Wescomb's study. A flicker of a smile came from his hostess.

"You say you trust this Fisher person?" Wescomb asked after considerable thought.

"Yes, I do, my lord. He has a solid head on his shoulders and is not prone to hysteria. Unfortunately, his intellect will demand more answers than I am free to give." Keats brushed his hands over the plate. He wanted more tea, but the threat of making a mess held him in check.

"The timing is ill," the lady observed. She shook her head in dismay. "The Conclave is anything but subtle these days."

"They dare not touch him or we'll have CID on our heads," Keats warned.

"Indeed. Nevertheless, often what appears to be a disaster may prove a boon. Perhaps it is time the world knew of us," Wescomb suggested.

Keats shook his head. "I disagree, my lord. The Chief Inspector weighs everything in relation to the danger it presents to Crown and Country. He is tenacious in that regard. We would, in essence, be the greatest threat he has ever encountered."

"Do you feel you can manage him without revealing our secret?" Lady Sephora asked.

"I have no choice. Fisher must be allowed to continue as Chief Inspector. We must remain hidden. I will just have to navigate a course between those two rocks."

Wescomb's silvery eyebrow ascended. "That is a lot for one man to take upon his shoulders."

"I know. I think I am capable." *I had better be.*

Lady Sephora leaned back in her chair, the tension draining from her face. She graced him with a saintly smile that warmed him to his toes. "I do believe you will succeed, Sergeant."

Keats was particularly susceptible to the lady's flattery. It was a near thing not to blush. "Thank you, Lady Wescomb. I value your confidence." He shot a concerned look at her husband. Wescomb had a grin on his face, aware of the effect his wife had on other men.

"Do keep us apprised of the matter," he said. "We will not mention this to The Conclave until it is absolutely necessary. What with Abernathy's illness—"

A series of taps on the door interrupted him. "Enter." The maid scurried in and handed an envelope to his lordship. As she left, he ripped it open and then donned his glasses to read the missive. He nodded, as if the contents were not unexpected.

"Ah, well, there it is. Abernathy summons us to his Death Rite, and requests that I be the Inquirer."

"Does he enclose a list of names?" Lady Sephora asked, leaning toward her husband in an attempt to read the document over his shoulder.

Lord Wescomb handed her the letter and pulled a separate sheet from the envelope. After a quick scan, he replied, "He seems to be two positions light of the required seven. He says that I should fill them as I see fit." Wescomb glanced over at Keats. "Will you do him the honor?'"

"I've never met him, but I shall stand at his Death Rite," Keats replied.

Wescomb turned toward his wife. "Sephora, will you accept the other position?"

She shook her head. "No, thank you. I have attended two others this month. I prefer not to see a third."

"Oh," Wescomb replied, clearly flummoxed.

"Why not Alastair?" Keats suggested. "He needs to be more involved in our traditions."

Wescomb nodded vigorously. "Capital idea! I'll send for him."

"He'll be at the hospital this time of the day, and none too pleased to be pulled away from his patients."

"Even better," Wescomb said. "He is one of us, whether he chooses to be or not."

Sephora returned Abernathy's letter with a pensive expression.

"Somehow, I suspect the doctor would most strenuously disagree."

✝

The man was a complete stranger. His crimson and black armband told the story—one of Alastair's kind was nearing the end of their life. He motioned the fellow into the hospital hallway, away from the curious stares of the nurses.

"Who is it?" Alastair asked in a low voice.

"Abernathy," the solemn man replied.

Alastair blinked. "There must be some mistake. I don't—"

A pale hand rose for silence. "Come. The Rite waits for no one."

The fellow turned on his heel and strode away, leaving Alastair with a myriad of questions. Biting back a scathing retort, he saw to his patient and then made his apologies for the abrupt departure.

His summoner waited by a carriage. Without a word, the man hoisted himself inside and beckoned to Alastair.

If he believed his escort would be more forthcoming once they were in the privacy of the coach, he was mistaken. Typically, a Death Rite was attended by close friends or family of the dying Transitive. This whole scene made no sense at all.

Alastair tried again. "Why am I to be part of this? I do not know this Abernathy. Surely he would wish one of his friends to be present instead of a stranger."

The summoner leveled his gaze on him. "You were requested, sir. That is all I know."

"*Doctor*," Alastair corrected, irritated at the man's tone.

"So you are." The fellow proffered an armband. Alastair jammed it into his coat pocket and fumed for the remainder of the journey.

The instant the carriage halted, Alastair disembarked. They were somewhere near Hyde Park. This Abernathy person was well heeled.

The interior of the house spoke of a solid income, though on the ostentatious side. New money, a few social rungs lower than the Wescombs, yet trying to give the impression they were equals. Most likely a prosperous merchant.

"Upstairs," his escort said and then added, "Doctor."

"Thank you." Alastair relinquished his outer garments to the maid and reluctantly donned the armband, ensuring the crimson stripe was at the bottom to signify his status as one of the Seven.

He was met at the top of the stairs by Keats.

"Ah, there you are. Come on, come on. It's nearly time," his friend urged.

Alastair snagged his arm and whispered, "You know this Abernathy?"

"No, never met him."

"Then why are we here?"

Keats raised his hands in surrender. "Because we are. Now stop fussing. Let's do what we must." He walked a short distance and entered a door demarked by black and crimson crepe. Alastair took a deep breath and followed him, his mind in turmoil.

The room was every bit as ostentatious as the rest of the house. A massive curtained bedstead dominated one wall near a blazing fireplace. Above the marble mantel was a vivid fresco of a vineyard, each vine bulging with ripe grapes.

Abernathy sat in a gilded chair, his grossly swollen feet propped on a fat purple cushion. He wore a heavy embroidered robe. On his balding head resided a crown of colorful flowers. A bottle of wine and a large goblet sat near him. He took a sip from the cup, using both hands to steady it.

Keats whispered, "Apparently a devotee of Bacchus."

Alastair nodded, disconcerted. Providing death was expected, each Transitive determined the setting in which they died. This one was a bit more garish than usual.

Lord Wescomb caught his eye and delivered a solemn nod in acknowledgment. Clearing his throat, he announced, "All are present." Abernathy gave a grunt of acknowledgement. "Let us form the Circle and witness the Rite."

As they took their positions around the dying man, Alastair's eyes skipped about the room. Besides Keats and Wescomb, there were four others present. He knew none of them. One in particular caught his notice, for he seemed out of place even amongst his peers. He was *en mirage*. Usually, the moment of change came later in the ceremony. Still, it wasn't the use of illusion that struck Alastair as singular so much as the aloof manner in which he held himself.

Wescomb began, "I stand as Inquirer for this most honorable *Rite de la Mort.*"

Alastair racked his brain for the required response and joined in with the others, his baritone voice ringing out. "We come to witness the End and celebrate the Beginning."

"Elijah Abernathy, are you ready to meet your Maker?" Wescomb asked.

"I welcome it," the man said, shifting uncomfortably on the chair, his color florid. Alastair's practiced eye surmised some disease of the blood, no doubt secondary to the man's passionate worship of the grape.

"Come forth, the Designated One," Wescomb ordered.

A young woman moved shyly forward, head lowered. She appeared in her early twenties. Clothed in black, her armband was reversed: a thick stripe of crimson with a narrow band of black at the bottom.

Abernathy beckoned to her with a weak motion of his hand.

"Come child, do not be afraid." She halted next to the chair, still looking down. Her body trembled, making her skirts rustle.

"Declare your name," Wescomb said, his tone softened.

"I am...Lynette, daughter of..." Her eyes rose and she smiled lovingly at her father. "Elijah Abernathy."

"Do you understand what is to come?" Wescomb asked.

"Yes."

"Then we shall bow to the one that finds Death's release. The Seven stand ready to witness the *Rite de la Mort.*"

On cue, Wescomb and the others dropped to their knees. The older man next to Alastair groaned with the effort.

With quaking hands, Abernathy uncorked a small bottle and poured the contents into his goblet. His grip betrayed him and the bottle fell to the floor. Ignoring it, he raised the cup to his mouth. Grimacing, he drank until it was empty, then set it aside.

Abernathy whispered, "Give me your hand, daughter." Lynette

did as ordered, a tear escaping down her pale cheek. "Close your eyes."

Alastair closed his eyes as well, though it was not required. He had no desire to witness the transition. He had lived through it, and it was not something he ever wished to see again. His beloved's Death Rite had not taken place in an opulent home, but in a clearing in the middle of a Welsh forest with her family clustered around her. There had been no need to hasten her death with some lethal potion. At her passing, two Transitives had been created. To Alastair's sorrow, he'd been one of them.

When he awoke from his nightmarish transformation, the man he knew was gone. Left in his place was an imposter, one who could change shape at will. Any form that he could visualize, he could imitate, even that of his dead lover. That had sickened him most.

Keats elbowed him, pulling him out of his past. The others had risen to their feet. He did so belatedly. Abernathy was dead. His daughter stood next to his body with an expression of utter incomprehension.

Alastair knew it well. No matter how someone tried to explain the sensation, it proved impossible to fathom. Her first few days would be unimaginable. Until the mind mastered the ability, the body would change at will with no discernable pattern. She would have to be hidden from view until she could control her shifts, until she understood the nature of what her father had bequeathed her.

"Welcome to our community, Lynette," Wescomb said.

Each of the Seven, in turn, offered their own greeting. When they reached Alastair, he gave a bow. He had no words of comfort for her, none that would explain how much her world had altered.

One of her arms shifted abruptly into that of an older woman. She stared at it in amazement. It changed back.

"Now it begins," Keats whispered. "God help her."

Alastair felt a frisson of apprehension rise within him as the others shifted into their particular forms. Lord Wescomb was as he'd seen him the night before, a younger version of himself. An elderly Keats appeared with a wise face and wrinkled hands. The haughty man gestured for Alastair to go *en mirage*. The doctor shook his head and stepped out of the circle.

"I think not." With an apologetic nod to the new Transitive in their midst, he strode out of the room. No one came after him. It was his choice whether or not he shifted, and the decision would be respected.

"For how long?" he asked under his breath, descending the stairs at a brisk clip. He removed the armband at the front door and handed it to the maid, collecting his coat and hat in turn.

"My condolences for your loss," he said. *And for what was created this day.*

7

Cynda's left breast hummed repeatedly, dragging her from a deep sleep. She groggily pulled herself upright and rubbed her eyes. The room was in twilight. Had she missed breakfast?

The pocket watch vibrated again. She extricated it from underneath the ruffle on her bodice. Before she communicated with TIC, she'd best figure out what had happened. Swinging her feet over the side of the bed, she allowed the vertigo to stabilize. The world around her was still red, like peering through a glass of cabernet.

Her mind clicked off events: arrived at boarding house, hit spider/doctor, slept, ate breakfast while dazzling the locals with her verbal brilliance. Then what happened?

She rummaged for the memory while buttoning her bodice. After she'd talked to Annabelle, she'd retreated to her room. The bed had called to her, and so she'd curled up for a quick nap. What could an hour matter?

She moved to the window and cleaned a patch of glass. Below, a lamplighter toted his ladder along the street, visiting each lamp along the way. Her hour nap had become a full day.

Oops.

The watch continued to reverberate like an irate bee trapped in a glass jar. Until she had something to report, it was best TIC didn't know of her physical condition. Once a Time Rover reached the point of no return—and they all did eventually—they were pulled from the field. Even Harter Defoe, the greatest of their lot, had been forced to quit. From what she'd heard, he'd not opted for a desk job, but vanished into legend. A classy *Exit Stage Left* after a career any Time Rover would envy.

Unfortunately, TIC's desk jockeys now disappeared in sync with the company's dwindling bank account. If Cynda couldn't time travel, she'd be without a job and a place to live. She'd end on her parents' doorstep, Off-Grid. Then she'd have to deal with her brother.

"I'll find Turner, then report. It won't be that hard."

By the time she'd laced her boots and donned her hat, gas lamps were lit as far as the eye could see. Cynda wound her way north to Wentworth, past the Victoria Workingmen's Home, and across the street to The Princess Alice. A three-story building with a classic bow front, it was reputed to be a favorite haunt of one of the Ripper suspects. If Cynda's luck held, Turner might be loitering there, observing the locals in their natural habitat.

Pushing her way past a couple of tipsy customers, she catalogued faces. The pub's interior reeked of cheap gin, unwashed bodies and cigar smoke.

"Shove off, luv, you're blockin' the way," a gruff voice announced. She obliged and moved further inside. In this sort of atmosphere she had to rely on the pocket watch. The interface would sniff the assembled bodies like a high-tech bloodhound, hunting for Turner's ESR Chip. Everyone from '057 had one. You got your Essential Subject Record Chip inserted at birth. Sort of like toting a portable filing cabinet with all your personal data. Without them, the PSI units were useless. In this case, no vibration from the watch meant no tourist.

And so it was. Pushing her way out the front doors, she set off for the next pub. A beer wagon lumbered by, the vehicle creaking under the load. She passed a young boy industriously polishing a gentleman's shoes while the customer scanned the evening newspaper.

Cynda paused at an intersection, blinking a couple of times in hopes of clearing her vision. Instead, the hallucinatory lightning fired again, bolts exploding around her as if hurled by a playful god. Preoccupied with the light show, she stepped in front of a carriage. A warning cry brought her back to reality. She lurched to the sidewalk with all the grace of an elephant on roller skates.

A man eyed her with concern, his grizzled face in need of a shave. "You best be careful, miss!"

"Thank you." He nodded and continued on his way.

"This is insanity," she murmured to herself. The East End was a dangerous place, and doubly so for those who saw things that weren't there.

Cynda retraced her steps to the boarding house, desperate for more sleep. Another day wouldn't matter either way, as long as she and the tourist were out of '88 before the 26th of the month.

TIC would be upset, but they'd have to live with it.

"Chapman Inquest News!" a newsboy called. She walked by him, ignoring his patter. "Police say murderer might strike again!"

Cynda halted in her tracks. Someone collided with her and issued a stern rebuke in blistering language. She swung around, fishing the needed penny out of a pocket and taking the paper.

"Thanks, ma'am," the lad replied, tapping his cap in appreciation.

"Thank you," she said without thinking. Positioning herself under the nearest gas lamp, she squinted at the masthead.

THE DAILY TELEGRAPH
TUESDAY, SEPTEMBER 25, 1888

"September 25th? What in the..."

A coarse shiver of vulnerability shot through her. She deliberately folded the paper and tucked it under one arm, struggling to keep the panic at bay. Straightening her hat, she set off for the boarding house. Outwardly, she appeared calm. Inwardly, her mind chattered like an inebriated monkey.

The Retrieval Order said August 24. I'm a month off. It's only five days from the double murders. Why is Turner still here? Why the hell am I here? No wonder Mildred and the others had been so concerned about her safety; she was in the middle of a crime wave.

Come on, it's not that dangerous. You know when and where the killings will be. Stay away from those places, and it'll be fine.

Her rationalization felt as thin as the leather on her boots.

Cynda halted at another intersection, mindful of the near miss she'd experienced a few blocks earlier. The drunken monkey had sobered with astonishing speed. She would contact TIC and demand an explanation. *If Ivan screwed up the chronsole setting, he's not going to live to see puberty.*

She was within one block of the boarding house when she spied him. Squinting in the darkness, Cynda judged the man against TIC's Vid-Photo. Same face, same hair, same approximate age.

A wave of relief flooded through her. "Professor Turner, I presume," she said. "A break, at last."

Turner observed her for a moment, then continued on his way.

Cynda followed, hiking at a strong pace despite the uncomfortable boots. If she was lucky, the professor was headed toward his new lodgings. They could collect his belongings, make sure the landlady was paid in full, and then spirit him down an alley and off to '057. Cynda would get her stuff from Annabelle's and follow in his vapor trail. In a few short hours she'd be lounging in her own bed after three luxurious showers. Maybe Chris would be back from his trip and they would work out their time lag the old-fashioned way—horizontal.

The man looked back again, as if to ensure that she was still following. That seemed odd; they'd never met. She kept up her pace. The edges of her vision began to unravel like a worn sweater. Radiant shafts of lag lightning blasted around her, leaving a wake of neon confetti sparkling downward onto the dark street.

In the distance Turner hesitated, executed a quick glance in her direction, and then disappeared into a passageway.

What's wrong with this picture? Hesitating at the entrance to the alley, her sixth sense fired warning rockets through her neural synapses. The interface wasn't vibrating. Not even a nudge.

She stepped gingerly into the alley, allowing the gloom to envelop her. No sound of retreating footsteps. A few tentative feet into the passageway, she saw something hanging from an intricate, free-form web. It was the biggest damned spider imaginable, the cerulean blue granddaddy of the one she'd accosted in her room.

It smiled at her.

"Go away!" Cynda waved to shoo it away, as if it were an annoying fly. "You don't exist." She blinked rapidly, hoping that might cure the problem. The spider remained, slowly lowering itself like a cheap theatrical prop until it was eye-level with her. Something darted past her feet. She jerked backward in surprise. The spider grabbed the rat with two of its legs.

She watched in fascinated horror as the arachnid proceeded to wrap the creature in its silken cords like it was a Christmas present. Over and over, the rodent tumbled in the spider's many legs, chittering in complaint. The moment the package was secure, the spider threw it over its shoulder like a grenade. It impacted the ground with a squishy squeak.

The compound eyes regarded her. "Next!" It beckoned with three of its eight feet while executing a smile worthy of a politician.

Hallucination or not, Cynda ran for it. She was a block away when the dry heaves hit. Bending over, she retched in the gutter until her stomach could no longer rise to the occasion. In the midst of her heaving, a couple walked by, shaking their heads. Cynda ignored them. Unless she could get control of the time lag, she'd have to return to 2057 empty-handed.

"The hell I will," she murmured. To go home without the tourist would mean her job.

"Miss Lassiter? Are you ill again?"

The doctor's voice. She groaned to herself. *Of all people...* A monogrammed handkerchief appeared under her nose. She wiped her face and mouth with it. Deciding he probably didn't want it back in its current condition, she stuffed it in her pocket.

A hand steadied her as she rose. "Yes, I am ill again. Now if you would be so kind as to walk me to the boarding house, I will go back to bed."

Dr. Montrose regarded her solemnly. "As you wish." He firmed his grip on her elbow and guided her at a leisurely pace. "Have you considered treatment for your delusions?"

"I'm perfectly fine," she snapped.

"Your actions say otherwise. You bolted out of that alley like the very devil was on your tail. Seeing spiders again, were we?"

Cynda gave him a sideways glance that would have dismembered a lesser man. Before she could respond, she wavered on her feet. His grip instantly tightened.

He studied her with a stern expression. "You must get your rest. You are near collapse."

"Look who's talking," she said. "At least my eyes don't have their own set of luggage."

He raised an eyebrow. "Your speech is quite unique."

"Americans are like that."

He shook his head. "No, I studied medicine in Baltimore. Your speech is singularly different."

Oops. Good going, Lassiter. "That's me, singularly different," she said, hoping he'd drop the subject. A flash of lightning struck at her feet and she jumped in response. The doctor shook his head at her antics.

"What was that? Another spider?" he chided.

"Lightning," she murmured. "It'll all go away once I get some sleep."

"Then by all means get your rest, Miss Lassiter," the doctor retorted. "If not, someone may feel compelled to have you committed until your hallucinations pass."

Cynda clamped her mouth shut, lacking a good response. The last thing she needed was to end up in a Victorian asylum.

‡

Once Dr. Montrose deposited her in her room, she used his handkerchief to stuff the keyhole so no one would see what she was about to do. It took time to crawl out of the heavy dress and petticoats and unlace the boots. She cautiously leaned over the washbasin—it was free of blue spiders. Sighing, she washed her face free of the street grime. After brushing her hair and teeth, she retrieved the pocket watch and flipped it open. As she wound the stem the appropriate number of times to activate the interface's communication link, she forced herself not to succumb to the rising desire to panic.

"I'll get it done. Everything will be okay," she told herself. She'd been in worse situations, like that time in 1906 during the San Francisco earthquake. It was all a matter of keeping focused.

The watch unfolded like a flower in her hand, petal by metal petal, until it reached the diameter of a large sandwich plate. A toothpick-size wand poked out the side—the only way she could access the miniscule keyboard. The dull orange screen lit the air above the device. Cynda sat on the bed, positioning the interface on the pillow in front of her.

She tapped in her password with shaking fingers and waited. She'd never quite understood how it all worked. Ralph had tried to explain, but all she got was that it was pretty awesome technology. She was happy to leave it at that.

The watch beeped reassuringly.

Cynda typed, *Log Ong.*

Unknown command.

She swore and entered the phrase again, taking more care.

Log On Complete, the tiny screen typed back at her. TIC's leering clock logo blinked at the end of the sentence.

Ralph?

Sure is. Where have you been?

She switched to their private code. *KATL.* Kick Ass Time Lag.

RB? Really bad?

RRB. Really, really bad.

Sorry. Any sign of tourist?

Just starting.

Keep me posted.

Why so short? He had a full-size holo-screen and keyboard and didn't need to be tight with words.

Big bosses here.

"Uh-oh." TIC's higher-ups didn't visit that often. Their presence was never a good sign. It usually coincided with more layoffs.

Something by tomorrow, she typed.

Sooner. Don't loiter.

She frowned at that. He knew she didn't like this time period. Why the nudge? Time to push back.

What was DOI? she asked.

A pause and then, *Date of Insertion 9/24/1888*

RO said 8/24/88.

Another pause. *No, Retrieval Order says 9/24/88.*

Cynda glared. She knew she'd read it right. *I'm not supposed to be here NOW.*

Neither is tourist. Corporate making payroll, no doubt.

Cynda stuck her tongue out at the interface as if Ralph could see her. She issued a deep sigh. So much for TIC's rules. They were easily bent when the bank account ran dry. *Find out what happened.*

Will do.

Need list of nearby pubs.

A list scrolled by—and scrolled by. It continued until Cynda's eyes began to blur. She waited impatiently until it ended.

How many are there? she asked.

Over 40.

Give me the most well known. Turner would hit the ones that held the best potential for academic research.

The list was shorter now. She studied the names and nodded to herself. Most of them she knew.

Thanks, Ralph.

Be careful.

I will. Log Off.

Logged Off.

She converted the pocket watch back to its usual size and tucked it under her pillow. Ralph was on her side. Between them, they'd get this done.

✝

Alastair heard the key in the lock, and then the sounds of the strange American woman rummaging around her room. She talked to herself, though he couldn't make out the words. It appeared her mental state was deteriorating with each passing hour. He'd been shocked to find her on the street in such a condition: the fear on her face genuine, the delusions of sufficient strength to frighten her witless.

He settled on a course of action, intending to consult a

physician familiar with ailments of the brain. Perhaps a particular treatment might aid the woman in retaining what degree of sanity she still possessed.

As he washed his face, he gazed into the shaving mirror above the washstand. Dark circles resided under his eyes. The sight caused him to laugh spontaneously. *She is correct; I do have my own set of luggage.*

He poked gingerly at the bruise and winced. It was darker now. Her violent act did not bode well. Would she degenerate into a raving lunatic, shouting obscenities at terrors only she could see? He'd made rounds at an asylum while in medical school. He knew what happened to young women in those places.

Pray God that is not her end. He splashed more cold water on his face. It seemed to steady him. *Perhaps the madness is temporary, as she says.*

The thought brought him no comfort. Miss Lassiter was going insane, and there was little medical science could do to stop it.

8

Wednesday, 26 September, 1888

Morning brought mixed blessings. On the plus side, Cynda's mind seemed fairly clear and her stomach was on the mend. On the negative, the world was still rose-tinged despite two doses of chocolate. And the worst news: TIC was noticeably silent. She'd flipped open the watch first thing, expecting a nudge to see how she was progressing. Nothing.

A shiver zipped through her. *Was TIC still in business? Surely, they wouldn't leave me here?*

They would if they could get away with it.

Despite laws against orphaning Time Rovers in the event of a bankruptcy, it was still rumored that folks just disappeared. Especially the ones who had no family to complain when their loved one didn't return. *Like me.*

No, Ralph was her lifeline. He wouldn't abandon her. He'd get her back home, no matter what it took.

"Home?" She shook her head. This small boarding house room had more charm than her corporate apartment, though it was a seventh of the size. Annabelle had tried to make it welcoming with a floral pattern pitcher and bowl on the washstand. The curtains, though slightly gray, were lace. A painting hung above the bed, a pastoral scene with a shepherd and his flock. In contrast, Cynda's apartment was Corporate Modern, as they called it. Corporate Sterile was closer to the truth. Since she lived there at TIC's whim, personalization wasn't allowed. She was as permanent as a bandage, her only possessions a book of poems by e.e. cummings and a stuffed, black-footed ferret she'd won at a county fair and smuggled back to '057. She'd named him Fred. Next to Ralph, he was her best buddy, the furry confidant who knew all her secrets.

Cynda heard the sound of a door closing, then the heavy tromp of footsteps on the stairs. Either Dr. Montrose or the bizarre Mr. Hix off to breakfast. It was her cue she needed to be out of bed.

"Move it, Lassiter," she commanded, rising to her feet. No fireworks erupted. She took that as a good sign. When the washbasin was arachnid-free, that brought more hope. "Happy days are here again."

Impatiently, she layered on the clothes—hose, boots and then the bustle and petticoats over the onesie. She never wore a corset if she could get away with it. Finally, the skirt and the bodice. Today, it was the navy outfit, though through her rose-tinted eyeballs it appeared purple. Buttoning the bodice was tedious, but eventually she looked presentable. The tapered design accented her tiny waist. *A proper Victorian silhouette.* A glance at her exaggerated rear end did nothing to improve her mood. *With a behind the size of Westminster Abbey.*

By the time she'd painstakingly negotiated the stairs, the dining room was empty. No need to worry about communing with the locals or enduring another patronizing encounter with the doctor.

Mildred puttered in, issued a good morning and told her to help herself to the food.

"Oh, can you do something for me?" Cynda asked. She dug the doctor's handkerchief out of her pocket. "This needs to be washed. It's Dr. Montrose's. He loaned it to me the other night."

Mildred took the item, gave her a curious look and then nodded. "He'll be glad to have it back. He's got seven of them you see, one for each day, and now he's down to four. He's rather put out that they're walking off. I spoke sharply with the washerwoman, but she said she didn't take any of them."

Cynda loaded her plate like she'd not eaten in weeks, the salty ham included. "Maybe he forgets he loans them out."

"Might be," was the response.

By the time Mildred returned a half-hour later, the serving dishes were empty. She nodded her approval, as if all women ate like dockworkers.

Burdened by a full stomach and the desire for a long nap, Cynda pointedly ignored the bed's siren call when she returned to her room. Something else caught her attention; the wardrobe door was open. A quick inventory proved nothing out of place.

"Probably Mildred." Cynda extricated more chocolate from her Gladstone and made sure to shut the door tightly.

The journey down the stairs wasn't as scary this time. When she reached the front door, she'd conjured up a good mood. Once outside, Cynda's good humor evaporated. Daylight did nothing for the East End's scenic appeal. Her rose-filtered mind played havoc with the scenery, causing the dull-yellow coal fire smoke to appear orange. In Cynda's world, a pumpkin-colored haze hung heavy in the air.

Yuck. The debris in the street was recognizable now. Besides the occasional dead rodent, piles of fresh horse droppings and rotting food dotted the ground. Two small children played near a decaying carcass, oblivious to the flies rising from what was once a dog. Cynda sighed. There was a desperate hopelessness at this time in history, as if humankind were caught in quicksand. The more they thrashed, the faster they sank.

"My God," she said under her breath.

"Depressing, isn't it?" a voice asked. She turned to find Dr. Montrose next to her. She'd been so transfixed she'd not heard him exit the boarding house.

"Yes, it is."

"And yet, in many ways, it speaks of hope," he said.

She frowned, not understanding. "How so?"

"Any improvement in their lot is a sea change. Something as simple as ensuring they have a safe place to sleep, or one nourishing meal a day makes a world of difference in their lives."

The simplicity of the theory intrigued her. "I hadn't thought of it that way."

"To move a mountain, all you need is a shovel and infinite patience."

She studied him with renewed interest. "Shoveling away, are you?"

He smiled while donning his bowler. "In my own way. How are you this morning?"

"Much better." That didn't seem adequate, so she added, "Thank you for asking."

"No visions?"

"No." *Unless you count the fact you've been hit by lightning twice while we've been talking, and the world looks like a burnt pumpkin pie.*

"That is good news." He tipped his hat politely and added, "Good day, Miss Lassiter."

"Good day to you, Dr. Montrose." She knew he didn't believe a word she'd said.

He descended the stairs and set off at a quick gait. A man with a purpose. "Good luck with your mountain, Doctor," she whispered. "You're going to need a lot of shovels."

The Princess Alice was a bust. The next four pubs were non-starters as well. As for the previous night's bogus sighting, Cynda chalked that up to time lag. Turner hadn't been there any more than the spider. The watch was never wrong. Sweating in the heavy garments, she trudged on. After another piece of chocolate, the East End returned to its usual sickly yellow.

The orange was better.

Heading east away from Commercial Street, Cynda struck pay dirt at The Alma. The moment she pushed inside the pub her breast began to vibrate, sending an unnerving pulse into her right nipple. She slid her hand under her mantelet and cautiously tapped the watch, ending the vibration. At the first opportunity, she'd have to reposition the thing.

Professor Turner sat in a far corner, puffing on a pipe just like one of the regulars, with a partially consumed porter in front of him. His eyes constantly scanned the room, surveying each patron with a clinical eye.

Sociologists—the ultimate people watchers.

Cynda skirted a couple of drunks and wound her way to the back of the pub. Without waiting for an invitation, she took a seat opposite her quarry. He assessed her openly.

"Miss, I am not inclined toward sexual proclivities, at least not at present." His upper-crust British accent marked him as a native, albeit a century and some change later. "However, this evening I might be willing to indulge you. You are far prettier than most."

Cynda leaned forward, delivered a devastatingly pleasant smile and replied in a low voice, "I am not a 'daughter of joy,' Professor Turner. I'm here to escort your butt home."

A chagrined expression blossomed across his face, as if he'd been caught *in flagrante delicto* with the Prime Minister's wife.

"Oh. I thought..." he stammered.

"You thought we'd not bother to find you, right?"

He gave a quick nod. His eyes saddened. Turner raised his hand to indicate the empty space around his wrist. "I thought since I'd misplaced the band..."

"How did you lose it?" she whispered.

"I'm not sure. I stopped to help a young woman. A while later, I noticed it was gone."

Oh, great. "Were you wearing it?"

An embarrassed look. "No, actually, I...ah...stuck it in a

pocket. It irritated my wrist."

Cynda kept the groan to herself. While Turner played the chivalrous knight, the woman's accomplice stole the band. It was a classic "distract the mark." Cynda would have to report the loss to TIC. They'd input the band code number and deactivate it. On its own, it wasn't capable of sending its owner through time. Still, losing one resulted in a ton of paperwork and that burden would fall on her.

"Come along, Professor. The omnibus is leaving and you're on it."

"But this is a most extraordinary time. It's so..." He waved a hand to encompass the bar scene. "...so rich in detail and human interaction. We couldn't...come to an arrangement, could we?" he asked, leaning forward conspiratorially.

Cynda wasn't surprised at the offer; a few Time Rovers took cash under the table to extend a tourist's stay, even if only for a few more hours. The money was useless in '057, but hard cash bought gems, and those could be smuggled home without much effort. Somehow, TIC always found out. Another one of those infractions that led to immediate dismissal, along with a visit from the tax authorities.

"No deal, Professor. The longer you're here, the more prone you are to..." She lowered her voice even more, leaning closer to him, "*their* diseases. So if you've been sampling the fruits of Victorian womanhood...for research purposes of course, syphilis is one of the many—"

Turner rose, siphoned off the rest of his beer and pointed toward the pub's entrance. "After you, madam."

Cynda kept the triumphant smile to herself. That line always got them right where it hurt.

As she led him out of the pub, one of the patrons called out, "Right fine one ya caught there, mate. Worth a poke, I'd say."

"Give it to her good," another chimed in.

Turner's face colored as he opened the door for her. Cynda couldn't muster any sympathy.

On the way to his boarding house, he waxed at length about the time period and how much research he'd conducted. She kept nodding—anything to keep him moving toward the future. Once they reached his room, she even helped him pack.

A few minutes later, he frowned as she rejected yet another site because of the amount of foot traffic. "Why not leave from my room?" he asked.

"If you disappear from the boarding house, it'll lead to

questions. We had that happen once, and the Rover was charged with murder, even though the cops couldn't find a body. Made a...mess of things," she said. *A helluva mess.* The week she'd spent in a Prohibition-Era jail cell taught her that lesson.

Finding the right location proved difficult. Most were full of people conducting some sort of commerce, illicit or otherwise. Finally, she located one that served their purposes. It was a dead end, with no windows overlooking the street.

Cynda looked around as she pulled the pocket watch from under her mantelet and flipped it open.

Turner offered a handful of Victorian currency. "You might as well have this."

"Professor, we've—"

"No, not as a bribe. They said not to bring any money back." He flashed a grin. "I was rather lucky at cards."

"As long as we agree it is not a bribe." A nod. "Okay, then I'll pass it onto someone who needs it." The doctor came to mind. He'd know an unfortunate or two who would benefit from a few regular meals.

"Thank you." Turner took a wistful look around, as if saying farewell to a lover. "I'm going to miss this."

You've got to be kidding. "Think of the really interesting stories you can tell at those dull academic parties."

He quirked a smile. "I can, can't I?"

She winked. "Especially the ones about the brothels."

He gave a mannish grin. "Just as long as the old *toil and strife* isn't around," he said, employing Cockney rhyming slang for his spouse.

Unfolding the watch, she logged on and typed in a retrieval order code. On the other end, chron-op would realize her charge didn't have a time band and after a quick sign-off from a higher-up, would send one. It cost TIC more money this way, but it got the tourist home. No doubt, the accounting department would try to stick Turner with the additional expense. While they waited, the professor fidgeted. Cynda tried hard not to do the same.

"Any moment now," she said.

She tensed as a couple walked by the alley's entrance. They continued on. A familiar hum echoed around them as a replacement band appeared near her right foot. She scooped it up, then regretted the move as her head exploded from inside. Someone flipped a switch and the world went orange again.

Cynda offered the band to her charge, waiting until he installed it on his wrist. She executed a mock salute and tripped the watch. The professor vanished. A chirp issued from the time interface a few seconds later. The tourist was home.

"Yes!" Cynda collapsed the watch and hid it for safekeeping, positioning it away from the more sensitive parts of her anatomy. She stuffed Turner's largesse in the top of her right boot, a feat in itself. Task accomplished, she strode out of the alley like a Roman conqueror.

As Cynda stood on a street corner waiting for the stream of carriages and carts to pass by, she felt a slight tug on her skirt. A quick grab netted her a grimy hand. The small boy attached to it squirmed like a snake, shouting at her.

"Nice try," she said, and then let him go. He fled, narrowly missing an old woman in his escape. Cynda put her hand in the pocket—the remaining piece of chocolate was gone. "Hope you enjoy it, kid."

‡

"Come on, come on," Cynda grumbled impatiently, tapping the little wand on the pillow next to the expanded pocket watch. It usually didn't take this long.

Logged On, the screen typed back at her.

Ralph?

Yes.

Leaving soon—30 min or less

Negative. New assignment.

"No, no, no!" she snarled. *KATL getting bad. Must come home.*

No go.

For a moment, she was tempted to type back a swear word, and then decided against it. TIC would review the logs, and cursing was penalized by a charge against your paycheck. She frowned and tapped the wand on her chin in thought. *Hadn't he been urging her to finish the assignment and get home?* Now it was just the opposite.

She pushed the envelope. *If I come home solo?*

There was a lengthy pause. *You don't want to do that.*

This time, she swore out loud. She was screwed.

Who is it? she asked.

Dr. Walter Samuelson. Details to follow.

The Retrieval Order dutifully trudged across the dinky screen. No photo was included. Another cost-cutting measure, no doubt. She skimmed through the minor details and then checked the tourist's retrieval date. Samuelson had gone AWOL four weeks earlier. That was a lifetime in TIC's world.

"What the hell is going on back there?"

Instead she typed, *Why didn't they act sooner?*

He's a psychiatrist. Check the hospitals and the asylums.

Why not sooner?

First Rover unsuccessful. Lost contact with second Rover three days ago. Last report stated tourist was being elusive, but Rover closing in.

Cynda rocked back in shock. Rovers did not disappear. TIC should be turning over every rock to avoid a governmental investigation. *Why didn't they mention this when they'd inserted me in this time period? Who could be missing?*

A bolt of fear shot through her. "Chris." She leaned forward again and typed the question with an unsteady hand.

Is it Chris?

The pause seemed to last hours. *Yes.*

"Oh, my God," she whispered. The last time they were together, he'd said he was going on special assignment, some high-paying contract job. He'd not given her the details, but then that wasn't unusual. Working as a freelance Rover, Chris alternated between the three time insertion companies. His hours were erratic. Often they didn't see each other for weeks. When they finally did connect, they were too busy working off the time lag in bed to talk about their respective jobs.

Why didn't they tell me before I was sent here? she typed.

CTA.

"Covering their asses," she translated. If the Rover caused a Time Incursion, there were substantial fines. It was probably why the dates on Turner's Retrieval Order had mysteriously changed. TIC would do anything to avoid the spotlight, especially with bankruptcy rumors swirling around them like dust devils.

I'll find both of them, she typed in uneven bursts, her hand shaking harder now.

Work fast and be VERY careful.

Cynda's blood chilled. Ralph rarely issued a warning so plainly.

Log Off, she typed.

Logged Off.

Cynda returned the pocket watch to its compact shape and clutched it between her palms. It felt icy against her skin, a reflection of the dread forming in her heart.

9

Ivan dropped into the chronsole chair, signaling a shift change. "How's it going?"

"Not great," Ralph replied. "Six out—four tourists, two Rovers. We got an issue in '88."

Thad crossed to the chronsole desk. "That's incorrect, Hamilton. The total is five out," their boss interjected. "Stone came back in."

Ralph shook his head. "Not from what I'm seeing. The log shows Chris is still in '88. His last update—"

"The log hasn't been updated. He came in last night."

That didn't wash. The chron logs were updated every quarter-hour. Before Ralph could protest, he felt a kick at ankle-level from Ivan.

"The logs have been running slow. They're about a day behind now," he explained.

The hell they are. "My mistake," Ralph said, casting a glance toward the kid.

"Hey, it happens," Ivan said, shrugging.

Thad made an approving noise. "That's settled, then. You're off-duty, Hamilton." The martinet turned on a heel and marched away.

"So I am," Ralph murmured. "And you're a lying SOB."

A furtive nod came from Ivan.

"Keep an eye on Cynda. Things are going wrong there," Ralph whispered as he bent to collect his backpack.

"I will." Something small tumbled into the pack from above.

"Read the file once you're out of here," the kid said.

"I will. Thanks."

"Later."

✣

Ivan's nano-drive delivered a succinct warning; scuttlebutt was that all the Senior Rovers' apartments would be confiscated at eight the next morning. Those poor unfortunates who were in residence would be evicted. Those on assignment would return to find their domiciles locked down, their possessions discarded.

Providing they ever got home. According to Ivan, the chron logs were being altered to avoid governmental fines. There were at least five Rovers in the Time Stream, including Chris. All indications pointed toward TIC orphaning the lot of them and hiding their crime by sanitizing the paperwork.

"Bastards."

Ralph waited for the LuggageBot to wheel itself into the center of Cynda's stark apartment. If a person's life could be judged by the amount of their personal possessions, Jacynda Lassiter was a phantom of someone's imagination. Clearly, she didn't see this as home. In retrospect, the piece of luggage was more than he needed. A good-sized box would have covered it.

While he packed her sparse wardrobe, he cycled through the Vid-Net Mail messages, deleting the sales pitches as he went. She always kept Chris' communications, and Ralph understood why. They were funny. Every time Chris returned from an assignment, he'd send a message to Cynda. Some included naughty limericks based on the time period he'd just visited. Others were frankly pornographic. All were hilarious.

"End of message queue," the computer announced. "Delete all?"

Ralph hesitated. "Negative," he said. "State date of last message from CStoneRover."

"Twenty-first June, 2057."

"No message received last evening?"

"Negative."

"Check status of CStoneRover mailbox."

"Mailbox full. Mail last downloaded twenty-first June."

A week ago. Thad's lie didn't hold water. Ralph sighed. Being right wasn't always pleasant.

"Send all messages from *CStoneRover* to *SilverHairGeek*," he ordered, forwarding them to his mailbox. Cynda would want them. He suspected she'd be bunking with him until TIC revived or died an unnatural death. The latter was the odds-on favorite.

"Messages forwarded," the computer reported.

"Delete remainder."

"Deleted."

And just to annoy TIC, "Lock account." It would take the geeks a while to hack the password, only to find the account was empty.

"Account locked."

Ten minutes later, Ralph tucked Ferret Fred into his pocket and shut the apartment door behind him. When Cynda gave him the apartment's pass code, she'd joked that he might need it if something bad happened to her. "Make sure Fred gets a good home," she'd said.

God, I hope it doesn't come to that.

☩

Wednesday, 26 September, 1888

Lord Wescomb's pacing proved exceedingly difficult in the cramped room that served as his study. He marched to the door, then to the east window, three wide strides to the mantel, and then to the far wall near the drinks cupboard. He was currently on his fifth circuit. Lady Sephora shifted her voluminous skirts out of the way to allow him a few more precious inches.

"How dare they?" he growled. As he marched by her once more, Sephora caught his hand. He glared, then softened his expression instantly.

"Really, John, you must sit down," she said. "We will find a solution together."

His anger dampened, Wescomb acquiesced. After crumpling into his chair and taking a large gulp of brandy, he swore, "God's blood." He gave his wife a chagrined look. "Sorry, my dear."

She waved it away. "I've heard worse."

"You've said worse," Wescomb retorted. They shared a smile.

"What has The Conclave done this time?" She retrieved her glass of Amontillado from the walnut table by the chair.

"They believe they've found Alastair's Achilles Heel."

"His clinic?" she asked. Wescomb dipped his head in respect for her astute guess.

"They will offer him monies to fund his work if he promises to leave town for the short term—at least until the murders cease."

"If Alastair declines their offer?"

"Then they will pressure the clinic's landlord to evict him."

Sephora's mouth dropped open in astonishment. "That is egregious, John. The clinic is his life. They'll destroy him."

"That's what I told them. They won't listen to reason."

"They are the most ignorant of men," she grumbled, tapping a finger on the rim of her sherry glass.

"I know that look, Sephora. The Conclave has ordered us not to interfere."

Her eyes flared. "They dare to demand we stand aside while they ruin his life?"

"Yes, they dare."

Sephora fumed. "They fear him that much?"

"They fear him and the volatility of the situation. The slightest mistake, and the world will know of our existence."

"It is too preposterous to think that Alastair is this fiend. He devotes his life to the care of the sick and injured."

Wescomb shrugged. "No matter his virtues, The Conclave wants him out of the city for the time being."

"They want him a puppet," she said, a frown firmly in place.

"That as well," Wescomb agreed. He finished his brandy with another gulp.

Sephora ran a fingertip around the rim of the sherry glass, generating a low-pitched hum. "When do they intend to inform him of their so-called offer?"

"They are having Keats deliver a summons tonight."

Sephora placed the empty sherry glass on the table and smoothed her dress. "At least we have Keats on our side," she said.

Wescomb nodded. "The ultimate mouse in the wainscoting."

"I had hoped they might bring him onto The Conclave to replace Abernathy."

"No such luck. Livingston is the newest member."

"He is an unusual man," Sephora said. "Difficult to read."

"Indeed. At present, we must bide our time, my dear."

She gave a deep sigh. "I so pity Alastair."

Wescomb shook his head. "There is more to that lad than they realize. His ability came from a Welsh Gypsy, did you know that?"

Sephora's eyes widened in wonder. "No, I did not."

"Keats told me. It is said they have capabilities beyond the rest of us." Wescomb rose to pour himself more brandy. He gestured toward the sherry. She nodded. "If Alastair can hold his own, we'll play those badgers for all they're worth."

Sephora gave a glittering smile. "Precisely my thought."

"To war, my lady," Wescomb toasted, raising his glass.

"To victory," she replied, clinking her glass against his.

‡

Stretched out on the bed, Cynda stared at the dingy ceiling. A slight breeze pushed aside the window curtain, flowing over her face. On the street, an eel-pie vendor touted his wares in a singsong chant. Her stomach growled, reminding her that food was a necessity.

According to Annabelle, neither Chris nor Dr. Samuelson had stayed at the boarding house during the past few weeks, though a young man matching Chris' description had called at the establishment and made inquiries regarding the missing shrink. That had been six days ago. The only other place TIC used in Whitechapel—Moody's Rooms on Green Street near the London Hospital—hadn't seen them either. With no photo of Samuelson to go by, she was reduced to trudging through the pubs asking about the elusive tourist and hoping the pocket watch would quake when she got close. That would be a supreme hassle. Better to go with Ralph's suggestion—check the asylums. Maybe someone would remember him.

If she were lucky, she'd intersect with Chris somewhere along the way. Cynda sought the memory of the last time they'd been together. It'd been a long, leisurely weekend full of quiet talk and vigorous sex. He'd just returned from Elizabethan England and the defeat of the Spanish Armada. In fine form, Chris had quoted Shakespeare while they'd made love. He always made her laugh. Now he was missing. If there had to be a last time together, it couldn't have been more perfect.

Cynda shuddered at the thought. *No way. He's just lost his interface, that's all.* In her heart, she knew her explanation didn't fly. If Chris had lost his interface, he'd stay put at the boarding house to wait for a Rover to fetch him home.

During one of their all-night sessions, he'd admitted he'd become a Rover for the money, and wanted to start his own business. Her needs were more primal; though she craved the security of a steady job and the means to help her family, it was the adrenalin rush that fueled her desire to leap time. Boredom was an abomination. Who else could say they'd ridden with Genghis Khan or stood on the deck of the Titanic moments before it kissed the fated iceberg?

"Who the hell would want to?" she muttered to herself. Well-adjusted people didn't seek risk. She was born to be a Time Rover. Now she felt trapped, just like that rat so snuggly cocooned in the giant spider's silken threads. Chris' disappearance had changed everything.

Now, the risk was personal.

✝

Cynda scanned the street, her vision clear for a change. Two men walked past her, giving her the eye. Did they think she was a prostitute, or were they after the contents of her purse? Hard to tell. If she'd been home, Cynda would have accessed the PSI unit on her left wrist. Hers was a wristwatch, though they were available in a variety of forms to suit the wearer. The interface would analyze the gents' ESR Chips and determine if they posed a threat. More expensive upgrades allowed you to access their marital status, financial rating and how many people they'd slept with. Depending on the upgrade, she could even snoop their college transcripts, blood type and current medical conditions. If she came under attack, a distress signal was sent to the nearest law enforcement center and a CopBot dispatched. The Personal Security Interfaces acted as the ultimate electronic guard dog while keeping tabs on you at the same time.

But not here. The Skeptics would love this place. No technology to speak of, at least nothing intrusive like the PSI units. You were on your own. You made a mistake, it cost you. Sometimes you only got to make one.

The two men halted at the end of the street, still watching her. A shiver crawled across her shoulders. The mission had changed; this was no simple retrieval. She needed help if she was to find Chris and the missing academic.

A door opened and closed behind her. It was the doctor. A quick glance revealed the pair was still at the corner.

Dour as he was, Dr. Montrose might prove the ideal remedy to her situation.

Once again, Alastair found Miss Lassiter on the stairs outside the boarding house. She was dressed in navy, and the color suited her complexion. As he exited the building, she stared at him thoughtfully, and then nodded as if some decision had been made.

"I have to find some food," she announced. "Would you like to join me?"

Alastair shook his head. "My...situation does not allow

such extravagances."

She appeared puzzled. He realized he'd have to be more candid. "All my spare income goes to the clinic."

"Oh, I see. What do you usually eat for supper?" she quizzed.

"I have an apple."

She blinked in amazement. "That's it?" He nodded.

"Nonsense. You have to eat."

"Miss Lassiter, I assure you that—"

"I still owe you for your treatment the other night. Consider a meal payment for your services."

He joined her on the sidewalk. "In truth, you do not owe me anything. I have an arrangement with Annabelle to treat her guests should they become ill. That arrangement compensates for a portion of my rent."

She frowned at him and tapped a foot. It was a girlish gesture that seemed out of place for a woman. "We are at an impasse, Doctor. I would like to pay for your supper. You are being...stubborn. How can we work this out?"

He frowned back at her. "I am not the one being stubborn."

More foot tapping, followed by a quick glance toward the corner. "It is likely that if I go out on my own tonight, I might have a relapse."

"Are you still seeing blue creatures?" he asked.

"Maybe," she replied. She looked down the street again. This time, his eyes followed. Two men loitered at the corner.

Are they the reason for her invitation?

"Are you requesting that I accompany you this evening, as your physician, lest you become incapacitated?"

"Exactly."

"And in recompense, you will purchase my meal?"

A quick nod, followed by a smile of triumph. He knew that look; Lady Sephora wore it when she was determined to get her own way. Lord Wescomb had once advised that when a woman adopted that expression, a man should just accept defeat and retire gracefully from the field.

He took her arm. "I know a dining hall that serves healthy food at reasonable prices."

"I knew you'd see it my way," she said and gave him a bright smile.

As if I had any other option, madam.

10

The doctor's choice of eating establishment proved ideal. The dining room was cozy, with a dozen or so tables, glowing gas lamps, a toasty fireplace and surprisingly attractive brocade wallpaper. For a moment, Cynda forgot she was in the East End. Even more important, the food proved plentiful and remarkably tasty. Her nausea abated for the moment, she ate heartily through the roast beef, potatoes, crusty bread and sticky toffee pudding.

Finishing off the dessert, Cynda resisted the temptation to lick her fingers. She pointedly ignored the giraffe sitting in the corner of the dining hall clad in a cutaway coat with a top hat nestled between its long ears. If it were really there, the Victorians would be serving it tea.

"You have quite an appetite, Miss Lassiter," the doctor observed, dabbing with a napkin in an attempt to obscure a smile.

"I always have. My family said I'm like a shrew: I can eat my body weight every day."

"I see," he replied, his amusement clearly growing. "I can't quite picture you with pointed nose and a tail."

She twitched her nose, and that set him to chuckling. "Did you know that some cultures believe that having a shrew in your house means you'll come into money?"

"Really? Then perhaps I should have you visit my clinic. How is it you know about such customs?" Alastair asked politely.

"I read a lot," Cynda said. "Have you tried to find funding for your clinic?" she asked, deftly shuttling the conversation in his direction.

He sighed and put down his fork. "Alas, yes. Money is difficult to come by. Donors prefer larger facilities than the clinic Daniel and I have created."

"And if you had adequate money?" she asked after a sip of tea.

Alastair leaned forward, his brown eyes suddenly ablaze at her question. "We would add more doctors and include newer methods of treatment. I envision a dispensary where we would hand out medicines on the spot. I would like to engage a doctor to visit those too ill to come to the clinic. And I would—"

He stopped abruptly and leaned back in his seat, the fire draining away. Picking up the fork, he shook his head. "I'm just dreaming."

"Dreams are what keep us alive, doctor," she said.

That earned her an intense look. "What is your dream, Miss Lassiter, if I may be so bold to ask?"

Cynda puzzled on that for a time. "To find a place that feels like home." That was the heart of it. She was always the stranger.

The doctor raised an eyebrow, the fork in his hand forgotten. "Certainly you feel at peace with your family."

"No, not really. I don't feel at home anywhere." *No matter the century.* "My family and I live in two different worlds. They have their lives; I have mine."

"Do you have siblings?"

"An older brother."

When she didn't elaborate, the doctor took the hint. "Then I hope you find your very own place, Miss Lassiter." To her surprise, he hadn't laughed at her, but appeared to comprehend the loneliness inside her. No doubt, he had his own.

"Call me Jacynda," she said.

"Alastair."

They studied each other for a time. The bruise on his cheek was darker now, though it didn't seem to hurt his looks.

"I'm sorry for hitting you, though I can plead diminished capacity at the time."

"I've been struck before, but never by such a fine-looking woman."

The compliment caught her off guard; she poured more cream into her tea to cover her self-consciousness. "I do need a favor."

He nodded knowingly. "As I suspected; this meal was not solely to repay me for accompanying you tonight. Does your favor involve that pair who were loitering at the end of New Castle Street?"

"They were paying far more attention to me than I liked."

"Perhaps it was because you are a truly handsome woman," the doctor replied.

"I honestly think you need glasses."

"No, my eyesight is fine. Perhaps your self-esteem needs adjustment."

Zing! Too close to home. She moved on. "Actually, I need to find someone. He was last seen in the East End."

"Professor Turner?"

"No, I've found him and...ah...delivered my uncle's message. There is someone else."

Alastair eyebrow arched. "For a missing person, I would recommend you consult the police. They'll no doubt be able to assist you."

"No cops," she said firmly.

His frown deepened. "Is this person in trouble with the law?"

"No, not as such."

He leaned forward, dropping his voice. "Who is this person to you?"

She hesitated for a second and then blurted out, "He's my lover."

There was a brief passage of chagrin over the doctor's face, and then it dissolved, replaced by an expression she found hard to translate. He looked at her empty plate and then gave a half nod to himself as if he'd worked out some puzzle.

"I have someone who knows the East End intimately," he said, his voice clipped. "I'll send him to you tomorrow."

"Perfect."

The doctor abruptly rose, dropping his napkin on the table. "It's time we were heading toward the boarding house."

She dusted the crumbs off her skirt as she rose. "Is there something wrong?"

"Nothing at all, Miss Lassiter."

She eyed him as he headed toward the door. He'd gone from warm and jovial to chilly and formal in a heartbeat.

All because I said I had a lover.

✝

The pair inside the restaurant appeared to be getting on splendidly. They were leaning toward each other, engaged in animated conversation.

"You never cease to surprise me, my friend," Keats murmured, peering in the establishment's front window.

Shaking his head in amazement, he returned to his scrutiny of the evening paper, skimming the newsprint for an overview of events in the East End. It was the Chief Inspector's technique; search for the little bits, and then weave them into a bigger picture. A missing carriage and a team of horses might not seem that important—at least to anyone but the owner. However, couple that loss with shovels, pick-axes and rope, all stolen on the same day, and new possibilities came into play. Just that sort of thing had happened last summer. Utilizing seemingly unrelated scraps of information, Fisher had captured a gang of Russian anarchists who had been busily tunneling into a silversmith's shop seeking the wherewithal to overthrow the Czar. Their arrest proved a feather in the Chief Inspector's cap. Keats wisely took note.

Tipping on his toes, he peered inside the window for another quick look. Time was running short, but he had no desire to interrupt. His friend so rarely dined out, let alone with a woman.

"Ah, excellent," he said as Alastair abruptly rose to his feet. "I won't have to fetch you." He leaned closer to the window, puzzled. The dynamics had changed. Up until a moment ago, the couple appeared to be getting on nicely. Now the chill of a crisp winter's day danced between them.

"Oh, lord, what did you do?" Keats muttered, shaking his head. *Leave it to Alastair to mess things up.* He dropped back on his heels and shifted the paper in his hands.

His friend spied him as the pair exited the building. A glower came his way. "What the devil are you doing here?" Alastair demanded.

Keats delivered a polite nod and then pointedly shifted his attention to the lady. Folding the newspaper, he tucked it under an arm and removed his hat.

"Good evening, ma'am. I'm Jonathon Keats," he said with a bow. She was thinner than he'd originally surmised, but well proportioned. An aristocratic face, complemented by light-brown hair and hazel eyes. Quite a striking woman.

"Good evening," she replied. "I'm Jacynda Lassiter."

"Pleased to make your acquaintance, Miss Lassiter," Keats replied. *Very pleased. Where have you been hiding this one, my friend?*

While they performed the niceties, Alastair fumed. Grudgingly required to move away from the restaurant's doorway to accommodate newcomers, he demanded, "How did you find me?"

"I saw you and the lady on the street." Keats lowered his voice. "I need to speak with you privately."

"Now is not the time."

"On the contrary. A particular...situation has arisen."

Alastair's glare withered, as if he'd divined the reason for Keats' presence. He swung toward his companion. "Please allow

me a moment to determine what this person wants." The lady
nodded and took herself a short distance away.

This person? Alastair made him sound like an irksome beggar.
Keats ground his teeth in annoyance.

The doctor turned back to him. "What is this about?" he asked,
keeping his voice low.

"*They* wish to speak to you."

"In regard to what?" Brittle anger flickered along every word.

In lieu of an answer, Keats pulled an envelope from inside his
jacket. As he handed it to the doctor, he whispered an address.

"They expect to see you sometime before ten this evening."

"I'm not some damned lackey," Alastair growled.

"I know that. However, you have little choice in the matter."

"What if I refuse their summons?"

Keats had anticipated that tack. "They will see that your clinic
is closed before the end of the week."

His friend blanched. "Good God, what kind of monsters are
they?"

"The kind accustomed to having their every whim fulfilled."
Keats cleared his throat and added, "Be sensible. Go see them.
Just don't expect them to play fair."

His friend's eyes narrowed. "You know what this is about, don't
you?"

"Yes, but I am enjoined from speaking of it further."

Another glower that mutated into a scowl. Alastair stuffed the
unopened envelope into his coat and checked on his dining
companion. She'd purchased a paper of her own and was concen-
trating on the front page, oblivious to their conversation. "Do me
the honor of escorting Miss Lassiter to the boarding house, will
you?" he asked. "I do not want her walking the streets alone."

Keats brightened instantly. "Most certainly. She's quite
handsome."

The scowl grew. "Yes, she is. However, Miss Lassiter has a
tendency to strike people for no particular reason."

"Is that where the bruise came from? I was wondering about
that."

A glare. "She is not well grounded, so do not try to take
advantage of her person."

Keats studied his friend closely. *Had he just been warned off?*

"She seems quite sane to me."

"No doubt to you she would," was the curt reply.

Is that jealousy I hear? How remarkable. "As always, I shall be
a gentleman," Keats replied solemnly. After another quick glance

at the lady, he returned to the bigger issue at hand. "Do be careful, Alastair. *They're* not thinking clearly at this moment. You're a perfect scapegoat."

"All the more reason to settle this matter once and for all."

✝

The young man escorting her to the boarding house was the antithesis of Alastair Montrose. A little shorter than the doctor, Jonathon had dark hair anointed with a modest amount of macassar oil, sparkling eyes and a precisely trimmed moustache that lightly curved upward at the ends. His attitude bordered on the outrageous. He'd immediately insisted she call him by his first name. No topic proved too personal, as if he were from her time. He harbored a spark of life that seemed to kindle the night air. She knew the type; he was like Chris, a Roman candle that would make a suitable lover, at least until his attention wandered. Still, Jonathon was a pleasant change from the mercurial physician.

"How long have you known Alastair?" he probed.

"A few days. We met at the boarding house. He treated me for a travel-related illness."

"I see. He's quite a good physician, I gather. I am surprised you got him out for a meal. He doesn't dine out often. Too tied to his work," Keats remarked, shaking his head in disapproval. "You'd think he was a monk instead of a doctor."

"Is his clinic nearby?" she asked.

"No." He twirled and pointed behind him, which drew a confused stare from a fellow pedestrian. "It's on Church Street near the Ten Bells."

"I should like to see it sometime," she said, more to herself than her companion.

"Rough neighborhood," Keats remarked, tipping his hat to an older woman. Across the street, voices rose as a pair of drunken harridans battled each other with considerable shouting and hair-pulling. A crowd gathered, urging them to greater violence with calls of "Give the old cow another!" and "That's the ticket!" Jonathon walked on, as if it were nothing out of the ordinary.

"Are you keen to see it right now?" he asked.

Cynda backtracked on the conversation. "The clinic?"

"Yes. Mind you, it'll be a bit dicey at night."

Her good sense told her no. She didn't know this man, other than that he appeared to be a friend of the doctor's. There was something odd about him; something that didn't track.

"No, that's fine. I'll go some other time."

Jonathon gave a quick nod of agreement. "It's probably best. What with the killer loose..." He pointed at the newspaper under her arm, the one that matched his. "You'll find a full report on the Chapman inquest in there," he said. "It makes horrific reading. It's a pity fellows like Alastair come under so much scrutiny during times like such as this."

Cynda puzzled on that last comment. Perhaps she'd heard him incorrectly. "Why Alastair?"

"He fits the profile."

"How so?"

"He's about the right height and weight, he lives in Whitechapel, is a solitary individual, and once told me that he'd assisted with surgeries in Baltimore. He keeps quite irregular hours and many of the clinic's patients are dolly-mops."

Cynda's confusion grew. "Dolly...mops?" That was a new one.

"Oh, pardon—prostitutes. It does give one pause to think my friend might be this blood-crazed murderer," Keats replied dramatically.

Oh, not going there. "How long have you known him?" she asked, shifting directions.

Jonathon accepted the change with grace. "A little over a year. I became acquainted with him right after he returned from his medical training in America. I've always found him a rather gloomy chap, but good-hearted. Of course, losing one's fiancée and posh position in Mayfair would put the glooms on anyone."

"Posh position?" she asked. Following the man's train of thought was like chasing a demented butterfly. Still, underneath all the verbiage she sensed a more subtle thread. The patter seemed to have a purpose. Jonathon spent the next two blocks painting a woeful tale of a talented physician made to choose between his sacred calling and the good life, fiancée included.

I bet you're an actor. "So he treated the boy and chose the Whitechapel clinic instead of Mayfair," she summarized. That wasn't a surprise, given what she knew of the doctor.

"Indeed. The last I heard, his former fiancée was being courted by a duke. No doubt her father's quite pleased."

"No doubt, especially if the duke isn't as grumpy as the doctor."

Jonathon beamed and winked mischievously. "I say, you are fun." It came dangerously close to a come-on. As if to reinforce it, he added, "I do hope to see more of you during your stay in London, Miss Jacynda. There are a number of sights I think you might enjoy, and I would love the opportunity to escort you. The

Crystal Palace, for example. An absolute marvel. It even has an aquarium!" There was a noticeable pause, and then, "Many things may be said about me, but I am not grumpy."

That *was* a come-on. Cynda chuckled anyway. This guy was fun. Pity she wouldn't be here that long.

"You are everything but grumpy, Jonathon."

That seemed to please him. To circumvent any further courting, Cynda bought another evening paper, different from the one she'd purchased earlier. He took it and added it to the stack under his arm. The Victorians were good about detailing little incidents, usually in garrulous verbiage. Perhaps one of the articles might point her toward Chris.

As they walked, she acquired more papers.

"I say, you do like to read, don't you?" Keats remarked, gallantly toting the substantial collection under an arm. It sounded like a compliment.

Why not ask him? He seems to know everything. "I'm trying to find someone. He went missing in the East End a few days ago. I thought maybe the papers might have something."

"I see. Where was he staying?" Jonathon asked.

That was the problem; she had no idea. "I'm not sure."

"Oh, that makes it a bit harder. Was he conducting business in the City?"

"No, in the East End. He didn't come home as planned. I'm worried about him."

Keats' face lost some of the youthful boyishness. "No doubt you should be, though there may be some innocent reason for his absence."

"Let's hope so."

"I would be happy to make inquiries for you. I have…connections, you see."

I bet you do. "His name is Christopher Stone. He's twenty-seven."

Her companion steered them under a gas lamp and unexpectedly handed her the pile of papers. Digging in his coat, he extracted a small notebook and a pencil.

"Height, hair and eye color?" he asked, suddenly all business.

"Five-nine or so, light-brown hair and eyes. No moustache."

"Identifying marks?"

"He has a four-inch scar here," she said, pointing below her right ear.

He scribbled more notes. His manner seemed out of place with the chattering magpie she'd endured since the restaurant.

"I will see what I can do for you," he said, tucking away the notebook and pencil. He retrieved the papers.

"I appreciate your help. Alastair had difficulty with the fact that Chris is my..." she hunted for a better word, "paramour."

"Ah, he's your lover, then. Well, Alastair's reaction isn't that surprising, really," Jonathon said as they arrived at the boarding house.

"I don't understand."

"A man does not like competition, Miss Jacynda. It is obvious that Alastair is quite smitten with you. To learn you had a lover would not set well."

Oh, lord. She hadn't even thought about that. "I see," she sighed.

"I agree with him. Where Alastair will become surly about the situation, I see it as a challenge," Jonathon replied, smiling widely.

Now I've got two of them going. This is ridiculous. To hide her dismay, she stretched out her hands to claim the newspapers. He took one, kissed it, then delivered the stack.

"I have had a delightful time with you, Miss Jacynda. I shall make inquiries and try to find your...particular friend." He winked, obviously not the least bit troubled that she was *experienced,* as the Victorians would put it.

"Thank you, Jonathon. It's been an interesting evening for me as well."

He doffed his hat, sweeping it downward with a flourish. Once she'd cleared the front door, he set off at a brisk clip toward the corner.

Instead of retreating to her room, Cynda took residence in the front parlor, doffing her mantelet and hat. Much to Mildred's consternation, she dropped the stack of papers on the rug and then sat on the floor, smoothing her skirts around her. As Mildred fussed off in search of tea and scones, Cynda opened the first paper, bending over to scrutinize the articles.

It was just a matter of finding a needle in Whitechapel.

✣

Alastair loitered across from his apparent destination, composing himself. His aggravation at Keats had succumbed to frank apprehension. He wasn't even sure he was at the right location. Alastair dug the engraved card out its envelope. Edged with royal blue, it was of significant weight and pedigree. To his annoyance, there was no street address listed. He'd just have to trust that Keats had given him the right information. That did not suit. All he had to work with resided in the center of the card.

The Artifice Club, #8.

The building was a grand, five-story affair a few streets from Covent Garden. Four massive Doric columns extended from the second to the third floors. The rooms facing the street were lit, and he saw figures moving behind curtains.

He maneuvered through the evening traffic, mostly theater patrons, and arrived unscathed at the building's front door. Comparing the card to the brass plaque near the door did not ease his worries. It listed no name, only *No. 43.*

"Playing their games again," he groused. He had no choice but to enter the lion's den, providing it was the right den.

He rapped on the door. Stomach clenched in a knot, he straightened his jacket and ran a hand over his hair. The portal opened smoothly. A skeptical face appeared. The rest of the person was clad in burgundy livery.

"Yes?"

"Is this the Artifice Club?" Alastair asked.

An eyebrow arched in disdain. "No," the man replied stiffly.

Irritated, Alastair shoved the card at him. "I was told to come here. If this is the wrong place, just tell me."

"You are not at the wrong place; you're just posing the wrong question," the fellow retorted, and then beckoned him inside.

Already disconcerted, the building's foyer further upset Alastair's emotional equilibrium. He'd been inside a gentleman's club before; Doctor Hanson had taken him round to his private club and Alastair knew what to expect. This foyer did not come close to his expectations. The two chairs positioned either side of the entryway were threadbare. The floor desperately needed polishing. The paintings appeared to be cheap imitations. Nothing was as it should be.

Artifice Club. Of course.

"This way, sir," the club steward gestured. They traveled the length of the hall and paused at a door, one of ten that lined the walls. All were identical. "Number Eight," the man announced.

Alastair stared at the door and then at his escort. There was no number to indicate this was the first door, or the eighth or the tenth. "How do you know that? Why isn't it that one, for instance?" he queried, pointing to the closest portal across the hall.

"Today, this is Number Eight. Tomorrow, it will be another door. It changes every day. I know this is the right one for today."

Alastair's mind strived to make sense of this peculiar logic. "What if someone else must take your place? How will he know?"

The steward solemnly tugged on his burgundy jacket in an officious manner. "There is no one else."

"If you are ill?" Alastair pressed.

"Then a number of important people will be severely inconvenienced," the man replied, as if that settled the matter. The steward produced a key, unlocked the door and pushed it open. "Two flights up, then to your right, sir."

"Thank you."

Alastair hiked upward. When he reached the first landing, he realized that the steward hadn't taken his coat and hat. But then, there'd been no place to store them in the entryway. Below him, the door closed firmly.

When he reached the top stair, he took a moment to catch his breath, then veered right as instructed. Another unmarked door. At least this time it was his sole choice. Steeling himself, he gave a firm knock. It was immediately opened by a man in royal blue livery, the exact color of the edging on the card clutched in Alastair's hand.

"Ah, Doctor, welcome." The liveried man waved him forward. "They are waiting for you. May I take your hat and coat?" Buoyed by the fellow's cheerful welcome, Alastair stepped into the antechamber and relinquished his outer garments.

"I'm Ronald, the 8th Room Steward. Should you need anything, just ask." Alastair had a number of questions, but kept them to himself. The answers would probably not be to his liking.

The antechamber was pleasant, warmed by a toasty fire. The painting on the wall was of infinitely better quality than the ones in the foyer. Intrigued, Alastair leaned closer to study it. A sharply turned-out butler stood at attention while his portly master labored behind a massive desk piled with stacks of gold coins. Clearly oblivious to anything but the wealth in front of him, the master of the house ignored his fine wife and two small children who played on the carpet with an energetic kitten. One portion of the painting echoed domestic bliss; the other a man's physical and emotional decline.

Beneath the painting, on the frame, was a gold plaque with a Latin inscription.

"*Pecuniae imperare oportet, non servire,*" Alastair quoted. His mind scrambled through the Latin. "Money should be mastered, not served."

Ronald fixed him with a pleased smile. "Exactly right, sir."

"Excellent advice. The fellow is neglecting what is most important."

"Indeed."

"Do any of *them* read Latin?" Alastair asked.

"Only one, and he found it quite instructive." Before Alastair could ask the logical question, Ronald inquired, "Are you ready, sir?"

"Yes, I am. Let's get this over with."

Right before he opened the door, Ronald murmured in a low voice, "Don't let them get your goat."

The doctor did not have time to respond to this astonishing advice before the steward swung open the door.

"Gentlemen, Doctor Alastair Montrose," he announced in a crisp voice.

Four heads bobbed upward in unison. Alastair stared at them in mute horror, his mouth agape. Facing him, brandy snifters and cigars in hand, were the Four Horsemen of the Apocalypse.

11

"What in the blazes?" Alastair muttered under his breath. He shot a quick glance toward the steward.

Ronald gave a bemused shrug. "They always fancy a good dress up, sir."

"Have a seat, Doctor!" War boomed. He gestured toward a chair, his face obscured by the visor of a red-plumed helmet. A naked sword perched on his lap. When he took a long puff of his cigar, whiffs of smoke poured out through the visor's apertures.

Alastair took the proffered chair. Ronald appeared at his elbow, offering him brandy and cigar. "No, thank you," he said. He had no desire to socialize with these men, not after their venomous threat against the clinic. The steward retreated to the back of the room on silent feet.

"It was good of you to be so prompt," Famine said. He sat clothed in judge's robes, a large brass scale resting at his feet. He swirled his brandy snifter absentmindedly. Alastair studied his face but could not determine who resided behind the illusion. The voices gave no clue, either. He was running blind tonight, and that did nothing for his confidence. *Why hadn't he paid more attention when Keats talked about The Conclave?*

"I had little choice but to be prompt, as you put it," Alastair replied, dropping the blue-edged card on the serving table next to him. "I was told to be here by ten sharp."

"Now, now, young man, no need to be that way," Pestilence said jovially. His illusion was the starkest. Clad in rough-woven linen such as a peasant might wear, his face bore pockmarks. A skeletal hand with blackened fingernails clutched his drink.

Alastair caught movement near the man's feet. An illusionary rat peered around a dirty boot, yellow teeth exposed. The doctor suppressed a grimace.

Death sat on Pestilence's right, clad in classic black robe and hood. A gloved hand held a scythe, its blade coated in dried blood. The hood obscured the specter's face. Alastair counted that as a blessing.

"Why am I here?" he demanded, keen to be away from this surreal masquerade.

War took the lead. "You need to embrace your unique ability and become an active part of our community, Doctor."

"And if I choose not to be party to this...delusion?"

Smoke huffed out of the visor. "You have no choice, young man. You are a Transitive, no matter how desperately you seek to ignore your heritage. Your peculiar behavior places us all at risk. I thought the Wescombs were clear on that point."

Alastair chafed at the man's lack of respect. "*Lord* and *Lady* Wescomb did present your case quite succinctly. Nonetheless, I fail to see why I am under scrutiny."

There was ponderous silence. War tapped a finger on the sword's hilt while Famine fiddled with his robes.

The fog cleared abruptly. "My God, you think I have something to do with the murders."

More silence, the condemning kind.

"You dare suggest that I would butcher a woman, no...*two* women, dissecting them as if they were mere scientific curiosities?" Alastair challenged.

"Do you view women as such?" Death asked. His voice was smooth, like ice on a tranquil pond. Hairs raised on the back of Alastair's neck. He heard the trap, satin-lined though it was. When he didn't respond, Death prompted, "They are, after all, just whores. What are a few more dead ones? Less to trip over when you take an evening stroll."

Alastair's anger burst into flame. "On the contrary; they are just as important as any of us. They're God's creation, though their unfortunate state argues against them."

"I would hardy equate an East End trollop with such as us," Pestilence replied tartly.

Alastair felt heat rise to his face. "There is little difference, gentlemen. We are all whores in our own way."

Another huff of smoke through War's visor. "It could be said, Doctor, that you have lost your objectivity. Perhaps some time away would be of value," he advised. He stubbed out the end of his cigar in a silver bowl. Ronald assisted in the lighting of a new cheroot and then stepped back into the shadows.

"Let us strike a balance," Famine said, gesturing toward the scales at his feet as if he'd made some clever jest.

"What are you suggesting?" Alastair asked.

War took up the cudgel. "We propose to mitigate the threat to our community while keeping you safe."

This trap had more teeth. "In what way?"

"We wish you to close the clinic and resign your position at the London Hospital until this madman is caught."

"Why would I do that?" Alastair demanded, astonished at the audacity of the request.

War continued, oblivious to his reaction. "We feel that you should leave the country until such time as the police, inept as they are, bring this lunatic to justice. For no doubt they will eventually bumble across him, and he will meet his deserved end."

"Yes, a trip to America would be ideal," Pestilence added. "You could visit your medical school chums. Of course, we would finance the journey and all expenses incurred." A pause. "Within reason, of course."

"But not France," Famine cautioned, waggling a finger in Alastair's direction. "Too close to London."

"If you wish to take someone with you, a young lady perhaps, that can be arranged," Pestilence said with a knowing smile. "You need time to rest, to reflect. Think of it as a sabbatical."

"I can't believe you're asking this of me," Alastair sputtered. It was one thing to threaten the clinic's closure, but to suggest that he shutter it voluntarily beggared belief.

War jumped in. "When the fuss dies down, you can begin anew. To show our appreciation, we will finance your clinic for two years."

"Within reason," Pestilence interjected.

"Really," Alastair said flatly. He shifted his eyes toward Death. The fourth member of The Conclave had remained silent during the bargaining phase. "And what do you say to this?"

"There will be more killings. If you stay in London, you threaten not only your own future, but ours." The specter rubbed a thumb along the scythe's blade. He continued in dulcet tones, "You have been noted by the constabulary. You fit their profile. It is best you are gone from London before the next whore's blood stains the cobblestones."

"You sound sure that there will be more deaths," Alastair said.

A low chuckle came from beneath the oversized hood. It sounded like wind washing across a gravestone. "I am Death. I know these things."

Famine leapt into the tense moment, his voice squeaky with

anxiety. "It's really for the best, Doctor."

"What if they never catch the killer?" Alastair asked, rising to his feet. There was a ruffle of unease amongst the three more vocal horsemen. None of them offered an answer. "I see. This might prove a permanent exile." He shook his head. "I must decline, gentlemen. I give you my word I have nothing to do with the murders. If you leave me to my work, then all will be well."

"We cannot accept that," War retorted. "Too much is at stake. If you do not do as we ask, we will be forced to take action."

Alastair took a step toward his tormentors. War held his ground. Famine and Pestilence shied back in their seats. Death watched impassively.

A trickle of sweat swarmed down Alastair's back. *Dare I make the threat?* He studied each one in turn. "Let me be plain. If you attempt to close my clinic, I will bring this matter to public view."

"What do you mean?" Famine asked.

"I will tell London about our existence."

"Good God, you can't," War spouted, surging to his feet. The unsheathed sword fell from his lap and landed with a clatter at Alastair's boots: a dark omen. Picking it up, the doctor dipped the blade toward the floor, resisting the temptation to use it.

"That's my counteroffer, gentlemen. You leave me to my work and all will be well. You interfere in my life, and I will deliver my own version of the Apocalypse to your doorstep."

Pestilence's mouth fell open. Famine continued to fidget with his robes, looking nervously at the others. Alastair suspected War was glaring at him, though he couldn't be sure.

Death, however, gave a nod that signaled respect, followed by an eerie chuckle. "A worthy threat," the robed figure said.

"No, a promise," Alastair said. He wheeled on his feet and marched away. Once he reached the anteroom, the steward claimed the sword and set it aside.

"Your coat and hat, Doctor," he said pleasantly, handing over the items.

"Thank you." Alastair's heart thudded in his throat. *Were they so arrogant as to believe I would abandon my patients just to appease them?*

The sound of raised voices. Death's chilly laughter reached them. Alastair suppressed a shudder.

Ronald put a hand on his arm and whispered, "Well played, Doctor. You're the first to decline their offer. You set them on their ears."

Alastair stared at him. "I'm not the only one they'd bullied?"

"Of course not. Once you see a little evil, you're inclined to see a lot."

Alastair couldn't hold back the smile. "You're a wise man, Ronald."

"Thank you, Doctor. Have a good evening, sir."

"I shall try."

✝

Given the peculiar nature of the evening, Alastair was not the least surprised when a carriage pulled next to him a block away from No. 43. He tensed, preparing for a fight.

Surely they wouldn't kidnap me off the street?

The door opened and a voice called out. "In you go, my friend."

It was Keats. Alastair remained on guard. It could be any one of his kind in illusion. He peered into the depths of the carriage and heaved a sigh of relief. Keats was alone and he sensed no one *en mirage.*

Alastair pulled himself inside and shut the door. As the carriage lurched forward immediately, he steadied himself on the bench seat. His coat slid toward the floor and Keats caught it, placing it across his own lap. Alastair nodded his gratitude.

"What were they tonight?" Keats asked, his face barely visible in the dim light coming through the carriage window. "Robin Hood and his Merry Men, or something else equally ridiculous?"

"Nothing so entertaining. They appeared as the Four Horsemen."

"What gall," Keats replied, shaking his head. "So what was their bait?"

"I thought you knew."

"I was not aware of all the details—just that they wanted to pressure you into leaving the city."

"They offered me a holiday from London of undetermined length, preferably to the States, all expenses paid. I could even take along a lady of my choice," Alastair said crisply.

"Ah, of course. Hoping you'd be too busy touring and fornicating to think about the poor wretches you left behind," Keats said, resentment laced around every word. "I hope you didn't accept their ludicrous offer."

"No, I made a counter proposal."

"Such as?"

"If they continue to pressure me, I will tell the world about our kind."

Keats' mouth fell open. "Good lord. You don't play Poker, do you?"

"No."

"You should. You'd easily win every hand with the ability to bluff like that."

"I'm not a gambler," Alastair replied tartly.

"Pull the other one, my friend. You're more of a gambler than I am, and that's saying a great deal. To have the gall to challenge The Conclave takes brass."

Alastair gave a curt nod. Keats was right; he'd gambled, and so far, he'd won. "Death seemed quite certain there would be more murders, and that the police have their eye upon me."

"Are you the killer?" Keats asked nonchalantly.

Alastair blinked in shock. "How dare you ask that!"

"Are you?"

"No!"

"Well, I was obliged to inquire."

"Sometimes you go too far, Keats."

"I'm curious—what did Death's voice sound like?"

Alastair resurrected the memory. "Like polished silver, but underneath..."

"Like Lucifer himself?" Keats asked, leaning forward.

His description jarred Alastair out of his reverie. "You have it precisely."

"Livingston," his friend announced. "Apparently, he's taken Abernathy's place."

"You mean the Abernathy whose Death Rite we attended? I didn't know he was one of The Conclave."

"You don't realize a lot, my oblivious friend."

Alastair had to give him that. He'd ignored the lot of them, hoping they'd return the favor. "Who are the others?"

"Hastings, Stinton and Cartwright. Hastings is ebullient, full of himself. Of the Horsemen, I'd say he'd choose War," Keats said.

Alastair nodded. "It fits. Famine was trying to make peace."

"That would be Stinton. And Cartwright is...a bit silly."

"Pestilence," Alastair muttered. Now he knew what manner of men hid behind the illusions, though not by sight. A thought occurred to him. "Were any of them at Abernathy's Death Rite?"

"Livingston was."

Alastair recalled the faces. "The strange man who stood next to Lord Wescomb?"

"That was him. Supposedly quite brilliant."

The one who can read Latin. "I don't remember hearing his name before."

"He appeared about four months ago and remained rather circumspect, at least in the beginning. However, with the murders in the East End, he's taken a more definitive role in our community."

"Apparently, others of our kind are being offered a free trip as well."

"From what I've heard, five have accepted their offer. Three are out of the country already; the other two leave tomorrow," Keats replied.

Sounds filtered into the carriage. Alastair leaned toward the window and studied the landscape. They were passing St. Paul's.

"I trust Miss Lassiter is safe at the boarding house."

Keats arched an eyebrow. "Yes, after I repeatedly had my way with her despite her vigorous protests."

Alastair deserved that one. "I apologize, Keats. I know you to be a decent fellow and—"

"You assumed the worse, however, or you wouldn't have felt compelled to issue the warning."

Alastair gave a conciliatory nod. "Again, I apologize."

A brusque nod. "She asked me to help find her missing paramour."

"I have that in hand," Alastair retorted. *Why did she ask you, of all people?*

"Really? What do you intend to do?"

"I will send Davy scurrying about. He knows all the nooks and crannies and will put the word out."

"A good start. I shall put the word out as well. I know a few people here and there who might be able to give us news of the man."

"I doubt he is lolling about the brothels or the gambling dens." Keats gave him a sharp look. Alastair sighed. "Well, whatever you wish. I suspect it is important we find him, if nothing more than for Jacynda's future."

Keats' brow wrinkled. "How so?"

"Given her bouts of nausea, followed by her raging appetite, I fear the missing fellow has planted his seed, and then taken to his heels when faced with the reality of supporting a family."

"Bastard," Keats murmured.

Alastair blinked. He'd expected a more frivolous answer. "I would appreciate you not mentioning my speculations to Jacynda if you see her. I can only imagine how upset she is."

Keats nodded. "I'll do what I can. Perhaps between the two of us, we can persuade the fellow to take his lumps and do the right thing."

Alastair stared at him. "I say, Keats, are you well? I never expected you to be so...mature about this."

His friend leaned closer, frowning. "I may be a ne'er-do-well in your eyes, Alastair, but I am an honorable one. Getting under a woman's skirts and leaving her the burden is hardly what a gentleman would do. My father was just such a scoundrel. Fortunately, my mother's family made him do the right thing...at gunpoint."

"Oh...dear," Alastair murmured.

Keats jammed himself against the seat and fell silent, his arms crossed over his chest. Feeling awkward, Alastair gazed out the window. They were on Whitechapel High Street now. He heard the unmistakable cacophony of a dance hall in full furor. The scent of fresh blood on the night air told him they were near one of the slaughterhouses.

The carriage halted at New Castle Street. Alastair stepped out, digging in his pockets to produce what few coins he possessed.

"Don't bother, I'll take care of it," Keats said, exiting. He handed Alastair his coat. "Oh, and Jacynda wants to see your clinic."

Alastair sighed and lowered his voice. "It may not be there for long, what with the financial problems."

"I'm sure all that will work out," Keats replied lightly. He handed over Alastair's coat and whispered, "Check the inner pocket."

He tapped his hat and hopped back into the carriage.

Under the first gas lamp, Alastair retrieved a piece of paper and a thick envelope from the pocket. The note was in Lady Sephora's fine hand.

To aid those who have no other champion but yourself.

The Wescombs had found a way to help him and, given the bulk of the envelope, done so in a most generous fashion. He tucked the paper away, his heart lighter than it had been in weeks. Despite the machinations of The Conclave, his clinic would remain in business.

12

"I know you're there," Cynda said. She searched around the parlor's floor, gingerly lifting newspapers and peering underneath. She made sure to keep her voice low so Mildred wouldn't hear her. From the clank of pans in the kitchen, she was probably safe. "Come on out. Don't be shy."

Nothing happened. Cynda refilled the cup of tea, setting it and the saucer some distance from her. Still nothing. She leaned over and added a teaspoon of sugar, mixing it in. No paper rustled. "Tough customer, huh?" Upping the ante, she placed the scone plate with its myriad of crumbs next to the cup and saucer. "You might as well come out. I'm not going to throw anything at you."

First one blue leg, then another gradually inched out from under one of the piles of newsprint. The spider, now the size of a chubby mouse, studied her soberly. Its feet were unclad. That was an improvement.

"Why the change in attitude?" it asked.

"I figure you're part of my life now, so we might as well get along. If you don't scare me, I won't hit you. How's that for a bargain?"

"Very practical," it said. She couldn't quite place the accent, but it sounded more British than American. In an odd way, that made sense.

The creature shambled across the piles of papers to the plate and proceeded to make the scone crumbs vanish, all the while keeping a weather eye on her—actually, weather eyes. Next was the cup of tea. It dipped a foot in the liquid and did a taste test. Apparently the tea met the arachnid's approval, for it hefted the cup and drank. Cynda watched in fascination as the numerous legs positioned the cup just right. Setting it down, the spider rubbed a leg across what might pass as its chin in a very human gesture. "Quite good."

"What's your name?" she asked. If she were going to have delusions, she might as well be on a first-name basis with the things.

"Whatever you care to call me," was the quick answer.

"How about Mr. Spider? Not very imaginative, I know."

"That'll do. Thanks for the cuppa." He gave her a wave and then skittered across the room, vanishing under an old bow front buffet.

"At least you aren't the size of an omnibus anymore," she said.

"I could be if you wish," the voice replied from under the buffet.

"No, thanks. You're fine just the way you are."

She returned to the newspapers. The reports were a mishmash of actual incidents and embroidered rumors: bodies found in the Thames or along the railroad tracks; a number of assaults upon persons, mostly due to the effects of excessive drink; and speculation about the identity of the Whitechapel murderer. Most believed the lunatic had to be a foreigner—no well-bred Englishman would ever contemplate such hideous crimes. The Jews were an odds-on favorite, especially as the East End was bulging with refugees from the Czar's pogroms. Those who labored on the Thames' cattle boats were on the list, as well as physicians, butchers and folks who worked in mortuaries. None of the guesses would ever bear fruit.

Then there were the droves of helpful citizens who wrote the papers, offering suggestions how to catch the killer. Some of the ideas were helpful, but most were pure fantasy. "Put constables on the street dressed as women," one wrote. Cynda had seen a couple of those; at least she hoped they were guys. By the time the murders reached their peak, a third of the City of London's constabulary would be dawdling on the streets. All for naught. Jack would vanish into foggy legend, adding to his cachet.

Cynda heard the sound of a key in the front door and Mildred's shuffling along the hallway to meet the newcomer. The doctor's voice answered the housekeeper's greeting and declined her offer of tea in the same sentence. Then Cynda heard her name mentioned.

"She's in the parlor, reading. Got the evening papers strewn all over creation. I don't know what it means," Mildred explained.

"I'll check on her."

"That would be grand. She seems better, but one never knows."

"No, one never does," Cynda murmured to herself.

A dark shape filled the doorway.

"Good evening, Doctor," she said looking up. He seemed to shimmer around the edges. She blinked her eyes and the illusion passed.

"Good evening," Alastair replied. He sounded cheerful for a change, a one-eighty from his earlier diffidence. "I see Keats got you home safely."

"He did. Your friend is quite the force of nature."

"It could be argued you are the same, Miss Lassiter," the doctor replied in an amused tone.

"Jacynda. And thank you, I'll regard that as a compliment."

"I would." He edged into the room and took a chair near her, bending over to consider her collection of papers. "Any luck?"

Cynda's neck cramped from the abnormal position. She massaged it just above the high collar. "There are a few unidentified bodies at the local morgues. I probably should check into them, though none of the descriptions sound like Chris."

The doctor turned solemn. "I sincerely hope that is not the case."

Reality struck. *What if Chris were dead? How would she get him to '057?*

"Jacynda?" the doctor asked. Apparently, her thoughts had registered on her face.

"I'm having trouble thinking of Chris in the past tense. He's so full of life, like your friend Keats."

Alastair leaned back in the chair. *Like Keats. What if that pest weren't around?* "That would be a loss," he said to himself.

"It's very important I find Chris and as soon as possible."

He heard the desperation. A single woman, most likely with child. How would she cope if her lover were dead? Would her family accept her condition or cast her onto the street? He grew heartsick at the thought.

"What's in the envelope?" she asked, pointing.

Alastair realized he'd been clutching it in his hand. He opened the flap with his thumb. Inside was one hundred pounds.

"Good heavens," he said, fanning the money onto his lap. He'd not expected that much.

"Been playing the ponies, have we?"

"No, it's a donation for the clinic."

"That's wonderful."

He stared at the bills as his companion rose. She reached for the cup and saucer, unsteady on her feet.

"I'll tidy for you," he offered, sensing her weariness. That earned him a grateful smile. She collected the newspapers, placing them under her arm.

"I'm glad things are working out for you," she said.

Before he could reply, she was climbing the stairs. Despite her hasty departure, she hadn't been able to hide the unspoken prayer. If things were working out for him, maybe they would for her.

"May God make it so," he whispered, tucking the donation into his coat pocket.

✝

Cynda woke to a peculiar sensation. It felt as if something had brushed against her cheek. She wondered if it was her personal delusion, but discarded that notion. This was softer, more tentative than an arachnid's hairy leg.

A shimmer in the air caught her notice. She blinked, but it remained. It couldn't be a trick of the light; there was little of it coming through the soot-begrimed window. As if realizing it was being surveyed, the shimmer vanished.

Rubbing her face in exhaustion, Cynda shook her head. "Great, now I'm seeing ghosts." She rolled over and fell back to sleep.

✝

The dream felt real, the room indistinct, as if viewed through fine lace. A set of boots positioned near the bed, a pair of stockings draped over them. Alastair moved closer, staring at the woman as she slept. Her rhythmic breathing made her breasts rise and fall under the bedclothes. Her hair, now unbound, lay scattered across the pillow in light-brown waves. She murmured in her sleep, calling a name. *Was it his?* He took a step closer, reaching toward her...

Alastair awoke with a sudden jerk and sat upright in the bed, causing the frame to creak.

"No!" Crossing his arms over his chest, he breathed deeply. The sensation passed. He was whole again.

His hands dropped into his lap in resignation. Rising, he dashed cold water on his face from the basin. It was not difficult to send oneself to another location while asleep—mere child's play to one of his kind. *Venturing,* they called it. It had been a lark at first, spying on people without them knowing. He'd learned of his father's midnight trysts with the housekeeper that way. Learned that a father's deeds were often at odds with his words.

Alastair returned to his bed, the frame creaking once again. He thought of the woman asleep in the room next door. What was it about Jacynda Lassiter? *Why am I drawn toward her? Pity, perhaps?*

With a long sigh, he rose and dressed. If he fell asleep, he'd return to Jacynda's room as he had every night since she'd arrived. If he succumbed and began to *venture* regularly, the desire to go *en mirage* would accelerate. He would become like the others, and The Conclave would win. He glanced at his watch after pulling on his outer garments. Just past two-thirty.

I'll go to the clinic. He wouldn't *venture* once he was there. The lure appeared to be the woman next door.

Careful to make little noise, he tiptoed downstairs, donning his boots at the front door. He made sure to secure the lock. After a troubled look at Jacynda's window, he jammed his hands in his pockets and set off toward Whitechapel High Street.

Oblivious to his surroundings, he failed to notice the figure following in his wake.

‡

There was activity on the streets despite the late hour: workers heading home, prostitutes trying to earn their coins for the night's lodging. Shifty men in dark corners watched him with jaded eyes. The chilly night air made him tug his coat collar up for warmth. Alastair knew he was acting the fool. Though he only had a few coins in his pocket, his clothes were worth stealing, if nothing more.

A woman called to him. He didn't bother to acknowledge the offer. Despite the killer's savage handiwork, they still worked the streets. They had little choice. Most clustered close to the pubs until they closed, following a set route from boozing-ken to boozing-ken on the troll for customers. Some pocketed the few coins they made and bought a bed at one of the doss houses. Others drank their income and went in search of more money. Once bright pigeons, they faded into drab nothingness until the cobblestones swallowed their bones. Every day, new arrivals flocked from the country, fresh-faced and eager, inexorably following the same path.

"'Ello, doc. Out for a stroll, are we?" a voice called. He turned to find one of the clinic's regulars staggering toward him. Aggie was in her forties now. Her pale, moon face registered a love of gin. She reached out to grab Alastair's arm to steady herself.

"Good morning, Aggie. I haven't seen you for a while," he said politely, though he really didn't feel sociable.

"Been pickin' 'ops in Kent. Got back 'bout a week ago."

"You should have stayed a while longer. It's safer than here," Alastair said.

"Ah, well, gotta die of somethin', don't ya?" She tightened her grip on his arm. "I tol' someon' to come see ya 'bout 'er chest, ya bein' a right fine doc and all."

"I would be happy to help her."

She shook her head. "Ya can't, 'less ya can raise the dead. Poor old cow. She's the one what died in 'anbury Street."

"You mean the Chapman woman?"

Aggie nodded. "I guess 'er chest don't trouble 'er none now." She gave a wan smile. "See, bein' dead's not so bad, is it?"

Alastair couldn't repress the shiver. "You shouldn't be on the streets, Aggie. It's too dangerous."

"Well, I got no choice, now do I?"

He dug in his pocket, found what coins he had and pressed them into her hand.

"Buy yourself a place to sleep tonight. It's not safe out here."

She stared at him as if he'd gifted her a pouch of gold. "Yer a godsend. I don't know what we'd do if ya weren't 'ere to 'elp us."

A wrench of emotion struck him. If The Conclave had its way, he wouldn't have been here tonight, or any night. "You come see me if your chest troubles you again. Don't wait like the last time."

"I will. I promise." She planted a gin-tainted kiss on his cheek. "I'll go to the doss 'ouse and get a bed. It'll be good to be inside for a night." She wobbled down the street. He watched for a time, and then continued on his way.

Pausing at the fringe of a small crowd, he listened to a patent medicine peddler. The man's grasp of medicine was dubious, though readily compensated by his showmanship.

"Banstrom's Egyptian Elixir! Blended from the secret potions of the Pharaohs! See clearer and further than ever! Improves your complexion and brings new vigor to your life!" he bellowed with theatrical fervor.

Alastair rolled his eyes. The sizeable amount of alcohol the elixir contained would make believers of anyone. Three tablespoons, and you'd be able to see Heaven without spectacles. Four, and you'd be as embalmed as the mummies in the Valley of the Kings.

He turned away and wandered along Wentworth toward Brick

Lane. Just south of the Frying Pan, another woman's voice called to him. He ignored her. A peculiar sensation engulfed him; she was one of his kind, *en mirage.*

In no mood for Keats' antics, he growled, "Leave off, will you?"

She tugged on his arm, pulling him into an alley. He squared off, furious at the interruption. Before he could launch a tirade at his friend, he squinted in the darkness, studying the woman in front of him. She didn't feel like Keats. A faint sound caused him to swing around, instinctively raising his left arm in a defensive gesture.

The truncheon blow struck his arm with immense force, arcing it into his face. He cried out, lurching backward until he impacted the brick wall behind him, his arm screaming in white-hot agony as wet warmth filled his sleeve.

His attacker moved forward, slapping a short truncheon into his broad, calloused palm. He had a scraggly moustache and the build of a dockworker. The woman was gone, the illusion replaced by the short figure of a man clad in ill-fitting clothes. He held a truncheon as well.

"I have no money on me," Alastair said, buying time while he assessed the damage. Though bleeding, the arm did not appear broken. He clenched and released his fingers in an attempt to mitigate the pain.

"Money isn't what we want, now is it?" the large man replied. He elbowed his cohort with a rough laugh.

"No, a few bob can't buy ya way out of this one, guv'ner," the other one said. He seemed a dwarf in comparison to his companion, his shoulders barely reaching Alastair's chest. They were a dangerous combination. What Stubby couldn't reach, Scraggly Moustache would.

"Then what *do* you want?" Alastair demanded.

"Send 'im a message, 'e said," Stubby replied. Moustache nodded with a black chuckle.

"He?" Alastair asked. Maybe they'd rise to the bait and supply a name.

Stubby shook his head. "We ain't stupid. Besides, 'e said you'd know anyways."

The Conclave. But which one— Livingston or Hastings?

"Is there no way we can come to an arrangement?" Alastair asked. He cautiously positioned one foot, then the other to ensure he had traction.

Moustache shook his head, slapping the weapon into his palm again for emphasis. It seemed to be one of his few skills.

"Do you know anything about the Welsh?" asked Alastair.

"Dirty, stealin' folk."

That was rich—the last time this one had seen water was probably at his christening, if he'd even been inside a church.

"They know how to fight," Alastair continued. "All those centuries of battling the English."

"We're ain't here for some bleedin' history lesson. Ya ain't Welsh anyway."

"How do you know?" Alastair punted back, flexing the fingers on his left hand. They were less numb now; the initial shock had worn off. He just had to wait for the proper moment.

Moustache spat on the ground, another one of his skills. "Ya can't understand 'em. They don't speak right."

Alastair would have laughed if the situation hadn't been so dire.

Stubby snorted, "'Sides, I don't see any of their lot about. Let's stop jawin' and get to it, 'eh?" He elbowed his companion, taking his eyes off the victim. It was the opening Alastair had hoped for.

He flung himself toward the larger target, sending him sprawling onto the refuse-covered cobblestones. Snatching Moustache's truncheon, he rolled, ducking Stubby's blow as it swooped by his head. Scrambling to his feet, he executed a strong backhand, cracking the weapon hard over Stubby's closest knee. A bellow cut the air, and he dropped hard onto the pavement. Howling, he twisted on the ground, clutching his leg.

Moustache rose, but he didn't remain vertical for very long. Alastair lashed out with the truncheon, catching his assailant on the shoulder. The man instinctively turned toward the blow and Alastair delivered the second strike, slamming the wood into the man's neck. Moustache crumpled to the cobblestones, moaning.

Tucking one of the weapons under his throbbing arm, the doctor pressed the tip of the other into Moustache's throat, applying enough pressure to make the man's eyes bulge.

Alastair gasped from the exertion. "Who...sent...you?"

"Don't know," was the choked reply.

Alastair shot a look at Stubby. The thug was in too much agony to talk, tears running down his dirty face as he struggled to regain his feet. A high-pitched keening noise came from his lips.

Blast. Alastair took a deep breath to calm himself. "A bit more about the Welsh. They taught me how to fight. Remember that if you decide to come after me again." Moustache had no comment, too intent on his next breath. "Tell your masters to leave me alone, or I'll bring the battle to them. That's how it works. You understand?"

Moustache gave a careful nod, the tip of the truncheon still pressing hard.

"I knew we could come to an arrangement," Alastair said, backing away.

"Ya bastard, ya broke me knee!" Stubby whined.

"Then consider yourself lucky," Alastair replied. "You came out of this alive." Stubby's eyes widened. He hobbled backward with jerky, incomplete steps, falling hard like a de-stringed marionette.

"All right, you lot, out you come," a voice commanded. An arc of light split the alley, moving upward as the constable hefted the bull's-eye lantern.

"It's the rozzers," Stubby hissed. Moustache dragged himself over to his companion. Showing surprising strength, he hauled them both to their feet. They hobbled away together, Stubby whimpering in pain with every footfall.

The lantern illuminated the twin truncheons as the cop cautiously edged into the alley.

Alastair let out a puff of air. *How can I explain this?* Before he could formulate an alibi, his senses tingled. He might not be able to see the figure behind the glowing lantern, but he knew who it was.

Keats. Thank God. The lantern lowered. A middle-aged constable surveyed the scene, shaking his head. His friend's choice of illusion had been inspired. "Keats?" Alastair inquired softly.

"Sorry, old man, I was delayed," came the barely audible reply. Louder, he added, "So what's all this, sir?" pointing toward the weapons.

Alastair went along with the charade, unsure of who might be listening. "I was assaulted, Constable. I...seized their weapons."

"I see. Are you wounded, sir?" Keats asked, pointing at Alastair's hand.

Glancing down, he found his palm streaked in blood. "Yes, I am."

"Any idea who those roughs were, sir?"

Best to play ignorant. Alastair shook his head. "No notion."

"Robbers, then?"

"I would suspect." Silent words of understanding passed between them.

"Sensible men are home in their beds at this hour, sir. Why are you not in yours?"

How remarkable. Keats sounds just like a copper.

"I was having difficulty sleeping."

"Well, then, you've learned your lesson. Do you wish to file a report, sir?"

"No need, Constable. I didn't get a good look at the fellows."

"As you wish, sir," Keats replied. "Come along, I'll see you home so you can receive proper treatment for that injury." He extended a hand for the truncheons. "I'll just take these."

Keats stuck the truncheons under his left arm and led the way, the lantern beam dancing ahead of them. Alastair followed, clutching the wounded limb to his chest. It pounded in cadence with each heartbeat.

The make-believe constable dropped the truncheons into the first garbage heap he found. Keats dusted off his hands in a satisfied gesture.

Alastair murmured, "How did you find me?"

"A certain titled lady asked that I keep an eye on you. She was concerned something like this might happen."

Lady Wescomb? Why would she ask you? He pushed the questions aside.

"Hopefully, the Horsemen will get the message," Alastair replied.

"Providing they're willing to listen."

13

The pounding flung Cynda out of the dream like a slingshot. She struggled to the door. A frowsy, dressing-gowned Mildred peered at her, eyes wide and hands fluttering in the air like startled birds.

"You must come right away. He's been hurt something awful!" she said in a forced whisper.

"Who?" Cynda asked, her brain still drowsy. *Chris?*

"The doctor. They tried to rob him! Can you believe it? Doesn't have a penny to his name and they try to rob him. You have to help." Mildred paused and then admitted, "I can't stand blood. Neither can Annabelle. I didn't wake her. She'd faint dead away for sure." She beckoned frantically.

"Let me get something on," Cynda said. The "something" was her black dress. She slipped it on without petticoats or the bustle. Ramming her bare feet into her boots, she tromped down the stairs unsteadily, struggling with the bodice buttons as she went. Her balance failed and she grabbed the rail for support. Once the world felt upright again, she continued.

"What was he doing out at this time of night?" she grumbled.

"Being an idiot," the policeman at the end of the stairs retorted. He tapped his cap. "Good...ah...morning, miss—"

"Constable," she said, fumbling her way around the newel post and toward the kitchen, still buttoning. She could hear Alastair protesting that he was fine and that there was no reason to wake Miss Lassiter.

"Too late," she said, flying into the room. She abandoned her effort with the small buttons. The last five gaped open, revealing a sizeable amount of cleavage.

The injured party sat in a chair at the kitchen table, his left arm lying on a thick piece of linen. Blood seeped onto the cloth.

The cluster of sweat on his forehead told Cynda that whatever had happened hurt like hell.

Mildred wavered on her feet, putting a hand on the wall for support, her face the color of fresh snow. Propelling her by the shoulders, Cynda pointed at the stove. "Make us some tea."

"It's really isn't that bad," the doctor said, his tone surprisingly timid.

Without asking permission, Cynda began unbuttoning his shirt. To her surprise, he didn't utter a word in protest. "Where's your bag?" she demanded.

"In my room."

She looked toward Mildred—it would be cruel to send the woman upstairs in her condition. The cop loitered in the doorway. *Might as well make him useful.*

"Give the nice constable your key so he can fetch your bag."

Yet again, Alastair complied without protest. The constable left the room on his mission, his heavy boots thumping down the hallway.

"Is that it?" she asked, pointing to the mess that constituted the doctor's left arm.

"I think that's plenty," he replied.

"What the hell were you doing out this time of night?"

Her profanity earned her considerable attention, both from the patient and Mildred, who stared at her over a shoulder.

"Sorry. I swear when I'm upset."

The doctor raised an eyebrow in disapproval, but didn't offer an answer to her the question.

"Soap?" she asked.

Mildred rummaged around for a rough-cut bar and handed it over, keeping her back to the patient the entire time. Hefting fresh water into the basin, Cynda lathered her hands vigorously. The soap burned like pure acid.

By the time the constable reappeared with the doctor's bag, she'd dried her hands and was inspecting Alastair's wound.

"Nasty. It doesn't look like a knife," she said, cautiously pressing on the bruised and lacerated flesh. The doctor gave a sharp intake of breath.

"It was a truncheon. I blocked a blow to my head," he said, sounding rather pleased with himself.

"Pity," she said, "it would have caused less damage the other way."

A derisive snort came from the constable who lounged in the kitchen's doorway as if he were family.

Cynda turned on him, in no mood for bystanders. "Is Dr. Montrose under arrest?"

"No. The singular lack of good sense isn't a chargeable offense or most of London would be in the clink," the man replied.

Alastair's frown skipped in his direction.

"Do you need to take a report?"

The two men traded looks. "No, I have everything I need," the cop replied.

"Then good night, Constable." A smirk from her patient.

The cop accepted his dismissal with good humor. "Right, then. Good night, all." His retreating footsteps clomped along the hall.

Pulling up a chair, Cynda examined the wound more closely.

"It's just a contusion," the doctor said, observing her with a benign expression. He seemed less tense now that the cop was gone. His eyes weren't on her face, but focused further south.

"What about the bone? Does it feel broken?" she asked.

"No. It might be cracked, but that's very hard to determine." His eyes hadn't moved.

"Enjoying the view?" she asked.

The eyes snapped upright, but there was no chagrin to accompany them. "Yes, I was, actually," was the straightforward answer.

Smart ass. "Any numbness in the fingers?"

"Initially, but not now. So where did you obtain your medical license?" he teased.

"My father's a doctor," she said. "He taught me a number of things."

"I see," Alastair replied, his tone more contrite. He studied the wound. "I don't think sutures are required."

"It wouldn't help much; it's more mashed than sliced," she said, scrutinizing him. His face had dirt on it, his usually tidy hair disheveled. Someone had worked him over with a vengeance.

As if in answer to her thoughts, he added, "I sincerely damaged one of the ruffian's kneecaps."

She inclined her head in respect. "Well done."

"I thought so. He didn't, of course."

Mildred jumped in. "After your clothes, I wouldn't doubt. I heard about a man they stripped and left in the street raw as the day he was born." She rattled the lid of the teapot as the kettle sang on the stove.

Alastair winked. Cynda returned it.

The doctor offered no further comments while Cynda cleansed the wound and dressed it, speaking only to thank Mildred for the tea that appeared near his uninjured arm.

"Do you have something in your bag for the pain?" Cynda asked, rummaging amongst its contents. It seemed an archaic jumble of bottles and ointment tins.

"It isn't that bad," the doctor allowed.

She eyed him and then sighed. "Well, it's your night's sleep, not mine." After one last examination of the bandage, she announced, "We'll change it again in the morning."

"Thank you. That was very well done."

"Now go to bed, will you?"

"I will." He wiggled his fingers on the injured hand. "You should be a doctor."

In this time period? You have to be kidding. She opted for "Thank you," instead.

Cynda followed him to his room, carrying the bag, handing it over once he'd opened his door.

A thought dropped into her mind. "Ah, Alastair?"

"Yes?" he asked. The sweat had returned to his forehead. She suspected he was regretting his decision to forego the pain medication.

"Has that constable ever been here before?"

A noticeable hesitation. "That particular constable? No, not as such."

Not as such? "Well, then, good night."

Once she'd locked the door, she slumped on the bed. Bouncing the skeleton key from palm to palm, she murmured, "Then how did the cop know which room was yours?"

‡

Thursday, 27 September, 1888

By the time Cynda hauled herself to the dining room for breakfast, everyone was gone. Mildred kindly fetched a plate for her, one she'd kept warm on the stove. While Cynda devoured her breakfast, the landlady brought her up to date. Mr. and Mrs. Bottom were touring the Victoria and Albert Museum, Mr. Everson was off to the wool warehouse, and Mr. Hix was "Heaven knows where."

"Queer fellow, that one. Keeps strange hours. He creeps about all the time, always wearing those gloves," Mildred said, shaking her head. "It's like he thinks we don't keep the place clean enough, or something." After the remainder of her report, none of which interested Cynda in the least, she announced, "Dr. Montrose asked that I give you this." She placed an envelope next to Cynda's nearly empty plate.

"Thank you. How'd he look this morning?"

"Tired, as usual. I don't think he slept much, what with his arm and all."

Surprise. Once Mildred puttered out of the room, Cynda ripped open the envelope. The doctor's handwriting flowed like a mountain stream, wide and expressive.

I have commitments this morning, but shall meet with you at Annabelle's at 2 sharp to assist you in your search.

Thank you for your expert care of my person,

Sincerely,

Alastair S. Montrose (Doctor)

Cynda rolled her eyes, stuffing the note into a pocket. "'*Expert care of my person*'...oh, brother."

She leaned back in her chair and was promptly reminded that her backside extended further than was sensible. Cursing under her breath, she wrestled with the bustle. It was always in the way. Why would any woman want to make her backside look bigger?

As she squirmed, she noted a newspaper on the chair next to her. Laying it on the table, she stared at the masthead while slicing the ham.

THE DAILY TELEGRAPH
THURSDAY, SEPTEMBER 27, 1888

"Three more days..." she whispered. Whitechapel's history would take a turn for the macabre on the 30th. Two more women would be dead, killed within an hour and a mere ten-minute walk of each other. Her mind flitted to the wounded doctor. Why had Alastair been roaming the streets in the middle of the night? He didn't appear the type to get his jollies in a back alley. Then again, why did she care? None of this was her concern. She just needed to do her job and let history take care of itself.

After wading through page after page of news reports with headlines such as "A Fire of an Exciting Nature," she found an article that stole all her hope.

An Unknown Found

Police are requesting the public's assistance in the identification of a young man recovered from the Thames, Monday last, near King James's Stairs, Shadwell. The deceased appears to be approximately twenty-five years in age with light-brown hair and eyes. In life, he would have stood five-foot nine, and was of slight build. A distinguishing feature may aid in his identification: a fine, four-inch scar situated behind the right ear. A partially consumed bottle of laudanum was discovered in the pocket of his jacket, and the coroner surmised that he took the opiate to ease his anxieties before casting himself into the river. A final note and numerous, weighty stones were discovered in the pockets of the dead man's garments. As reported in yesterday's edition, an inquest was held and a verdict of Suicide returned. The body is available for viewing at the parish mortuary at St. George's-in-the-East, Cable-street.

"Chris." Cynda lovingly brushed her hand over the paper, fingers staining dark from the ink. Considering the scar a badge of honor, he'd refused to have it removed, though most of their contemporaries thought any blemish unacceptable. *"How many people can say they survived an Ottoman Turk's blade?"* he'd joked.

"Not very many," she whispered. Chris had been pulled from the Thames the night she'd arrived in Whitechapel.

‡

Even before she entered the room to view the body, the pocket watch announced her lover's presence.

Oh, God, no.

Christopher Stone rested on a rough wood table, a grayed sheet tucked around his narrow hips. His pale skin was marred by dirty cuts and he stank of the river. She could imagine what he'd say about that. Fortunately, Chris was beyond caring.

From his perch near the door, the mortuary attendant watched her with disinterested eyes. "Ya know 'im?" he asked in a gravelly voice, a curl of smoke coming from his mouth.

"Yes."

A huff of approval. "Put his partic'lars on that piece of paper over there," he ordered, pointing toward a table. "Cor'ner will need it for the death certif'cat."

Cynda gently pushed a clump of mud-caked hair off her lover's face. Cold skin numbed her fingers. "What was the...cause of death?"

"Too much water," the man said. He chuckled thickly at his black joke.

She glared at him, resisting the temptation to take his smoldering cigar and stuff it up his red-veined nose. He saw her expression. "Sew-ee-cide, that's what the cor'ner says."

"What about his clothes?" she asked, eyes lowering to her lover's body. Chris was bruised and battered, no doubt from the time in the water, rolling over and over, smashing into... She swallowed hard as her stomach careened.

"Clothes is over there." He pointed to a sodden pile on the floor. "If the cor'ner says it all done proper, where ya want the body sent?" he asked, like she'd just purchased a fish at the market.

Cynda gave him a piercing look. *2057, you ass. Think you can manage that?* "Put his clothes in something so I can take them with me."

With a bored shrug, the man collected the pile of wet garments and hiked out the door, a choking trail of cheap cigar smoke in his wake.

Cynda bent over the body, studying the exposed flesh. A red welt encircled both his wrists. Exposing his ankles, she found no marks. Hearing the heavy tread of the morgue attendant, she returned the sheet to its former position.

He stuffed a wrapped parcel into her hand. As he did, he made sure to squeeze her breast. Tempting as it was to deck him, she let it pass. If she nailed the jerk, he'd take his wrath out on Chris' body. Right now, her lover had no way to protect himself.

"I'll send someone for him," she said, retreating out of groping range.

The attendant gave her a leering smile. "Or ya could come back for 'im yerself."

She shook her head. "If I do, you'll have to learn how to hold your cigar with your toes."

‡

It took another half-hour before all the *partic'lars* were complete, including an uncomfortable discussion with the coroner. The man launched a barrage of questions: What was the name of the deceased, his age, address and profession? Had he spoken of ending his life? Where had he purchased the laudanum? Who was the next of kin?

Cynda had bluffed her way through, fabricating answers as the coroner made notes for the death certificate. Then the alleged suicide note was produced: penciled letters on a wrinkled sheet of paper.

DEATH BECKONS AND I OBEY.

More questions: Was the deceased in the habit of writing in block letters?

She gripped the note tightly. "Yes, when he was upset," she lied. She memorized the words, searing them into her brain.

"That's all I need," the coroner said. "I am sorry for your loss, miss."

Not as much as I am.

Sitting in the mortuary's courtyard, Cynda unwrapped the parcel and sorted through her lover's clothes: a suitcoat, trousers, shirt, but no boots. Even his lucky piece of turquoise was gone, the one he'd carried for years. More important to TIC, his time interface was missing.

No surprise. If it had been in Chris' possession at the moment of death, his body wouldn't be here; it would be auto-returned to 2057, courtesy of the *Dead Man Switch,* as the Rovers called it. It did little to help the dead Rover, but it kept history reasonably tidy.

The bottle of laudanum was tucked inside a coat pocket, half empty, the chemist's label distorted by its time in the water. Holding it upright, she struggled to read the writing.

"Os...?" she speculated. It was nearly impossible to judge what with the water's effect on the ink. She dug deeper into his clothes, wrinkling her nose at the stench of raw sewage and dead fish. In an inside coat pocket, adhered to the lining, she found a piece of paper. Written in pencil, the word was barely legible.

"Drogo?"

She tucked the paper into her own pocket, folded the clothes and repackaged them in the damp paper. TIC owed her lover a proper set of funeral clothes. She'd be sure he got them.

14

By the time Jacynda reached the boarding house, tears pressed against her eyes like a spring flood. The moment she closed the door to her room, she sank to her knees, sobs spilling forth. Cupping a hand over her mouth so the landladies wouldn't hear her, she rocked back and forth in silent agony as the tears surged downward.

Chris Stone had built his own niche in her heart. He'd often shared his dreams with her after they'd made love. All those were gone now, washed away with the tide. She'd never again savor his hands holding her close, his jokes or his impish smile.

Rovers weren't supposed to die. They weren't part of history, and yet someone had brutally altered Chris' timeline. Raw, primal rage built inside her. By God, if given the chance, she'd return the favor, history be damned.

It took several minutes before she had the courage to open the time interface and send the news into the future. How would TIC react? Making the arrangements would be difficult, but Time Rovers always returned, no matter what. If the roles were reversed, Chris would make sure she got home.

"I owe you that," she said, logging onto TICnet. Fortunately, they couldn't see her tears.

Logged On, the screen typed back.

Ralph?

Yes. What's going on? Why haven't you reported in?

She had no way to blunt the news. *Chris is dead.*

There was no reply for a time, and then, *I'm so sorry, Cyn. How?*

Looks like murder.

Oh, God.

Need to transfer him home, she wrote.

I'll get Thad to approve it. There was a long pause, then the screen displayed, *Do you have his time interface unit?*

That had to be Thad—Ralph wasn't a callous jerk.

No. It's missing. "Or he'd be home, you fool."

Find it.

Yeah, that was Thad. "And where do you suggest I start?" she growled. She opted for a fib. *Bottom of the Thames. What about Chris' transfer?*

Unable to do so at this time.

What??

Use TIC funds for suitable burial in that time period.

"What? You cheap son of a—" *Chris has to come home. He has family,* she typed in a fury of letters.

Not possible. Maybe in the future.

She stared at the screen, incredulous. "Future? What are you going to do, come back and dig him up in a couple of centuries?" She tried a new tactic. *What about a potential Time Incursion?*

Not your concern. Have you found tourist? the screen asked.

"You cold bastard. All you care about is that bottom line." *No. Been busy at the morgue.*

Find Samuelson. Your job depends on it.

She forced herself not to pummel the watch into minute pieces and ruin her chance of doing the same to Thad sometime down the line.

Cyn?

That had to be Ralph. *Yes?*

Sorry. Not good here. What can I do to help?

God bless him. *Tell me about the tourist.*

The man's dossier appeared. She skimmed through it, anger still bubbling in her veins while her fingernails dug into her palms. Samuelson's primary area of research was the care of the insane during the Nineteenth Century—hence, his trip to Victorian London.

Any luck with a photo? she typed.

Not in the file.

Why not?

Things are getting that way here. Anything else?

Check the word Drogo for me.

Hold on. 12th C. Patron saint of bodily ills, cattle, coffeehouse owners, insanity, orphans, sheep, and unattractive people.

Unattractive people?

Yes. Thad's got his own saint.

That made her chuckle, despite the tears. *Has tourist*

been here before?

Can't access those files either.

Are things that bad?

Worse.

Give me a list of asylums.

Her screen filled with name after name. She pushed the cancel key.

Narrow it down!

Can't. There were lots of them.

Check tourist application, she typed. Maybe Samuelson had filed a proposed itinerary.

Can't access that, either.

What the hell is going on? A long pause. *R?*

I'll get the info for you. Check back later.

She groaned. *Hurry.*

FYI—your apt. is gone. TIC took it back. Your stuff is at my place. I got everything, Fred included.

"What?"

Realizing Ralph couldn't hear her, she typed, *What????*

Sorry...no choice.

"Ah, no," she muttered. Not that she had that much stuff, but still...

Cyn?

Thanks, R, I owe you. Is TIC going to make it?

Jury's out on that. Just come home safe, okay?

Got it. Log Off.

Logged Off.

A tremor worked its way from her tailbone to the crown of her head. Cynda converted the watch to its usual size and then stuffed it under the pillow, huddling under the bedcovers in a futile attempt to get warm.

No Chris, no apartment, potentially no job. What am I going to do?

She punched the pillow. *What would Defoe do?*

Touted as the greatest of their ilk, Harter Defoe's inventiveness was legendary. He'd always found a creative solution to any problem. "Probably all PR," she muttered. "Besides, he's not here."

"But *I* am."

The spider sat on the chair near the wardrobe. He'd nestled into the folds of her mantelet, multiple eyes peering brightly in her direction.

"Thanks. It's good to know some things are constant."

"As the time and tide," the spider replied, pushing a recalcitrant fold into a more comfortable position and then settling with an exaggerated ease that reminded her more of a cat than an arachnid.

"Time and tide waits for no Rover," she murmured. "Even Chris."

"Sorry about that," the spider said. "How will you get him home?"

That was the dilemma. It wasn't as if she could hug his dead body to hers and then effect the transfer. His ESR Chip would tell TIC what she was up to. Once they sensed his presence, the transfer would be denied. Even if she removed the chip, they'd notice the excess weight. They'd retrieve Samuelson in a heartbeat. He was a tourist.

"I need to get Chris to '057 without them realizing he's along for the ride," she mused. "But how?"

Lying on the bed, she closed her eyes, letting her mind wander. Memories, like rambunctious toddlers, scampered around in no particular order. The explosion of the atom bomb, the streets of Imperial Rome filled with cheering hordes, the final death throes of the Hindenburg as it sank to the ground in a boiling mass of flames. Ash and smoke filled her nose, followed by the horrific roar of Vesuvius' wrath as it engulfed Pompeii.

"Fire and ash..." she murmured, and then swung herself upright. A cunning grin formed. "Why not? As long as he's home..." The grin quickly faded. "But if I cremate him, we won't know how he died."

She placed her face in her hands. "Autopsy." Her eyes darted toward the wall that adjoined her room with Alastair's.

"Dr. Grumpy owes me one," she said, rising with purpose.

✝

2057 A.D.

Time Immersion Corporation

Cold rage made it hard to concentrate. Ralph rose deliberately from the chair and leaned across the chronsole counter toward Thad. His voice pitched low, like a growl. "You told me Chris was back in."

An unconcerned shrug.

"You're fudging the numbers, aren't you?" Ralph demanded. "How many others are still in the time stream? How many are you planning to orphan?"

Faces swiveled in their direction. The room collectively held its breath.

"We're not orphaning anyone," Thad replied in a practiced tone. "That's against the law."

"Then why haven't the other Senior Rovers been in here to complain about losing their apartments?" He looked at the computer screen. "The logs are telling me they're all in. Why aren't they stringing you up by your balls, Thad?"

"None of the Seniors are lodging complaints. They understand it was purely a fiscal decision to aid the company during its rough patch. The attitude problem appears to be yours."

Ralph leaned closer. "Bring Chris Stone home. You owe him that."

"No, we don't. His contract didn't specify retrieval in the event of termination. He should have paid closer attention."

"Decency demands—"

"Decency doesn't make payroll, Mr. Hamilton," Thad snapped.

"What about Cynda?"

When his boss turned away, ignoring the question, Ralph's fury exploded. "You're going to leave her there, aren't you? You lying weasel. You've got your nose so far up the bosses'—"

Thad whirled and banged his fist on the chronsole counter. "You're done, Mr. Hamilton. Clear out your stuff. I want you out of here in less than a minute."

Ralph snagged onto his nemesis' collar, raising a fist. Thad squeaked and tore himself away, tapping at his PSI unit as he skittered to the other side of the room. Out of the corner of his eye, Ralph saw one of the customer reps throw him a thumbs-up. He returned it.

The security specialists were in front of him within thirty seconds.

"What kept you guys?" he chided.

"Traffic. It's been a busy day. You're not the only one," a guard remarked.

"Good to hear it."

While Ralph waited on the transport platform for the next Grav-Rail train, flanked by the two guards, he took one last look at the building that had once housed his mighty employer. The massive pocket watch logo above the front entrance flickered ominously, portent of TIC's future.

I'll get you home somehow, Cynda. I swear I won't leave you there.

✝

Thursday, 27 September, 1888

The cup of tea sent an inviting spiral of steam into the air. Keats ignored it and consulted his notes from his latest assignment. It had been an exercise in futility, given what he'd discovered.

Clearing his throat, he addressed his superior. "The barrister's son has a penchant for gambling and expensive courtesans. Nevertheless, he possesses a solid alibi for both murders. He is not in debt that I can gather. In fact, he's rather lucky at cards."

Fisher arched an eyebrow. "What does that tell you, Sergeant?"

"That someone wished to discomfit him or his father. Settling scores, I think. Perhaps by someone who wasn't quite so lucky at cards."

Fisher nodded with approval. Keats returned to his notes.

"The Conservative noble's nephew is inclined toward...he was in France during the second murder, spending time with his lover, the son of a winery owner. Two separate sources state that he has no interest in women at all. He spends most of his time in Paris."

Fisher nodded. "Avoiding a charge of gross indecency, no doubt."

"Most likely. As for the chemist, he is so blind he has to hold medicine bottles against his nose to read the labels. He couldn't cut someone's throat if he tried, let alone extricate a woman's womb in the dark."

"And the dentist?"

Keats took a hurried sip of tea. "A bit more promising, but not likely. His servants swear he was in bed the night of both murders. His colleagues speak well of him, and he has no history of violence against women. His sole crime, if you call it that, is an overriding passion to study the murders in detail. He collects all the newspaper accounts and regales his patients with theories as to the murderer's identity."

"Like the majority of London's citizens, I wager. In your opinion, all of these were for naught?" Fisher asked, riffling through the closest file on his desk.

"Indeed," Keats replied, barely stifling a yawn. "However, if I ever need a barrister or someone to pull a tooth, I know whom to consult."

"Not an entire waste of time, then," Fisher replied with a hint of a smile. "I have one more for you." He pushed a piece of paper across the desk.

Keats collected the sheet. A cold sweat bloomed underneath his shirt as he read the name. His eyes darted up and then down again.

Fisher continued, "The fellow is a doctor in the East End. Apparently, his behavior has attracted someone's attention. Do check him out, Sergeant."

Keats swallowed heavily. The name wouldn't change, no matter how many prayers he uttered. *Had The Conclave lost their collective minds? Surely they wouldn't dare to...*

"Sergeant?"

Keats put the sheet on the desk, his hand steadier than it had a right to be. Fisher had been honest with him about the dying Transitive. That trust had to be returned.

"Alastair Montrose and I are well acquainted, sir. I consider him a valued friend."

Fisher's face grew pensive. "I see."

"I hold him in extremely high regard, and that would color my report."

Fisher refilled his cup with deliberate calm. "Tell me about him."

That wasn't unexpected. His superior wouldn't let him off the hook easily.

"I've known Alastair for about a year, just after he returned from his medical studies in Baltimore. I met him through a mutual acquaintance."

"Does he have surgical skills?"

"Some."

"Married?"

"No, though he was engaged for a time. I have found Alastair to be a man of high moral standards, though a bit rigid in his viewpoints. He is an excellent physician and completely dedicated to the care of his patients, often to the exclusion of everything else in his life."

"Is he a fanatic of some sort?" Fisher asked, stirring cream into his tea.

"No, just committed, sir. He shares a clinic with another doctor. Both men invest every spare moment in its operation. They treat an average of thirty to fifty patients an evening, those with little recourse other than the hospital."

Fisher gave a shudder. "Not an appealing alternative. You said that Dr. Montrose was engaged at one point. Explain that."

With great care, Keats related Alastair's life-changing decision and how it brought him to Whitechapel.

Fisher tapped his chin. "Quite extraordinary. Nevertheless, for a moment let us assume that whoever brought his name to our attention has a valid reason for doing so. In your opinion, is Dr. Montrose capable of these murders?"

Keats took some tea to steady his nerves. *Could his friend be the killer, convinced in some irrational fashion that he was mitigating their suffering?*

He had no choice but to speak the truth. "Alastair is quite capable of harming someone, Chief Inspector. He was instrumental in a man's death in Wales, though it was in self-defense."

Before Fisher could pose the question, Keats cut him off. "I verified his story with the police in Caernarfon. It was indeed as he reported." Keats exhaled a puff of air. "Would Alastair tear women apart in such a frenzy? No, that is not in my friend's nature."

"Are you sure? You checked his story, despite your regard for him. That implies you didn't entirely trust him to tell the truth."

Keats closed his eyes and then gave a slow nod. "I wasn't sure then, but I am now, sir. I have watched him give his last pennies to the poor, forgoing food so they might have a bed for the night. My friend's obsession lies in mercy, not murder."

Fisher did not reply, but rose and drifted to the window. He stared at the street scene for a time. When he finally turned around, he proclaimed, "Write a report to that effect, and I will consider Dr. Montrose cleared."

"Sir?" Keats asked, astounded. "I could be mistaken as to Alastair's character, Chief Inspector."

"And it's possible that blind chemist could be a ravening butcher and we've given him a free pass. Our job involves making judgments. On occasion, we make the correct ones."

"Yes, sir," Keats said, taking that as dismissal.

"One last thing, Sergeant."

"Sir?"

"Get some sleep, will you? You look exhausted."

"I am, sir. However, I must keep an eye out for Flaherty."

"Nevertheless, if you're too weary to think properly, you will make mistakes." Fisher pulled out his watch and flipped it open. "Take a few hours off, have a good lunch and a lie-down. Consider that an order."

Keats grinned. "If it is an order, sir, how can I disobey?"

"There's a good man. I'll need your reports by tomorrow morning, though."

"Yes, sir."

Keats remained oblivious to his surroundings until he was out of the building and savoring the mid-morning sunshine. Jamming on his hat, he hurried toward the omnibus stop. He would do precisely as his boss had ordered, providing his mind would stop hounding him with questions for which there were no answers.

☩

2057 A.D.
TEM Enterprises

The man sitting across from him was legendary; yet somehow, T.E. Morrisey wasn't what Ralph had expected. The Vid-News reports made him appear older, less careworn. In person, he seemed like any other geek, though better dressed than most. His British accent was the most notable feature, apart from his penetrating eyes. Currently involved in an online Vid-Call, he'd motioned for Ralph to take a seat. Or actually a pillow, as there were no chairs in the room.

Ralph gingerly parked himself and tried to calm down. The summons to TEM Enterprises had caught him offguard and sent him into an uncharacteristic panic. He'd always dreamed of meeting the man who had created the amazing software that powered the Time Immersion industry. Now he sat across from him.

While he waited, Ralph took a visual tour of the room. It was unique, just like its owner. State-of-the-art time technology equipment rubbed elbows with priceless paintings and exquisitely carved marble statues. A Bach cantata played in the background, circumventing the hum of the machinery. A pleasant marriage of old and new.

Then things got odd: the furniture was set low to the ground so that you were required to sit on small pillows to access the holo-keyboard and the terminals. It reminded Ralph of a Japanese tatami room with computer equipment. The paintings were positioned about three feet off the ground, as if designed to be viewed by toddlers.

Before he could puzzle further on that discovery, Morrisey ended his call and turned toward him. "Pardon the intrusion, Mr. Hamilton."

Ralph took a breath and pushed aside the desire to gush. Instead, he focused on the more important issue—the orphaned

Rovers. "Not a problem. How can I help you?"

Morrisey shook his head. "More to the point, how can I help *you?*"

Ralph frowned. "The only way you can help me is to retrieve a few TIC Rovers, but I suspect that isn't why I'm here."

"First lesson, Mr. Hamilton: Never make assumptions. That will be paramount if you are to work for me."

Ralph started in astonishment. "Me...you?" he sputtered. Distrust set in, fostered by the lessons learned at the hands of his former employer. "Why?"

"We share a common goal, Mr. Hamilton. We both want the Rovers retrieved."

"What's in it for you, other than good PR?"

Morrisey stiffened. "Good public relations has nothing to do with it. Rovers are not disposable."

"Okay, I apologize. So, why me? I'm just another time jockey."

"You have a good reputation, you possess a conscience, and I need your knowledge of TIC."

Ralph furrowed his brow. "You'll bring every Rover home, no matter how long it takes?" he asked.

A solemn nod from Morrisey.

"Well, I'll be damned." Ralph grew pensive. "Do I have to sell my soul to you or anything?"

A muted chuckle. "No, just the standard contract."

"Same thing," Ralph muttered. He pondered for only a half-second. "Tell me what you want me to do."

A reassuring nod. "TIC's been altering the chron logs for the last few weeks. We need to verify exactly how many Rovers are in the time stream. Once we know, we will access their time interfaces and begin the retrieval process. I want all of them out in a very short period of time so TIC doesn't realize what we're up to. Is that clear?"

That made sense. Once the Rovers returned, all hell would break loose; TIC's lies would be revealed, and the government would step in. "I'll see what I can find out. I have contacts inside TIC who can help me figure out what's really happening."

"Indeed you do."

Ralph blinked. "How do you know that?"

Morrisey avoided the question. "Do not mention my name when you're making your inquiries. It is important that no one be aware that you are in my employ, at least at this point in time."

"You know that one of the Rovers has died in 1888?"

Morrisey's eyes grew distant. "Yes." He looked away. "Do your research Mr. Hamilton. We need answers as soon as possible."

A few minutes later, Ralph was positioned on a pillow in front of one of the low tables, working his contacts via the Vid-Net Mail system. His back complained about the lack of a chair. He was having second thoughts. Joining forces with Morrisey might be a gigantic mistake. Everything he'd heard about the guy had been filtered through the media—not the most reliable of sources. Was he being played for a sucker? Did Morrisey really intend to honor his word?

I've got no choice. Cynda has to come home.

Behind him, he heard Morrisey rise. Ralph hazarded a quick glance over his shoulder. The genius had arranged himself into a Lotus position on a large pillow facing one of the masterpieces and was inspecting the art with a surreal intensity that bordered on obsession.

That's why the pictures are so far down on the wall.

Shaking his head, Ralph returned to his work. Typing furiously, he wondered how long it would be before the White Rabbit made an appearance, muttering about his ears and whiskers.

‡

Thursday, 27 September, 1888

Alastair found her just outside the main entrance to the hospital, leaning against one of the brick arches. Her face was unnaturally pale, a handkerchief knotted in thin fingers. He lightly touched her elbow.

Jacynda's red-rimmed eyes rose to meet his. "I found him."

Without a care what others might think, he wrapped his arms around her, giving a gentle hug. "I am very sorry, Jacynda."

Feeling awkward, he released his embrace. She didn't appear to have taken offense at his gesture.

"They say he committed suicide."

"My lord," Alastair murmured. *Why would a man do such a thing?*

She actively kneaded the handkerchief with both hands. "He didn't kill himself."

"This must be very difficult for you—"

"No!" she retorted. Her tone earned them a startled look from a passerby. "I know Chris. He did *not* kill himself."

Caught by her ferocity, he acquiesced. "What do you intend to do?"

"I want you to examine him."

He shook his head. "I have no expertise when it comes to...post mortems."

"Do you know someone who does? Someone who is...discreet?"

The last question puzzled him. "Yes. My partner at the clinic, Dr. Cohen, has performed autopsies. I could request he examine your...particular friend."

"*Lover,* Alastair. He was my lover!"

"I'm sorry...your lover."

Her anger seemed to fade. "How do I get him to the clinic?"

"Where is he?"

"St. Georges-in-the-East, the parish mortuary," she said, stuffing the handkerchief into a pocket.

"I'll make the arrangements. I'll send someone for you after Daniel has completed his examination."

"No, I want to be there. When shall I meet you at the clinic?"

"An autopsy is no place—"

"When, Alastair?" she pressed.

He sighed. She wasn't going to permit him any quarter. "Allow me three hours." If all went well, the autopsy would be complete before she reached the clinic. He disliked lying to her, but no woman should see such a sight.

"Thank you. I appreciate your help."

"Do you need me to summon a hansom?"

"No, I want to walk. I need to think things through."

He leaned closer, returning his hand to her elbow. "You are not alone in this. I will help as I can. It is not right for you to face the coming months alone."

A puzzled expression was his answer. Before he could pursue the matter further, she fled down the steps to the street.

☦

Daniel Cohen gave his partner a dubious look over the top of his glasses. "You do bring mixed news. The donation was a godsend. However..." He gestured toward the body on the examining table. "What have you gotten us into, my friend?"

Alastair sat at the other table rolling bandages, creating a neat stack. "I promised we'd determine this poor soul's manner of death. It has been ruled a suicide. I doubt that will change."

Daniel shoved his glasses up the bridge of his nose. "I see."

"Just review the coroner's findings. It is Jacynda's opinion that the fellow did not kill himself."

"Jacynda?" When he received no reply, Daniel stepped closer and studied the corpse. "Did he leave a final note?"

"Yes. Rather cryptic according to the coroner," Alastair grumbled. "He believes this fellow took a hefty dose of laudanum before flinging himself into the river."

"Attempting to escape the previously mentioned lady, perhaps?" Daniel queried.

Alastair's bandage rolling grew more agitated. "Hardly."

"Who is this Jacynda person? You've never mentioned her before."

"Miss Lassiter lives at the boarding house."

"Ahhh. Now the murk clears a bit." A pause and then, "Shield the table, will you? We don't want our patients to think we do a brisk business in corpses like Burke and Hare."

Alastair rose and positioned a movable screen to shield their work. "It's a sad commentary that we'd make a better income by grave-robbing than treating the living." He made a final adjustment. "How long will this take?"

"We should have sufficient time before the clinic is set to open," Daniel replied. He leaned over, inspecting the body. "Handsome young man." He opened the corpse's mouth. "River debris present. Amazingly healthy teeth, the like of which I've never seen." Glancing up, he offered, "If you wish to return in an hour or so, I'll be able to tell you more."

Alastair shook his head, removing his coat and tossing it over a chair. Rolling up his sleeves, he replied, "Go on. I'll assist as I'm able."

"Good lord, what happened to your arm?"

Alastair eyed the bandage, which sported a sizeable patch of dried blood. "I was assaulted in the street. It's the sole injury. Fortunately, I didn't have the donation with me at the time."

"Thank God on all accounts. Did you file a report with the police?"

"No need. I couldn't identify the rogues if I stumbled over them," Alastair fibbed. He'd know them, all right; one would be limping and the other using hand signals to communicate. "After you finish, I'll be in need of a dressing change."

A nod returned as Daniel bent over the deceased's head, examining something that had caught his notice. "Now that's particularly interesting..."

✠

Alastair watched in fascination as his partner thoroughly examined the body and then performed the autopsy. Daniel muttered to himself the entire time and refused to explain what he'd found until his work was complete.

"You see the rope fibers embedded in the flesh?" Daniel asked. He held a candle close as Alastair trained the magnifying glass on the dead man's wrist.

"I do now. I never would have thought to look for them." He shook his head in amazement. "I am astounded at what you've found. I had no notion of what a corpse could reveal to the trained eye."

"The wound on his head was the tip-off. I found wood splinters in it."

"A truncheon, perhaps?" Alastair asked, recalling the pair in the alley. Any number of street toughs carried them for protection.

"Possibly. As with some of the other injuries, the head wound occurred before he went into the water. Most of the marks were from being pummeled by debris in the river. I hazard to state that he endured some degree of...coercion before his death."

"You mean he was tortured?" a woman's voice asked.

The doctors turned in unison. Both had their sleeves rolled to the elbows. Dr. Cohen was shorter than Alastair, dark in complexion with an unruly shock of hair.

"You shouldn't be here," Alastair cautioned.

Her eyes drifted to Chris' recumbent form. She jerked them away, focusing instead on Alastair's disapproving face. Beneath her mantelet, the time interface buzzed in recognition of Chris' ESR Chip. After she gave the watch a tap, it fell silent.

"Are you Miss Lassiter?" the other physician asked, stepping away from the body to wash his hands in a basin.

"Yes."

"I'm Daniel Cohen. I am sorry we meet under such unpleasant circumstances."

"Thank you."

Daniel explained, "In answer to your question, he wasn't tortured in the conventional sense. However, he was vigorously questioned."

"Meaning?"

"He has considerable bruising over his right ribs. One of the ribs is broken. The injuries occurred before his death."

Cynda finally allowed her eyes to rest on her lover. Though

decently covered from the waist down, his chest displayed an incision from the Adam's apple downward, closed with neat stitches. Nausea rose at the mutilation. *What had she expected them to do?* They couldn't him put on a Post-Bed and have the computer spit out the autopsy results. They'd have to open the body. *At least Chris' family wouldn't see him this way.*

She hid her hands behind her skirt so the docs wouldn't notice their shaking.

"Did he drown?"

Toweling his hands, Daniel shook his head. "He was deceased before his time in the Thames. There is no river water in his lungs."

Cynda took a deep breath and let it out in relief, her hands falling to her sides. "Thank God," she whispered. She saw their puzzled looks. "Chris was mortally afraid of water. It would have been the worst way for him to die, to feel it close over him." She bit her lip to hold back the tears. "That's how I knew it wasn't a suicide."

"Then that is some comforting news, at least," Daniel replied.

Cynda dug in a pocket. "They found a bottle on him." She handed it to Alastair. He squinted at the label.

"I cannot make anything of it." He passed it to the other doctor.

After a moment, it came right back. "Neither can I," Daniel replied. "It's too damaged. That is a pity, for I suspect the laudanum was a diversion."

"Diversion?" Alastair asked. He filled the washbasin with fresh water and scrubbed his hands vigorously.

Daniel settled onto a chair, propping his feet on a nearby bench. "A diversion to misdirect the coroner's attention away from the ligature marks, the lack of water in the lungs, and so forth."

"How did the coroner miss all that?" Cynda pressed.

A shrug. "Often they see what seems most logical, and are disinclined to look much further. A combination of elements would have directed his decision: the final note, the stones in the pocket, the laudanum. In his defense, a coroner's pay is not the best. With the recent spate of killings, they have far too much work piled up."

"Daniel!" Alastair barked sharply.

The medico's face blossomed in embarrassment at his insensitive remark. "My apologies, miss. I meant no disrespect to this gentleman."

"None taken, Dr. Cohen," she said. Her attention returned to Chris. He seemed so somber, unlike the prankster she'd known. She expected him to leap off the table, tear off the fake stitches and shout, "Gotcha!"

"The police must be notified," Alastair said as he toweled his hands.

"No police. I will handle this myself," she said.

"Miss Lassiter," Daniel began, "it is our duty as physicians to report a suspicious death. Surely you would rather have—"

"No police."

Daniel shook his head. "I am sorry, but there is no choice in this matter."

Alastair rolled down his sleeves and retrieved his coat. "I'll go to the Commercial Street station," he offered.

Caught up in the emotions surrounding Chris' death, Cynda hadn't thought this through properly. She'd never meant for them to take this any further.

"You can't report this," she insisted. "If the police try to trace him, it will create too many awkward questions."

Alastair ignored her and headed for the door.

"Wait!" she commanded, stepping in front of him.

He halted in his tracks, frowning. "You are being irrational, Jacynda. One moment you wish to know the cause of your paramour's death, and now that we do, you will not allow us to proceed. Please step aside."

"Ah, damn," she grumbled. "I didn't want to have to do this."

Alastair's frown grew at her profanity. She pointed toward the body. "Chris is not from here...he's..."

Both physicians stared at her.

Now what? If they make this a murder case, they'll have to reopen the inquest, call witnesses and...

She had no choice but to set her own agenda. "I'll show you why you don't want to go to the police."

"I doubt you have an argument that will prove compelling," Alastair replied, clearly aggravated at her behavior.

"Lock the door." He didn't move. "Do it!"

After a quick glance at Daniel and a lengthy sigh, Alastair did as she instructed.

Cynda removed her mantelet and hat, placing them on a bench. Digging her interface out of its hiding place, she ran it over Chris' left arm. A hollow beep sounded. Swallowing hard, she zeroed in on the location of the ESR Chip, the task made difficult by the postmortem swelling.

"See this?" she said, tapping on the swollen skin just above the elbow.

Daniel leaned forward and palpated the area with his fingers.

"There doesn't appear to be anything there." He shot Alastair a disgruntled look, as if she were pulling his leg.

"Just make an incision."

"What is it?"

"I'll show you once you take it out."

Muttering under his breath, Daniel fetched a scalpel. He made the cut, and then enlarged the incision until he encountered a tiny flat disk. "There is something there. It is incredibly thin." Removing it, he held the disk between his thumb and forefinger, transfixed. "It appears to be some sort of…" His voice trailed off, replaced by a pensive frown.

Cynda demanded, "I need your word as gentlemen that you will *never* speak of what I'm about to show you. Is that understood?" The two physicians traded perplexed looks.

Daniel nodded in resignation. "You have my word."

"You have mine, as well," Alastair said. "Must you be so melodramatic about this whole thing?"

Ignoring him, Cynda placed the watch on Chris' chest. As it began to unfold, she heard both men gasp. She didn't want to think how many laws she was violating.

The doctors stared in frank awe.

"What in heaven's name?" Alastair murmured.

Taking Chris' ESR Chip from the bewildered Daniel, Cynda plugged it into the watch's input portal. The interface pondered for a moment before a holographic screen appeared eight inches above the corpse's unmoving chest. Chris' face lit the screen in full color, a stark contrast to the ashen copy that resided beneath.

Cynda steeled herself. Now would be the hardest part.

"Hi, I'm Chris Stone," he said in a cheery tone. "But then you know that from the chip. I love beer and I hate water. And I love to time travel. That's what I do best. I'm one of the best Time Rovers there are, except for maybe the crazy lady."

Cynda jammed her lips together to keep them from trembling, lowering her eyes until Chris' face disappeared.

A chirp resounded. "Task?" a synthetic voice inquired.

"Run vital statistics including most recent employment," she ordered in a voice made thick with tears. She thought for a moment and added, "Do not include sexual history stats." She didn't want to hear Chris' list of conquests. It was enough to know she was the last one.

The dead man's blood type, medical history, education and employment record, including each one of his time leaps, appeared on the holographic screen above his unmoving chest. Chris' foray to the Ottoman Empire included a note about a near-fatal neck wound incurred while protecting a tourist from an enraged husband who'd caught him in bed with one of his many wives. A final beep ended the holographic resume. A technological tombstone, minus Chris' date of death.

"My God," Daniel murmured.

Cynda looked up into the astonished faces of two Victorian gentlemen who had just seen one hundred and seventy years in the future.

"No police," she insisted. "They can't investigate the murder of someone who hasn't been born yet."

15

Cynda reduced the watch to its usual configuration and hid it under the ruffle on her bodice. Her companions remained silent. She could only imagine what was going on in their minds.

It was Alastair who broke the silence first. "Well, that explains your odd diction," he said quietly.

She turned toward him in surprise. Of the pair, she'd expected him to be the most skeptical.

"What year are you from?"

"2057. Chris and I are time specialists for a company called Time Immersion Corporation."

"You actually believe all that?" Daniel asked, shifting a dumbfounded expression between Cynda and his partner.

"I find it improbable," Alastair said. "However, I lack another explanation." He gave her a soft smile and placed a reassuring hand on her elbow. A simple gesture, yet it held such power.

"Thanks," she whispered.

He nodded. "Someday, I may ask the same leap of faith from you."

"Nonsense—utter and complete nonsense," Daniel spouted. "Man cannot travel through time. It is not physically possible."

Cynda shrugged. "Unfortunately, it is. A hundred years ago, the telegraph, gas lights and antiseptic didn't exist. Give humans nearly two more centuries, and you'd be surprised what we can come up with." *And not all of it is good stuff, either.*

"Those discoveries are a far cry from what you propose," Daniel protested.

"Perhaps in your way of thinking. Still, I'm here, and so is Chris, and neither one of us was born in this century." Cynda trailed her fingers along her lover's arm. "We don't usually die on the job."

"Is that why you see spiders and lightning bolts?" Alastair asked.

"Yes."

"You see things?" Daniel retorted. "Oh, heavens, come now. You can't possibly make me believe that you're from twenty-whenever. I do not know what it is we just witnessed, but my mind cannot accept it. It has to be some trick."

"And what would be the purpose of that?" Cynda said, her anger rising. "Gee, I'm bored. I think I'll just pop over to Whitechapel and baffle a couple of physicians this afternoon."

Alastair's hand returned to her elbow. "Jacynda, you must give us time to adjust to this most unusual state of affairs."

She gazed into his eyes and then nodded. "I'm sorry. I don't have any other proof to show you." *None that won't seriously screw history, at least.*

Turning toward his partner, Alastair gallantly took her side.

"During the autopsy, you stated that this fellow had remarkably healthy teeth, the like of which you've never seen, and that the old wound on his neck was closed so fine you couldn't see the sutures."

"We don't use them," Cynda interjected.

Daniel glowered. "Indeed, I will give you all that. Still, the technology required for man to traverse time—"

"Could just be possible. We have no notion of what the future holds, Daniel. Either this woman is capable of an extraordinary illusion, or she comes from another century. I feel that the latter makes more sense."

Daniel crossed his arms and addressed Cynda. "Then if this is true—and mind you I am still dubious on that point—what were you two doing here? Collecting souvenirs?"

Cynda chuckled, despite the circumstances. "No, collecting missing academics. In our time, people pay good money to come to your time and nose around. Two of our tourists went missing. I found mine, Chris…" She left out a deep sigh and let her gaze fall to the sheet-draped form.

"Your first morning at the boarding house, you inquired about Professor Turner. Was he one of your…clients?" Alastair asked.

"Yes, he was."

"That doesn't surprise me. When he first arrived, he seemed very unsure of his surroundings, as if concerned he might make a mistake. I thought him peculiar, to be honest. He just didn't fit."

"Like me."

"Precisely."

"Turner didn't return when he was supposed to. It was my job to find him and get him home."

Daniel pulled the sheet over Chris' body. "Who was this unfortunate fellow hunting?"

Cynda sensed a subtle shift toward acceptance. "A psychiatrist named Samuelson. I believe you call them alienists."

Daniel shot his companion a sidelong glance. "Your verdict, Alastair?"

"I have no desire to explain to the police why they will not be able to trace this person. As it has officially been ruled a suicide, I suggest we leave it at that. There is enough hysteria in Whitechapel at present. If the papers discover this man's origin, all sorts of strange things might happen. We'll be right in the middle, and the clinic will suffer for it."

Daniel scrunched his face in thought, then threw his hands up in exasperation. "So be it. I shall go along, but I do not feel this is proper in the least."

"Thank you, gentlemen," Cynda said, meaning it. "The future doesn't need any more problems than it already has."

"I still think it's highly improbable," Daniel added, as if he just had to have the last word.

"As long as Chris' death remains a suicide, the thread of history isn't threatened." *I hope.* "History is pretty resilient. You really have to work hard to muck it up."

"How remarkable," Daniel muttered, shaking his head. "I never imagined I'd be having such a conversation."

"I will hold you to your word, gentlemen."

Nods returned from both physicians.

"I'm certainly not going to speak of this," Daniel said. "I value my practice too much for that."

"Precisely," Alastair said.

"What is the future like, if I may ask?" Daniel queried.

Cynda shook her head. "It's good and bad. Technology may change, but people don't. We still want the same things—love, respect, three meals a day. And we're still willing to kill for them."

"Have you learned how to cure *all* diseases?" Daniel asked, his eyes wide with wonder.

"Most." She gazed at the sheet-draped form. "We still die, some sooner than they should."

There was a silence, one that seemed proper. Both doctors bowed their heads, if they were standing at a graveside. The gesture touched Cynda's heart.

"I would like to have Chris cremated and placed in an urn, one that doesn't weigh a ton."

"I'll see to the arrangements," Alastair offered.

"You'll need money." She parked herself on a bench and unlaced one of her black boots. Once it was off, she extracted Turner's currency and handed the money to Alastair. He counted it and returned most of it.

"This shall be plenty," he said, sticking the bills in his trouser pocket. "Why do you store money in your boot? Is that how it's done in your time?"

She laughed. "No, just when I'm here. Your *toolers* are far too adept at picking pockets."

"Ah, well, you have that right."

She struggled to lace the boot while cursing under her breath. To her amazement, Alastair knelt in front of her, assuming the task despite his damaged arm.

"If I had any doubt you're from the future, your ineptitude with this task puts it to rest. Only small children are incapable of lacing their own boots," he said, bemused.

She watched as he expertly worked the laces. "Small children and Time Rovers."

"I am very sorry about your *inamorato*," he said in a lowered voice, pitched so that only she could hear him.

"Thank you. Chris was a good guy. We hadn't decided where it was all going, but we were less lonely when we were together."

"I understand." Their eyes remained locked for a second. He returned to the lacing. Once it was finished, she rose, dusting off her skirts absentmindedly.

He offered his arm. "Let me walk you home. I want you to rest."

She shook her head. "No, thank you. I'll be fine."

"What do you intend to do if you find your lover's murderer?" he asked.

An intense calm filled her. "It's best you don't know that."

She swept out the door before either of the physicians could offer advice. It was best they didn't know what she had planned for the bastard who'd taken Chris Stone away from her.

‡

Perhaps it was a case of nerves that drove Keats to the clinic, an intense need to validate his endorsement of Alastair's character. Or maybe it was instinct, now that he thought about it. From the moment he knocked on the clinic's door, the encounter had taken a disagreeable turn. Alastair cracked the portal and stared at him as if he were an unwelcome beggar.

"Yes, Keats?" he asked in a chilly voice.

"I wished to ask you a few questions regarding Miss Jacynda's missing paramour. I have an idea how we might be able to track him," Keats said, choosing his words carefully so Alastair wouldn't deem him a threat. He'd already noted the doctor's disapproval when it came to his involvement with the American lady.

A vigorous shake of the head. "No need. He's been found. The coroner has ruled his death a suicide," Alastair retorted. He started to close the door.

Keats slammed a palm against the wood, making the door quake. "Wait a moment. That's not good enough. Why did he kill himself? Perhaps there is something else involved here. Coroners often make mistakes."

Alastair's face grew wary. "Nonsense, Keats, you're letting that overactive imagination of yours run riot. A man does not throw himself into the Thames without adequate cause. The fellow must have had personal issues of some dire nature of which we are unaware. My task is to help Jacynda adjust to the loss. You have no part in this."

Your task? Keats' jaw clenched at the sharp rebuke. Leaning forward, he poked a finger at Alastair's chest and exclaimed, "Stop treating me as if I were still in knee pants."

Alastair studied him with cool disdain. "Then if you're so keen to play detective, find the chemist who sold this. It was found in the dead man's pocket."

The doctor thrust a small bottle toward him. Keats snatched it out of his grasp. The label was waterlogged. His friend had just given him a nearly impossible task.

Send the pest on a fool's errand, is that it? "I shall accept your challenge," he said. "Good day to you, *sir.*"

Keats retreated to an obscured location across the street, his hand rhythmically opening and closing his pocket watch to burn off some of his anger. Alastair's treatment had singed him deeply, especially after he'd put his career on the line for someone he considered a friend.

Perhaps my assessment of you has been flawed from the start.

A short time later, a wagon rattled up the street, a plain coffin in the back. When it stopped in front of the clinic, curiosity overtook him. Keats watched from the shadows as the coffin was ferried inside the clinic and then back out again.

"So who's in the box?" he murmured. "Jacynda's lover, perhaps?"

The deceased came to rest at Owens & Sons Mortuary. Keats waited until the coffin was inside, and then knocked on the door. With the right approach, he'd learn the identity of their latest customer. That would settle one of his questions.

While he waited for someone to answer, he retrieved the bottle from his pocket and held it to the light. It was half-empty. The exterior smelled heavily of the tide. He removed the cap and took a sniff. "Laudanum," he muttered. His mother's lengthy illness had imprinted the smell in his memory. Studying the ornate border on the upper part of the label, a smile crept across his face. Fortune had dealt him a card that even the self-righteous Alastair Montrose couldn't play.

✠

Malachi Livingston swept his gaze over his three companions, striving to keep boredom at bay. In their private room on the second floor of No. 43, all was the picture of apparent contentment. The hearth blazed, ample food arrayed itself on a long table against the wall. Ronald, the adept steward, hovered nearby.

"What's a six letter word for *peril?*" Cartwright asked, squinting at the newspaper crossword puzzle in his lap, his face screwed up in concentration.

Hastings shrugged, florid from two brandies. Though located the furthest away from the fire, a glint of sweat hung on his broad brow. Stinton appeared not to have heard the question, industriously polishing a jacket button with his sleeve as if preparing for a military inspection.

"Six letters? Menace," Livingston replied. "It comes from the Vulgar Latin, *mincia.*"

"That's it!" Cartwright said, penciling in the letters.

Livingston's eyes darted toward the mantel clock. Beneath his monk-like calm, he analyzed the vibrations in the room. Something was wrong; Hastings usually drank one brandy before supper. Ronald had just poured the old warhorse his third. Stinton, though a fool, had somehow sensed the unease, his button polishing a means to compensate. Cartwright was oblivious, as usual.

A tap on the door. Ronald exited and then returned nearly in the same breath, bearing a message. He bent low to speak a few words in Hastings' ear. Cartwright's pencil-scratching and the crackle of the fire made it impossible to overhear any of the whispered conversation. The steward placed the message in the man's beefy hand and stepped back into the shadows.

Cartwright tapped the pencil against his cheek in thought, puzzling over the next word. Stinton shot a nervous look at Livingston, then at Hastings.

"Ill news?" Stinton ventured, his button polishing forgotten.

"Humpff? Yes, quite," Hastings replied. He crumpled the note and tossed it toward the fire. It bounced off an andiron. Livingston retrieved the ball of paper and after rubbing it between his fingers, pitched it into the blaze.

Settling into his chair, he gave his fingers a quick sniff. *Fish.* "So what have you done, Hastings?" he asked, wiping his fingers on his trousers and then tenting them in front of his face. To his annoyance, the smell remained.

The older man's eyes narrowed. "A business venture has not gone as planned—nothing more."

Liar. "Would this business involve...us?" Livingston asked, including the others in a sweeping gesture.

Hastings' expression darkened. "In some ways."

"In what manner did it not go as planned?" Livingston persisted, his hands now resting on the arms of the leather chair.

"I dispatched two men to have a discussion with our young doctor. I thought that if he were presented with the consequences of his rebellion, he would fall in line and accept our generous offer."

"Ah, the two fish market bullies."

"How did you reach that conclusion?" Hastings asked, clearly piqued.

"I am aware that you employ thugs on occasion, especially those who work at Billingsgate Market. It was rather easy to deduce, what with the barely legible scribbling on the note, the crude variety of paper upon which it was written and the unmistakable scent of rotting fish."

Hastings took an unseemly slug of brandy. "The plan did not work as I had envisioned. One of the ruffians has a broken kneecap and the other some difficulty with his throat so that he is unable to converse above a whisper."

Hence the note. "And the doctor?"

"I gather he was injured in some way, though not seriously."

"Good lord, Hastings, what have you done?" Cartwright asked. "We never agreed upon violence."

"I felt it worth the gamble. If we frightened him, perhaps he would take our offer and leave London."

Livingston scowled. "Given your ill-advised behavior—without our consent, I might add—you are fortunate he has not come in person to deliver his displeasure in a more forceful manner."

"Nonsense," Hastings huffed. "I've seen his type before. All bluff. He just needs to be brought down a peg or two."

"The more you apply pressure to Doctor Montrose, the harder he will push back," Livingston warned.

Hastings waved dismissively. "You attribute too much to this fellow,"

Livingston leaned forward in his chair. "You misjudge him. Though the doctor is a man of conscience, he has a level of violence within him that would astound you."

"That I doubt," Hastings huffed.

"What do you know of the fellow?" Livingston challenged.

"That he is a physician who works with the poor and disdains our traditions. What more do I need to know?"

"That he has already killed one man."

Hastings' mouth dropped. "Surely not."

"It is a matter of documented fact. We have made our offer in good faith, and he has sent us packing. Harassing him will only cause more harm. That would not be in *your* best interest, Hastings."

The two men eyed each other.

"You are junior here, Mr. Livingston."

"Not any more." Livingston glanced toward the clock. Sixteen minutes. He rose, straightening his jacket.

"I say," Stinton began, "we cannot have one of us running roughshod over the others."

Livingston swung toward him; Stinton quailed. "On the contrary, Hastings has put the spurs to the two of you more than once."

Cartwright's eyes widened, but he wisely kept his mouth shut. Stinton gnawed on a lip, his eyes darting around like a hare in a trap.

Livingston gave a sharp nod. "If you will excuse me, gentlemen, I have another engagement. I suggest that you all have another glass of brandy and help Cartwright complete his puzzle."

In the anteroom, the steward handed Livingston his cloak, top hat and cane.

"Thank you, Ronald."

"My pleasure, sir. Do you need me to arrange transport for you, sir?"

"No, I shall walk."

"As you wish, sir."

In the other room, Cartwright's edgy voice protested, "Did you hear what he said? How can he treat us that way?"

"He is too arrogant by half," Hastings grumbled to the clink of the brandy decanter's glass stopper edging out of the bottle. "As for the doctor being a killer, I don't believe it for a moment."

As Livingston descended the stairs, a smug smile kept him company.

What a delightful trio of morons.

✣

Leaning against a cask, Livingston allowed his eyes to adjust to the cellar's dim confines. A faint trickle of water competed with the thud of heavy boots overhead. If this room had a particular bouquet, it was of wine and mildew.

There was a noise on the stairs as his factotum descended into the gloom. William trod deliberately, as if assessing hidden dangers with each step.

"Good evening, sir," the fellow said.

"Good evening, William," Livingston replied. He extricated a pipe and tobacco from a deep pocket and began packing the bowl. "What do you have to report?"

His subordinate cleared his throat. "I followed Sergeant Keats as you asked. He seems to spend most of his time wandering the streets of Whitechapel."

"Any particular route?"

"The pubs mostly, though he's only drinking for show. He's looking for someone."

"Ah..." Livingston applied a match to the packed pipe and took a series of puffs. The smell of fine Virginia tobacco, redolent of black cherries, filled the air. "Who might that be?"

"An anarchist, one named Flaherty."

"That's interesting. What else?"

"There are six tenants at the boarding house at present; a wool merchant, an accountant, the doctor, a couple from Dover here on holiday and a lady from New York."

"How did you learn that?"

"I spoke with the butcher. One of the landladies is quite chatty."

Livingston took a few more puffs. "Go on."

"I've watched the doctor's clinic for a few days. This afternoon, a body was delivered there from St. George's Mortuary."

Livingston frowned. "To the clinic? You'd think it would be the other way round."

"That's what got me curious. After a few hours, it was moved on to Owens and Sons Mortuary. The doctor asked that it be cremated as soon as possible, and an urn delivered to the boarding house in care of Miss Lassiter, the American lady."

"How did you find that out?" Livingston asked, intrigued.

"I chatted up the mortuary's maid."

"Why was she so forthcoming?"

A hint of a roguish smile formed at the corners of William's mouth. "I put a bit of brass in her hand and bought her a new bonnet."

This one is brighter than most. He knows how to use people.

"You've shown initiative."

"Thank you, sir. I wasn't the only one interested in the body—Sergeant Keats had a sharp discussion with the doctor and followed the coffin to the mortuary."

"Really? Now that is interesting." Livingston took another puff of his pipe and let the smoke curl into the air. "Learn what you can about this Miss Lassiter and her relationship to the deceased. Find out what you can about the anarchist. Then meet me in front of the Lyceum Theater at 6 sharp tomorrow evening."

"Yes, sir," the man replied, seemingly unfazed by the multiple requests.

Livingston fished in a pocket and tossed the man a sovereign. That got an immediate reaction.

"Thank you, sir," the fellow said. He had the good sense not to bite the coin to verify its authenticity.

"Tomorrow then, William."

"Sir," the man replied. He executed a slight bow, one that betrayed a clue to his background. Hiking up the stairs, he tucked the coin out of sight.

William's speech patterns marked him as someone who'd spent considerable time amongst the aristocracy. "A manservant or a groomsman," Livingston said under his breath. "Probably dismissed for giving the mistress of the house better than her husband."

After finishing his pipe and tucking it away, Livingston shifted form. He had a couple of visits to make in Whitechapel and the illusion of a costermonger would make him nearly invisible amongst the masses.

16

Cynda found it odd how the mind recorded ridiculous details at times like this; seven steps to the black crepe-bedecked mortuary door; solid brass name plate, highly polished; *Owens & Sons - Serving Since 1863;* tall man clad in deepest black with a somber expression permanently stamped onto his face.

"Miss Lassiter," he said and gestured her inside. Before Cynda could question how he knew her name, she found Alastair waiting in the vestibule. His hair was carefully combed and his suit pressed. He wore a black armband. That struck her heart.

"May I offer you my sincerest condolences, madam," the mortician said.

"Thank you. Are you one of the Owens?" she asked, struggling to make proper small talk.

"Yes, madam. I am Clyde, the second son," the man intoned.

She wondered how many times he'd had to say that over the years. Always the second son. Never good enough.

"I trust madam will find the arrangements to her liking."

"I'm sure I will, Mr. Owens."

Alastair stepped forward, taking one of her hands. "Jacynda." The look in his eyes somehow steadied her.

"Thank you for being here," she said.

"It is only proper."

The mortuary was so quiet it seemed like it was shrouded in heavy fog, cut off from the outside world. The wooden floors made no squeak of protest. The viewing room smelled of roses. Gas lamps whispered along the walls. The coffin was polished pine, but of good quality. She wondered if it would be consigned to the flames with her lover.

"How are you?" Alastair asked softly near her ear, a comforting hand at her elbow.

"Okay." *So far.*

"Do you wish me to remain, or do you prefer privacy?"

She thought for a moment. "Please stay."

An expression of gratitude appeared on his face. Unwilling to unravel what that meant, she advanced toward the coffin, one deliberate step after the other.

The last five feet were the hardest. She paused just short of her goal.

I can do this.

Moving forward, her mouth parted at the sight.

Christopher Stone was the model of a Victorian gentleman. Alastair had been extremely attentive in his choice of suit, ascot and waistcoat. They fit perfectly, as if her lover had been born to this century. Chris' hair was clean and neatly styled, his hands crossed over his chest. Other than the unusual pallor, he looked quite handsome.

Somewhere in the distance a clock tolled the hour. She counted the chimes...eight. Chris was the ultimate Rover now; he'd learned how to transcend time. The clock could strike nine, ten, a thousand times and it would not matter to Christopher Stone. He resided in eternity.

Cynda bent over and tapped his arm, like she used to when he'd fallen asleep in her bed. She half expected him to open his eyes and wink at her.

"I'll miss you, Chris," she whispered. "You taught me how to laugh. Now you've taught me how to cry. I promise I'll get you home, no matter what it takes."

Tears crested and she leaned back, not wanting them to fall into the coffin. A crisp handkerchief appeared and she took it, dabbing at her eyes. The embroidered initials seemed stark against the white linen.

"He was a very handsome young man," Alastair said.

Cynda nodded. "He had a wicked sense of humor. That's what I will miss the most." She raised her eyes upward. "Thank you, Alastair. He looks wonderful. You've gone to a lot of effort for someone you never met."

To her surprise, the doctor's eyes grew misty. "It's the last time you'll see him. I wanted you to remember him in a positive way."

She touched his forearm, squeezing it. He promptly winced.

"Oh, sorry. Wrong arm."

"Mr. Owens will have the urn delivered to the boarding house in a couple of days. I hope that meets your schedule."

She gave a shrug. "Until I find Samuelson, I'm not going anywhere."

The quiet was split by the sound of booted feet stomping along the long hallway toward the viewing room.

"I assure you madam, this is not the—" Owens' voice called.

A woman stormed into the room. She appeared to be about Cynda's age, with frowsy blond hair and worn clothes. The delicate smell of roses gave way to cheap gin.

"I am sorry," Owens began.

"Mind you, I knew he was doin' me no good." She tottered toward the coffin, weaving unsteadily in her boots. "I told ya this would happen if ya kept going with that tart. Now ya see, ya randy old stoat?"

"Madam, please lower your voice," Owens insisted, unbridled panic pushed all other expressions aside. "I assure you this is not—"

"She weren't no good for him, and her man, he's a right devil. Evil-like. But did ya listen to me? Now look at ya, all laid out like a king. Ya stupid fool."

The woman stopped short of the coffin and whirled, raising an accusing finger in Cynda's direction. "Are ya one of his luvy ladies? Don't deny it. I know he had a string of 'em from Paree to Portsmuth. My mum always said never go with a sailor, and she were right." The woman gave Cynda the once-over. "Yer a right posh one. Ya must work the Strand. Get a good bit of brass there, I hear. Toffs like the fresh ones, they do."

Cynda leaned toward Alastair and whispered. "What is she talking about?"

"She thinks you are a..." Alastair cleared his throat. "Ah..."

The confusion cleared. "Dolly-mop?" Cynda said, recalling the term Keats had used.

A curt nod. "Indeed."

The woman brushed Mr. Owens aside and marched the final distance to the coffin. She squinted at the deceased, then drew back.

"Bloody hell, what have ya done to him? He looks so young." She leaned closer and then shook her head. "This ain't me Robbie. Ya got the wrong one." Another weave and then, "Nice lookin', though. Pity, I'd a given him a go. I bet he was worth liftin' yer skirt for."

"That is what I was attempting to tell you, *Madam*. This is not your...person," Owens flummoxed. "We do not have a Robert Stone in residence at present."

The woman clucked, shook her head, and then turned her full fury on the hapless mortician.

"Why didn't ya tell me?" she snorted. She paused for a second near the bouquet of roses, pulled one out of the vase, and then made for the door. Another pause near Alastair, then a lewd chuckle. He jumped as she passed, his face coloring.

She started to sing, bellowing a bawdy tune about a sailor and a maiden.

Let me show ya my riggin', the sailor said he.
No dear sir, for it shall not be.
For I am a maid and wish not to see.
But mine is the finest ya'll spy in the land.
All tall and proud and made to stand.
No, dear sir, it shall not be.
A maid I am and a maid I shall be.

By the time the woman left the building, Owens was a gibbering wreck, sputtering apologies and wringing his hands repeatedly.

He mopped his forehead with a handkerchief. "We've never had this sort of...situation in over a quarter of a century. I deeply regret—"

"It's not a problem," Cynda said, choking back the laughter. She dabbed at her mouth with Alastair's handkerchief to keep the giggles inside. The man withered, misreading her emotions. Before her control evaporated, she scurried for the front door. Behind her, Mr. Owens continued his litany of apologies. Alastair commiserated to no avail.

"Blast that abominable woman," Alastair grumbled. He had gone to such effort and she had ruined it all.

He found Jacynda leaning against a lamppost for support. Agonized, he murmured, "I am so sorry. That had to be horrible for you."

She looked up at him. Instead of the devastated grief he expected, he saw something entirely different. Something that puzzled him.

"Come on," she said, tugging on his uninjured arm. "I can't hold it in much longer." She dragged him into the closest passageway. "That was so..." She clamped a hand over her mouth, tittering, her eyes sparkling over the top of her fingers.

"I don't know how I can make it right, but I shall try," Alastair said, sincerely aggravated. "I wanted that to be so perfect and—"

She dropped her hand and shook her head. "No, no, you don't understand. Chris would have loved it!"

"Pardon?" he asked, bending nearer. That made little sense.

"You didn't know him," she said. "He was a clown. Any chance he had to make people laugh, he went for it. He absolutely detested funerals."

"You have totally confused me," he admitted.

"It couldn't have been more perfect! He would have loved it! And that song of hers...about the rigging and all...I about died."

Alastair blinked in confusion. "You're not upset?"

"No! What did she say? '*I bet he was worth liftin' yer skirt for.*' She got that one right." Jacynda winked libidinously. Chuckles followed, then deep, unrepentant belly-laughs. She clutched her stomach and rocked back and forth, oblivious to the scene it presented.

Astounded, Alastair watched her revel in the mirth. When she seemed to gain control of herself, a smile crept onto his face.

"After she stole the rose, she pinched my bottom," he revealed.

"You're kidding!"

"No, right on the buttock, bold as brass."

"Well, your bum is quite nice. I can see the attraction."

He cleared his throat, fighting the embarrassment. *Was there nothing this woman wouldn't say?*

She continued on, "Poor Mr. Owens. I thought he was going to have a stroke."

"He is quite convinced you'll file a complaint with his father and he'll get the sack."

"Oh, God, no. He was great." She looked around the alley and wrinkled her nose. "Let's go somewhere and find food. I'm hungry."

Alastair opened his mouth to protest, but stopped the moment she raised her hand. "My treat. Don't argue, or I'll start crying again." She waggled an eyebrow and grabbed onto his arm, tugging him toward the street. He yelped in pain; she'd chosen the injured one yet again.

"First stop, Owens and Sons. I want to reassure Owens Number Two that he's not in hot water. And then, I want lots of food. And maybe some wine. We'll lift a glass in honor of Chris," she said.

Alastair gave an approving nod. "I deeply regret I never met him."

His companion's face saddened. "I have regrets, too," she said, her voice darkening at the end.

I pray you can bury yours with your lover. Mine haunt me every day of my life.

✢

The mullioned windows displayed a myriad of storage vessels. Above them, a gold-lettered sign proudly proclaimed: *Oswander Dispensing Chemists.*

Keats hadn't stepped inside the shop during his previous inquiry, preferring instead to interview the neighbors as to the chemist's character. Once he'd peered in the shop windows and noted Oswander's severely limited eyesight, that had been the end of the inquiry. Now he had no choice but to enter the shop and face old memories head on.

Opening the door elicited a merry tinkle from the bell above him. The scent of the place brought forth a vivid scene from his childhood in Canterbury: a seven-year-old Keats standing on his tiptoes, calves cramping, peering eagerly over the wooden counter while the chemist sifted, weighed and wrapped his mother's numerous medications. His father stood nearby, impatiently tapping a finger on the top of his cane.

As a child, the chemist's shop had filled Keats with wonder. So many incredible sights, not the least of which was the huge blue earthenware jar full of leeches that sat on the counter. He'd so wanted to have a look inside, but his father wouldn't hear of it. Instead, he'd amused himself by trying to sound out the strange names on the bottles and carboys, like *Aqua Rosea* and *Veratrum Albo*. His mother had died a few years later, the chemist shortly thereafter. He'd heard the shop had closed. There'd never been a chance to peer inside the big blue jar.

Oswander's voice pulled him back to the present. "May I help you, sir?" To Keats, he appeared like an albino mole, his blue eyes accented by pale skin.

Clearing his throat, Keats stepped toward the dark wood counter. Behind it sat an astonishing array of bottles and bins all carefully labeled and in immaculate order. He'd decided at the tender age of eight that he would be a chemist when he grew up. By the time his mother died, that desire had vanished; now he avoided anything to do with lingering illness and death.

"Sir?" the chemist asked again.

"Sorry, I was woolgathering." Keats placed the bottle of laudanum on the counter. "I need to ascertain who purchased this medicine."

"Why do you wish to know that, sir?"

Keats positioned his card next to the bottle. "I'm Sergeant Keats, Special Branch. I am conducting an investigation."

The older man placed a monocle in an eye-socket. The card brushed the end of his nose as he studied it. Tilting his head in thought, the chemist asked, "Are you the young jack who's been asking about me, wondering if I go about all hours of the night?"

Keats had anticipated that. Neighbors talked, especially when a copper came calling. "Yes. I assure you that the answers have been most satisfactory, Mr. Oswander. You may rest assured that line of inquiry has been closed."

"How'd you hear my name in the first place?"

"You were one of many I was assigned to investigate. Apparently, you've upset someone."

The man nodded. "Old lady Barstow, probably. I keep telling her I won't add rat poison to her husband's sleeping powders, but she still badgers me every time I fill the order."

Keats' mouth fell open. "But sir, if she's trying to kill her husband—"

"No, no, nothing of the sort. Just her way of complaining about him. The two of them are like peas in a pod. She'd be lost without him. But that doesn't keep her from making threats."

"If you're certain," Keats muttered. He filed the name for future reference, lest the unfortunate Mr. Barstow failed to wake one morning.

The chemist put the card on the counter and picked up the bottle, repeating the monocle maneuver.

"It's one of mine, all right. How'd you know?"

"The filigree on the label. I saw one exactly like that while conducting my inquiries. One of your neighbors was quite put out by my questions, and insisted on showing me all her medications, even the empty bottles."

The eye regarded him with increased respect. "Mrs. Grimshaw?" Keats nodded. "A corker, that one," Oswander replied, shaking his head. "Takes all kinds." He returned the bottle. "See those numbers amongst the garland at the upper-right corner?"

It was Keats' turn to hold the bottle close to his nose, the numbers were so miniscule. "Yes. What do they mean?"

"It's the order number. That was filled sometime this week."

Keats frowned in confusion. "Certainly given your..." He hesitated, not wishing to antagonize the fellow. "Your limited eyesight would make it impossible for you to inscribe that on the label."

"Ah, you're right there. My daughter has a fine hand and excellent eyes. She inscribes a number on each label. I use them in turn. That way, we can reference back if there is a question."

"Why make the numbers so small?" Keats asked, intrigued.

"Had someone try to change one so he could claim I gave him the wrong powder and sue for damages. Now we do it this way so there'll be no messing about."

"Does this number correspond to some sort of ledger?" Keats prompted.

"Right it does. You seem to know a bit about a chemist shop, lad."

"I spent a lot of time in one when I was a child."

Oswander pulled a thick leather-bound book from underneath the counter and flipped it open to a page.

"Order number 88-1551," he said, skimming his hand over the page. "The first two numbers tell me the year, and the next tells me the actual order." Bending over until it appeared as if he were worshipping the print, he announced, "Order filled four days ago, on the 23rd: a bottle of laudanum." Oswander squinted harder. "88-1552, as well, for chloral hydrate."

"Were they signed for?" Keats asked, trying to see around the man's semi-bald head. Oswander straightened up and turned the ledger in his direction.

Keats trailed his index finger down the page to the two numbers. On each line, a wide, flowing hand met his eyes. His mouth fell open.

He closed the book with a pronounced thump.

"Do you remember this gentleman?" Keats quizzed.

"Yes, as best as I can see a person, that is."

"How tall was he?"

"About your height."

"Not taller?" Keats pressed.

"No. I can judge height pretty well; I just can't see details."

"Coloring?"

"Lighter than yours."

"Right- or left-handed?"

The man pondered. "Left. He took his time signing the ledger; that's why I remember."

"Did he pay for the medicines or put it on account?"

"Paid in cash. Seemed to have trouble counting out the money."

"Really? That's odd. Was he a foreigner?"

"No, still something didn't feel quite right about him, if you know what I mean," the chemist said, shaking his head.

164 | Jana G. Oliver

The bell announced a new customer. Keats stepped aside to allow a lady to make her way to the counter.

"Thank you, Mr. Oswander, you've been very helpful."

"Good to hear it, Sergeant," the man replied. "Be sure to come back if you have need of my services."

The new customer gave Keats a quick glance, followed by a shy smile. Disconcerted by what he'd discovered in the ledger, he tipped his hat and left the chemist to his work. It was only later that he wondered if Oswander possessed a jar of leeches.

17

The dining room hadn't changed, except that the giraffe was nowhere to be seen. Around them, patrons spoke in hushed tones and cups rattled in saucers.

"I believe we mollified Mr. Owens," Alastair observed while arranging the napkin in his lap. "You were extremely considerate of his feelings."

"It's not easy being the second son."

Alastair gave her a penetrating look. "I detect the voice of experience, though you are hardly male."

"My brother believes he rules the world, and never lets me forget it."

"Does your family approve of what you do?"

Cynda shrugged. "Sort of. They don't live inside anymore, so it's hard to judge."

"Inside?"

She gave a quick wave of her hand. "Never mind; it's hard to explain unless you're from there."

"I see."

The server appeared with two bowls of beef soup. The scent was heavenly. Cynda launched into its consumption.

"Apparently, your nausea has improved," the doctor observed.

She gave a quick nod. "I'm not seeing as many of the strange things anymore."

"The spider is finally gone?" Alastair asked. .

"No, but he's the size of a mouse now. At least the world's the right color for a change."

"I don't understand," he said, face drifting into a frown.

Cynda gave a quick look around; their fellow patrons seemed to be involved in their meals or dinner companions. She leaned across the table, lowering her voice.

"When you travel as much as I do, you see all sorts of odd things. Eventually, the hallucinations don't go away."

"Then what will you do?" he asked, leaning toward her, a spoonful of soup forgotten in his hand.

"I have to quit. When sleep doesn't clear the weird things, it's time to find another job." *Just what might that be...*

"The nausea is part of this travel-related illness?"

"Oh, definitely, along with the need for chocolate and..." She paused and then added, "and other things."

His eyebrow rose while the spoon continued its belated journey to his mouth. After delivering its contents, he set it down.

"Then I owe you an apology, of sorts."

"For what?"

"I had thought you were...enceinte."

Cynda frowned. The word sounded familiar. "Meaning?" she said.

He cleared his throat, dabbed at his mouth and whispered, "With child."

"Oh." She burst into a grin. "No way. Not an option with my job. Traveling does nasty things to little growing people."

"I see."

The solar bulb went on. "You thought Chris was the father, didn't you?"

A stern nod. "I was intending to speak to him about his...duty to you."

"That's sweet," she said. *And so old-fashioned.* "Fortunately, we've dealt with that sort of thing. We have babies only when we want to."

"Pity we don't have that ability, though I suspect the government would never allow it. They don't seem to understand that most of the poverty in the East End could be averted by reducing the birth rate."

"You're quite enlightened for your time," she said.

A stern look. "I trust you're not patronizing me."

"No, just stating a fact."

The plate of roast beef arrived. As she cut a sizeable hunk and put it on her plate, along with the roasted potatoes and a warm slice of bread, the doctor watched her every move.

"Why are you staring?" she asked.

"I was just wondering what you will do when you can no longer *travel.*"

She sighed. "That's the problem. I don't know anything else."

"Is it possible you might become stranded during one of

your...sojourns?" he asked.

"God, I hope not," she said, wondering where that question had come from.

"You once said you'd never found a place that felt like home."

She resumed eating. The conversation was getting too close for comfort. Maybe he'd let it drop.

"Jacynda?" he asked, his voice polite, but insistent.

"No, I've never felt at home. That's why I travel. The closest I've come was Pompeii."

A slow nod, as if he were thinking something through.

"Perhaps you will change your mind," he said.

"Miracles do happen." *Why is he so curious?*

The one glass of wine made Jacynda giddier than Alastair would have preferred. As they walked toward the boarding house arm-in-arm, he found she possessed a rich singing voice, though he couldn't quite understand the song's lyrics—something to do with tulips and the act of tiptoeing through them. When he complimented her on it, she gave a slight bow and nearly toppled over. He tucked his arm around her waist.

"You don't drink often, do you?"

"No, hardly at all. Traveling intensifies the alcohol's effect. One glass equals..." She waved a hand to indicate infinity, narrowly missing a lamppost.

"Then why did you—"

"Had to honor Chris," she said resolutely. "He would have done the same for me."

Eventually, she fell silent, an unnerving change from her earlier frivolity. He'd tried to engage her in conversation, but to no avail. By the time they reached her room and she fumbled to unlock the door, his concern had grown.

"Jacynda?"

She turned toward him, her bottom lip quivering. He could see the glint of tears in the dim light.

Alastair took both her hands and gave them a light squeeze. "He's in God's hands now."

She blinked rapidly to try to forestall the tears. "I realized that I'll never know if we had a future together." Then she was gone, the door closing behind her. He heard the squeak of the bedsprings, and then quiet sobs.

Alastair retraced his steps to the street. He had no words of comfort, no healing balm he could apply to Jacynda's heart. If there were a remedy, he would have readily offered it.

And prescribe a liberal dose for myself.

‡

2057 A.D.
TEM *Enterprises*

It took Ralph longer than he'd hoped to find the answer—nearly two hours. During the entire time, Morrisey meditated on the artwork. It was a photograph of some remote galaxy, pinwheels of swirling light and shadow circulating around a dark core. Quite interesting, but not worth two hours of anyone's time.

Before Ralph could figure out how to interrupt him without being rude, Morrisey asked, "What is the final count, Mr. Hamilton?"

"Five Rovers, one tourist."

"You're including Mr. Stone in that number?" Ralph nodded.

Morrisey returned to his position behind the low granite table that served as his desk. After performing a couple of stretches, he tossed a small object toward Ralph. It was a nano-drive. "TIC's latest set of access codes. You'll need them to get into the logs and the IA settings."

Ralph plugged in the drive and logged into TICnet. He noted his access name was *Watson*. He didn't remember anyone of that name at TIC. Working his way through the maze of files, he reached the Interface Attributes Cluster.

The files were empty.

Ralph accessed the files again, just in case he'd screwed up. The Attributes were gone. An icy chill washed through his veins.

"Mr. Hamilton?" Morrisey quizzed.

Ralph turned. "Someone at TIC purged the Interface Attributes settings. I don't know if it was deliberate, or if some file jockey thought they weren't needed anymore. Either way, I can't get the Rovers home without the—"

"I know," his boss snapped, his face darkening.

"God," Ralph muttered, shaking his head. "I never thought they'd do that." Without the Interface Attributes, there was no means to communicate with anyone in the Time Stream. No way to initiate a transfer.

TIC had severed the Rovers' lifelines.

Morrisey's fingers danced over the holo-keyboard in front of him. Ralph heard the characteristic beep of an outbound Vid-Net Mail message. A few seconds later, another beep indicated an answer. His boss exhaled loudly. Apparently, the query hadn't paid off.

Morrisey grew pensive. "In every failing organization, there is someone who has the foresight to cover their arse. Work your contacts. Someone would have made a copy of the Attributes in case there's an investigation. If you have to offer money to obtain them, do it. If they need other incentives, let me know. Remind them of the gravity of the issue, that orphaning a Rover is a Grade Four Capitol Offense."

Ralph wondered what Morrisey meant by *other incentives*, but decided not to ask. He mentally generated a list of TIC employees who might be able to help him—starting with Ivan. *Could he be...*

"Who is your mole inside TIC?"

A raised eyebrow. "I have a number of them."

"Ivan, the chron-op?"

A nod.

"That's how you got the access codes."

Another nod. "Find out what you can as quickly as possible, Mr. Hamilton. History takes a dim view of stranded Rovers."

History isn't the only one. Ralph repositioned himself in front of the terminal, his backache forgotten, and worked the keys like a man possessed.

‡

"There's a Mr. Keats here for you," Mildred said, her hands nestled inside her apron. From the line of flour marking her left breast, she'd been in the midst of making bread when the visitor arrived.

"Thank you, Mildred, but I'm not really in the mood for visitors. Please deliver my apologies, and tell him I'll see him tomorrow."

"As you wish, miss."

Cynda closed her door and leaned against it. Bad news did travel fast. She watched through the window as Keats exited the boarding house. He seemed upset, his strides redoubled.

Shaking her head, Cynda leaned against the windowsill. Nothing from TIC. By now, she'd figured Thad would be bugging the hell out of her. She stared at the pocket-watch dial, and then flipped the lid closed. Contacting them would only stir things up.

She had two choices: sit in her room and cry all night, or find

Chris' missing tourist. Sitting on the bed, she tightened her bootlaces for what lay ahead. The only way she'd find Samuelson was to put a few more miles on the shoe leather.

‡

For a man on duty, Keats was sucking down the beer in record time. When the publican pointed at the empty and asked if he wanted another, he shook his head. He did want another—quite a few, in fact—but getting drunk wasn't going to solve his problems. Things were getting too complicated. Up until this week, all he'd had to worry about was his job. Now there was the business with Fisher and the Transitives, Alastair's inexplicably petty behavior and the confusing Miss Lassiter. He'd been making too many mistakes: trusting Alastair, for one. Not finding Flaherty for another.

He mentally shook himself out of his reverie and took stock of his surroundings. He was sitting in the Paul's Head Public House, *en mirage* in his sailor persona. The pub was doing a brisk business, not all of it legal. This was rough territory, where daydreaming could easily become fatal.

A figure slid into the chair opposite him, beer in hand.

"Crowded tonight," the fellow observed.

"Always is," Keats mumbled. He didn't know his informant's name, only that he worked at one of the stables and was always keen to earn a few bob on the side. "Anything new?"

A shake of the head. "Whatever's gonna happen must be big."

"Why do you think that?"

"Folks is nervous," the man replied. "They're not sayin' much. Fearful like."

Keats snorted. "Got that right." He pulled a crown from his pocket and set it under his empty glass. "If you hear anything…"

"I'll find ya," the man grunted.

A figure passed their table. Keats glanced up, then did a double-take.

Jacynda Lassiter was standing only a few feet away from them, blinking in response to the pall of smoke. She slowly tracked through the room, as if searching for someone.

Keats' informant followed his gaze. "Ah, that's a right smart one. Not been on the game long, I bet."

The woman in question drifted out the front door. Keats gave a surly nod to his contact and followed her, indignation and worry battling for supremacy. She had refused to meet with him earlier, though according to her landlady she'd been out to dinner with the doctor. Now she was blithely wandering around one of the most infamous parts of Whitechapel, unaccompanied.

Have you no notion where you are? Perhaps she didn't. She was from New York, after all. He shook his head and continued after her.

After a stop in the Horn of Plenty, she set off along Dorset Street.

He didn't dare risk revealing his true form on "Dossers Street," as the locals called it. Even constables regarded this patch of pavement with respect bordering on fear.

What are you doing, you silly woman? He pushed on, praying she'd make it to Commercial Street before someone decided to give her a lesson in East End "courtesy."

‡

Cynda realized she was in trouble the moment she stepped outside the Horn of Plenty. Her preoccupation had taken her somewhere she shouldn't be, especially at night. The threat increased with each step. The denizens of Dorset Street openly assessed her. Young, female, alone. Her clothes, though plain, were posh for this neighborhood, painting her as a suitable victim.

Really dumb, Lassiter. Is this what happened to Chris? Probably not. If he'd been killed on this street, they wouldn't have bothered to drag his body to the Thames, but left him in an alley for the rats.

Cynda took stock of her situation. She had no weapon. Her ill-fitting boots and cumbersome skirts precluded hoofing it if attacked. She'd just have to bluff it out. Clenching her jaw, she trudged toward Commercial Street, her heart hammering.

Ahead of her, two men lounged in a doorway, sizing her up. They were dressed in dirty clothes and black felt hats. She could almost hear their thoughts: *Tasty bit, good clothes. We could have a bit of fun and score some brass, as well.*

Her only advantage was that she wouldn't react like they expected. Squaring her shoulders, she pressed on, passing the ominous pair.

She heard the sound of boots shifting position and mumbled words. She readied herself. When a dirty hand grabbed her shoulder, she reacted instantly, driving her elbow back with tremendous force. When it impacted, she felt a rib crack, followed by a piercing bellow of pain. The man staggered away, hunched over, fighting for breath. A moment later, he was on his knees, retching. Spying his short truncheon, she retrieved it.

"Yer a right witch, aren't ya?" the other rough snarled, spitting on the street.

He was thickly built, and the glare in his eyes promised payback for hurting his cohort. He marched forward, a curved knife in his hand.

"Hey!" a voice called. The tough turned. There was a solid thud, and the man sunk onto his knees, dazed. When her foe began to rise, Cynda delivered her own blow and sent the fellow nose down onto the pavement.

"Are ya all right, miss?" a man in rough garb asked. He held a stout piece of timber in his hands and peered at her with concern. When he saw her eyes on the makeshift weapon, he tossed it away.

"Just fine, thank you." She weighed the truncheon in her hand. "Useful little thing. I think I'll keep it as a souvenir." She stuck it in her skirt pocket. The handle protruded until she covered it with her mantelet. After a quick check to ensure the pocket watch was where it should be, Cynda called another "Thanks," and set off toward the main road.

Keats watched her hike away, shaking his head. She'd dropped the first thug on her own, and from the looks of him, he'd not be messing with anyone for quite a while. "Amazing," he muttered. He followed in the lady's footsteps.

When he caught up with her, she shot him a wary look.

"I'm not up for trouble, miss," he said. "I'll walk ya to where ya needs to go. Y'aren't safe here."

"Thank you for helping me."

"Ya looked like ya were doin' right fine on yer own." A shrug. "Where ya headed?"

"The Britannia."

He nodded. "That'll do."

When they were across the street from Crossingham's Lodging House, Jacynda slowed her pace, and then stopped outright. She edged forward, peering into an archway with a sober expression.

What are you doing? "Miss?" No response. "Ah, miss, we should be goin' now."

"What?" she asked, distracted. He eyed the passageway which so closely held her attention. It was nothing special, just like any of the squalid courts in the area.

He looked back over his shoulder. The two thugs were on their feet now. One held a cloth to his head and pointed in their direction.

"We gotta go, miss!" he urged, tugging on her arm.

She nodded and hurried along the street, still preoccupied.

Keats breathed a little easier once they reached the pub. No one was following them, as least as far as he could tell.

At the entrance, she took his hand and pressed a sovereign into it—a fortune in the East End.

"Buy yourself a drink or two on me."

"God bless ya, miss."

He tipped his hat and wandered into the bar. She followed him in, had a look around, and then left. Keats counted to forty before easing out the front door. In the distance, he saw her heading south. Once away from this part of Whitechapel, he could safely change forms. He had a few questions to put to Miss Lassiter, and it was best if they came from Jonathon Keats.

If not for her height, he would have missed her in the crowd. She was listening to an organ grinder. When the tiny monkey skittered up to her, dapper in his red uniform and gold braid, she knelt and placed a coin in his cup. The expression on her face reminded Keats of a little girl, so full of wonder.

The little creature chattered, doffed his cap, and rattled the cup again.

"I don't have any more," she said, and then laughed.

"Here, let me help you," Keats offered, kneeling beside her and offering a couple of pennies.

The smile moved in his direction, warming him. "Thank you, Jonathon." She took the coins and gave them to the monkey. The cap popped off again, and then the primate hurried to his master to deliver his largesse. "He is so cute!" she said, beaming. "I've never seen one of them before."

Keats offered his arm, and they rose together. "I'm glad I happened along, then."

He'd figured she'd be shaken by her earlier encounter, recounting it in horrific detail. Instead she was composed, as if nothing untoward had happened.

Remarkable. Reticent to ruin the moment, he walked for some distance before posing the question.

"Why are you out on the streets alone?" he asked.

"Just needed to take a walk," was the prompt reply.

And visit every pub? "There are parts of Whitechapel that aren't the safest, you realize."

"So it seems," she said.

"I would have happily escorted you, if you'd given me the

opportunity."

She gave him a long look. "I wasn't in the mood at that moment. I'm doing better now."

"Yet you dined with Alastair."

Another guarded look. "That is not your business," she said sharply.

He stopped abruptly. "If you find me an annoyance, have the decency to say so."

Confusion covered her face. "You're being ridiculous." She yanked her arm out of his, gnawing the inside of her lip.

Ponderous silence. Being a copper warred with acting the gentleman. Instead of sharing Jacynda's grief, he was flogging her with it because she had dinner with his friend.

"I am...sorry," he began. "I am in particularly bad temper this evening. When I saw you on the streets, alone, I was very concerned. I've articulated that rather badly."

A cold look. "I'm not in good humor, either. It's been a very long day."

"You have my sincere condolences."

"Thank you."

The next block passed in silence. Finally, he hedged an offer. "When you are feeling up to it, I would like to escort you to the aquarium. It is most remarkable, and I feel it will lift your spirits considerably."

A slight smile, as if she appreciated the rapprochement. "I will consider that."

That seemed the best he could expect. He heard the call of a newspaper boy just up the street. He halted at an intersection.

"I wish to buy a paper." Without waiting for a reply, he left her behind, keen to have a moment's breathing room.

As he waited for the lad to finish serving another customer, Keats observed his companion. She stood at the kerb, unaware of his scrutiny, a forlorn figure gazing into nothingness. Alone in the midst of a crowd. Sadness clung to her like a shroud.

Blast. He'd been overly harsh with her. Why was he so unusually volatile?

After buying the paper, Keats noted a flower vendor a few paces away. Determined to make amends, he dug in his pocket for the required coins.

Cynda waited at the kerb, uneasy after the events of the evening. She'd escaped the assault on Dorset Street by sheer luck and the intervention of a civic-minded bystander. Jonathon's sudden appearance had been odd, but somehow reassuring. Her gut told her he knew something wasn't kosher. She'd already pushed the envelope with the doctors; telling anyone else about her origins wasn't an option. Her groan was lost in a chorus of shouts and applause. She turned toward the commotion, welcoming the distraction. Youngsters cheered and pointed at a gaily painted beer wagon rumbling down the street. Two men perched on top in crisp uniforms. A pair of massive roans pulled the heavily laden wagon, their hooves fringed in silky hair and the size of dinner plates. Gleaming metal and colored tassels adorned their harness: a rolling advertisement for a local brewery.

Cynda stared at the team in frank awe. "Wow," she whispered. Grav-Rail didn't hold a candle to these guys. They moved with an easy grace, despite the load. The crowd around her agreed.

"Mummy, look at the big horses!" a little boy shouted. He tugged on his mother's arm in earnest and pointed.

"They're called Shires," the woman replied and gave Cynda a wink. "Big ones, aren't they?"

"That's prime horseflesh, all right," another person added.

Shires. Wow, they're pretty. In high school, Cynda had visited a farm, one of those "that's the way it was" tours kids were forced to endure. She remembered the trip because of the horses. Were these big boys' noses as soft as the ones she'd caressed as a teenager?

Realizing that Jonathon was missing all the excitement, she hunted over her shoulder in an effort to find him. The newsboy was counting out change to a well-dressed man, but it wasn't her escort. Certainly, he wouldn't abandon her...

A sharp jolt from behind propelled her into the air. She landed on her hands and knees, pain sheering into both arms as she skidded on the rough pavement. Before she could stand and give someone hell for their prank, a shout rent the air. Then a woman's scream. When Cynda raised her head, her vision was dominated by muscled legs and huge, pounding hooves.

18

Cynda flung herself sideways in a desperate attempt to avoid the slicing hooves. The uneven pavement slowed her movement, digging into her ribs as she rolled. Straw and dirt clung to her. With a shout from the teamster and the snap of the harness, the horses abruptly stopped. Cynda's roll to freedom ended as one of the enormous hooves trapped her trailing mantelet and skirt beneath it, the truncheon in her pocket embedding itself into her side.

"Get away from them!" the teamster yelled.

Once on her hands and knees, Cynda furiously tugged at the trapped garments without success. She didn't dare strike the horse's leg or the beast might bolt, pulling the wagon over her. She fumbled with the mantelet's clasp. The effort only tightened it around her neck, causing her to gag. Ducking, she wrenched the short cape over her head. It caught on her hat, pulling the hatpin free with a sharp stab. Throwing all her weight into the effort, she ripped the skirt from underneath the hoof and landed hard on her backside.

Freed, Cynda gave a crow of triumph.

Startled by the sound, the nearest Shire skittered toward her. One of the massive hind hooves shot out and clipped her shoulder. The blow drove Cynda flat onto the filthy pavement, knocking the wind out of her. She heard another shout as the horse kicked again. Digging her fingers into the bricks, she crawled away from the panicked beast.

The commotion caught Keats' attention. He hurried toward where he'd last seen Jacynda.

"What has happened?" he asked, trying to see over the crowd.

"Some fool woman threw herself under the wagon!" a man said, pointing toward the street.

Keats pushed his way through the crush of bodies to the kerb. He found chaos. One of the uniformed teamsters battled with a huge horse in an attempt to keep it from bolting. The beast threw its head back, nostrils flaring as the man clutched the bridle. The other horse had no such counterweight, but harnessed to its mate, it could not rear into the air. Instead it shied sideways into the street, leather straps straining from the pressure, its eyes wild. Screams rose around them, terrifying the horse further.

Keats thrust his paper and flowers into a woman's hand and rushed into the street, heedless of the danger. He launched himself at the panicked animal. The horse's hooves struck the ground in a shower of sparks. He grasped the bridle. The beast shook its massive head, viciously wrenching his arm. He dug in and began a spirited tug-of-war.

"Steady, steady!" he called.

The horse flung its head again, preparing to rear. Finding resistance, it fought him. Keats continued to offer soothing words and a strong counterbalance. Finally, the beast began to settle. He brushed a hand along its nose. "That's it. Nothing to be worried about."

Continuing to soothe the horse, Keats stared into the crowd, trying to catch Jacynda's eye. When he couldn't spot her, a sense of foreboding rose.

Oh, God, she wouldn't...

Still holding the bridle, he leaned out into the street in time to see a figure rise from the cobblestones.

His mouth fell agape. The straw and muck-covered figure wavered for a second, then righted itself. When Jacynda turned toward him, he sighed in relief.

"Thanks for your help, mate," the teamster called from his perch.

After a nod, Keats relinquished control of the horse and hurried toward the bewildered woman in the middle of street.

Cynda brushed the hair from her face and surveyed the scene. Wide eyes stared at her from all directions. *So much for staying out of the limelight.* A hansom cab passed unnervingly close, reminding her it was dangerous to loiter. Spying her hat, she picked it up. Mindful of the horses, she turned away to bang it against her thigh in an unladylike gesture and plopped it back on her head. A gasp came from some of the females in the crowd, followed by a wolf-whistle.

Why am I so cold?

Before she could address the issue, Jonathon hurried to her side, the trampled mantelet in hand.

Giddy with the euphoria of survival, she beamed at him.

"Well, that was fun, wasn't it?"

"Are you all right?" he blurted. His eyes tracked toward her backside, his eyes widening in surprise. "You're...exposed."

Cynda turned to survey the damage—the back of the skirt was gone, as were most of the petticoats. By Victorian standards, she might as well be nude. She took the mantelet from her companion and wound the garment around her waist, replacing some of the missing fabric. The appreciative whistles ended.

"Better?" she asked.

Jonathon gave a shrug, mischief in his eyes. "Well, it depends. I rather liked it the way it was."

Surveying her handiwork, she chuckled. "Who knows: maybe in a couple of months this will be all the fashion." A horrible thought overtook her and she tapped at her breast for the interface. It was gone. Casting her eyes on the ground, she found it near a pile of trampled manure. Forgetting her makeshift garment, she bent over and the wolf whistles started up again. Cynda cleaned off the watch and tucked it away as her escort watched in amazement.

Jonathon leaned closer and flicked some straw off her chin. "Your shoulder is bleeding."

She'd known about that, but hoped if she ignored it the thing wouldn't hurt. Jonathon's observation ended the delusion; the arm roared to life with sizzling ripples of pain.

Staring at the wound, she groaned. "You just had to mention it, didn't you?"

The teamster called from the top of the wagon. "What in heavens were you thinking, miss? Jumping in front of the beasts like that. I can't stop a team that fast!"

She angled her eyes upward. Telling him the truth would draw the cops and land her name in the Daily Telegraph.

"You're absolutely correct!" she called back. "I'm sorry for being a nuisance." As she lowered her eyes, they caught Jonathon's. He looked skeptical.

"We should go," he said, tugging on an elbow. As they approached the kerb, the young lad who'd admired the team raced up, his mother in tow.

"You forgot these, sir!" he called, thrusting out the roses and the paper.

"Thanks, lad," Jonathon said, pulling a couple coins out of his pocket and exchanging them for the items. The boy grinned. The lad's mother leaned close and spoke to Keats in a lowered voice. He frowned, and then nodded his understanding. He extracted one of the roses and handed it to her.

When Jonathon rejoined Cynda, he presented the remaining flowers with a decided flourish. "Please accept these as an apology for my earlier...churlish behavior."

The scene had to look ridiculous. She was in shredded clothes, coated in whatever noxious stuff they left on the streets, and he was giving her flowers as if they were off to a grand night at the opera.

One thing was clear: Jonathon Keats was a hopeless romantic.

Cynda managed to choke out, "Thank you," and took the roses in a grimy hand. Holding the flowers close to her nose eradicated the other smells, most of which came from her. Cheers erupted from the crowd around them. They loved a show, and they'd had a ringside seat for this one. Jonathon tipped his hat in acknowledgement, and then led her away.

She counted to one-hundred and thirteen before he posed the question.

"What really happened back there?"

‡

The fussing began the moment Jonathon ushered her inside the boarding house. Mildred put her hand to her mouth in shock and hustled off to collect her sister, moving at a far faster clip than her bulk would suggest possible.

"Now I've done it," Cynda said. Jonathon nodded grimly, his jaw set. He'd been that way ever since she told him she'd tripped and fallen into the street, courtesy of her bootlaces. He'd asked a series of pointed questions and she'd deflected each one with vague replies.

"Thank you for coming to my aid," she said, "and for the beautiful roses." He gave a curt nod. The fury radiating off him was enough to light the darkest East End alley.

He knows I'm lying. The sisters returned in force. Cynda chose not to fight the battle and called out another "thank you" as Jonathon was shown the front door.

"Don't worry, ducks, we'll take care of her," Mildred advised, and then closed the door in his face.

And care they had. As Cynda steamed away in a tin bathtub

located in a room off the kitchen, she heard the sisters debating how to salvage her ruined dress. Annabelle thought it a total loss; Mildred wasn't so sure.

"Luckily I have a another," Cynda murmured. What she didn't have was a spare life. The near-miss with the Shires had driven that point home with more force than necessary. Someone was intent on killing her, no doubt the same someone who had murdered Chris.

"Why?" she asked, sinking further into the water. It made her shoulder throb and burn, but the rest of her loved it. "I'm not a threat to anyone."

"How you doing, luv?" Mildred asked, peering in. "Do you need more hot water?"

"No, I'm just going to wash my hair and get out."

"Then I'll put the kettle on for you. You want some scones with your tea?"

Cynda nodded her head. A piece of straw landed in the water. She threw it over the side of the tub as the door clicked shut.

Grateful for the silence, Cynda sank into the tub as far as she could, the hot water a balm to her bruised body.

Someone had declared war. It was time to go on the offensive.

‡

Keats arrived at the clinic like a gale-force wind. Unusually testy, he brushed aside Alastair's protests at the interruption, insisting they had to talk at that very moment. Not wishing to upset his patients any further, Alastair donned his coat, offered a mumbled apology to Daniel and followed his friend outside. To his surprise, Keats crossed the street, marching up the street toward Christ Church. Alastair had no other choice but to follow him.

"What is wrong?" he demanded, striding to catch the retreating form. Instead of providing an answer, Keats kept marching, his boots striking the ground with considerable force, as if trying to ground his fury into the earth.

Alastair grabbed the man's arm and spun him around. "Now see here…"

Keats retaliated by jabbing a finger in his direction. "Someone tried to kill Jacynda tonight. She was deliberately pushed into the path of a beer wagon. Fortunately, she's of strong constitution, or you'd have to order another coffin."

The two men eyed each other.

"You don't seem surprised about this," Keats observed.

Alastair shook his head. A few days earlier, he would have believed Keats' rampant imagination was at play. Christopher Stone's body said otherwise.

"She lied to me, of course; told me some cock-and-bull story about tripping because of her bootlaces. Absolute humbug."

Alastair didn't reply, not knowing the best way to play the situation. He'd never seen Keats this angry.

His silence caused the other man to explode. "Tell me the truth. Did her lover commit suicide?"

Alastair turned toward the clinic, hoping Keats would cool down and stop asking questions that shouldn't be answered.

Keats' hand caught his upper arm in a solid grip. "Tell me, damn you."

"You sound like a Blue Bottle. Why do you care so much?"

"I act like a copper because...I want to know the truth."

"The truth?" Alastair shook himself free. "So be it, then. Mr. Stone was murdered."

"You've informed the police?"

"No. Jacynda is adamant that we not do so. There are...mitigating circumstances."

"Such as?"

"I am not at liberty to speak on that."

"Holding your silence nearly got her killed this evening."

"I had no choice in the matter," Alastair shot back.

Another savage finger jab to the chest. "Why didn't you bother to mention this little discovery when you sent me on that fool's errand?"

"I didn't feel you should be involved."

The glare grew tenfold. "Silly old Keats, always a bother. Doesn't have a brain in his head, is that it?"

"I would have acted differently if I'd known this would happen."

"Somehow, I doubt that." Keats rammed his hands into his pockets. "You must report this to the police."

"Jacynda does not want Mr. Stone's death investigated for...personal reasons. I have been unable to convince her otherwise."

"A crime has been committed and as a physician—"

"The body has been cremated. You can raise a fuss, but it will have no effect other than to bring unwelcome notoriety upon Jacynda...and the clinic."

Keats opened his mouth to argue, then promptly closed it. He slumped against the stone wall, his eyes downcast.

"Tell me what happened tonight," Alastair urged.

His eyes rose to meet Alastair's. "I made a condolence call, only to find you'd already been there squiring her around."

"Good lord, you're jealous."

Keats' jaw tightened. "Yes, I guess I am."

"Well, that explains a great deal."

"Meaning?" Keats snarled.

"Meaning we both care for the woman. Nevertheless, now is not the time for petty animosity. We need to work together to keep her safe."

A grudging nod.

"Please tell me what happened tonight," Alastair urged.

Keats acquiesced. By the time the tale concluded, including Jacynda's encounter on Dorset Street, Alastair let a loose a blast of air through pursed lips. "Bless you for coming to her aid," he said.

Keats shook his head. "She would not tell me why she was on the streets. I honestly believe she knew where she was—that it wasn't a misjudgment."

Alastair nodded. "Jacynda was there on purpose, I wager. She's not thinking rationally at this point."

Part of him wanted to bolt for New Castle Street and see Jacynda in person, to ensure she wasn't injured beyond what Keats had reported. He heard a noise and turned toward the clinic—another patient shuffled inside.

"You're sure she wasn't hurt more than she let on?" he queried.

"Yes, I'm sure. She walked back to the boarding house without my assistance. It appears her shoulder took the brunt of the damage. Her landladies are seeing to her."

"Thank God."

"Indeed."

Another patient limped into the building. Alastair let out a deep sigh. "I'd best help Daniel, then I shall go to the boarding house without delay."

"I will rest easier knowing you will see to her."

Their eyes met yet again. There were words held back on both sides. "Why is someone trying to kill her?" Keats asked.

"I have no idea."

"You must go to the police."

"The coroner has ruled the death a suicide, and Mr. Stone has been cremated. The matter is at an end."

A snort. "You might as well know, I traced the bottle you gave me to the chemist who dispensed the medicine. It was purchased four days ago, and signed for in the shop ledger."

"Then, by heavens, we have him!"

Keats shook his head. "No, we don't. We only have more questions."

"What do you mean?"

"The man who signed the ledger shares something in common with you."

"Which is?"

There was a tense pause. "Your name."

"What? My God, you don't think I..." Alastair's voice faded in horror.

"I'll be honest, I had my doubts for a time, but the description of the fellow did not sound like you."

"Why in God's name would someone forge my signature?"

"Another question without an answer. This whole affair is a complete tangle," Keats allowed. "We must press Jacynda to leave London."

"There are mitigating circumstances. For the time being, she may be forced to remain in London."

Keats straightened up, deep in thought. "Indeed." He gestured. "They're queuing outside the door, now. I'd best leave you to your work."

"Thank you for looking out for Jacynda." Keats didn't reply. He strode away, the pensive expression still in place.

Alastair retreated to the clinic. As he motioned the next patient forward, his mind demanded answers. *Why would someone want Jacynda dead? Who had tried to implicate me in a murder?*

Keats was right. This whole affair was a complete tangle.

19

Friday, 28 September, 1888

Morning brought new, painful discoveries. As she examined her limbs in the wardrobe's small mirror, Cynda found it hard to believe there weren't more bruises. Her right arm, the one that had tangled with the horse's hoof, was swollen half again in size and a brilliant blue and black. She wiggled her fingers; they moved fairly easily. The shoulder didn't.

"As long as it's not broken, I'm fine," she coached herself. She knew what broken things felt like. This was just one big ouchie. In some karmic fashion, the bruise offset the one she'd given the doctor. All in all, her dance with the Shires had turned out better than she'd had a right to expect.

Dressing brought more than one oath to her lips. Buttoning the navy dress proved impossible. Admitting defeat, she took her semi-dressed self to the kitchen in search of one of the landladies.

"You must be more careful, Miss Jacynda," Mildred warned, deftly buttoning.

"It was just an accident," Cynda lied.

"Shouldn't you rest today?" Annabelle asked, peeling apples at the table.

"No, I'm fine. Just a little sore."

Mildred admired her handiwork. "There, you look proper."

"Don't forget the doctor's note," Annabelle cautioned.

"Ah, yes," Mildred replied. She pulled an envelope from under the teapot and handed it over. "Dr. Montrose asked me to give you this."

"Thank you."

Cynda didn't read the note until she was out the front door, clad in Annabelle's spare cloak.

I was unable to tell you with the landladies present last evening—Keats is now aware of the particulars of Mr. Stone's death, but nothing further. I shall be available at the clinic after three if you need further care or wish to speak about the 'Accident'.

That was cold. No "I'm sorry you nearly got trampled to death" or anything remotely resembling concern.

Why did you tell Keats? Shaking her head in irritation, she stuffed the note into a skirt pocket and went in search of a cabbie. Her day was full enough without a rendezvous at the clinic.

✝

Though Cynda's shoulder ached with every bump, the hansom ride refreshed her soul. The further westward she traveled, the cleaner and wider the streets became. Even the air seemed less dense. The route took her past St. James Park and Buckingham Palace. The last time she'd seen the place it was merely Buckingham House, serving as a residence for George the Third, his wife, Charlotte, and their umpteen children.

"Definitely an improvement," she murmured, marveling at the edifice. Missing was the memorial statue to Queen Victoria, so prominent in later decades. It'd be a few years before that came to fruition.

As they clip-clopped their way to fashionable Belgrave Square, Cynda marveled at the contrast between the upmarket West End and the dingy sadness of the East. Gaily dressed young women appeared on the streets as the morning wore on, like elegant silk flowers seduced outdoors by the sun. Dapper young men in crisp morning coats and top hats paid them court. One particular woman's gown, a rich emerald green tipped with silver, caught Cynda's eyes. She sighed with a combination of envy and frustration. Clothes were no longer elegant in her time, merely functional. Here they were sumptuous, moving canvases.

Despite the trip, the Medico-Psychological Association office gave her nothing to work with. The only Samuelson they knew of was British born and bred, a curmudgeon in his mid-eighties. Ignoring the constant throbbing ache in her right shoulder, she pressed on. After a hearty lunch at a dining hall near the Law Courts in Holborn, she took a hansom across the Thames to Lambeth and one of the most infamous institutions in all of Britain.

✝

Cynda heard the voices even before she entered the building. Not the inmates' otherworldly howls, or the bizarre cackles that bounced off the stone walls, but the infinitesimal whispers of those who were no longer here. Had they graced this structure with their madness before they departed, bequeathed it into the very stones?

"Welcome to Bedlam," they said. "You are no different than us. Why are you free and we are not?"

Cynda shivered from crown to toes. Something pressed against her mind, clawing as if it sensed her sanity and sought to possess it. She closed her eyes and took a series of deep breaths to stem the unreasoned panic blooming inside her. The howls of the damned grew in response.

"Miss?" a voice inquired.

Cynda forced her eyes open. A male attendant stood in front of her, a quizzical expression on his whiskered face.

"I need to see who's in charge."

He beckoned and she followed meekly, though it took more courage than she thought she possessed. As they turned a corner, a woman tromped by in jerky movements, a human wind-up toy. Minus a few teeth, the scowl on her face seemed to be etched into her genetic code. She hissed like an angry cobra, narrowing her eyes and craning her thin neck.

"Go 'way. No place for you 'ere," she said in a thick Irish accent. "Go 'way, go 'way. You'll take their food. Go 'way, go 'way!"

With one last venomous look, she returned her eyes to the floor, thrusting her head to the right and then the left as she tromped away.

The attendant leaned close to explain. "That's Mad Sammy. She feeds the mice her food. That's why she doesn't want us here. Figures we'll eat all the victuals and the mice'll starve. She's better'n some of 'em, I can tell ya."

"A woman who values mice over men," Cynda mused.

"That's it for a fact," the man said, beckoning her forward.

"Don't the sounds bother you?"

He gave her a peculiar look and then shook his head. "They used to. I don't hear them no more."

Oh, God.

"Dr. Samuelson?" the resident officer asked, looking up from the stack of paperwork on his desk. "Yes, he was here."

"When?" she asked, leaning forward in anticipation.

"And just who are you in relation to him?" He removed his glasses and laid them carefully aside.

Cynda readied the lie. "His niece. There is an illness in the family, and we must find him as quickly as possible."

"Oh, I see. Well, it's been well over a month since I've last seen him."

Cynda's hope dwindled. "Do you have any idea where I can reach him?"

"He was staying somewhere near Fenchurch Street Station. I don't know precisely where."

"Did he mention any other asylums that he intended to visit?"

"Quite a few actually, but I cannot remember them at this point. Not speaking ill of your uncle, but he is a rather odd fellow, to be honest."

"Yes, he is," Cynda agreed. Anything to keep the man talking.

"If time is of the essence, I would suggest you send telegraphic inquiries to those institutions closest at hand. It would save travel time and expense. You might consider placing a personal notice in the paper."

Why not? "I shall do as you suggest," she said. "Thank you, sir."

"Doctor," he said. "Good day, miss." He bent over his paperwork, the minutiae of the mad, mumbling something under his breath about interruptions.

The walls continued to talk to her even as the hackney pulled away.

What would it be like if you could never leave?

⁜

"Bane of a good copper," Keats muttered under his breath, setting one page of his report aside and starting on the next. Fisher was a stickler about paperwork and had, on occasion, required Keats to rewrite a report if it didn't meet his exacting standards.

The work would have been finished earlier if his mind weren't playing leapfrog with him. He'd start thinking about how close Jacynda had come to harm, then he'd wonder what else Alastair had been hiding from him during their argument. His mind had waged war with him all night, demanding he take the matter of Mr. Stone's death to his superiors.

But that could backfire. Though he still did not believe either Jacynda or the doctor to be capable of murder, would Alastair's

188 | Jana G. Oliver

earlier brush with the law condemn him anyway? Would they be charged and convicted based on Keats' testimony that they sought to hide the true cause of death?

He'd been to hangings; he knew what they were like. The thought of the rope entwined around Jacynda's delicate neck...

The pen shuddered, and he had to cross out a word. Irritated, he crumpled the paper. With some effort, he tugged his mind back to the job, beginning the botched sentence anew.

The telltale sound of inspector Ramsey's heavy footfalls echoed in the hallway. Keats' fellow cops tidied their coats and earnestly hunched over their paperwork to avoid scrutiny. They need not have bothered; once Ramsey spied him, Keats would be his target.

Ramsey halted near the desk. He cleared his throat to attract attention.

"Well, well, is that Sergeant Keats? This is a surprise. Don't see much of you around here. Too busy playing detective, I hear."

Keats looked up from his report. "Good afternoon, Inspector."

"Mind you, my lads don't see you on the street, either. They see the other coppers, but not you. That tells me something. You know what that is?"

That your lads couldn't find their bums with both hands? "No, sir," he answered politely.

"That tells me you're running a game on us. I bet you're warming some tart's bed while drawing your pay." Ramsey pointed a sausage-shaped finger at him. "One of these days, I'll catch you at it. Fisher might think the sun rises in your arse, but I know better."

There was no need to argue with the fellow—he wasn't known for his brains. "As you say, sir." Keats selected another piece of paper and continued his report.

"So, what are you working on?" Ramsey asked, glowering.

Keats looked up again and faked a smile. Then the devil got the best of him. "Not doing much, sir. Just running my game, as you put it."

The man's fist rapped hard on the desk. "Someday, I'll catch you and I'll have you by the nads. You got that?"

"I believe so, sir. Someday, you intend to handle my bollocks."

Ramsey reddened, the fist flexing. Keats continued with his paperwork, as if nothing were amiss.

The inspector muttered an oath under his breath as he marched out of the room. Whispers erupted amongst the other cops. Keats kept his head down, eyes fixed on the report. He wondered how long it would take before the details of the conversation reached Fisher's ears. He could hear his superior now—"Really, Sergeant, must you aggravate the man at every opportunity?"

Yes, twice over.

Keats blotted the ink on the last line of the report, tidied up the desk and toted the paperwork to the proper people. One day, he'd go too far with Ramsey and pay heavily for his insolence. Fortunately, it did not appear to be today.

His mind elsewhere, Keats hopped into a crowded omnibus, scrunching up next to a parcel-laden woman.

Jacynda had stirred up a memory. He knew of only one way to exorcize it.

‡

The woman in the dark brown dress glowered from the doorway. By now, Cynda was used to the look. This was her seventh boarding house near Fenchurch Station, and so far she'd struck out at every one.

The landlady had her hands on her hips, the universal "why are you wasting my time?" gesture.

"Dr. Walter Samuelson," Cynda repeated.

"There was a fellow here by the name," the woman admitted. "Why do you want to know?"

Yes! "I'm his niece. A family member has taken ill."

The landlady eyed her. "Well, then you've not heard, have you?"

"Heard what?" *If he ended up under a beer wagon...*

"He's gone home."

Home? "When?"

"About three weeks ago. Mind you, he was all too fond of those mad people." She paused and then frowned. "I suppose you'll be wanting his things."

Cynda heard the resentment. No doubt, the woman thought of selling them to augment her income. "Yes."

"Follow me, then."

Dr. Samuelson had left very little: a pair of dirty socks, a rumpled shirt and a book about psychiatric diseases clad in a worn leather cover. When the landlady wasn't looking, Cynda checked the book's copyright date—2017—and winced. Someone at TIC wasn't doing their job. All tourists were to be vetted for anachronistic items before transfer. Luckily, the landlady wasn't the curious type.

Cynda left the socks and shirt and retraced her way to the boarding house. It was nearing five. Her shoulder was so stiff she couldn't move properly. A hot bath would help, along with liberal helpings of tea and scones.

She'd narrowed her quest to within a few weeks. If her flurry of telegrams didn't pan out, then she'd make the rounds of the morgues. If worse came to worst, Walter Samuelson might be heading home in an urn just like Chris.

‡

The fire crackled in the background and the kettle was just coming to a boil. Settled in his favorite chair, Keats held the book as if it were a rare gem. It was hardly that, but it exacted as much awe for him as any diamond or ruby. He'd selected the proper one from amongst its many companions—his mother had kept diaries since she was in her teens—and this particular volume was where Keats came into her life.

The binding was cracked, and bits of dried leather flaked onto his lap. He could have it repaired, but then someone else might read her tortured words. He couldn't let that happen.

He smiled in remembrance of the woman who had loved him unconditionally. She had left him too soon, though now that he knew of her pain, he understood how death could bring such sweet respite.

There was no need for him to open the book: The words had been seared into his heart from the first time he'd read them.

I am with child.

At first I rejoiced, for it is a miracle. Then my joy burned away, like Icarus soaring too near the sun. If I had known what kind of man Hiram would become, I would not have succumbed to his flattery, his bold pronouncements of love, his licentious ways. I saw in him honor and grace, a man I could admire. Now the serpent rears its head.

When I told him of our child, he spurned me, laughing at my misfortune. He denies his responsibility to the life in my womb. I am ruined, and he does not care. God forgive me, I have had thoughts of ending this torment, of slaying myself. The child within me stays my hand.

If it is a girl, I pray she never fall victim to a man's smooth tongue. If it is a boy, then I beg God that he becomes the antithesis of his father. If ever faced with such a moral obligation, I hope he would do the honorable thing, outshining the brute that so callously sired and then denied him.

In the end, it had taken Keats' maternal grandfather to force the nuptials into reality, employing the lure of a sizeable monetary settlement, coupled with the threat of physical violence. Because of the old man, Jonathon Davis Keats had been born legitimate. Until he read his mother's diaries, he'd never understood the gulf that resided between his sainted dam and the cur she'd married.

Keats gently kissed the book. It smelled of old leather and his mother's lilac perfume. Jacynda came to mind. What was it like to carry the child of a dead man, knowing he could not restore your honor from the grave?

Tucking the diary away, he rose and dusted off his suit. He knew what he must do. In all ways, he was resolute: He would be a better man than his father.

☨

"You're sure someone pushed her into the street?" Livingston asked.

"It is the only explanation, sir. One moment she was admiring the horses; the next, she was underneath them," William reported.

"And the body at the mortuary?"

"Suicide. A young man named Christopher Stone. Pulled from the Thames."

"What relation is she to him?"

"I'm not sure on that, sir."

Livingston arched an eyebrow. "Did Miss Lassiter take any harm during her misadventure?"

"An injury to her shoulder. It did nothing to slow her progress today. She has been inquiring after a man named Samuelson. He is an...alienist."

"Is she seeking treatment?"

"I do not believe so. She was putting it about that she is his niece. She visited Bedlam this morning, and then boarding houses near Fenchurch Station."

"Bedlam? Good God," Livingston remarked, deftly flicking some lint off his coat. Knots of theatergoers waltzed by, chattering amongst themselves. "Why is this Samuelson so important?" Livingston pondered.

192 | Jana G. Oliver

"Perhaps he has something to do with Mr. Stone's death."

Livingston gave his companion a look of respect. "I think you might be right on that, William, especially in light of the attempt on Miss Lassiter's life." He delivered a nod of approval at his subordinate. "You have performed outstanding service." He extracted another sovereign and handed it to the man.

The fellow blinked. "Thank you, sir. You've been extremely generous."

"You've earned it. For the time being, continue to follow Miss Lassiter. If you need to contact me, leave a message at the Artifice Club. The steward will forward your message."

A nod. "If someone should try to harm the lady in future?"

"If you can intervene without revealing yourself, do so. Until I am sure of her part in all this, it is best she remain alive."

"Yes, sir," William said, executing an abbreviated bow. After a spin on his heels, he made his way into the evening traffic.

Livingston tapped the head of his cane in thought. "I wonder what it all means." Flipping open his pocket watch, he gave a satisfied nod. Time remained for an excellent supper before the play began at the Lyceum. He had much to ponder—there was a hidden player in this game, one with a penchant for murder.

✝

It was becoming an evening ritual—Jonathon Keats at the front door, hat in hand. Tempting as it was to have Mildred tell the man to go home, Cynda couldn't be that callous. His sincerity was endearing. Besides, in another day or two, she'd be back in her own time, and all this would just be a fond memory.

Jonathon shot to his feet the moment she entered the parlor, bowler clutched in his hands.

He cleared his throat nervously. "Good evening, Jacynda. I wished to see how you were faring."

"Good evening, Jonathon. I'm doing fairly well, considering. Thank you for asking." She gestured and he returned to his place on the couch. Before she could take a seat, he cleared his throat again.

"Ummm, if you are amenable, I would appreciate it if you would, ummm…close the door. I have something of a personal nature to discuss."

"Certainly, Jonathon." She closed the door.

Cynda chose to sit in the chair, not on the couch, which caused a brief look of disappointment to flit across her visitor's face.

"I...uh..." A tug on his shirt collar. "Your shoulder, how is it today?"

"Stiff and sore, like something heavy tromped on it," she said.

"Of course." His eyes darted around the room and then back to his hat.

"Jonathon?" she asked as sweetly as she could. *Get on with it!*

"Alastair has informed me of the particulars regarding the death of your lover. I must strongly urge you to go to the police."

She shook her head. "That is not possible."

"I know it will be difficult, but—"

"This is not open for discussion." She rose. "Now if you will excuse me..."

He looked painfully uncomfortable. The hat did a quick spin in his hands. "Please, sit down. I have something else I wish to speak to you about."

She lowered herself into the chair. "Go on."

"...I feel it is imperative that you return to New York as soon as possible. If money is an issue, I would be willing to purchase the ticket and escort you to Southampton to ensure your safety." He rose before she could reply. "I understand there is another issue at stake...ummm...and know that it would present a difficulty for you to return to your family in your...ah...state," he stumbled on, the hat now spinning in time with his agitation.

She gestured for him to continue, at a loss as to where this was leading.

"I am fond of you, Jacynda, and have no desire that your reputation be sullied. I personally do not mind that you are...ah...*experienced*. Why should it be so morally indecent for a woman to have a lover, and yet a man may take as many as—" He stopped abruptly, his face blooming crimson. "Well, you understand."

"Sit," she said, pointing at the couch, "and please speak English, Jonathon."

He sank onto the cushions. Another tug at the collar, though plainly it wasn't tight. The hat twirled. She gestured and he reluctantly handed it over. With nothing to muss with, his hands tumbled into a pile in his lap.

"Go on," she ordered, her patience nearing what promised to be a tumultuous end.

"I apologize; I've done this badly. I am here to offer my hand in marriage, to ensure that your...unborn child is not a...that he or she be seen as legitimate. I have personal knowledge of how...devastating that can be to a woman." He blinked in conster-

194 | Jana G. Oliver

nation. "Not that I, personally, have caused such a situation, however..." He hesitated and then tried again, "We can wed as swiftly as the law will allow, and then you may leave for New York where you will be safe. With my name, you will not face criticism for your condition. Should anyone inquire, you may say the child is mine. I will come to visit you as soon as possible. We can make arrangements for your return once we are sure you are in no further danger."

Child? Marriage? Apparently, Alastair had shared his misdiagnosis with the honorable Mr. Keats.

The expression on Jonathon's face was so serious she didn't dare laugh. There was no deception on his part; he was genuinely offering to marry her and accept another man's child as his own to protect her reputation. In 2057 it wouldn't matter either way. To the Victorians, this was a big deal.

Clearly uneasy at her silence, he pressed his case. "I have a steady position with a decent salary, though my hours are rather irregular. I rent comfortable rooms in Bloomsbury. We can move to another location if you wish, as long as it is within London. If, in time, you find me acceptable, I would like to have children of our own. I am quite taken with you, Jacynda, and do not make this proposal lightly."

Oh, heavens. Cynda lowered her eyes to the hat in her lap. Its solid and straightforward appearance was at odds with its owner—at least the man she remembered from the first night they'd met. The lighthearted Keats had vanished, and what was left behind confused her.

Why are you making this offer? There was something deeper here, but Cynda knew it would only cheapen his gesture if she asked. She took her time formulating the answer. When she raised her eyes, she found his riveted on her.

Rovers weren't supposed to face this kind of thing. *Just a Visitor, Never a Participant,* that was the mantra. Still, how could she not be touched by such a humane gesture?

Cynda made sure her tone was soft and full of respect. "You are an incredible gentleman, Jonathon." That earned her a smile. "I am honored by your offer. However, I am not pregnant."

Frank surprise replaced the smile. "Oh...oh...ah...but I thought..." A perturbed frown. "Alastair said he thought you were."

"Well, Alastair may be a brilliant physician, but he is not always right. I'm not hatching." That garnered a chuckle. "And I am not leaving for New York quite yet." The humor vanished.

Before he could protest, she continued, "I'm staying a little while longer. I promise I will be careful."

"Alastair said you would be difficult on that point."

"He would be right about that."

"Do you have any notion why someone would kill your lover or want to harm you?" he asked.

"No, I honestly don't."

Keats drummed his fingers on a knee. "And my offer of marriage?"

Startled, she realized she'd not officially turned him down. "I assumed it was contingent on me being pregnant."

He opened his mouth, and then shut it.

"I am honored, but I must decline. We know little about each other and that is not a good basis for a marriage." *You have no clue.*

Jonathon gave a slow nod and then a wider smile of relief. "I agree."

He rose and collected the bowler. As he did, he leaned close and brushed a kiss on her cheek. "You are a remarkable woman, Miss Lassiter."

She lightly kissed his cheek in response.

"Not as remarkable as you are, Mr. Keats."

Once on the street, Keats took a deep breath and slowly let it out. Instead of disappointment, he felt some odd kind of rapture, as if he'd narrowly escaped some hideous fate. That puzzled him. Being married to Jacynda wouldn't be a penance: she was an intelligent, enchanting woman and no doubt quite passionate.

And yet... Had his father thought the same of his mother, only to learn that she despised him and would not allow him to touch her?

"I am not my father," he muttered, clapping the bowler on his head. "Far from it." He marched toward the main road, whistling a tune, attempting to push his nagging doubts aside.

20

"No, luv, never seen him," the woman replied. "Sounds like a right nice lad, though."

"Yes, he was..." Cynda said, visualizing Chris in his Victorian finery.

"Fancy an apple?" the woman asked, holding up a prize specimen.

"Yes, thank you." Cynda purchased the fruit and gave it to the first urchin she found. The child stared at her like she'd handed over the Crown Jewels.

Weary of trudging the same old route, and leery of Dorset Street, Cynda went west along Aldgate High Street toward St. Botolph's Church. She stopped at the first pub, The Bull Inn, and made the circuit inside. No Samuelson, and the publican didn't remember Chris, either.

While trying to decide where to go next, Cynda leaned against the building, adjusting a boot. Horses came and went from the livery stable next door with a noisy clatter.

Two women exited the pub. One waved farewell and walked toward the church. The other remained by the entrance, adjusting her red neckerchief. She removed her bonnet and ran her fingers through her dark auburn hair. Though thin, her face had a puffiness that suggested ill health.

"Troubles with your boot?" she asked, noting Cynda's battle. The woman repositioned her hat and rammed the hatpin back home.

Cynda nodded. "They pinch all the time. I just can't seem to get them right."

The woman eyed her. "You're not from hereabouts, are you?"

"No. I'm from New York. Don't worry, I'm not taking any trade tonight."

A shrug. "Don't bother me none. I got my doss money. What's New York like?"

"Pretty much like here," Cynda said, straightening up. "Good and bad."

A snort. "If you're not earning your crust, why are you here, then?"

"Looking for a particular fellow," Cynda replied, working on the other boot.

"He do a runner on you?" the woman asked.

"In a way." She supplied Chris' description.

"Sorry, luv, I just got back from Kent. Been hoppin'. Not a good year for it."

"Oh, I see. Sorry."

"Right fine hat you got there," the woman added.

"Thank you. Yours is quite nice as well."

A smile. "Well, best be off to Shoe Lane before it gets too late."

"Be careful," Cynda warned.

"Oh, I'm not fretting about the killer," the woman said, winking conspiratorially. She sang her way up the street.

"Then you're about the only one," Cynda murmured.

‡

Saturday, 29 September, 1888

Fate was a cruel mistress. The telegram read: *Samuelson in residence, Colney Hatch Asylum.* Cynda's jubilation faded the moment Alastair insisted they take the Underground Railway from Aldgate Station to King's Cross.

"It is really quite safe," he cajoled as they wended their way through the throng toward the train platform. To Cynda, it seemed as if they were miles under the street level. Despite the cool weather, it was stifling hot inside the tunnel. The crush of bodies made it worse.

"First time?" he asked.

"Yes." That wasn't quite true: she'd been here before. In 2057, it held Grav-Rail trains—quiet, clean and boring transportation. '88's Underground was anything but.

"Can't we take a hansom?" she asked for at least the third time.

"No need. Much faster this way. Once we reach King's Cross, we'll change to the Northern Line; then it's only twenty-one minutes to Colney Hatch," Alastair said with an air of pride. "The

Underground is one of the marvels of our time, like the new bridge near the Tower. You should experience it while you're in London."

Cynda eyed him. "This isn't a marvel to me, Alastair. This is penance."

"Oh…still, it's quite a bracing excursion. Certainly not as bad as traveling from…" He gave an offhand gesture to indicate the future.

Cynda glowered. "You're one of those technology-worshippers, aren't you?"

"Certainly! Who isn't?" Alastair asked, surprised. "Technological advances such as this will allow our society to grow," he said, attempting to gesture expansively but not having the space to do so. "If society flourishes, the less fortunate will benefit."

"Right," she muttered. "You sound like a politician."

"I see you're going to criticize everything I say," he replied, sounding hurt.

"No, I'm just…"

"Afraid?" he shot back.

"No." The doctor raised an eyebrow. She sighed. "Yes."

"Well, it won't last too long," Alastair said, returning to a reassuring tone.

"Long enough to kill me," she grumbled.

A blast of noise welled out of the tunnel, followed by the massive bulk of a steam engine. Chaos ensued the moment it halted at the platform.

Alastair gripped her left elbow tightly. "Stay with me," he shouted over the din, his face alight with joy.

Even if she'd wanted to turn and run for it, there was no chance, not with the tide of people pushing her forward and Alastair's steering grip. Someone bumped into her right arm and she winced from the pain. They made it onto a carriage and took their seats with mere seconds to spare. The doctor beamed like an enthusiastic child.

"A bit dicey there for a moment, but we made it!" he crowed.

Shouts and bells rang out, doors slammed. With a horrendous lurch, the train heaved forward. Cynda was on her feet in a flash. Alastair caught her and forced her down on the seat.

"It'll be fine," he shouted near her ear.

"You lie," she shouted back and then jammed her eyes shut, squeezing his hand as hard as she could.

Darkness enveloped the car as they sped along the rails, the stench of sulfur and pipe smoke invading her lungs until she was sure each breath was the last. As they roared through the tunnel, Alastair leaned close to her ear and recounted the wonders of the Metropolitan Line, just like a tour guide. She focused on his words, desperate to shut out all the ominous sounds.

"The line opened in 1863, and is quite safe and efficient," he said. "It moves thousands of people a day. They even created special vents to ferry the steam and smoke to the surface to keep the tunnels free of the fumes."

"Not working," Cynda said into Alastair's handkerchief, currently positioned over her mouth. She rose at each station, only to be gently tugged back onto the seat.

"Just a few more. We're almost there," he said. "This is quite an adventure."

Cynda stared at him, astonished at his boyish zeal. She never would have believed anything could undermine his emotional armor.

The train pulled into a station. This time, he was the one doing the tugging. "This is it." She couldn't fathom how he knew. They pressed their way toward the door and out onto the platform. In what only seemed a second later, the train chugged away leaving behind the stench of coal dust, oil lamps and overly warm bodies.

"I have to have air," she whispered, her head swirling.

The exalted look on the doctor's face vanished. "This way out," he said, pointing.

The day was clear and autumn crisp. Cynda reveled in the slight breeze as she sat on a bench, sighing after each deep inhalation. Alastair hovered nearby, watching her closely.

"Are you better now?" he asked.

"Yes, thank you."

"You did very well," he said. "Other than trying to abscond once or twice."

Tempting as it was to kick him in the shins, she resisted. Certainly, hurtling through time was a lot more dangerous and unpredictable than riding in a steam train deep in London's sooty cellar. *Why did this frighten her so much?*

"You're right." She rose, dusting bits of who-knows-what off her skirt. Probably coal cinders. "How do we get to the asylum?"

"I'll inquire which train we should take," Alastair offered and headed toward a railway employee.

Once he was out of earshot, she grumbled, "Bracing excursion, my ass."

Colney Hatch Asylum resembled a ducal estate rather than a mental institution. The Italianate building soared above landscaped grounds, belying the horrors within. Cynda and Alastair traded looks.

"Not like Bedlam," she said. Her companion nodded.

The hackney driver called down, "You want me to wait?"

"Most definitely." Alastair pulled a few extra coins out of his pocket and pressed them into the man's hand.

The jarvey touched his hat in respect and then shot an uneasy glance at the edifice in front of them. "God help them."

"I am sure He does," Alastair replied.

Cynda dropped the telegram on the desk. "No, no, there is some misunderstanding."

The medical superintendent gave her a disgruntled look and shifted his attention toward Alastair. Before she was cut out of the conversation altogether, she tried again. "We need to speak to *Dr.* Walter Samuelson, not one of your patients. You sent me a telegram saying he was here."

"On the contrary, I did not realize you were making an inquiry regarding an *actual* physician," the man replied in clipped tones. "We have an inmate here by the name of Samuelson who claims to be a doctor, but in no wise is he genuine."

"When did he arrive?" Cynda demanded.

The superintendent consulted a large book. "On the seventh of this month."

The timing was right if Samuelson's landlady was accurate.

"I wish to see him." If it were the missing shrink, the time interface would tell her. The superintendent gave Alastair a disgruntled look and stood in a huff.

"Come then, I will show you this man, and put an end to the matter. Then you can go about your business."

They hiked along the longest corridor Cynda had ever seen. Individual cells lined one side, each housing some poor unfortunate. Unlike Bedlam, this building didn't attempt to shoehorn itself into her brain. This felt more like a hospital, not an island full of the insane.

As the super unlocked a door, Alastair bent closer to her and whispered, "Patience is a virtue."

She gave him a withering look.

The man inside the cell was perfectly composed. He sat on his bed, a piece of wood on his lap upon which he scribbled notes. An inkwell perched precariously on the nearly flat mattress, a mound of foolscap nearby.

"Samuelson?" the superintendent called.

"Humpff?" the fellow asked. His appearance was disheveled, but there was no hint of madness in his eyes.

Cynda reached under the cloak, extracting the pocket watch from her bodice. The interface was silent; this wasn't the right man. Her hope exploded into tiny slivers.

Tucking away the watch, she stepped forward, selecting one of the pieces of paper. It was full of bizarre markings.

"As you see," the superintendent said in a lowered voice, "he is quite content to slave away on his notes, as he calls them. They make no sense at all; just mindless drivel. Random letters and symbols, no doubt some language of his own making. We hope to reorient him to rationality and then release him when he is deemed cured."

She turned and gave a wan smile, tossing the paper back on the pile. "He isn't the fellow I'm looking for."

"As I knew," the super said with barely concealed smugness.

Cynda took one last look at the inmate on the bed. The fellow delivered a distracted smile and went back to his writings, pausing every now and then to gnaw on the top of the pen between sentences.

The door creaked shut, leaving the lunatic to his work.

Engaging the lock, the superintendent added, "As long as we keep him supplied in paper and ink, he is docile. I wish the same could be said for some of the others."

The moment they climbed aboard the hansom, the jarvey set the horse off at a trot, keen to be away from the place.

"I'm sorry it wasn't the right fellow," Alastair said.

Cynda rubbed her face with her hands. Her best lead had turned out to be a dead end. Back to square one. Maybe one of the other telegrams or the note in the paper would pay off. If not, she would be returning to '057 empty-handed and unemployed.

She leaned toward Alastair. "What time is it?"

He retrieved his pocket watch and studied it. "Half past four. Why?"

"Let's get some supper before we go back to London."

"Are you sure that's wise? A full stomach might not be your best friend while riding the train."

She gave him a dazzling smile. "Train? Heaven forbid. We're going to return to London in style."

He arched an eyebrow. "In a carriage, I suppose?"

"Indeed, Dr. Montrose, in a carriage. I'll even pay for it."

"It will take infinitely longer," he hedged.

"Yes, it will," she said, nodding happily. "It appears I have plenty of time."

21

"Have you always courted danger, or is this a recent development?" Alastair asked, flicking some cinders off his bowler as they rode back to London.

"My family tells me it all started when I was about ten months old. One day when my mom wasn't looking, I wobbled into a street of…vehicles," she began, carefully scripting her response not to reveal too much detail. "My father saved me at the very last moment. He nicknamed me Daredevil, and I've been living up to his moniker ever since."

"I was never like that. I took risks, but not of the physical sort. Keats is always going on about how stuffy I am," Alastair admitted.

She smirked. "You *are* stuffy."

"Well, not always," he replied, sounding miffed she'd agreed.

"Then tell me about a time when you broke the mold—acted on impulse."

He frowned in concentration. "I went to Wales on a whim once."

"Why?"

"A friend dared me to go with him, so I took off. My father was quite upset when I cabled him from Cardiff and told him what I was about."

"So what did you learn on that trip?"

He looked away. "That love is fleeting," he murmured.

Caught by his sadness, Cynda took his hand and squeezed. He gave a wan smile in return.

"*'Without a hurt, the heart is hollow,'*" she said.

Alastair gently ran his finger along the side of her jaw. Bending forward, he tentatively kissed her. When she didn't pull away, he gave her another, stronger and more insistent. Cynda felt the passion behind the gesture. In another time or place, it

204 | Jana G. Oliver

would have been readily welcomed.

She gathered her skirts and moved to the other side of the carriage.

He blinked in surprise. "If I have offended you—"

"No, you didn't. It's just…" She felt heat rise to her cheeks.

"Go on," he prompted.

"I don't want to make it harder to go home than it already is."

Alastair issued a low sigh and dropped his gaze. "I agree. It is best we do not take this any further." He leaned back into the seat, crossed his arms over his chest and closed his eyes.

Over time, the gentle rocking of the carriage worked its magic. Alastair drifted off first, his head propped against the side of the moving vehicle. A lock of hair fell over his face, giving him a rakish appearance. Cynda smiled at the sight, painting a picture to take with her when the time came to leave. Taller than Jonathon, five-foot seven or eight, with a fair complexion. Aristocratic brow, nimble mind. Jonathon's mind was equally sharp, though his height was closer to hers, his complexion a shade darker. The glint in his eyes spoke of untold mischief. Alastair's reflected duty.

What a pair. No wonder they get on each other's nerves.

Weary from the travel and the demoralizing lack of progress, she closed her eyes. It would start to rain sometime after nine. Shortly after the deluge ended, two more prostitutes would be dead. The news of the so-called "Double Event" would encircle the globe. If Samuelson were caught in the police dragnet and pulled in for questioning…

She fell into a light sleep, the movement of the carriage not allowing her to rest properly. Something lightly touched her face. It repeated the gesture. Cynda opened her eyes to find Alastair sitting beside her, caressing her cheek in that way of his.

Except it wasn't Alastair. He was still asleep on the seat across from her.

She swiveled to get a better look at the apparition. A misty version of the original, she could see the carriage through it. The phantom's eyes widened, as if it realized it was being scrutinized.

It wasn't one of her hallucinations. "Gotcha," she said.

Across from her, the doctor jolted from sleep, his mouth agape, murmuring something indistinct. The illusion faded from view.

"So, what was that?" she asked.

"I don't know what you're—"

She waved him off. "What was it?"

"You must be seeing things again."

Cynda shook her head. "You've done it before, in my room."

The doctor leaned forward and placed his head in his hands. Cynda let the silence stand. When he finally raised his head, she saw the pain in his eyes. "I don't know how to explain this."

"It can't be any odder than what I told you the other day."

He frowned. "In that, you might be wrong."

She slid sideways on the bench and patted the empty spot next to her. "Sit here. It'll be easier to hear you."

He didn't move. She patted the seat again. He moved warily to her side and then stared at his hands for a time, marshalling his thoughts.

"I'm a Transitive." He waited, but she didn't reply. "Surely you have them in your time?"

Cynda shrugged. "I'm not sure. I don't know what *they* are."

"We are shape-shifters, masters of illusion," he explained. "We can mimic any form we choose."

"Whoa, now *that* is weird. How do you do it? Is it magic?"

"The exact process is not known."

"Do you chant spells, or something like that?"

"No."

"Have you always been one of these...shifters?"

"No," Alastair replied. "It is an endowment we receive from another Transitive at the time of his or her death."

"Sort of like passing on the family silver, I guess," she joked, hoping to lighten the moment.

He frowned again. "Not quite."

Cynda tempered her enthusiasm. "So, you could look like me?"

A nod.

"Would someone be able to tell the difference?" she asked.

"Unlikely. The mimicry is an imprecise art; however, we are close enough for the average person not to notice."

"But you'd still sound like yourself?"

He shook his head. "My voice would change, and any tell-tale physical deformities would be hidden, as well."

"But I saw a hazy version of *you*, not someone else."

"When we sleep, sometimes we *venture* from our bodies, especially if we have not been *en mirage* recently. During that time, we appear as ourselves."

"Sort of like sleepwalking?"

"Somewhat. We do not physically move, but our...essence does."

Cynda was silent for a moment. "You don't like having this ability, do you?"

"No. I am attempting to subvert the inclination. I do not think it is entirely healthy."

"Why not?"

"It's unnatural. Why should I be allowed to appear as someone else?"

"What's the harm in it?" she countered. "It could be pretty awesome." *Lots of fun, actually.*

He straightened up, his eyes lit from within.

"Allow me to provide you an example, one that illustrates the dangers of this predilection. Let us suppose that I have a carnal interest in you; however, you're married. Using this ability, I could wait until your husband is out of the house and then suddenly return, mimicking his form. I could slip into your bed and you would deny me nothing, believing me to be your husband. I could have my way with you under false pretenses."

Cynda winced. "Oh. Hadn't thought of that. Like Uther Pendragon, except Merlin had to help him with that one."

"You would swear the man you'd had relations with was your husband, even though he would think you were lying."

"Which could lead to all sorts of nasty complications."

"Precisely. What if you became pregnant and the child did not resemble your husband? You could easily find yourself divorced and on the street with your baby. Even worse, what if you are assaulted and you give evidence against a man who is not the one who ravaged you? An innocent would go to prison."

"Oh, lord. Didn't think of any of those, either."

"If not handled properly, the ability to change forms is a license for immorality."

"Have you done any of those things?" Cynda challenged.

He stiffened in response. "God, no."

"Then where's the problem?"

He cleared his throat and tugged on his collar, unwittingly copying Jonathon's gesture. "You appear to have a singular effect upon me, Jacynda. I've been venturing into your room every night since you arrived. I cannot stop myself. You are so beautiful," he said. "You have every right to think me a monster."

He thought she was beautiful? That earned him a pass. "Well, at least now I know it's you," she said with a relieved smile. "I thought it was one my hallucinations."

"You're not upset?" he asked, astounded. "I am a voyeur of the worst sort."

"I'm the one who sees omnibus-sized spiders, so I'm not one to talk."

He returned his attention to his hands, still clearly ashamed.

"I've not heard of anything like you in our time," she said. "That doesn't mean they're not there. I would guess they're being careful about exposure."

"We have similar concerns. The Conclave is pressuring me to—" A long sigh. She could almost hear the internal debate: clam up or tell her more.

"The Conclave?"

"Our...leaders, as it were. They are pressuring me to shift like my fellow Transitives. When I refused, they grew angry. That night Keats met us at the restaurant, I was summoned before them. They demanded that I close the clinic and leave London."

That's why you were so upset. "Why make you leave? You have patients to care for."

"They fear one of our kind might be the Whitechapel killer. As I work in the East End and am a doctor, they feel I might be a logical suspect."

"You told them to go to—" She cut off the swear word, knowing he wouldn't approve. "You told them no, didn't you?" He nodded. "It doesn't make sense to force you to join the pack. If you don't want to, you shouldn't have to."

"It is believed that if we don't honor our true nature, mental illness ensues," Alastair explained.

"Use it or go mad, huh?"

He looked up; a slow grin creased his face. "I guess you could say that."

"What scares you about shifting?" she asked.

The grin slid away. She'd struck home.

"I owned up to my fear about the train," she insisted. "You owe me."

He looked away for a moment, and then back. "Perhaps I fear a loss of control when I take another's shape."

"You can't get stuck or anything, can you? Go around looking like a mailbox or hat rack for the rest of your life?"

That elicited a chuckle. "No. We cannot mimic inanimate objects very well, though it is rumored that some try."

"How can you ever trust anyone?" she asked, musing on the implications of his revelation.

"Once you know we exist, trust is the first victim," he said.

"Can you tell if someone else is one of these shifters?"

"I am able to discern the difference between some of them, and only when they are *en mirage*. Keats, for instance..." He shook his head at the slip. "I'm telling you too much."

"And showing you twenty-first-century technology doesn't

amount to a hill of beans?" she shot back.

A prolonged sigh. "You're right. You've been as honest as possible with me. I should be the same."

"The constable who brought you home the other night—was that Keats?" The doctor gave a nod. "He slipped up," she remarked. "He knew where your room was without being told."

Alastair's eyes widened. "I am impressed. You are quick."

"Not quick enough, or I wouldn't have ended up under those horses."

"Indeed."

Which means the man who tried to kill me could look like anyone. Is that why they never caught the Ripper?

Or maybe..."Alastair?"

"Humm?" was the quiet reply. The doctor raised his head, his eyes distant, as if focused on some harrowing memory.

"How is this ability transferred at the time of death?"

"By touching the dying Transitive. The Death Rite allows us to gift the ability from each hand—two at a time, if the dying Transitive so wishes."

"Where did your ability come from?"

"My journey to Wales gave me this..."

Curse. She heard the word, as if he'd spoken it. "I'm sorry." Her mind raced forward. "Is it possible to take this ability from a Transitive while they're alive?"

"No. If that had been the case, I would have discarded it years ago." He slid closer to her, as if sensing the fire flickering in her mind. "What are you thinking?"

It was too far-fetched to believe the murders were anything more than a psychopath getting his thrills. "Nothing, nothing. Just wondering how it all works." *Love is fleeting, he'd said.*

"Was the woman you loved a shifter?"

A nod, one laced with loss. She took his hand, pulled it up to her mouth and kissed it gently. His moist eyes acknowledged the gesture. He reclined against the seat, his face betraying a parade of emotions. His hand remained in hers, and Cynda saw no reason to change that.

✠

The remainder of the trip to Whitechapel passed in silence. Cynda laid her head on Alastair's shoulder and they held hands, the simplicity of their connection resonating without need for words. The respite ended the moment they entered the boarding house.

"Doctor?" Mildred called, scooting down the hallway in an uncharacteristic bustle. "A young lad was here for you. His name was Davy. He came to get you about his mum. Said she was quite ill."

Alastair halted at the bottom of the stairs. "How long ago?"

"An hour or so. He said it was something to do with her lungs."

"Yes, it would be. I'll go straight away."

Cynda waited as he flew up the stairs, two by two, and returned clutching his medical bag.

"I'll go with you," she offered.

"No need."

"No, I want to go."

"As you wish."

After purloining an umbrella from the stand near the front door, she fell in step once they reached the street. He halted for a moment as if to give argument, and then shook his head. After that, she struggled to keep up with his punishing pace as they hastened up Whitechapel High Street and onto Aldgate.

"Where are we going?" she called to the figure striding five feet in front of her.

"To Bury Street," was the terse answer.

"Why are you so upset?" No reply.

Alastair's pace slowed when they encountered a knot of people on the sidewalk. A constable knelt next to a woman lying on the ground while the crowd murmured amongst themselves.

Alastair elbowed his way through. "I'm a doctor. May I be of assistance?"

"Not unless you can cure her of drink," the constable replied. He hoisted the inert form to her feet and butted her up against the side of the building. She promptly slid back to the ground, insensate. "Anybody know this woman?" There were no takers.

Cynda pressed through the throng as Alastair knelt by the incapacitated figure. Something about the scene tugged at her memory. She studied the woman's clothing: the usual Whitechapel attire of a black jacket with cheap fur around the collar and cuffs, a green skirt, a dirty apron and a pair of men's boots. Her black straw hat was askew.

Hat. That was it. The woman had complimented Cynda on her hat at the pub the other night.

A second constable arrived, and after more discussion, Alastair returned to Cynda's side. "They're taking her to the police station," he reported, turning up his collar. "It's just as well. It looks like rain. At least she'll be inside on a night like this."

Cynda stared at the woman intently. Something clicked. "Which police station?"

"Bishopsgate."

"What time is it?"

He pulled out his pocket watch and studied it. "About half past eight."

"We're on Aldgate, right?" she asked.

"Yes. Why?"

Eight-thirty. Aldgate High Street. Two constables. Bishopsgate Police Station.

The dots connected. She covered the shiver slithering along her spine by rearranging Annabelle's cloak. "Nothing," she whispered.

The cops pried the drunk off the ground with considerable effort. She wobbled between them in an oblivious stupor. In five short hours, she would join the list of the dead, her name forever remembered as one of the Ripper's victims.

Alastair continued his forced march, heedless of Cynda's internal torment. The chill settling into her marrow had nothing to do with the night air. Being a Rover meant taking risks, visiting time periods that were anything but picturesque. Now it felt as if history had turned the tables, sweeping her along like a branch caught in a raging torrent. In its wake, all would perish.

She trailed behind Alastair, paying little attention to where they were going, the face of the drunken woman filling her mind. He turned right onto a side street and then left into a passage, with Cynda ten steps behind. The moment she stepped out of the passage and into the open, her throat tightened. Though it was dimly lit, she could make out the giant lettering on the building to her right.

Kearley & Tonge.

Her eyes tracked the doctor's movements, his footsteps echoing as he crossed the deserted square. *Why did he come this way?* She quickened her pace, her eyes instinctively drawn to a stretch of ground to her left near the back of a building. In a few hours, that piece of pavement would be covered by the rapidly cooling corpse of Kate Eddowes, the woman currently on her way to Bishopsgate Police Station.

Cynda bolted through the carriageway and onto Mitre Street, as if the killer were on her heels.

Alastair turned at her sudden rush. "Is something wrong?" he asked. He looked back the way they'd come. "Is someone following us?"

"No," she said, "I just..." *God, I don't want be here. Not tonight.*

"We're nearly there," he said, taking her elbow and steering her on with increased haste. "I pray we're in time."

22

A young boy ran in front of them, shouting a greeting. Alastair winced as the lad urgently tugged on his injured arm.

"You came!" the boy cried. Then he became grave in an instant. "She isn't good, doc. All stove up in her chest."

"Don't worry, Davy, I'll do what I can," Alastair replied. "I am sorry we weren't here sooner. We were out of London for the day."

"It's all right; you came. I knew you would." The boy shifted his attention to Cynda. He was probably about twelve years old, though judging the age of a street urchin was nearly impossible. Dirty face, ragged clothes, a slight limp.

Right out of one of Dickens' stories.

The boy tapped his cap in respect. "Miss," he said.

"Good evening, Davy."

He waved them forward. "This way. Mind the floor," he warned.

From Cynda's point of view, calling the structure they were entering a "building" would be overly generous. It stank of mildew, and where the floor didn't have gaping holes, it was covered in refuse. As she followed the pair, she stepped on something soft. Jerking away in surprise, she saw that it was a dead cat. Cynda swallowed hard to keep her supper from joining it.

Midway up the staircase, the doctor paused. "Davy, you help Miss Lassiter up, and I'll go tend to your mother."

"Right, doc."

Before Cynda could reply, the doctor was on the move, dodging right and left like a climber working up the side of a treacherous mountain. As she approached, she realized why he moved in such an erratic fashion. There were jagged holes in some of the stair treads, and no railing. The remaining stairs looked spongy, ready to collapse as soon as you put any weight on them.

"Mind you, don't touch the walls. They move," Davy advised.

"Move?" she repeated incredulously, peering more closely at the nearest one. The boy wasn't jesting. The wall rippled as if something were living underneath it. Lots of somethings. Somehow, she didn't think they were illusionary.

"Oh, great," she muttered.

"Here, take me hand, miss," the lad offered. "I'll help you."

"Thank you." *Why didn't I stay at the boarding house?*

Her skirts proved a liability, catching on the jagged boards as she ascended. The tenants were aware of which steps were sound and which were not: It was all a matter of practice. Put your foot wrong, and you fell through and snapped an ankle. Simple enough.

"The landlord should fix these," she sputtered.

"He don't do nothing but collect the rent," Davy said, "and offer to cut a little off if me mum would go with him." Cynda stared at the boy when she realized what he meant. "She tells him no," Davy added.

"Good for her."

By the time Cynda reached the second floor, she was sweating through her dress. Davy set off like a shot for the last door at the end of a dismal corridor. As she followed, an argument rose in the apartment to the right, followed by the screeching howl of a baby.

She found Alastair sitting on a rickety chair near his patient's bed. Davy's mother was so pale, Cynda thought she might be carved of ice—so thin, she nearly melted into the bed. A low, rasping sound came from her lungs, like pushing air through syrup. Davy huddled near the head of the bed, holding his mother's hand. His lip quivered, a flicker away from sobs.

"When did the fever start?" Alastair asked, returning his stethoscope to the Gladstone. The woman started to answer, and he shook his head. "Let Davy answer. You work on breathing." A feeble nod.

"This morning. She went to work 'spite of it. Said they'd give her the sack."

Cynda ground her teeth at the thought. A visual tour of the meager hovel didn't improve her mood: a tiny table, a couple of chairs, the single bed, a pallet near the cold fireplace. Two books sat on the tabletop. She leaned over to study them. One was a Bible. She peered at the verse. *"The Lord is my shepherd; I shall not want,"* she whispered. A child's primer sat open to a lesson; a grimy piece of paper adorned with writing sat in front of it, the stub of a worn pencil resting on top.

"I...can't...pay...you," Mrs. Butler croaked.

"No payment required," Alastair said. "Davy helps out at the clinic, and he's a good lad. I want you to take some medicine every three hours. It will ease the pain in your chest." He looked up at the boy. "Ensure she takes it. Don't halve the dose to save it for later. Use it all. It will help her breathe. When you run low, I'll bring more. Do you understand?"

"Right, doc. How much does she take?" the lad asked, his voice stronger now. The task appeared to buoy him.

"I'll show you," Alastair said, rising from the bed. He beckoned Davy near the single candle on the table and demonstrated how to measure the medicine. The boy scrunched his face in concentration, nodding occasionally.

Not knowing what else to do, Cynda sat near the ill woman, taking her hand. It boiled inside hers. She looked about Cynda's age, maybe younger.

"Take...care...of...my...son."

Cynda's heart sank. The woman knew how ill she was.

"We will until you're well enough to take care of him yourself."

A painfully slow nod. Cynda smoothed back the woman's damp hair. *What must it be like to live like this?*

Alastair returned from his tutelage and administered the first dose while Davy watched intently. The bottle looked like the one they'd found in Chris' pocket, except this label was intact. Once the task was complete, the doctor gestured Cynda to join him near the empty fireplace.

"She needs nourishing food and some coal for the fire. Can you go with Davy and purchase some?"

Down those stairs again? "Sure." When he began to dig through his pockets, she shook her head. "I've got money."

He looked at her feet. "Best to retrieve it now than on the street."

"Good idea."

"If you can locate some clean linen, I'll make a chest poultice to help draw out the infection."

"I'll see what we can find."

Alastair grew solemn. "Please be very careful."

"Don't worry, doc; I'll watch out for her," Davy said with more bravado in his voice than boys twice his age.

Alastair patted him on the shoulder. "I'm sure you will, son."

After Cynda liberated money from her boot, much to the lad's amusement, they retreated down the stairs. The sound of pouring rain greeted them, right on schedule. She flipped open the umbrella and Davy shifted the coal scuttle in his hands to crowd underneath.

"This way, miss," he said, pointing into the rain.

"Jacynda," she replied.

"David Edward Butler," he said proudly, and they shook hands. "Sounds right posh, don't it?"

"Yes, it does."

"I'm named after me dad." The boy's face lost its smile. "Mum's not goin' to get better, is she? She has that look they have right before they go away. Me sister and me brother looked the same."

Cynda put her hand on his shoulder. "Doctor Montrose will do his best."

The boy nodded sadly. "He did right by me. He wouldn't give up. Others would have let me lay in the muck and die, but not him. He's a saint, he is, and I'll have none say a word agin' him."

"Yes, he's a saint," she agreed, marveling at the heart of the man.

Davy gave her penetrating look. "Are you his lady?"

"Me? No, just a friend."

The boy brightened. "I'd like him to take a shine to me mum. She'd be all right for him."

"She's a very nice woman."

The boy gave a nod. "She'll make a fine angel someday."

Davy proved an excellent escort, despite the deluge. The rain was a mixed blessing: It soaked their clothes, but also drove the nastier folk off the street. On their rounds through some of the most desolate back alleys she'd ever encountered, they found stew, fresh bread and a couple of apples. Another stop netted them reasonably clean linens, which Cynda tucked under her clothes to keep dry. Throughout their journey, folks called to the boy by name, asking about his mother. He put on a brave front and returned the banter without revealing the truth.

Pleased with their finds, the lad's spirits continued to rise with each step.

"Mum will love the apples. She never gets to eat them. They'll put her right for sure."

"Good. Now, where do we find coal?" Cynda asked, examining the sodden-gray world around them. How the child found his way in this Stygian darkness baffled her. No wonder the Queen had harped about the lack of streetlights in the East End.

"This way," Davy said, pointing. He set off at a brisk clip.

Once the coal scuttle was full and covered by a piece of burlap to keep the rain off, they headed back toward Davy's *crib*, as he called it. When they encountered any suspicious figures, he glowered and puffed himself up. A couple of them chuckled at his antics, but none challenged him.

Fearing she'd stumble and drop the food, Cynda made Davy climb the stairs first, provisions in hand. By the time she reached the top step, sweating and out of breath, he'd already made his delivery and raced back.

"It's good the landlord...isn't where I can get...my hands around his neck," she gasped.

Davy stared at her in surprise. "You'd *strangle* him?"

"I would, at least until he promised to fix the damned stairs." A moment too late, she realized she'd sworn. Davy's eyes grew wide. "Sorry."

"Best not say that in front of me mum," he advised. "She's got some wicked soap and she'll use it on you."

"I'll behave myself," Cynda promised with a wink.

He winked back and took her hand, guiding her the remaining few steps to his home.

The nourishing food and warm fire seemed to revive the patient. The poultice—some gruesome-smelling concoction the doctor made from whatever was lurking in his bag—proved as helpful as all the other treatments. In time, Davy's mother fell asleep, her breathing less labored.

"Give her the medicine as I ordered," Alastair whispered near the lad's ear, "and I'll be back in the morning."

"I'll do it, doc."

"If there is any change, come for me at once." Davy gave a nod, then a long yawn. "And wash your face, will you?" A grin this time.

There was no conversation as the doctor and Cynda negotiated the treacherous stairs. Rain pelted the open entrance in endless torrents, sending a fine spray in their faces.

Alastair looked back the way they'd come. "She has an infection in her chest. If I can break her fever, she'll live. If not..."

She'll make a fine angel. "If she dies, what happens to Davy?" Cynda asked.

"He'll either live on the streets or go into one of the orphanages."

"Just like Oliver Twist," she murmured.

Alastair nodded. "I intend to see that doesn't happen. His mother and I spoke while you were out. If she passes on, I'll support the lad until he's grown."

She stared upward into the doctor's rain-dampened face.

"How? You have barely enough money as it is. You were living on the 'one apple for supper' plan a short time ago."

"I will take on other work as needed."

"You already work more hours in a day than—"

He raised his hand to silence her. "I promised the woman I would look after her son and I shall do it, no matter the personal cost. He may not seem like much to you, but given a decent upbringing he could become a doctor, or even a member of Parliament someday. All he requires is a chance."

She tipped up on her toes, placing her palms on either side of his face. He smiled at her touch.

"You're incredible, Doctor Alastair Montrose. You refuse to give up."

"Much like you, Miss Jacynda Lassiter."

"What I do is not important. You make a difference."

A snort. "I'd debate that."

"It's too wet to argue; let's go home." She hesitated. "What time is it?"

He pulled out the watch and angled it until he could read the dial.

"Half-past eleven." He looked up, snapping it closed. "You are very curious about the time."

"Part of the job."

Alastair crowded under the umbrella. After some fumbling, they switched tasks to accommodate their injured arms; she toted the Gladstone in her left hand while he held the umbrella in the right to shield them from the deluge.

"We'll take the royal way home," he announced.

"Pardon?"

"King Street to Duke Street. It's as close to royalty as either of us will ever get."

"Speak for yourself. I've met King Henry the Eighth."

He blinked in astonishment. "I'm surprised he didn't take you to wife, or at least to bed. He was a lecherous old sod."

She waggled an eyebrow. "He chatted me up, but I'm no fool. I know how that story ends."

His laughter rang out, momentarily warming the night. "Queen Jacynda. You would have been as good as Old Bess."

She beamed. "Thank you. That's quite a compliment."

He swept downward in a bow, getting drenched for his gallantry. "Your Grace."

"Your Lordship," she purred back, executing a tolerable curtsey. "It is time we seek our beds, sir, and the respite of sleep," she said, taking his arm.

"You're sounding more like a native with each passing day," he observed.

I know. I know.

✛

The boarding house was quiet, except for someone's aggressive snoring. The doctor waited while Cynda fumbled with her key. Once her door swung open, she swept inside, wet skirt dragging behind her.

Alastair spied a square of white on the floor. "Something for you," he said, bending over and retrieving it. Cynda lit the candle and sank into a chair to study it.

"It's from a hotel called Morley's, postmarked this afternoon," she said. Her name was written in a wide hand, the ink smeared after her damp passage across it. At first glance, she would have thought it to be from her companion, the penmanship was so similar. She ripped the letter open.

Miss Lassiter,
It has come to my attention that you are seeking my person. I suspect this is in regard to the matter of my "future." I will meet you at Paul's Head Public House (Crispin Street) tomorrow evening (Sunday) at eight sharp so that we may put this matter right.
Sincerely,
Samuelson, W.J. (Dr.)

She dropped the letter into her lap with a sigh.

Alastair knelt by the chair, gazing upward at her. "Is it your tourist?"

"Yes. He wants to meet tomorrow evening."

The doctor's face fell. "So soon." She handed him the letter and he scanned it. "Then you'll go home tomorrow," he said so softly she could barely hear him.

"Yes. I'll need to collect Chris first."

His eyes returned to the letter. "I shall miss you."

Cynda could only nod, her emotions too tangled for conversation. Alastair rose in silence. She heard the door to his room open and close, followed by the sound of water splashing in the washbasin and then the creak of his bed. She could imagine him staring at the ceiling.

Unlacing her boots, Cynda strained to pull them off. She arrayed the rest of her damp garments over the chair in the vain hope they'd be dry by morning. Sitting on the bed, she massaged her reddened feet. This would be her last night here. The thought saddened her. She would bring Chris home, but never solve his murder. That felt like a shard of glass to the heart—a wound that would never heal.

23

Sunday, 30 September, 1888

Somewhere, a door closed and footsteps echoed in the hall. Cynda jolted out of her sleep, rising from the bed in slow-motion. Muzzy, she dragged herself to the window. A shadowy figure paused under the gas lamp. It was the doctor.

"Don't you ever sleep?"

Retrieving the pocket watch from under the pillow, she pried it open. 12:30.

"No, no, you idiot! What the hell are you doing?" Within a half an hour, another woman would be dead. He couldn't be on the streets now.

Unless he's...

There it was: the question that had taunted her from the moment Keats mentioned the doctor and the killer in the same breath. There was only way to find out if the saint possessed the twisted soul of a madman. Frantic she'd lose him, she dressed in a blur, battling her wet stockings. The sodden bootlaces refused to go through the holes. Swearing, she wound them as tightly as possible around her ankles and tied them in a bunchy knot. The damp petticoat and navy dress slipped over her body, generating goose bumps. As if knowing it was best not to fight her, the bodice buttons closed without much effort. Stashing the pocket watch into its hiding place, she grabbed the cloak and fled the boarding house, heedless to the noise she made.

Alastair was gone by the time she reached the rain-sluiced street. The pavement glistened from the downpour, but gave no indication which direction he'd gone.

"Where are you?" she murmured. "Davy's? No, you weren't

carrying your bag. Clinic? Maybe..." Cynda slammed her open palm against the cold lamppost in aggravation. She could make guesses all night and still not find him.

Use your head, Lassiter.

She knew where the murders would be committed; all she had to do was go to the crime scenes and pray Alastair Montrose wasn't anywhere near them.

But he's a shifter. How will I know it's him?

By the time she reached Whitechapel High Street, she knew her makeshift arrangement with the boots wasn't going to work. Choosing a reasonably dry set of steps, Cynda sat and fiddled with the lacing, blowing on her fingers to warm them. All the while, her heart hammered in her chest. She had no reason to be out on a night when two women would die; one who would be "ripped up like a pig in the market," according to the constable who would discover the body. Being a Time Rover gave Cynda no immunity from a blade. If she arrived too early, catching the killer at his handiwork, she could become a victim of old Jack.

"That'd piss off TIC," she muttered. "Talk about buggering history." A Time Incursion of epic proportions. Once an event became "embedded," it was damned difficult to reverse—especially if there was a body.

Cynda angled onto Commercial Street at the intersection where it met Whitechapel High Street. Despite the earlier rain, people were going about their business, headed home after a long day of work or seeking entertainment of the liquid or female sort. And there were females to be found. After three weeks and no further deaths, the prostitutes appeared to be weighing practicality with safety. Coins had to be made for food, rent or gin.

It wasn't until Cynda hurried along Back Church Lane that her doubts resurfaced with stunning intensity. *What the hell am I doing? Does it really matter if Alastair's the killer?* By tomorrow night she'd be home, and all of this would be behind her. Knowing that the doctor wasn't the Ripper would make no difference.

Or would it?

She leaned against a brick wall to give one of her boots a vicious tug.

"Curiosity and cats," she said. One way or another, she had to know. It was just one of those things.

A couple years back, right before she'd started her travel into Victorian England, she attended a presentation on the Whitechapel killings. The lecturer, a dull, graying academic with a stultifying monotone, had rambled on for two hours about the deaths. His dry recitation had stuck with her solely because it had sounded so devoid of emotion.

"*'Elizabeth Stride, found at one in the morning between No. 40 and 42 Berner Street, throat cut. No mutilations. Catherine Eddowes, found at 1:45 a.m. in Mitre Square, throat cut, extensive bodily mutilation.'"* A grim recitation of statistics, rather than lives lost. It had grated on her then. Now, on the streets of Whitechapel, it felt obscene.

She hesitated at a narrow passageway connecting the lane to Berner Street. Though there was a gas lamp mounted on the wall at the entrance, further in was far too dark for her liking. It would make an ideal escape route for the killer once he'd finished his work a block away.

"I have to know," she said.

After a deep breath, she inched into the passage, sliding a hand along the rough wall to navigate. She took one cautious step at a time, her knees shaking.

She'd gone a short distance when something snarled in the dark. She jumped in fright, swearing under her breath. The luminescent glow of cat's eyes glared back at her, a dead rat hanging from its mouth.

Cynda sighed in relief. *It's all yours. I'll get the next one.*

The cat skittered away. Cynda continued to make slow progress, twitching at every sound.

There was another snarl, followed by a high-pitched yowl. Someone had just stepped on the beast.

Cynda crammed into a doorway, the bustle digging into her back. Steps grew closer, hurried, but not running—solid footfalls, like someone wearing heavy boots.

And then they stopped.

Cynda held her breath. *A lag hallucination?* Not likely. *Why doesn't he move? Had he heard her?*

As if in betrayal, her injured shoulder cramped, causing her to gasp aloud.

Silence. A half-second later, a shout cut the air. She slammed herself back into the niche.

"Murder! Police!" a man's voice cried.

Liz Stride's body had been discovered.

No sound from the passageway. She edged outward. If the body had been found, would the killer be loitering? Most likely he'd be headed toward Mitre Square and his second engagement.

Unless there were two killers.

Knowing she could stay rooted in fear until dawn, Cynda

summoned her courage and hurried back the way she'd come. As she fled, she listened for the sound of pursuing footsteps. There were none.

Once she reached Back Church Lane, her nerves collapsed. Nauseous, she leaned against a wall, swallowing repeatedly to keep from vomiting. There was no need to check her watch; it would be just past one in the morning.

The shrill howl of a police whistle rent the air: Constable Lamb summoning aid. Shortly, Berner Street would be chock-full of the morbidly curious.

Cynda retraced her steps along the lane. She'd been too late to glimpse Liz Stride's killer. If she hurried, there was still a chance to learn the truth.

⚜

Jonathon Keats stood at the edge of the crowd attempting to appear innocuous, his gut in knots. *En mirage* as a sailor, he had no desire to trigger the interest of the numerous constables prowling between him and Whitechapel's latest murder.

Moving around for a better view, he tipped up on his toes to peer at the victim. A man was kneeling beside the body, examining it in the light of a bull's-eye lantern. The dead woman was lying on her left side with her feet drawn up in a fetal position, blood clotting at the neck. She wore a black cloth jacket, and pinned to the right side were red and white flowers. Her bonnet lay on the ground nearby.

He sighed in relief as he lowered himself. It wasn't Jacynda.

Someone near him asked, "Who's the bloke looking at her?"

"A doc from up on Commercial Road. Blackwell's his name," another answered.

"Was she done like the others?"

The first man nodded. "Cut her throat."

"Bless her soul," a woman murmured, crossing herself.

Keats slid away. His night had been filled with unpleasant choices. To his supreme irritation, the Fenian remained elusive. Despite covering a half-dozen pubs and dozing through a spiritless lecture on *Socialism and the Common Man* at a workers' hall, he'd not encountered a whiff of Flaherty.

Hiking along Whitechapel High Street in a foul mood, he'd spotted Alastair loitering under a lamp. He'd intended to challenge him, but his friend set off at a brisk clip toward Aldgate Station. That was when Keats spied Jacynda inexplicably heading east, into the heart of Whitechapel.

It had been an ugly choice: Alastair or the pretty lady. His choice of the latter now put him squarely in the middle of a crime.

"What are you doing out here?" Keats growled under his breath. *I would have thought the other night had cured you of this sort of nonsense.*

He caught sight of his target near the brewery on Commercial Street. The way she walked, it appeared her feet were hurting. Her shoulders drooped. He tensed when a man approached her. There was a brief exchange, and she walked around him with a shake of the head. The fellow continued along the street until he encountered another woman, this one more amiable to his proposal. She nodded, and they walked away together.

In his heart, Keats preferred not to think that Miss Lassiter stole along the streets earning her room and board, but as a cop, he'd seen worse. He once questioned a well-bred young woman from Knightsbridge who dressed in shabby clothes and made her way to Whitechapel, earning coins from filthy men in exchange for sexual favors. When he asked her why in God's name she would do such a dangerous thing when she obviously did not need the money, the response had stunned him. "For a lark, Sergeant," she'd said. "Life is so dull in Knightsbridge." A few months after he'd spoken with her, she'd been committed to an asylum to shield her family from public ridicule. He shuddered at the memory even now.

Jacynda sped up her footsteps, sensing his presence. To her credit, she did not look backward in panic. After a brief hesitation at New Castle Street, she turned toward the boarding house. He paused, watching her disappear into the distance.

"Thank God. Now stay there," he said, flipping open his watch. 1:18. As he closed the lid and tucked it away, his stomach growled, reminding him he'd not had any food since that afternoon. There was a chandler's a few blocks away; he'd eat and then try to locate Alastair. Hopefully his friend had a realistic alibi, or there would be more questions come morning.

‡

The man who'd trailed behind her continued on his way, reducing one worry. If Cynda's mental map of Whitechapel was accurate, she could go north for a bit, angle west and then south toward Mitre Square. A quick peek at her watch told her she'd have to hustle. The roundabout way would chew up precious minutes, and history wasn't inclined to wait for anyone—even a Rover.

Despite a wrong turn, Cynda's timing was nearly perfect. She positioned herself at the north end of Duke Street, checking the watch every few seconds in nervous distraction. The door to The Imperial Club at No. 16 opened. A trio of men exited, talking amongst themselves. Unaware of her presence, they sauntered south, toward the main road.

Hiding the watch, she took a few tentative steps forward. It was vital she not be seen or her description would be splattered across the morning papers. The men continued on, chatting back and forth, ignorant of the role they would play over the next few minutes.

In the distance, past the synagogue on the right, a couple loitered near Church Passage. As the trio passed by, one of them hung back to study the pair. As if satisfied, he caught up with his companions and they walked on toward Aldgate High Street, leaving the couple behind.

Cynda crept forward. If she were lucky, she could pass by Kate and her killer right before they entered the passage to Mitre Square. If luck were with her, the man wouldn't be Alastair Montrose.

What if it is? If he'd shifted, how could she tell?

Her folly reared its head. *What if he hadn't changed form?* What did she expect him to do when she recognized him—nod as if to say *'You caught me,'* and then go about his infernal business?

"It's not him," she whispered like a mantra. "It can't be."

The couple continued their conversation, oblivious to her approach. Kate looked in better shape than earlier while on the way to the police station.

Why didn't you go the doss house? Why are you here with him?

Cynda grew closer. She kept her pace, as if in no particular hurry. The man appeared to be roughly the same height as Alastair. He had a moustache as well, though fuller than the doctor's. He held himself differently. Wouldn't a shifter do the same, mimicking the illusion he or she had created?

It can't be him.

The man braced himself against the wall with his left hand, leaning toward Kate as he spoke to her in hushed tones. She nodded and tapped his shoulder lightly, laughing at whatever he'd said.

'Come into my parlor,' said the spider to the fly.

As Cynda walked by, the man averted his face. He leaned

further in toward his victim, the loose salt and pepper-colored jacket swinging forward. Cynda's eyes were riveted on the red handkerchief at his neck: the perfect way to clean the blade after he'd finished.

Kate looked over, recognized her and winked, then returned to her conversation.

Cynda forced herself not to look back until she reached the main road. When she did, the street behind her was empty. An electric shudder surged through her. Had Kate reached the darkest corner of the square with her john? Were his hands around her neck, snuffing the life out of her? Or was he drawing the long blade from its hiding place beneath the loose coat and cutting away her clothes?

Cynda fled, tears burning her eyes. The man with Kate Eddowes couldn't be Alastair—not unless his arm had miraculously healed to permit him to so casually loiter against a wall, allow him to strangle another human being. Her morbid curiosity had been fed.

The truth was poor consolation for the woman dying in Mitre Square.

24

Cynda stumbled up the street, block after block, oblivious to her surroundings. Tears streamed down her face for Kate, and all the others who died in back alleys. If there were ever a demarcation in Cynda's life, it was now: A jagged red line separating indifference from brutal reality. In the past, she'd zipped into a time period, did what she needed to do and zipped back out, untouched by the people she'd met, more fascinated with the places than the inhabitants. As the Rovers' black humor put it, "Here today, dead tomorrow."

Chris had joked that it was like theater. You watched the play, but when it was all over, you shuffled out of the building, never caring what happened after the curtain closed. Now all Cynda saw were the actors, each and every one of them. She was part of the play, caught up in it. Instead of revulsion, now she marveled at the small things: the flower vendor selling vivid crimson roses that appeared in lapels and pinned to women's jackets; the smell of fresh-baked bread and yeasty beer; the raucous singing that flowed out of the dance halls at all hours; the tiny monkey who flipped his hat for coins while his master ground out a tune on the barrel organ.

Behind her, a police whistle screamed in the night air like a banshee. Cynda's hand flew to her mouth. Constable Watkins had just entered Mitre Square and discovered the most horrific sight of his entire police career.

Leaning against a lamppost, tears threatened again. As she fought for control, her mind conjured up the grainy autopsy photograph, the patchwork quilt of a human being that had once been Catherine Eddowes. If being a Time Rover meant not caring, then Cynda's career was over. She could never again look into the face of a prostitute without thinking of Kate, remembering that last laugh with the man who would destroy her.

There was the sound of approaching footsteps. She ignored them. A hand grabbed her arm; she spun out of its grasp. Grappling for the truncheon in her pocket, she pulled it free.

"Hold on!" Keats demanded. He was dressed in his usual dark suit and bowler, his eyes glowing angry. "What in God's name are you doing on the street alone at this hour? Have you no notion of how dangerous it is?" Before she could answer, he pointed at her face. "You've been crying."

"I was trying to find Alastair," she snapped, slapping away his hand. "Why are *you* here?"

"I was..." he hesitated, and then his anger dissipated in a stream of air from his lips. "Doing the same." They stared at each other.

"He went out earlier," she said.

"I know. I followed you instead. While you don't give a fig about your life, some of us do."

"A fig?" she asked, amused. She stashed her weapon into the skirt pocket, covering it with the cloak.

"A fig," he repeated, his face set, clearly not in any mood for humor. "Come, let's get you home." He reached for her arm, but she pulled away.

He sighed. "You are so stubborn."

They walked on in silence. From behind them, another police whistle. Keats half-turned, pensive. "What the devil?" he said. "It couldn't be..."

"Sir?" a voice called out.

They turned and found a policeman a few feet away, a hand resting on his truncheon.

"Yes, Constable?" Keats replied.

"Just wishing to know your business, sir, given the late hour."

"I am escorting the lady home," Keats replied.

The constable's attention shifted to Cynda, using her clothing to measure her social status. She could almost hear the mental calculations; not posh but clean and tidy. Probably not a whore, but if so, one who commanded a living wage. Definitely a woman with no sense to be out at this hour.

"Your name, sir?" the constable asked, moving his attention back to her companion. Blessedly, he'd not noted she'd been crying.

"Keats."

"Occupation?"

There was a hesitation, a murmur under his breath, and then

Keats produced a card from his coat pocket. The constable moved forward and took it, squinting at the print.

A blush of embarrassment. "Oh, sorry, Detective-Sergeant. We're under orders to speak to every couple we encounter after midnight. Just checking all is right, you understand."

"Quite proper."

"Right you are, sir," the constable said, returning the card to Keats. "It's been a nasty night. First the one in Berner Street, and now..."

"Another one? Where?"

"Mitre Square, sir. And this one's..." The constable stopped abruptly, gave Cynda an uncomfortable look, and then his eyes returned to Keats. "A right bad one, they say."

"Good God," Keats murmured, shaking his head.

"Are you headed to your homes, sir?" the constable asked. Apparently, he'd written them off as being harmless, but he was still doing his duty.

"Yes, we are."

"Very good, sir. I shan't keep you."

"Good luck in your hunt, Constable."

The man touched his cap in respect. "Thank you, Sergeant. Good morning, miss."

Once the copper was out of range, Cynda grabbed Keats' arm and pulled him toward her. "Detective-Sergeant?"

He gave a boyish shrug, as if he'd been caught with his hands in the cookie jar.

"City of London or Metropolitan Police?"

"Special Branch."

The big boys. No wonder Jonathon had been so thorough in taking Chris' description. *And Alastair told him how Chris died.*

"Alastair doesn't know you're a cop, does he?"

"I'd prefer he not know until I tell him."

"Why all the secrecy?"

"I am on an assignment that demands it."

"You're after the Rip..." She glossed over her near-blunder, "the...Whitechapel killer, aren't you?"

"No, I'm not."

That caught her off-guard. "Oh."

"The last I saw Alastair, he was on Aldgate, headed west. I suspect he is communing with that new bridge they're building on the Thames. He seems to have a morbid fascination with it."

"He's a techno-junkie," she said without thinking.

"Pardon?" Keats asked.

"Ah…he's quite keen on technology."

"Ah, yes. He says he does his best thinking whilst staring at the thing. Makes no sense to me."

She waited for him to ask about Chris, but he didn't. An uncomfortable thought rose. *Does he think Alastair killed him?*

Her mind raged with questions until they reached the street that led to the boarding house. Cynda stopped and placed a hand on Jonathon's shoulder. For a second, Kate flashed into her mind. "I can walk the rest of the way."

"Are you sure?" he asked, scanning the street for threats. "I should escort you to your door."

"No, I want you to find Alastair."

He studied her, and then gave her a brusque nod. "Have a safe trip back to New York, Jacynda. I shall miss you. I do wish you would write me when you can."

"That might prove a bit difficult, Jonathon," she said. *More than you realize.*

Instant chagrin. "I see."

"It isn't because I don't want to write you, it's…"

Oh, God that sounded pathetic.

Knowing no other way to apologize, she stepped forward, placed her hands on either side of his face and drew him toward her. The kiss wasn't hurried. If anything she lingered, savoring it. His arms went around her waist and drew her in, making her shoulder protest.

When the kiss ended, a sad smile appeared.

"I shall miss you even more now." He stepped back, and then strode away without giving his signature bow. She wondered if it was to keep her from seeing his eyes.

‡

As predicted, Keats found his friend parked on a bench along the Thames, hands folded over his chest. The doctor nodded, as if not surprised to see him, and then returned his concentration to the incomplete structure.

"Our masters send you to fetch me?" the doctor asked sourly.

"No."

"Then why are you out at this hour? Just rolling out of some dolly-mop's bed?"

Keats' mouth twitched. "I've been trying to locate you."

"Why?"

"Stand up and take off your coat," Keats ordered.

Alastair's head swiveled around. "What?"

"Do as I say. I must verify there is no blood on you."

"Blood?"

"There's been two more murders."

"Where?"

"Berner Street and Mitre Square," Keats replied.

"Good heavens. I walked through Mitre Square just this evening."

"Why?"

"To see a patient on Bury Street."

Keats pointed. "Take off your coat."

"How dare—" Alastair stormed, rising to his feet.

"Just do it, damn you!"

Alastair stripped off his coat and flung it at his friend. He extended his hands like a child commanded to show he'd washed properly, flipping them over to expose the other side. "Do you want me to strip naked as well?"

Ignoring his sarcasm, Keats studied both hands, paying particular attention to the fingernails. He surveyed the coat and then knelt to examine his friend's pant legs. There was no sign of blood.

"Thank you," he said curtly.

Alastair snatched his coat. "How dare you suggest that I—"

"For God's sake, Alastair, use your good sense! You were out on your own when two women were murdered. You need someone to vouch for you. Jacynda was worried—"

"Jacynda?"

"She heard you leave the boarding house and followed you."

Alastair blanched. "Oh God. Tell me she's safe."

"She is unharmed. I escorted her home."

Alastair sighed in relief. "Thank you for that."

He sank onto the bench, staring into the flowing darkness. "She knows I'm a Transitive."

"What?" Keats exclaimed.

"I fell asleep in the carriage from Colney Hatch. I *ventured,* and she caught me. I had no choice but to confess."

"Oh, lord," Keats moaned. He slumped on the bench next to the doctor. "Yet another complication."

"I inadvertently revealed your secret, as well. She has figured out that you were *en mirage* as a constable the night I was injured."

"Oh, bloody hell!" A furious frown. "What else can go wrong?"

"Jacynda won't be inclined to speak of her discovery. She is not entirely without her own secrets."

In the distance came a rhythmic splashing as a rowboat oared its way along the Thames. Keats gazed out at the twin pylons.

"Why does this bridge enchant you so much?"

A moment passed. "It looks so powerful, yet it was created by man. That means it must be flawed. Only God is perfect."

"God created man, and *we're* hardly perfect," Keats observed.

"You are agnostic, aren't you?" Keats nodded. "I must admit, I wonder sometimes. Why *would* God make man so flawed?"

"Perhaps to watch us learn and grow," Keats said.

"Well, He must be deeply disappointed. We're not very quick students, are we?"

"No, we're not. Come, let's find a hansom and I'll drop you at the boarding house. I need to get some sleep."

"Did I interrupt your appointed rounds tonight?" Alastair asked, his tone more sociable.

"In a way, my friend; in a way." *You may have complicated my life beyond measure.*

‡

The knock at Cynda's door wasn't a surprise. She knew Keats would find the errant doctor, who would then learn about the killings. And then Alastair would think about her real job and what that entailed. *How can I justify what I don't believe?*

When she cracked the door, Alastair was standing on the other side. Under his exhaustion lurked another emotion: moral outrage. Not waiting for her invitation, he pushed into the room.

Cynda closed the door and leaned against it. *What if she'd been wrong and the man she'd seen near Mitre Square was in her bedroom at this moment? Had he fooled both her and Jonathon?*

"You knew," he said in a low whisper, like a cold draught over the moors. "You knew and you didn't stop it!"

Mindful of the others in the boarding house, Cynda whispered back, "I couldn't, Alastair. It's what happened."

"Last night, you constantly asked as to the time. I thought it odd then, but now I know why. You knew precisely when those women would die."

She didn't reply. He stormed on. "Do you realize we walked through Mitre Square on the way to Bury Street?"

"Yes."

"Yet you didn't think to mention that someone would die there a few hours hence?"

"No. A Time Rover isn't allowed to—"

"To hell with that!" he spat in a hoarse whisper, shocking her with his oath. "If your beloved future is so uncaring, so full of itself that you'd let two innocent women be slaughtered, then I wish you'd never come here in the first place."

"In some ways, so do I."

Moving forward, she grasped his arm over the top of the wound, squeezing hard. He winced visibly and yanked it away.

"Why do you insist on doing that? You know that hurts me."

"Because the killer in Mitre Square tonight was leaning against a wall with that arm."

His eyes widened in the dim light. "You *saw* him?"

"Yes."

"My God, do you know how dangerous that was?" he hissed.

"Yes." *Oh God, yes.*

"Why were you there? Bloodthirsty curiosity?"

Their eyes met, and she saw the moment he understood. "You thought it was me..."

"I had to know."

He looked away, disgusted. "Yet you won't go to the police and tell them what you saw."

"I can't change history, Alastair. If I'd warned the two victims and they didn't die, then maybe two others would...ones who weren't meant to."

"No death is acceptable if you can prevent it," he said, glaring back.

She shook her head. "I hate to tell you, but your East-End sadist is a novice. In a couple of decades, you'll be able to rub elbows with a revolutionary living in Whitechapel. When he finishes his reign of terror in Mother Russia, more than thirty million of his countrymen will be dead. Could you creep up behind him and put a bullet in his brain, knowing you'd change the course of history? Could you play God, Doctor Montrose?"

Alastair's body shook. "How can you be so heartless? You know the faces of these poor women, you know their final death agonies, and yet you ignore the chance to save them."

"I am not here to fix things, Alastair. I'm here to collect a tourist and go home."

"Then do your accursed job. The sooner you are out of my life, the better." He flung open the door. Angry footsteps thudded in the hallway and onto the stairs.

Cynda closed the door, but made no effort to go to the window. She knew he'd be striding down the street, righteous indignation in every step.

"I had no choice," she whispered.

25

The scratching of pen on paper filled the candlelit room.

Sunday, 30 September, 1888
Eternal riddles. One sliced, the other assayed. Centuries hence, they shall puzzle on my night's work. Frustration abounds. My quest bears no fruit. Can it truly be so deeply hidden, or am I blind to it? If that is the case, then there is no hope.

‡

The tightly wound mountain of bandages on the examining table testified to Alastair's emotional turmoil. As he rolled the linen, his mind performed the same maneuver, his problems tumbling over and over like a feather caught in a turbulent whirlwind.

Had he been wrong to expect Jacynda to have a heart as big as his? What so deeply attracted him to her? Once she returned to her time, would she laugh at his quaint morals, jesting with her friends about the stuffy doctor who had fallen in love with her?

Exhausted beyond the need for sleep, he rose and leaned in the clinic's doorway as the East End came alive. Things were different this morning. News of the killings had spread fast. Most of the populace seemed to be milling about on the streets, though it was barely past dawn. Clustering in knots around one of their literate neighbors, they listened with rapt attention as he read from the latest edition. Women dabbed at their eyes with handkerchiefs; men sported grim expressions.

"'E'll kill us all in the end," one woman said. "'E's the devil's own."

"The devil's own," Alastair repeated in a coarse whisper.

Locking the clinic, he tracked his way to the boarding house and collected his medical bag. Some part of him was relieved when he didn't encounter Jacynda. Too many ill words had passed between them—ones he didn't feel could be retracted. Hix met him on the stairs, uncommunicative as usual, his eyes concealed behind those smoky spectacles.

Alastair found Davy's mother alone, the room still warm from the coal fire. She rested in bed, a cup of tea, half an apple and the medicine he'd prescribed nearby. The level in the bottle was noticeably lower, and that meant Davy had taken his job seriously. A wan smile from his patient. She straightened the thin blanket over her lap.

"Davy's selling papers. Said...more women died...and he could make...good money. Everyone wants...to read about it," she explained in weak bursts of speech that corresponded with her need to breathe.

Alastair nodded soberly. There was always money to be made in tragedy. It was a reality of life. "It is all the sensation on the streets."

"Where's your nice...lady friend?" the woman asked faintly.

"She's..." He hesitated and then sighed, "returning home today."

"Ah. She's a pretty one."

Alastair sat on the chair next to the bed, warming the stethoscope between his palms. When he deemed it acceptable, he listened to the woman's lungs. They still sounded like bubbly sludge, but were clearer, her skin less fiery to the touch.

"Much better," he said, embroidering the truth. "Your fever's abating."

"I thought so."

His mind wandered as he checked her pulse. Soon, Jacynda would be gone. He'd no longer hear her going up and down the stairs with tentative steps, or be able to chide her about seeing things.

In his anger, he'd branded her heartless. His eyes moved to his patient. Was his professional demeanor any different? He'd kept up a brave front for Mrs. Butler and her son, never revealing the complete truth about her illness. Was that any different than Jacynda's insistence that she couldn't meddle with history?

To his embarrassment, he realized he'd been holding Mrs. Butler's hand and not counting her pulse.

"Sorry, a bit distracted," he said.

"I understand. It's been a...hard night for you."

"Not as hard as yours." A weak nod returned. "I am pleased with your progress."

"It's because of...you and your lady. Davy told me...she gave him hope. It meant a lot...to him."

"I didn't know."

"She gave him money. Told him to buy...proper food. He wouldn't tell...me how much it was. She's got a good soul, that one."

A good soul. "We have to find you a better situation. Your lungs can't tolerate the char work you do." A nod. "You've not been eating right, either. Giving most of it to your son, I suspect." She flattened the blanket again, avoiding his eyes. "I'll see if I can find you somewhere to work that isn't so hard on you."

The woman's brown eyes moved toward his. She took his hand and squeezed it. "You're a good man, doctor. I don't fear dying...knowing you'll watch over Davy."

Alastair stuffed the stethoscope back into his bag, unable to find a suitable reply. She had ultimate faith in him. In truth, he was impotent as any man on the street. He couldn't forestall death any more than could the lady from the future.

‡

"It is being said that we are spending too much time trying to find Flaherty and not enough on others of his ilk," Fisher remarked.

"He'll surface," Keats replied, in no mood to admit his assignment was foundering on the rocks. He'd already heard the rumbles on the way to his boss' office. The 'Ram' was making pointed remarks about how Fisher didn't have his sergeant on a leash, as if he were some high-strung terrier.

"Our superiors have a limited tolerance for the lack of progress," Fisher continued patiently.

"Well, that's their problem," Keats grumbled.

"Pardon?"

Keats's eyes popped up to the Chief Inspector. Realizing he'd been surly, he stammered, "My...apologies, sir. I'm a bit worn out."

"That is obvious. At the rate you're going, you'll age twenty years in a week. And trust me, Sergeant, fifty is not a walk in the park."

That made Keats smile. "No, sir."

"You're trying too hard, young man. I have done the same in your position. I suspect it's not only to bring a criminal to justice but, perhaps, to impress one's superiors along the way?" Keats gave a conciliatory nod. Fisher continued, "Experience has taught me that sometimes you have to let things play out for them to come to fruition. You're pushing yourself beyond what's humanly possible, Keats."

"I want these bastards, sir."

A smirk at his strong language. "Indeed. I want them as well—preferably before they blow up someone important."

Outside Fisher's office, a pair of detectives strolled by, laughing at some joke. Turning back to business, the Chief Inspector asked, "Any luck with your inquiries into the explosives firms?"

"I've heard back from all but two. I'll press them today."

"Are they local?" Keats nodded. "Go see them in person," Fisher ordered. "Impress upon them that when Special Branch makes an inquiry, it is best they respond promptly."

"As you wish, sir."

"What has Doctor Montrose been up to?"

Keats blinked, and then shook his head. "How'd you know I'm still following him?"

"I suspected as much. You've put your good name on the line. If it were I, I'd be watching him closely just in case I were wrong."

Keats nodded in resignation. Fisher was always one step ahead of him.

"Alastair was wandering around alone after midnight last night."

"Really?" Fisher asked, leaning forward, always a sign his attention was captured. "Did you have him under observation during the murders?"

"No. However, I rather rashly examined his person after the fact, and there was no evidence of blood. I also spoke with a constable..." He paused, dug out his notebook and flipped a few pages. "PC Rogers. He verified that Alastair was located on a bench overlooking the Thames at one in the morning when he went off-duty. The constable did not challenge him, as he appeared to be sober and well behaved."

"I see. So he couldn't have been involved in the first killing." Fisher leaned back. "What about the second?"

A shrug. "Alastair admits to being through Mitre Square last night on the way to treat a patient. I will find out who that was and question them…discreetly."

"Does he know you're a copper yet?"

"No. I'm not ready to tell him."

"Good." Fisher selected a file and placed it in the center of his desk, signaling to Keats their discussion was nearing an end. "See to those explosives firms. If there have been no thefts, write up your report and we'll move on."

Keats opened his mouth to protest, but Fisher held up a hand. "We have no choice on this. Word from On High," he said, extending his right index figure toward the ceiling.

"It's a mistake, sir."

Fisher gave a knowing nod. "Precisely."

Keats cocked his head. He knew that tone. Fisher gave him a conspiratorial wink and then shooed him away with a handwave. "Off you go, Sergeant."

"Yes, sir."

As he left Scotland Yard, Keats had the definite impression that he and the Chief Inspector walked a fine line between duty and insubordination. One stumble and Fisher would be in line for a reprimand, making Keats' future exceedingly murky.

"I just to have to find Flaherty," he said. "How difficult can that be?"

†

The evening streets were visceral, packed with roaming citizens whose moods veered from fearful to combative. Some shouted their derision at the police, while others demanded that someone, anyone, be arrested and hung for the crimes. Finding a hansom proved impossible, so Cynda hiked until she reached Bell Lane and then headed north, shifting her bag back and forth as she went. As she traveled, she became privy to all the latest theories.

"He could be a rozzer, for all we know," a costermonger remarked to a customer while he awaited payment for a used pair of boots.

A cop? Keats had said he'd been tracking Alastair the night before. *Was he telling the truth?*

Cynda shook her head. Soon, she'd be pinning the murders on Ralph in '057. What was it about Jack that so captured the imagination, making everyone a potential villain?

She nudged her mind to lighter matters. *Had Alastair found the envelope yet?* She could imagine his face when he stared at the bank papers awarding him a sum of money just over two hundred pounds. TIC would probably quibble about her signing the money over to the doctor, but the way she saw it, it wasn't theirs in the first place. During her last trip to 1789, TIC had ordered her to open the "emergency funding" account for Rover use and then stiffed her for it when she came back, debiting the sum from her paycheck. "No deposit receipt," they'd said, "no refund." No matter how much hell she'd raised, they wouldn't reimburse the money. Ergo, this two hundred pounds in 1888 was hers. Now it belonged to Alastair Montrose to do with as he chose.

He'll make a difference, unlike TIC.

Cynda shifted the hefty Gladstone from one hand to another. She'd had to leave the ruined dress behind, but managed to wedge the truncheon inside the bag, deeming it a souvenir. Chris' remains and urn added another nine pounds to her load. The weight made her fingers ache; she couldn't carry it for long on the right side, or her shoulder retaliated with bolts of fire into her chest. Hopefully, TIC wouldn't notice the extra weight. Maybe they'd think she'd gone heavy on the toffee pudding.

"May I help you with that?" a familiar voice asked.

She looked up with a sigh of relief. Alastair was walking beside her. Rather than anger in his eyes, she saw purpose.

"Yes, that would be great. Chris is heavier than I thought."

He took the bag from her and groaned. "Good lord, he is."

They walked silently for a block before she had the nerve to broach the subject. "I didn't think I'd see you again."

"I realized that I couldn't just let you...disappear—not after what I said to you. I felt I should make amends."

"No need. Some of what you said was right. I've been too...isolated. Last night cleared away a lot of the fog."

"I was still wrong. You're not a heartless person, and I apologize for saying you are."

"Thank you. Still, what's the point of what I do if I'm always a bystander?" She shook her head. "How is Davy's mother?"

"Improved. I believe she will recover. She said you gave the boy money."

"It took some doing. He didn't want to accept it." She eyed him. "Have you been to your room yet?"

"No, not since this morning. Why?"

She flashed a smile. "I left a surprise for you. Consider it a gift."

Alastair suddenly grasped her elbow, drawing her out of the pedestrian flow. Setting the bag on the ground, he pulled her close and cleared his throat. "Send your tourist wherever he needs to go and stay here with me."

Her mouth fell open. "Alastair—"

"You said you've never felt at home, no matter where you are. I think you could here. We could make a life...together."

Did he just...

She was shaking her head before she spoke. "I can't do that," she said. "Going native isn't allowed."

"I don't have much to offer, but I swear you won't have to work the streets to eat." He looked away for a moment, as if gathering his courage. When his eyes returned to her, they were lit with bright fire. "I believe I am in love with you, Jacynda. I don't want you to leave."

She drew in a long breath. *This can't be happening...again.* Before her mind could begin to contemplate what their life would be like, she shook her head again. "I can't stay, Alastair. I just can't."

The doctor's face lost its intensity. "Is it Keats?"

"Jonathon? No, he's..."

"Very keen on you."

"Yes, I think he is." *But not in the same way you are.* "Apparently, you'd led him to believe I was pregnant. He felt honor-bound to do the right thing and asked me to marry him. Of course, I refused his offer."

The doctor blinked in frank surprise. "Oh, dear, I am sorry. I shared my concerns with him and, well...I never would have thought him capable of such a gesture." He kissed her hands. "What prevents you from staying here?"

His query hung in the air between them. She'd been asking herself the same thing, though she'd never dared speak it aloud.

There was little in '057 to call her own: a good friend, a stuffed ferret and a remote family. But to stay here meant making a commitment, believing that in a few months, or years, she'd still find Alastair Montrose a decent man, still worthy of the sacrifice she'd have to make. What if admiration was the best she could give? What if she never grew to love him with the same passion he promised her? Would that be enough?

It was the decision every Victorian woman faced—love versus security.

"I'm not a Victorian," she whispered, pulling her hands away.

Alastair stepped back. "I see." He pulled something out of his pocket. "I believe you will want this."

She took the paper-wrapped item, cautiously opening it. Inside was a photograph of Chris in his coffin, a classic Victorian memorial portrait. Closing her eyes to subvert the tears, she failed.

"I know it was a bit forward of me to have it taken," he mumbled.

"You are such a good man, Alastair."

"Not good enough, it appears."

Before he could move away, she kissed him delicately on the lips and then caressed his jaw line.

"I will never forget you," she said.

His jaw clenched, then released. Hefting the bag, Alastair averted his gaze. "Come, we should hurry, or you will miss your appointment."

Over Alastair's protests, Cynda went inside the Paul's Head alone. Saying goodbye one more time was beyond her capability; crying in the midst of the smoky pub would be wrong.

While she waited, her mind and heart wrestled over her future. She let them thrash it out, desperately attempting to keep a dispassionate distance. Her "quick trip" to 1888 had become a personal nightmare, both physically and emotionally. Instead of returning to Chris' arms, she was bearing his ashes home in hers. Then, there were the two Victorian gentlemen. Jonathon's offer of marriage had seemed solely based on honor—an uncharacteristic gesture, according to the doctor. Alastair's proposal came from the heart, and was harder to set aside.

I don't belong here. And yet, in some odd way, she knew she did. This time period had captured her imagination with more ferocity than any other.

She pulled her lover's photograph out of the bag. Besides the heartfelt decency of the gesture, the doctor was gently telling her that Chris was in her past, and that he offered her a future.

Cynda propelled a stream of air out the side of her mouth. That earned a glower from the pub owner, probably because she didn't have a drink in front of her. She rewrapped the photo, placed it in the bag so it wouldn't be squashed by the urn, and retreated to the street.

Depression soon gave way to irritation. "If this jerk stood me up..." she murmured.

"Miss Lassiter?" a voice called. The interface buzzed under her mantelet. She gave it a tap.

Standing a few feet away was a nondescript gentleman with a graying beard and moustache. As he moved closer, she noticed one iris was darker than the other.

"Dr. Samuelson?" she asked, cradling the heavy bag in her arms.

"Indeed."

She waited for an explanation for why he was late, but it didn't come. Instead, he observed her with guarded eyes.

"Shall we?" she said, gesturing.

"Indeed."

The longer they walked, the more the man annoyed her. He didn't offer to carry her bag, there was no apology for his late arrival, and he didn't give way on the sidewalk to women. He marched right down the middle as if he owned it.

God complex. She'd seen the type before. The shrink wasn't toting any sort of luggage. Tourists always brought back souvenirs: copious notes, rare books and the occasional collection of naughty postcards from Half Moon Street. *What was with this guy?*

Cynda scrutinized each alley for departure potential. She shared that trait with the whores—hunting for a dark corner to conduct her business.

Her eyes slid toward her companion. "Where have you been all this time?"

"Working," was the crisp reply.

"Did another Rover contact you?"

He shot her a sidelong glance. "I did not care to return, so I did not make myself available to be *contacted,* as you put it."

You arrogant creep. "Your contract with TIC specified when you were to return."

"My contract is not your concern, Miss Lassiter."

She felt the corner of her mouth twitch. "Why do you want to go home now?"

"I've completed my work."

That didn't ring true. Given the number of asylums in this country, Samuelson could be here for life and never visit them all. Unless his disease shield was wearing off...

"How's your health?" she quizzed.

"Fine."

This guy was a fountain of information. *Weren't psychiatrists supposed to be a bit more chatty?*

She shifted the bag into her left hand and scratched her wrist. Instead of diminishing, the itching increased.

They paused near a passageway that seemed suitable, waiting for a couple to leave. As she leaned against the brick wall, a flash of blue caught her notice. Perched on a broken barrel stave at her feet was her personal delusion.

Along for the ride? she asked silently.

"Always," the spider replied. Its many eyes shifted toward the psychiatrist. "Something's not right with this one."

What do you mean?

"I wouldn't go with him, if I were you."

She muttered under her breath about paranoid arachnids.

"I'm serious!" it spouted.

Cynda rolled her eyes at the delusion. All she wanted to do was get the hell out of here. It didn't matter if Samuelson was a self-centered jerk, just that he got home.

Turning back toward him, she asked, "Did you learn anything at the asylums?"

"Yes," was the terse reply.

I moved heaven and earth to find this cold fish?

The couple from the alley wandered by. The woman spied Samuelson and said in a cheery tone, "Mind he doesn't cut your throat or nuthin'."

"I'm sure he won't." Cynda dug harder as the itch on her wrist flared up. She was scratching right over the top of where her PSI unit would usually be located. Without it, she had no idea what was going on.

"Let's get this done," Samuelson said, striding forward.

"You get lost for over a month, and now you're in a rush?" Cynda asked.

Her reply was the sound of his footsteps in the narrow passageway.

She found a portion of the alley that was a bit darker than the rest, without any windows overlooking it. Setting the bag down, she pulled the watch from her bodice. Instead of preparing for the transfer, Samuelson stared toward the street, tense.

"What the hell is going on?" she demanded, turning to look for herself. "Are you in trouble or something?"

A shake of the head. He turned back, gesturing impatiently for her to continue.

Desperate to put an end to this torture, she flipped open the watch. Would TIC transfer them both, or just the tourist?

Only one way to find out. "You still have the time band?"

"No."

She shot a glance at Samuelson. Another hassle. His odd eyes regarded her with what appeared to be anticipation. "Figured it out yet?" he asked.

"Figure out what?" she demanded.

A malevolent grin formed. "You're as dense as the other one."
Chris? "You said—"

"I lied."

She flipped the watch shut. "Just what the hell is your game?"

Her answer came as a line of silver lancing through the murky darkness. Cynda lurched backward instinctively as the knife slashed toward her. Grabbing the bag, she pulled it up in front of her. Her right shoulder failed to support the weight, and the bag dropped. The knife slashed along the leather with a ragged, tearing sound.

Before she could recover, Samuelson lunged toward her again. This thrust hit home, deftly negotiating between two ribs. Forcing his weight into the blade, his eyes drew close to hers. She saw ecstasy in them.

He pulled the knife out in one swift tug. Her grip loosened and the bag slipped to the ground, landing with a solid thud. Staggering backward, Cynda bumped into the wall and began sliding down the rough bricks, one by one. Blood bubbled around her fingers as they probed the wound. An eerie suction pulled at her palm with each frantic breath.

"Why?" she gasped.

Her assailant retrieved the watch from where it had fallen and placed it in her free hand, wrapping her fingers around it.

"Why?" she repeated, this time barely above a whisper.

He didn't answer. There were voices at the end of the alley and he sent his attention toward the noise. "Not yet," he murmured. He looked back at her, dropping to his knees. "Come on, die, will you?"

She raised her head. "The...other Rover?"

"Of course I killed him," he spat back, as if it were a silly question. Over the sound of her thudding heartbeat, she thought she heard an accordion. There wasn't enough air to permit her to shout for help. Each breath grew noticeably shallower. Dull gray formed on the edges of her vision, like a fog creeping along the sides of a narrow tunnel.

Samuelson rose to his feet, retrieving the knife from his pocket. It had something white wrapped around the handle, now stained with her blood.

"Not fast enough," he said. He stepped to her left side and grabbed her hair with his right hand, pulling her head back. She felt cold air caress her throat. The silver blade hovered in the air in front of her.

"No..."

26

Alastair's progress toward the boarding house was painfully slow. Part of him didn't care that more than one woman eyed him with frank suspicion, as if he'd brandish a knife at the first opportunity. His mind was on Jacynda. Was she gone now? Was there any chance he'd ever see her again?

She refused me. Though his practical mind told him they had no future, his heart had hoped otherwise. The only thing he had to offer was himself, and that wasn't much. In another month or so, the Wescomb's donation would be exhausted, and then he'd be skipping supper again. It was an uncertain future he'd offered, and she had been wise to decline.

Perhaps it is for the best. His heart said otherwise.

In the distance, he saw a familiar figure puffing through the throng. Alastair called to him. Keats veered, diving for him like a drowning man would a life ring.

"Where is she?" Keats demanded, perspiration coating his face. When Alastair didn't answer quickly enough, he repeated, "Where is she?"

"She's gone home."

Keats dragged a handkerchief from a pocket to mop his face. "I've been hunting for you for the last hour."

"Why?"

Another deep breath. "I found where Jacynda's lover was staying before he died." Keats dug in a pocket and produced an envelope. "Mr. Stone's landlady discovered this envelope while cleaning the room. I thought perhaps Jacynda might know this person, and it could aid in your investigation into Mr. Stone's...death."

Alastair grabbed it from his hands and stared at the return address.

"Morley's, Trafalgar Square." Over Keats' protests, he opened the envelope and scanned the note.

"Oh, God," Alastair said, whirling around in the direction he'd come. "Perhaps she hasn't met him yet."

"What's wrong?"

Alastair waved the note. "Cynda received a similar missive last evening. She is meeting this same man tonight."

Keats' face blanched.

With a grim nod, Alastair set off at a furious pace. Keats hurried to catch up, hooking onto an arm to slow him down.

"Do not run. This crowd is too volatile. They nearly strung up some poor bloke this afternoon just because he tried to chase down a constable to report a robbery."

"I don't give a damn. She may be in grave danger."

"In that, you may be right. Nevertheless, we will be of no assistance to her if we're hanging from a pair of lampposts."

Nodding brusquely, Alastair marched on, Keats at his side.

I should never have left her alone.

"She took off a bit ago. Wasn't drinkin' at all," the publican complained, and then turned away to refill someone's pint of bitter.

Outside the pub, Keats surveyed the streets with worry. "Where would they go? Victoria Station?"

Alastair ignored the question as the answer would be too improbable. "You search that side of the street, I'll take this one. If you find her, bring her to the pub and wait for me. Understood?"

Keats gave him a petulant frown and then scurried across the street. Alastair began his own hunt. Maybe it was of no concern that both notes had come from the same establishment. Perhaps her lover had been waylaid before he'd made his rendezvous. None of Alastair's rationalizations eased his fears.

Each alley he scrutinized made his hope rise. Perhaps she was already gone, safe in her time.

Squinting into a passageway, he saw two figures, one bent over another. His eyes caught the flash of metal in the air. Disregarding Keats' warning, he bellowed and broke into a run.

The watch slipped through Cynda's fingers to the ground with a metallic tinkle. She had no strength to retrieve it. Her existence collapsed into distinct images: the unholy gleam of the knife's edge, each raspy breath, the dull throbbing ache in her side, the sure knowledge she would die here.

The hand tightened on her hair, arching her head further back, exposing her. Perversely, her mind noted her attacker was left-handed, like Alastair. *Like the Ripper.* She thought of the two Victorian men who would see her in the coffin. Would the doctor have a photograph made of her? Would Jonathon arrest her killer and watch in grim satisfaction as he was hung?

"Don't..." she whispered.

"Nothing personal, I assure you."

"Who are—"

"Who am I?" A rough laugh. "I'm Dr. Montrose, don't you know?" he said.

"No. He's—"

An enraged shout, followed by pounding footsteps.

Her assailant swore. The blade moved closer. She drove her left elbow backward, aiming for his groin. It impacted his thigh instead, causing his grip to tighten.

A sharp cry from her foe. As he spun away, the blade sliced at an imperfect angle. He cried out again, tumbling to the cobblestones.

Clutching the side of his chest, he regained his feet, breathing heavily, searching wildly for his unseen attacker. There was another shout from the approaching figure. Collecting the knife, the killer took to his heels.

Cynda sagged against the brickwork, hand to her throat and blood washing across her fingers. Strangely, there was no pain—just the heightened sense of diminishing time.

The sound of skidding boots on pavement. Alastair's frantic face filled the tiny window her vision afforded.

Prying her fingers away, he dabbed at her neck with his handkerchief. It didn't spray like an arterial wound, and for that he was grateful. Still, her face was alabaster, lips blue-tinged. She shook like a sapling in a gale. There had to be another wound, one more grievous than the cut on her neck.

"Where are you hurt?" he demanded.

"Chest."

His eyes tracked downward. Blood frothed out of her side. His slender reed of hope snapped. Her lung was punctured, collapsing inward with every breath.

He leaned in close, nearly touching noses with her, ensuring she could see him. "There is nothing I can do."

She gave a slow nod. "I...know..." A wet cough. "Watch..."

Watch? "Where is it?"

Her left hand moved feebly to indicate the ground. He fell on all fours, rummaging in the patchy darkness.

The crunch of boots on pavement came closer, along with someone humming a tune. He saw a glint of yellow on the dark stones and grabbed at it, offering a prayer of thanks as he clutched the cold metal.

The boots stopped short a few feet from him. He stared upward into the eyes of a heavyset woman. Her gaze slipped from his face, to his bloody hands, to Jacynda's dying body. Her mouth opened, but no sound came forth. Then a sharp shriek rent the air as she fled, growing higher-pitched as she skittered round the corner in a rush of petticoats.

Alastair held the watch out to Jacynda. "I have it."

"Open...it."

His blood-slicked hands took three tries to pry open the case. Handing it to her, he watched her methodically performing a series of windings, each slower than its predecessor, as if she had difficulty remembering the sequence. She looked up and nodded.

Brimming with tears, he offered the only solace he could. "I love you," he whispered in the closest ear. It felt cold against his lips.

Another faint nod, followed by a shuddering, gurgled breath. Her free hand flailed in the direction of the Gladstone. He hefted it onto her lap and she leaned over it.

He waited, but nothing happened. A bubbly breath. She raised her head, her eyes wide.

"They wouldn't...leave me..." A single tear rolled down her face. Her eyes closed, and she slumped against the bag.

Alastair's heart broke. Had this all been her delusion? Had he not seen a glimpse of the future? Why were they not saving her?

"Oh, God, no," he whispered, reaching out to touch her.

Astonishment overrode horror as an iridescent halo sparked into life, causing him to yank his hand back in surprise. The halo encompassed her and collapsed to a fine point, like an angel ascending to heaven. It left in its wake tenfold darkness.

Alastair remained on his knees. Drawn by morbid fascination to a piece of bloodied cloth on the ground, he plucked it up. The monogram appeared familiar.

ASM.

He knew it intimately. It was his.

✝

Terrified screams attracted Keats' attention. Discarding his own advice, he bolted across the street, shoving aside pedestrians. A woman was fleeing an alley, howling at the top of her lungs. Keats flew down the passageway to find Alastair on his knees, his hands crimson, staring at a bloodied handkerchief. In front of the doctor was a sizeable patch of fresh blood.

"What happened?" Keats demanded.

No reply. Keats dropped on his knees near the prostrate man. "Damn you, what has happened? Where is she?"

"Gone," was the hoarse reply. "Gone forever."

"Down there!" someone cried.

Keats shot to his feet. A group of ten, maybe fifteen men marched toward them, some brandishing bricks or boards. He forced Alastair to his feet.

"Run for it!"

The doctor didn't move. Keats grabbed his wounded arm and squeezed. The pain seemed to drive a wedge into Alastair's befuddled brain. He swore, jerking his arm away.

"Come on, you idiot!" Keats urged, tugging him along.

Alastair stumbled forward and then broke into a run, the riotous mob in step behind them.

‡

Three streets away, winded and staggering from the exertion, they ducked through a gateway into a side yard. Keats flailed his arms to indicate he could run no further without a rest and leaned against a post, his breathing ragged. Alastair bent over to catch his own breath. Their pursuers were relentless. Shouts of "It's the killer, lads!" and "We have him!" only added to their number.

They took refuge behind a shed. Reaching into his pocket to mop his dripping face, Alastair discarded the idea. His hands were too bloody.

Her blood.

"You must shift," Keats insisted. "We can shake them if we change form."

Alastair shook his head vehemently.

"You have to—"

"No!"

Keats balled his fists in frustration. Hearing the shouts of their pursuers, he began to go *en mirage*. Effortlessly, he grew taller, his hair and moustache lightening until he matched the doctor precisely.

"What are you doing?" Alastair demanded.

"You and your damned principles have left me no choice. Go to Bishopsgate Police Station. I'll meet you there."

"They'll catch you," Alastair warned.

"I know Whitechapel better than they do." Keats clapped a hand on Alastair's shoulder. "Bishopsgate, and don't mention my name to anyone!" He hurried back the way they'd come, toward the danger.

"You're a lunatic!" Alastair shouted after the retreating figure.

"You would know," Keats taunted. The instant he stepped onto the street, their hunters bayed like hounds, pounding after him.

"May God keep you safe," Alastair whispered. He headed in the opposite direction, working his way toward the police station through the back alleys. He soon learned that Keats' heroic gesture hadn't decoyed everyone.

"Come on, he's here somewhere," a deep voice urged. "We'll have him and string him up before Johnny Law can find him!"

"We'll show 'im a bit o' fancy knife work, see 'ow 'e likes it."

Alastair ran blindly, careening through knots of people on the street. Barreling around a corner, he nearly collided with a carriage, the horse rearing as he flung himself out of the way.

A hand grabbed at him. "What's up, mate?"

Alastair shoved the man away and shot into the street. He darted between a wagonload of coal and a hansom cab, causing both drivers to curse at him. Swinging through a gate, he found a dark corner and sank onto his haunches, his thigh muscles quaking from the exertion. His hunters wouldn't tire; their desire for revenge was too deep. If he didn't shift soon, Keats' heroic gesture would be in vain.

Keats. "Oh, God, I hope you're safe." The moment the words came out of his mouth, they felt absurd. Of course, his friend would survive. To think otherwise was too much for him to bear.

"Down here!" someone called. He heard gates slamming and the sound of someone hammering on a door, demanding entrance.

Panicking, he rose, searching for an exit. There was none. He had trapped himself.

Feeling the bile rising in his throat, Alastair closed his eyes and visualized the form he would take, cursing himself for his weakness. The prickling began at the back of his neck, and then traveled downward like a sea of molten lead. He gritted his teeth and bore it out, the pain excruciating—penance for not shifting in over three years.

In time, the boiling sensation ended. He opened his eyes and stared downward, turning his hands first one way, and then the other. They were delicately small. He could feel the blood drying beneath the illusionary black kid gloves.

There was no need to look in a mirror. For a few minutes longer, Jacynda Lassiter graced the streets of Whitechapel.

☦

The low, vibratory hum of the Thera-Bed was Cynda's first clue she'd survived. It automatically adjusted as she took a deeper inhalation, monitoring her oxygen level while increasing the amount of neuro-blockers to reduce the pain. Despite all the high-tech coddling, each breath hurt like someone jamming a wooden stake into her chest. *Is this what vampires had to look forward to?*

Another breath, along with a corresponding beep from the bed. She hated these things. They healed you, but she'd always thought there was something creepy about them.

Must be alive. I'm already bitching about technology.

She opened her eyes; the bed beeped three times to signify the change.

"Hey!"

"Ralph?" she whispered, still not sure if she dare take a deeper breath.

"You got it. So how's it going?" The dark circles under his eyes told her this hadn't been a picnic for him, either.

"Okay. What's my pain level?"

He leaned over, peering at a screen located next to the bed. "Seven."

"Euuu..."

"Yeah. Well, it's better than when you came in."

"What the hell happened? The transfer didn't work. At first I thought..."

Silence.

"...I thought they'd left me to die."

More silence.

She glared at him. "Ralph?"

"TIC denied the transfer. They wiped the Interface Attributes."

Oh, my God. "Why?"

He looked at his hands. "They planned on orphaning you."

The terror in the alley washed over her again, the blunt force of the knife slamming between her ribs. "Who brought me home?"

"We'll talk about that later."

"How'd you get the attribute for my watch?"

A satisfied smile. "Remember the customer rep with

the designa-tush?"

Cynda delivered a cautious nod.

"You owe her a thank-you. She got a copy of the attribute file from Thad. Apparently, he's got a thing for nostalgia heels and well-padded behinds."

"I owe my life to Thad and the blonde airlock brain?"

A finger waved in front of her nose. "Ah-ah, be nice."

"Why did Thad have them?"

"Covering his ass for when the government starts issuing indictments." He turned serious. "How did you get hurt?"

"The tourist knifed me. He admitted killing Chris."

Ralph blinked in stunned astonishment. "Whoa..."

"Yeah, tell me about it. I barely got the watch out of my pocket, and he nails me. It just doesn't make sense." She remembered her other task. "Chris?"

"We delivered the urn and a copy of the photograph to his family this morning. I kept the original for you. I thought you'd like to have it."

She nodded. "Who's 'we'?"

"Later."

"Is TIC still in business?"

"No."

She jammed her lips together to keep the tears from appearing.

Ralph rose. "Get some rest, and we'll talk about this later." Then he was gone, the door whooshing closed behind him.

Her right side flamed, causing an instant teeth-gritting grimace. Once she could catch her breath, she commanded, "Neural-blocker on full." The resulting rush of sleep-inducing painkiller let her drift into a dark haze. The last thing she remembered were the faces of the two men she'd left behind.

‡

Mindful to keep his stride in check, Alastair moved like a diminutive woman, focusing on each step. His heart thundered so loud he swore his pursuers could hear it. The mob's wave charged toward him, fanning out into the yard, wrenching open the door to the privy to the right of him. Having no faith in his abilities, Alastair steeled himself for discovery.

"You seen a bloke?" one of them called.

Alastair shook his head and kept moving. Behind him, the mob scattered in search of their prey.

A short distance from the police station, he found a deserted niche and shifted back to his usual appearance. The shock of the change made him retch until his stomach emptied. Standing upright, he wiped his sweaty forehead on his coat sleeve. The sight of Jacynda's blood on the cuff made him double over and retch again.

His heart sank the moment he drew near the station. A crowd clustered on the street, their mood volatile. One fellow had raised himself above the masses on a costermonger's cart, expounding on the ills of the East End, how the police did not intend to find the killer until all the women were dead. The outrageous claim drew shouts from the mob and demands for vengeance.

Alastair jammed his hands into his pockets to conceal them. Why hadn't he stopped and washed them along the way? Was it because the blood was the only thing he had left of Jacynda?

Angling around the crowd's periphery, he intended to remain outside until Keats arrived. A couple of men eyed him and he moved to a different location. He kept glancing around, searching for Keats, but there was no sign of the man.

He kept close to the front door, no more than twenty feet away, in case someone recognized him from the alley. Two constables flanked the entrance, truncheons in hand, eyeing the assemblage uneasily. Alastair kept his hands in his pocket, avoiding eye contact.

Suddenly he stumbled over a broken brick in the street and pitched forward, bracing his fall with his hands. Eyes turned in his direction. As he rose, a burly man pointed at him.

"Hey, what's with your hands, mate?"

A woman leaned closer. "That looks like dried blood." She stared at him and then backed away in horror.

"It's him!" another shouted.

"Grab him before he scarpers!"

As Alastair flung himself toward the front door, rough hands tore at him, ripping his jacket and shirt. Hot breath scorched his neck. Someone's fingers dug into his wounded arm, making him cry out.

"For God's sake, help me," Alastair shouted to the constables, flailing in the sea of angry faces.

Belatedly, one of them waded in with his truncheon. "Hey, get off, you lot," he bellowed. The building disgorged three more bobbies, who joined their companion in the melee. Fists flew. Rough hands hauled him toward the station.

A minute later, Alastair found himself on his knees just inside the door. His head spun and his right ear burned from a blow. He rose to his feet, adjusting his torn garments with some measure of dignity.

"This way," a cop ordered, pointing. Alastair trailed behind the constable, grateful to have escaped with his life.

To his supreme irritation, they stuck him in a cell for *safekeeping,* as they called it. The small enclosure was dirty and smelled like its last occupant, who had apparently worked in a slaughterhouse. Alastair parked himself on the hard bed, rubbing his palms together to flake the dried blood onto the floor.

"I pray you lived," he whispered.

He turned his mind to what would come next. He'd have to explain what had happened in the alley. Well, most of it, at least.

The cell door creaked open. A man entered, flanked by two constables. He was clad in a black suit, and the way he moved told Alastair he was senior in rank.

"Right, now, let's get this hashed out," he said. "What's your name?"

"Doctor Alastair Montrose."

"Where do you live?"

"At a boarding house on New Castle Street."

"Where do you work?"

"London Hospital and at a clinic on Church Street."

"Any surgical training?"

"Some."

The two constables traded knowing looks. One smirked.

"How did you get blood on yourself?" the senior cop quizzed.

Alastair spun the tale as best he could, though he'd never been much of a liar. He left out almost all the details, other than how a particular friend was to meet a gentleman at the pub on Crispin Street. Fearing for her safety, he'd tracked her to an alley and found her wounded.

"Is this woman a prostitute?" the man asked.

"No, she is not."

"Where is she now?"

"I'm not sure. I chased her assailant away. She was gone when I returned."

"Which alley?"

"I'm not sure. It is somewhere near the Paul's Head."

"Take off your jacket."

Alastair removed it and his questioner explored the pockets. When he came up with the bloody handkerchief, that earned Alastair a long look. Then he produced the clean one.

"You usually carry two?"

"No, not usually. I must have forgotten I'd already put one in my pocket."

The coat came back to him and he placed it on the bed. His inquisitor pointed at the bandage on his arm. The wound was bleeding again, courtesy of the crowd.

"I was assaulted the other evening," Alastair explained.

"Where?"

"Near my clinic."

"Robbery?"

"I think so, though I had no money on me at the time."

"Which was?"

"Pardon?"

"The time?"

"About two or three in the morning."

"Why were you out that late, Doctor?"

"I couldn't sleep." In his mind, Alastair could hear the hole deepening with every answer he supplied.

"One of my men says he saw you last night on Aldgate High Street, that you stopped to help him with a drunken woman."

"Yes, I did. There wasn't much I could do for her."

"Do you know her name?" Alastair shook his head. "Were you in Mitre Square last night?"

Alastair's throat tightened. "Yes. I crossed through the square to go to Bury Street."

"What's there?"

"A patient of mine, a Mrs. Butler. Her son helps us at the clinic."

"Did you see the drunken woman later in the evening, perhaps on your way back to your lodgings?"

"No." *Why is that important?*

"Are you in the habit of associating with dolly-mops?"

Alastair frowned. "I offer medical treatment for their ailments. Do I consort with them? No."

"Are you sure you didn't encounter the woman later in the evening, perhaps demand some personal payment for your earlier treatment?" There was a low snort from one of the constables.

Alastair's temper flared. "That's insulting. To suggest I would expect a woman to—"

"You wouldn't be the first." The officer continued, "Where were you the rest of the night?"

"I left Mrs. Butler's at approximately a quarter to midnight. Once I returned home, I went to bed." The lie sounded hollow. *What if they talked to Keats? What would he tell them?*

"Rather precise with times, aren't you?"

Alastair shrugged.

"Any witnesses?"

And there it was. His witness was gone. "Yes. Miss Lassiter accompanied me to see Mrs. Butler, and returned with me to the boarding house." He inwardly winced. That sounded wrong. "Miss Lassiter lives at the boarding house, as well," he quickly added.

"Ah. Then we'll have to talk to her."

"If you can find her. She is the woman who was injured tonight in the alley."

"Well, that's right handy, isn't it? Do you have anyone else who can vouch that you were in your own bed?"

Before Alastair could answer, there was a tap at the door. A clerk of some sort hurried in and whispered into the senior man's ear. His message caused a grimace.

"Blast them. How did they find out?" he asked.

The fellow shrugged and shot Alastair a quick look.

"Right then, we'll step back until they get here. But if that mob breaks through, I'm not risking my men for someone who isn't my responsibility. You tell them that." The clerk bobbed his head and left.

His questioner gave him a sour look. "Seems you're too hot for us to handle." Alastair heard the resentment and envy. With a final glare, the cop slammed the cell door behind him. Someone had just pulled rank.

Who had that kind of power? And where in the devil was Keats?

27

Monday, 1 October, 1888

Once he'd shaken his own pack of hounds and shifted form, Keats made his way toward Bishopsgate. Listening to the crowd outside the station told him Alastair was already in residence. Pushing his way to the door, Keats displayed his card and was readily granted entrance. A few minutes later he was on the move again, not bothering to see his friend. He was in no mood to tip his hand just yet. If the truth were to be discovered, he'd need to perform his investigation before the street court passed its verdict.

Admittedly, he'd played Alastair like a pawn; the incident in the alley fell in Metropolitan Police territory, yet he'd sent his friend to Bishopsgate—a City of London police station. He banked on the time it would take for the two divergent organizations to work through the issue of jurisdiction. That was his edge.

He dispatched a telegram to Chief Inspector Fisher with the terse message, *Dr. A.M. now in custody Bishopsgate, possible assault on woman. Concerned for safety. Might you intercede?*

Returning to the alley where it had all begun, he found the scene altered. Someone had spread straw over the bloodstains and added a wilted flower, no doubt believing this to be another example of the Whitechapel killer's handiwork. He swallowed heavily at the poignancy of the makeshift tribute. *Had he so misjudged Alastair that it had cost Jacynda's life?*

No matter how hard he searched, the scene yielded no clues. As expected, the witnesses had scattered. He went door to door interviewing those few folks who had heard the commotion. To the person, they'd ignored the ruckus and gone on with their lives.

An hour later, he found the woman who had stumbled over Alastair, drunk and holding court at the Britannia, telling her tale to anyone who would buy her a drink. From her condition, it appeared she'd been talking for a long time. The tale had grown with each recitation.

After introducing himself, Keats asked, "What did this fellow look like, madam?"

"About six feet, bushy eyebrows, I think. He had a wicked scar on his cheek. He spat and waved his knife at me. I ran for it, I did." A couple of the locals gave a cheer, and she executed a curtsey that nearly toppled her over.

"On which cheek was the scar?" Keats asked.

She thought and said, "Left one, it was," while pointing to her right. Keats made note of that.

"Hair color?"

"Black as coal."

"Eyes?"

"Red, like the devil."

"How old was this fellow?"

"Oh…" The woman pondered for a bit while the small group around her bent closer in anticipation. "I'd say about fifty. Shabby genteel, he was. And he had a black flowin' cape and a big bag."

"What color was the bag?"

"Black." A hiccup. She demurely put a hand over her mouth and giggled.

"What was he doing when you first saw him?"

"Crawlin' around on the ground, sniffin' like a hound."

"Pardon?"

"He was crawlin' around on all fours like a dog. I thought it right queer. Then he looks up at me and leers. I ran for it. I ain't no fool."

That might be debated. "What about the woman?"

"She was dead. He'd cut her throat."

"Had he…disarranged any of her clothing?"

"No. She was propped up against the wall like a puppet."

"Did he say anything to you?"

More thought, and then a nod. "'You're next, luv.'"

"Your name and where you live, madam?" *Lest we ever need your ridiculous testimony.*

"Katherine Miller," she said. "I live on Sandy's Row."

"Thank you, madam," he said, tucking the notebook away.

"You catch him, you hear? I want to see him swing. I want a front-row seat."

260 | Jana G. Oliver

"Yes, madam."

Keats paused outside the pub to wipe his face with his handkerchief. Fate had delivered a witness who was useless. It was a safe bet that if Alastair were tidied up and placed in front of her, she'd not recognize him.

Thank God.

He made another pass through the alley. This time, he got lucky.

"I saw a man go down there with a lady," the cobbler said. He had a pair of patched boots in his hands, apparently on the way to deliver them to their owner. "She weren't one of the whores."

"How could you tell?"

"She was carrying a heavy bag, a brown one. Whores don't do that. They wear all their clothes."

"That's sound reasoning," Keats replied. "What did the man look like?"

"Well dressed, graying moustache, older gent. Seemed out of place. Too posh for here, that's why I watched him. His shoes were right fine."

Keats kept the smile to himself. A cobbler would notice the man's footwear.

"Did you overhear any of their conversation?"

"I did. The lady asked him where he'd been all this time, and whatever he said upset her. She was angry at him."

"Did he seem to threaten her in any way?"

"No. But there was something not right about him. Felt cold, like the grave."

Keats made note of the man's name and address. "Thank you for your time. If you should think of anything else," he said, offering his card. The fellow's eyes descended southward to Keats' boots.

"I can make you a better pair; they won't hurt your feet like those, I promise it. I'll give you a good price, you being a cop."

"I'll come to your shop as soon as I can."

"Right. Good night, sir."

"Good night to you."

Keats hailed a passing hansom and jumped aboard. "New Castle Street," he ordered. Perhaps he'd learn more at the boarding house.

A few blocks from his destination, he spied a telegraph office. Dismissing the cab, he hustled inside and sent a wave of messages across Whitechapel in hopes of locating Jacynda Lassiter. Once he'd finished, he made his way to the boarding house, knocked on the door and presented his card.

"You're a copper?" Mildred asked, frowning at him. "Funny how you never mentioned that before."

"Right now, the police are not held in high regard."

Her frowned deepened. "So, what do you want?"

"I wish to examine Miss Lassiter's and Dr. Montrose's rooms."

"Miss Lassiter's gone," was the quick reply.

"I know. I still want to see their rooms."

"Why?"

"The doctor is in custody with regard to an incident earlier this evening involving Miss Lassiter. I am investigating the matter."

The frown turned ominous. "He wouldn't hurt her."

"I agree, but I still must investigate."

"I thought you were his friend," Mildred charged.

Keats nodded reluctantly. "I am. Which makes this doubly hard, madam."

The frown dissipated. She reluctantly waved him in. After asking her a few pointed questions, he tromped up the stairs, his heart like a leaden weight. *How had it come to this?*

Keats began in Jacynda's room because he knew it would be the hardest. Fortunately, the landlady hadn't cleaned it yet. Inside the wardrobe he found a crumpled chocolate wrapper, one of the feathers from Jacynda's hat and her ruined black dress. The garment brought back memories of the beer-wagon incident and her brush with death. *Had someone succeeded in his quest? Then where was the body? Why carry it off?*

Tucking the feather into his jacket pocket, Keats used the landlady's key and entered Alastair's room. It was much like the man: tidy in a sparse sort of way. Medical books stacked high on a table, his spare suit in the wardrobe, exhibiting wear at the cuffs and elbows. A shirt, a few pairs of socks. Not much to show for once having a lucrative practice in Mayfair. No doubt Alastair had sold the rest of his wardrobe to fund the clinic as monies ran thin.

Tucked under the hairbrush on the dressing table was an envelope addressed to his friend. With a pang of guilt, Keats slit it open.

Alastair,

I know you will be able to make a difference with this money, so I leave it to you. The account is now in your name. You'll need to buy a new shovel every now and then as you move that mountain of yours...

You will always be in my heart.

Jacynda

Keats' eyes clouded, and he blinked hard to clear them. Had he been so blind as to think he'd had a chance with her? He flipped to the paperwork. "Two hundred and fifty-eight pounds," he murmured. *Where had she gotten such a sum?*

"More puzzles," he muttered, returning the letter and the bank form to the envelope. He tucked it into his jacket and continued his search. So far, he hadn't uncovered a reason why the doctor would want to harm Jacynda Lassiter, nor had he discovered a reason why Alastair hadn't. *Maybe I'm not the only one who isn't what they appear.*

Mildred met him at the door. Keats knew the look on her face; she was having second thoughts.

"I...well...I suppose you should know," she began.

"Know what?"

"They had an argument. He was quite put out with her. Stormed out of here in a fine rage."

"When?"

"In the middle of the night, near on to three, I think. They were trying to be quiet, but I heard them."

"What was the argument about?"

"I don't know."

"Thank you, Mildred."

With a half-hearted nod, she left him at the door.

‡

Exhaustion caught up with him; despite the stink of the mattress. Alastair fell asleep, Jacynda's ashen face parading through his dreams. He roused when the door swung open, stifling a yawn. The newcomer reminded him of a somber patrician with a well-trimmed graying goatee, moustache and tailored clothes.

"Doctor Montrose?" the man inquired. It was a voice with strength behind it—someone accustomed to exercising authority.

"I am he. And you?"

His visitor didn't reply, waiting for a constable to place a chair in the cell. "Thank you. You may leave us. I'll call when I need you."

"Are you sure, sir?" the fellow asked, eyeing Alastair dubiously. "If he's the bloody bastard who's been ripping up those—"

"Then as long as I'm not a prostitute, there shouldn't be a problem, correct?"

The constable frowned and then nodded, pulling the door closed with a hollow thud that echoed throughout the cell.

The newcomer moved the chair to within a foot of the bed. Removing his coat, he draped it over the back. Once seated, he dusted a smudge of dirt off his knee.

"I am J.R. Fisher," he announced, as if Alastair should know the name.

"You're a policeman?" A nod. Alastair made a guess. "However, not at this station."

"No."

"I'll be honest, Mr. Fisher; I shall not be inclined to say much more until I know who you represent."

"*Chief Inspector* Fisher," the man replied. Each took the measure of the other. "I am with Special Branch."

Alastair's eyes narrowed. "I am no dynamitard, Chief Inspector. I eschew violence."

A slight tilt of the head. "You may not be an anarchist; however, you might be the most crazed madman this country has ever bred."

"Sorry to disappoint."

"I shall be blunt, Doctor. I've been hauled out of my bed and told an improbable tale. Perhaps you may clarify precisely why I'm here."

"I have no notion."

"Then tell me how you came to this station."

With a deep sigh, Alastair recounted the evening's events, careful to leave Keats out of the picture. Fisher listened with rapt attention, giving little indication if he accepted the tale or not.

"Do you believe this Miss Lassiter is still alive?" he inquired.

"If my prayers have been answered." Fisher regarded him with increased intensity. "I am not this monster, Chief Inspector. I am a physician who works with the poor, and I have a good reputation."

Fisher's eyebrow arched. "Yet, you've killed a man."

Alastair blinked in stark surprise. "How do you know that?"

"My sergeant told me."

"Who knows my personal business so intimately?"

"Detective-Sergeant...Jonathon Keats."

Alastair couldn't prevent his mouth from falling open. "Keats? No, he's a..."

Oh, lord. It'd been Keats' idea that he come here. Had his so-called friend made him a sacrificial lamb?

"He failed to mention his true vocation," Alastair replied, his astonishment fading into cold resentment.

"He does not widely publicize it."

"Apparently not even to those he blithely calls 'friend'."

Fisher donned his coat. "We shall speak further on this matter when I have more information."

"I'm sure I'll be here."

"Not if the impatient citizens of Whitechapel have their way."

‡

Time had not improved the situation at Bishopsgate Police Station. The crowd, now swollen in size and volatility, rang with open calls that the building be breached and the murderer hung from the nearest gas lamp. Keats found his superior waiting in an office, cup of tea in hand. Fisher gestured for him to close the door, then pointed to the chair next to him. Keats complied, dread rising in his chest.

The Chief Inspector leaned unnervingly close. "Why am I here, Sergeant?" he asked in a dark whisper.

"I was concerned that Doctor Montrose would be hanged before we learned the truth."

"Truth about what?" Fisher retorted.

"Concerning the disappearance of Miss Lassiter, sir. I trust you are aware of the events of this evening."

"To some extent. I have heard his story. It makes little sense. Either way, this is not Special Branch business unless Abberline deems it so. The locals are quite capable of handling this inquiry."

"I am aware of that, sir. However, as we have vouched for the man, I felt it best we keep an eye on the investigation."

Fisher's face clouded. He leaned back in his chair. "That's a patently thin argument, Sergeant."

"Not entirely, sir. If, God forbid, he *is* this murderer, it would be better that we discover our own error."

Fisher did not reply for almost a full minute. During that time, Keats saw his career flaming into oblivion.

"Give me your report," Fisher commanded.

Keats painstakingly related everything he'd learned and handed over the envelope he'd taken from Alastair's room. While Fisher read through the documents, Keats studied his hands.

"How did you know he was in custody?" Fisher asked, tucking the papers into the envelope.

"There was a commotion in the streets, and I went to investigate. I found Alastair in a dazed state with blood on his hands. When the mob began to chase us, I sent him here."

Fisher's eyebrow shot up. "He did not mention you were

present at the scene."

"I asked him not to."

"Why?" his superior demanded.

"I did not want Special Branch implicated at the onset."

Fisher's eyes narrowed. "Did he have a weapon on him?"

"No."

"You searched him?"

Flustered, Keats shook his head. "I had no time, given the mob."

"He might have discarded it along the way."

"Yes, that is possible."

His boss was studying him with an intensity that made sweat pop out on Keats' forehead. "There's more here than you're telling me," Fisher hissed. "Out with it, man!"

"There was an apparent attempt on Miss Lassiter's life two nights earlier. She was pushed in front of a wagon. Fortunately, she was quick in her response and took little injury."

"Was this reported?"

"No. She asked that it not be, dismissing it as an accident."

"Why would someone wish to harm her?"

"Of that, I am not sure. According to the doctor, she received a note to meet a fellow at the Paul's Head last evening, which she apparently did. The cobbler I interviewed was quite precise in his description: an older gent with a cold demeanor."

A loaded sigh from his superior. His boss took a lengthy sip of his drink, as if to buy time. Grimacing, he slammed the cup on the desk so hard Keats thought it would shatter.

"Nothing worse than cold tea," Fisher growled. Looking up, he advised, "I dislike this situation intensely, Keats. At first blush, it feels like someone is mimicking our East-End killer. Nevertheless, I sense more is going on than you or Montrose are willing to impart. You will put the next round of questions to the doctor. It is time you squared your personal loyalties."

Ashamed, Keats nodded. "Yes, sir."

"I will arrange for a transfer to our patch. He'll be safer there."

Jarred out of his misery, Keats blurted, "Oh, God, thank you, sir."

Fisher's eyes turned flinty. "You're not out of it yet, Sergeant. There's a great deal of your story that doesn't track. We'll talk more about this later."

The feeling of dread grew. Keats could only murmur a contrite "Yes, sir."

✣

As he washed his hands in the bucket of cold water, Alastair blessed the dim light for affording one benefit: He was unable to see Jacynda's blood staining the water. Toweling dry, he heard the bolt slide free. He shielded his eyes from the light. Two entered: Chief Inspector Fisher and the man he'd once considered his friend.

"Shut the door," the senior cop ordered. A constable complied with a noisy bang.

Alastair scowled, flinging the coarse towel away. "Ah, *Sergeant* Keats. Come to torment the accused?"

Keats stared at the floor.

Did you tell them about Chris Stone? Of course you did. You played me for a bloody fool.

"Detective-Sergeant," Fisher urged.

There was a low sigh. Keats pulled something out of his jacket and tossed it on the mattress. "It appears you are now rather well-heeled."

"I don't know what gives you that notion," Alastair retorted.

"That is a letter from...Miss Lassiter. She left you a considerable sum of money on deposit at the Bank of England."

Alastair shuffled through the papers, his mouth agape. "This is incredible," he said, looking up. "I had no idea that's what she meant."

"Meant by what?" Keats demanded.

"She said she'd left a surprise in my room."

"When?"

"Right before she went into the pub."

Keats took the papers from him, returning them to the envelope. "Where you see philanthropy, others may see a motive for murder."

Alastair flared, "You think I would harm her for money?"

"There are lesser reasons for mayhem," Keats replied. "According to your landlady, you two traded words."

"We were at odds over an unrelated matter."

"Which was?"

"It is a private concern." Alastair shot a look at Fisher. "I am not a killer."

Keats jumped on that. "You've done it once; why not again?"

Alastair gritted his teeth. "You know that was self-defense."

A noncommittal shrug. "What really happened in that alley?"

"It's not believable."

"Where is she?" Keats pressed.

"I don't know where she went. That is God's truth."

"I had thought you would be more reasonable—"

"Reasonable?" Alastair snarled. "I am not inclined to be reasonable with a man who pretends to be my friend and then betrays me."

"That is not the issue!" Keats shouted. "Jacynda is the issue, in case you've forgotten."

"Is this your petty revenge because she refused your offer of marriage?" Alastair shot back. "Well, she did the same to me. It appears that neither of us measured up to her standards."

"Well, well, well. So there's the missing link," Fisher said, shaking his head. "I should have known the woman would be at the bottom of this."

Keats gave his superior a panicked look. "Sir—"

Fisher waved him into silence. "There are too many half-truths flying in this room. Perhaps a bracing ride to Scotland Yard will clear *both* your minds."

Alastair gestured toward the door, "After you, Inspector. You, I trust." Keats looked away, his fists knotted.

Fisher hammered on the cell door to summon the constable. "You would do well to trust no one at this moment, Doctor."

28

As Cynda rested in the semi-lit room, enveloped by the monotonous thrum of technology, her ears still reverberated with the cries of eel-pie sellers and creaking carriage wheels on uneven cobblestones. She thought she could smell naphtha lamps and the fresh tang of horse sweat. God help her, she missed Victorian London.

"Forty-five degrees upright," she commanded. The bed smoothly took the requested position.

A movement on the bed caught her notice. He was still blue, the one constant in her life.

"Posh digs," he said, gesturing with a leg. "A bit flat for my tastes, mind you. I like Covent Garden better."

"Yeah, real posh. I wasn't sure you'd make the journey."

"I'm here for the duration."

"My brain's that fried?"

The spider gave what passed as a nod and bustled over to the side of the bed until he reached a small mound of bed clothing. Settling on top of the mound, his multiple eyes watched her intently.

"Thanks for warning me," she said. "I should have listened."

"You will in the future."

"You can bet on that one."

"He put the watch into your hand after he hurt you," the spider commented.

She concentrated on that, pulling up the memory. Her assailant had played with her, taunting her. *"Figured it out yet?"*

Then he'd deliberately placed the watch in her hand after driving the knife deep into her chest. *Why?*

Cynda glanced toward the spider for input, but he appeared asleep. It seemed to be the best solution to her problems. It wasn't like she was going to go back to '88 and ask the bastard.

‡

Monday, 1 October, 1888

The moment Alastair stepped outside the cell, he could hear the low rumble of the crowd. Noting his dismay, a constable smirked and drew a line across his neck. "That would solve all your problems, wouldn't it?"

They were met at the side door by a sergeant with a florid face. "It's not getting any better, sir. They just keep coming."

Fisher sighed wearily. "We'll need one of your blankets for the duration, and a constable to serve as guard on top of the carriage. We need to move now—daylight will only serve to complicate matters."

The journey to the carriage was accomplished in near-darkness, at least from Alastair's perspective. With the blanket obscuring his vision, Keats helped him forward, murmuring directions as they exited the building. Banging his shins on the steps, Alastair hoisted himself inside the carriage, falling heavily into the seat. He immediately extricated himself from beneath the scratchy cover.

Across from him, Fisher adjusted his coat. Keats entered next, latching the carriage door behind him. He held a truncheon.

"We're sending out another carriage in hopes of distracting your well-wishers," Fisher explained. "If we're lucky, we'll make it to the Yard unscathed."

"If we're lucky," Alastair muttered, shooting Keats a glare. His betrayer looked away.

They'd gone only a short distance when a burgeoning roar came from somewhere nearby.

"Most likely the other carriage has been intercepted," Fisher observed in a remarkably calm tone. "Hopefully, the good citizens of Whitechapel will be too busy with that one to notice ours."

"Am I under arrest?" Alastair asked.

Keats and the Chief Inspector traded looks. "No, not technically," Fisher said.

More shouts. "Hey you, get off!" their driver yelled. A whip cracked through the air, followed by an enraged oath. The carriage lurched to an abrupt halt, nearly pitching Alastair into the Chief Inspector's lap.

"So much for our diversion," Fisher said, shaking his head.

"Official police business. Stand aside," a voice announced from the top of the carriage.

"O-ffish-al my arse," someone called. "Let's 'ave 'im out of there."

"Well, that's splendid," Alastair grumbled. "I might not be under arrest, but I can still be hung."

"Keep quiet!" Fisher whispered. He turned to Keats. "Cover him with the blanket. I'll go throw my rank around and see if it will do any good. If not, your first responsibility is to the prisoner, do you understand?"

"Yes, sir," the sergeant replied, weighing the truncheon in his hand.

Prisoner?

The blanket flopped over Alastair, casting him into shadow. He heard the door open and someone, presumably Fisher, step out. The door slammed. Under the cover, it quickly grew hot and stale.

"What is the problem here?" Fisher demanded in a stentorian tone.

"We want 'im, guv'ner. There's too many of us for you to say no. Just stand aside."

Alastair recognized the voice—it was one of the men who'd accosted him on the steps of the police station.

The carriage jostled, as if someone were putting weight against it. Fisher immediately protested, but his words were drowned out by the shouting.

"He's not going to be able to stop them," Keats said. "You know what you have to do to stay alive."

"Why would you care?" Alastair growled, his voice muffled under the blanket.

"Stop being an ass. I don't want to see you hung."

"Why the hell didn't you tell me you were a cop?"

"I was on special assignment. I…"

"You didn't trust me. And now it appears I shouldn't have trusted you."

"We can hash this out later. Just do what you must to survive. Getting hung will not allow us to help Jacynda."

As he'd hoped, mentioning the American lady did the trick.

"What about Fisher?" Alastair finally asked. "Certainly he's not one of us."

"Don't worry about him —we'll work it all out later. For God's sake, don't be a damned fool and throw your life away just to make a point."

Keats opened the door and stepped outside. Most of the faces arrayed in front of him were in shadow, half-lit by torches held throughout the crowd. A quick look around proved they'd not moved very far from the police station. *Were reinforcements on the way?* Not likely. The station would have its own problems at present.

When Keats' face became clearly visible, disappointment rolled through the crowd, followed by a chorus of boos.

"That ain't him," someone called. "He's a rozzer for sure."

"Constables will be arriving any moment, and we will press charges if you do not disband immediately," Fisher announced.

Good bluff. But will they believe it?

A man stepped forward, slapping a thick piece of wood into his palm.

"Po-lees bizness, ya say? We got bizness ourselves. If ya don't want to get yer nice suits all mucked up, ya best step aside."

"Absolutely not," Fisher replied. "This person is in my custody. I will not allow—"

A brick smashed into the side of the carriage, splintering the wood. That triggered the throng. Keats ducked a wildly-thrown blow, fighting to keep his position near the carriage door. His superior disappeared into the swarm, roaring his outrage. The constable on top of the carriage blew his whistle in increasing panic, then dropped from on high into the fray. The boiling mass of bodies caused the horses to spook, and the carriage pitched forward as the teamster struggled to hold the beasts in place.

Someone wrenched open the carriage door and blindly rummaged inside.

"Got 'im!" the man cried, and then stumbled backward in surprise.

The crush moved forward, intent on bagging the prize and earning bragging rights at the pub once they'd done their civic duty. Keats lunged for the door but made little progress, pinioned by men stronger than he.

"Come out of there!" someone bellowed.

A slim head dipped into the doorway, the black veil obscuring the face of its owner. A delicate hand clad in a black glove clasped the side of the carriage.

The chief agitator stepped forward. "'old on. What's this?" he asked, baffled.

Keats sighed quietly in relief. Shaking off his captors, he took his place at the bottom of the stairs. As he reached out his hand, the woman's gloved palm met his and she cautiously exited the conveyance. An astute observer would have noted the carriage adjusted more than would be required for a woman of her slight weight.

If Keats had any doubt of the doctor's feelings for Jacynda Lassiter, his personification of her laid that to rest. Alastair had created the illusion with the uncanny accuracy born of a man who idolizes a woman.

"Sergeant, why are these men accosting us?" his friend asked.

Keats' throat tightened. It was *her* voice. If he had not known Alastair was behind the illusion, he would have sworn it was Jacynda.

He cleared his throat. "There are some ruffians, miss," he said, glaring in the direction of the crowd. "They were mistaken as to who was inside the carriage."

"Heavens!" Alastair retorted, drawing a hand to *her* mouth just as a frightened woman would. But not like Jacynda. She'd be giving this lot a going-over. That would have been a delight to watch.

Fisher waded into sight, his coat askew and bowler missing. Blinking at the vision in front of him, he shot a bewildered glance at his sergeant.

"The young lady is unharmed, sir," Keats announced, as would be expected. *Please, please don't make a scene, or we're all dead.* Alastair was not that proficient at shifting, and it had to be a tremendous strain for him to keep the illusion in place. Any disruption in his concentration...

Fisher straightened his coat, no doubt to allow himself time to deal with his confusion, and then strode to Keats' side. "So it seems, Sergeant," he replied, as if nothing were amiss.

A stocky sailor pushed through the crowd and stuck his head inside the carriage. He swung around and demanded, "Where the hell is he?"

Keats rounded on him. "Mind your tongue in front of a lady!" The man cowered backward and blended back into the throng, his bravado gone.

The chief instigator spat on the street and nodded in respect. "Smart ones, ain't ya? Well, we'll find 'im and do 'im proper."

Fisher shifted to stand eye-to-eye with him. "The man you're hunting is not connected to the Whitechapel murders. We wish to speak to him on another matter. If you take justice into your hands, you'll be the one sized for the rope."

That drew murmurs from the crowd.

"Then 'oo's this one?" the fellow asked, pointing toward the illusionary woman.

"That is not your concern. We're escorting the lady to Scotland Yard for her safety. If any of you wish to join us..."

There were more murmurs, and then the horde thinned into groups of two and three, merging with the night. Fisher turned to hand the lady back into the carriage.

A rough fellow poked the chief inspector's hat at Keats.

"Sorry, mate," the man whispered.

Keats nodded and followed his superior inside the carriage. Once the door closed, he let out an explosion of pent-up air. Fisher retrieved his hat, dusting it off with his handkerchief. Every few seconds, he shifted his attention from the hat to the woman seated across from him. Aware of his scrutiny, Alastair deftly rolled the veil upward and tucked it into the hat.

The carriage bumped forward at a brisk clip. Keats knew Fisher would easily discern what had just happened, given his experience with the dying Transitive in Rotherhithe. *How long would it be before he learns my secret?*

"Is your landlady discreet, Sergeant?" Fisher asked, still working on the hat.

"Ah, yes, sir, she is."

"Then inform the driver of the address."

"Sir? I thought we were—"

Fisher set his hat on his lap and gestured toward Alastair. "It appears we need considerable privacy to discuss this newest revelation. We most certainly will not find that at Whitehall."

"Yes, sir." Keats surveyed his friend. Alastair sat stone-silent. How do you explain the impossible?

29

2057 A.D.
TEM Enterprises

Testing her endurance, Cynda swung her legs over the side of the bed and took a few deep breaths. The pain was blunt, but tolerable. She felt her neck; there was a line of raised skin where the knife had cut into the flesh. Leaning over, she swiveled the Thera-Bed graphics board around and checked her status. The thick blue line was pushing in the right direction. Lots of blue meant you were healing. No blue meant you were a memory.

"Nearly healed," she said. "Pretty amazing."

"Indeed." A lean figure floated into the room with the same quiet precision she'd expect of a robot. That's where the resemblance ended: salt-and-pepper hair, black turtleneck and tailored slacks.

Standing ramrod-straight near the window, he ordered, "Open twenty-three percent." The window covering complied, allowing a soft glow to inhabit the room.

Twenty-three percent? Who calibrates blinds that closely?

He studied her intently. "I am pleased to see you are improving." His sober voice was overlaid with the soft veneer of a British accent.

"And you are...?" Cynda asked.

A bemused expression. It made him look less like a statue. "I am T.E. Morrisey. Perhaps you've heard of me."

"Morrisey?" *It couldn't be...* "The guy who created the *Fast Forward* time-travel software?"

"Among other things."

"My friend Ralph thinks you're a god, you know."

A wry chuckle. "So he's said."

Studying him, she made an educated guess. "You brought me home?"

"Yes."

"And paid for all this?" she said, waving to encompass the technology, making sure to use the arm on the opposite side of the chest wound.

"Yes."

"Why? What's in it for you?"

"You, Miss Lassiter."

She blinked in astonishment. "Me?"

"Second to Harter Defoe, you're the best Rover TIC employed. It would be difficult to offer you a job if you were dead."

"Job?" She shook her head. "My roving days are over. I'm having serious lag-induced hallucinations."

Ralph sidled into the room at that point and took a position near the door, leaning against the wall.

"Hey," she said.

"Hey yourself."

A concerned frown from Morrisey. "Your hallucinations do not resolve with rest?"

"No, not really." The spider was missing at present, but she knew he'd not wandered far.

"Well, that is unfortunate. However, my plans are more...esoteric."

"Meaning?"

"You would be in what I call the 'mending' trade. It requires less travel, more hands-on."

Cynda rubbed the bridge of her nose to quell an itch. "In English, Mr. Morrisey."

She heard a sharp intake of breath from Ralph. Apparently, you weren't supposed to challenge the genius. Morrisey stared at her, but there was no anger on his face.

"You've been in the London Underground?" he asked.

"Yes. Just recently, in fact. Smelly place in '88."

"In *our* time period?" Morrisey asked.

"Yes, a couple of years back."

"Ancient, isn't it?"

"Yup."

"And yet, though they are nearly two centuries old, the tunnels are in remarkable shape. They still serve their purpose, albeit with a new mode of transport."

She nodded. "Grav-Rail beats the hell out of the old steam

engines. A lot less messy."

A slight flicker of irritation. "The point is they are still intact, and that is because someone takes the time to patch them on a regular basis."

"Which means?" she asked, spreading her hands. Her right side cramped in response. Gritting her teeth, she breathed through the discomfort rather than up the neuro-blocker.

"Time is no different than the tunnels, Miss Lassiter. It requires patching to prevent collapse."

Feeling perverse, she lowered the painkiller a couple more notches. The ache rose proportionally. She ignored it, needing as clear a brain as possible for this topic. "That's a no-no," she hedged.

Morrisey's eyebrow headed upward. "And cremating the body of your lover and transporting him to the twenty-first century, contrary to the direct order of your employer, is acceptable?"

"Chris," she whispered. The sadness returned, stronger than she'd anticipated. She looked away to control the tears.

Morrisey's voice softened. "Indeed. If you hadn't made the effort, Mr. Stone's remains would not be home with his family at this moment. You brought them considerable comfort."

A single tear rippled down her cheek; she wiped it away, embarrassed. "If TIC had told me he was missing, I would have gone earlier. I would have found him. Maybe he'd still be alive and..."

Morrisey shook his head. "Or both of you would be dead. At this point, it's academic. His death is embedded in the time stream and can't be altered without...consequences."

"Did his family accept that?"

When Morrisey didn't answer, Ralph spoke up. "It was hard. They didn't understand why we couldn't make it right."

Cynda blinked away another tear. "I can imagine." *We can sling your boy through time, but we couldn't keep him from dying. Sorry. That's the breaks.*

Morrisey abruptly cleared his throat. "Anyway, back to the matter at hand. You're sharp, and you know how to circumvent the rules. Where TIC did not appreciate those traits, I find them to be of value."

Cynda countered, "I was taught that time is pretty resilient, that it will spring back to its original path if given the chance. Unless, of course, you really bugger up something major. So how can you mend it?"

"Some time threads are more fragile than others—more

susceptible to manipulation or disarray. The time flow you just occupied is one of the most strained. Fortunately, that fragility diminishes as you reach the new century."

"Why is it like that?" Cynda asked, genuinely puzzled.

"The physics are rather complex. For an analogy, consider time as individual threads woven into a piece of fabric. Some threads are weaker than others, due to wear or to an issue with the initial construction."

"Initial construction?"

"If you 'wish me to lecture on the intricacies of Inter-Momentuary Quantum Physics—"

Cynda held up a hand in surrender. "No, no. Please don't do that. I'll just accept that '88 was built by an inferior contractor, how's that?"

A smile bloomed, and then promptly vanished. "A fair assumption. My 'menders,' as I call them, search out the weak intersections and patch them so they'll stay on track."

"But how do you know if something is going off the rails?" she asked, captivated both by the conversation and this most unusual man.

"I have developed a means to sense the 'shift' and 'drift' of events. If undisturbed, time continues on its way. If it's altered, the movement can be abrupt—a shift—or gradual—a drift. Either way, it is headed in a direction that wasn't the original thread."

"So, the guy who knifed me in the alley—was he a shift or a drift?" Cynda cracked.

Morrisey sighed, taking her question seriously. "I have no idea. We're at a loss as to his motives."

Cynda shook her head. "I've had tourists hide from me, try to bribe me, but never one who tried to kill me. It doesn't make sense." She frowned. "He didn't have a time band. Could it have been someone else's tourist?"

"No, it was Samuelson," Ralph replied. "The interface registered his ESR."

"He put the watch into my hand after he stabbed me. When I didn't die fast enough to suit him, he tried to cut my throat."

"The Non-Life-Sign Interact," Morrisey said, and Ralph nodded his agreement. "It would have triggered the transfer."

"Can't have stray bodies cluttering up history," Ralph said ruefully.

"However, he didn't do that for Mr. Stone," Morrisey observed.

The memory of her lover's bruised body provided the answer. "Maybe he wanted Chris' interface," Cynda offered.

"What's he going to do with that?" Ralph asked. "Unless he knows how it works, it's a fancy pocket watch."

"I think Chris told him," Cynda said.

"Not likely." Ralph replied.

"He didn't have a choice. Chris had been beaten before he died."

Morrisey stared at her. "Are you saying he was tortured?"

"Vigorously questioned, at least," she said, softening the truth. Her benefactor looked away, his jaw tightening.

Cynda caught Ralph's eyes, surprised by Morrisey's reaction. Her friend shrugged. *Something isn't right.*

"Did you ever find the tourist's photo?" she asked.

"Sure did," Ralph replied, "after the fact. It took some doing. TIC's file was corrupted, so we had to access his academic record. For some reason, it wasn't on that database, and they had to pull it from a backup."

"I want to see it."

"Happy to oblige." Ralph triggered a small panel near the door. It neatly unfolded to display a holo-keyboard projected on a small tabletop. He tapped away at the keys.

Morrisey gave her a stern look. "What about my job offer, Miss Lassiter?"

Cynda shook her head. "I don't want to travel anymore. I want to do something else." *Something that doesn't tear my heart out.*

"There is little else you can do, Miss Lassiter. Your PLIS rules out nearly every other legitimate profession."

Cynda wondered when he was going to mention that. Her Personal Life Index Score had always been a problem. She'd answered a few too many questions inappropriately, at least from society's point of view. Her honesty had earned her the Adrenalin Reactive label, reducing her employment opportunities at the same time.

"Maybe I'll go Off-Grid," she mused. "My folks could always use an extra hand raising turnips, or whatever it is they grow."

"You will not be at liberty to leave after the charges are filed," Morrisey replied.

Cynda sat up again. The bed beeped in response. "What charges?" she asked in a bare whisper.

"Supplying goods to Off Gridders."

"I—"

"The government's been watching your trips to the deli," he replied.

"How do you know that?"

"He knows everything," Ralph murmured from his place near the door, still pecking away at the keyboard.

"Unfortunately, you won't be the only one charged," Morrisey continued.

Eli. This guy knows exactly what buttons to push. He's worse than TIC.

"Got it," Ralph's voice announced, cutting through their standoff.

The image of Walter J. Samuelson, psychiatrist and erstwhile time-traveler, suspended itself in the air a few feet in front of Cynda. She blinked, and then swore.

It was the man in Colney Hatch Asylum.

✝

Monday, 1 October, 1888

"Idiocy is its own reward," Livingston mused, surveying the wreckage. A thin strip of wood hung from its torn hinges— remnants of the clinic's door.

William crunched his way across the broken glass after a cursory tour inside. "Not much left, I'm afraid," he reported. "I asked around. The crowd was whipped up by two men."

"One who could barely speak above a whisper and the other with a bad limp?"

William nodded his assent. "The two thugs threw around a few bob and that was all it took."

"Any word on where the doctor is being held?"

"Bishopsgate is what I heard. A fair number have gone there in hopes of settling the matter of the two dead doxies."

"Yes, I wouldn't doubt." Livingston's index finger tapped the head of his cane in thought. "That will be all I need tonight, William. You've done well by summoning me. I believe you may have diverted a larger disaster."

The man glanced toward the rubble and then back again, as if he intended to challenge the notion. Instead, he nodded, tipped his cap and trudged away.

As Livingston headed west toward Bishopsgate Street, his mind took stock of the situation. True to form, Hastings had struck again without consulting him, no doubt hoping that the clinic's destruction would force the erstwhile physician to leave town.

"How little he understands human nature," Livingstone murmured. He doubted Hastings knew of the doctor's arrest. The fool charged like a bull without any great amount of thought. As usual, it had worsened the situation. Now it was up to Livingston to put it right.

30

Alastair maintained his illusion during the entire journey, fearful of what his stomach might produce from the shock of changing form. When they reached Bloomsbury, Fisher exited the carriage first, surveying the street as if expecting trouble. Keats helped Alastair out of the carriage, maintaining the charade while the two men on top peered down at them.

"I still don't know how you got the lady in there, sir, but it was right slick," the driver said, shaking his head.

"Yes, well, we had a bit of luck with that," Fisher replied. "We shall not need your services from this point on."

"Right, sir." The driver traded a look with the constable at his side as the carriage rattled off, the sound reverberating in the empty street.

"I'll make us some tea," Keats offered, leading them toward the red brick building.

As he ascended the stairs to the second floor, Alastair was keenly aware of Fisher's devout scrutiny, every movement captured and analyzed. As he waited for Keats to unlock the door, Alastair realized he'd never been inside the man's lodgings. That didn't speak well of their supposed friendship.

The door swung open. After a few moments, the gas lamps revealed a compact, yet tidy room. It offered a nicely appointed couch, two chairs and a bookcase filled to the brim. No stray bits of women's clothing or a deck of cards to be seen. Keats' deception had been masterful.

Their host gestured for them to take a seat. Fisher deposited his coat and hat at the door. Alastair sank into the nearest chair, his head swimming. *How do the others go about en mirage for hours at a time? It is so draining.*

Kneeling in front of the fireplace, Keats plucked coal from the

282 | Jana G. Oliver

scuttle and vigorously applied the bellows. Once the fire took shape, he rushed off into another room and returned with a teakettle. Placing it on the hook over the fire, he dusted his hands and then looked at his two guests with open anxiety.

Knowing he could wait no longer, Alastair leaned back, closed his eyes and clenched his teeth. The transition came in roaring waves, like molten lava boiling over his skin. Gasping aloud at the discomfort, he bent over, elbows on knees, breathing deeply to quench the nausea.

Keats knelt next to him, offering a wetted cloth. Alastair stared at it. One moment, the fellow was savaging him with questions—the next, treating him like a long-lost relative.

So confusing. He reluctantly took the cloth and applied it to his face, savoring the cool dampness.

"I'll have tea pretty soon," Keats announced.

Alastair was vaguely aware of their host twittering around for a few more minutes. Keats finally settled into a chair near the fire, apprehension pouring off him.

As expected, Fisher opened the conversation. "I am quite impressed, doctor. I would have sworn I was sitting across from an attractive young woman in that carriage." He leaned forward, rife with curiosity. "Was that Miss Lassiter?"

Alastair nodded. After a look toward Keats, he added, "Apparently, you are aware of the nature of this...transformation."

"I have learned of it only recently, and not in complete detail." A sidelong glance at Keats.

"If I could have escaped in any other manner, I would have done so."

"Sir, I—"

The teakettle shrilled over Keats' interjection. He rose and poured the boiling liquid into the pot, his hands shaking noticeably. Though his friend had stood firm in the face of a ravening mob, the sergeant's panic was rising with every passing minute.

Fisher doesn't know he's a shifter. Alastair returned his attention to the senior cop. "I can hardly deny what you saw, so put your questions to me as you wish. I will endeavor to answer them as honestly as possible."

"How do you refer to yourself?"

"We are called Transitives."

"I see. How does one become such as you?"

Alastair explained the process with as little detail as possible.

There was no guarantee this conversation would not come back to haunt him.

Keats offered his superior a cup of tea. Not wishing to be distracted, Fisher snatched it out of the sergeant's hand and set it on a small table next to him with a loud rattle. Keats retreated to his place next to the fire, his fidgeting accelerated.

"You sound disquieted about this...talent," Fisher remarked. "Why?"

"I do not believe it is honorable," Alastair replied.

Fisher stared into the fire, brows furrowed. "You call yourselves 'Transitives'. How remarkable. Are you able to tell if one of your kind is...*en mirage?*" he asked, repeating the new words carefully.

"To some extent," Alastair admitted.

"Are you able to tell when Keats is in that state?"

Their host's mouth fell open, and then quickly closed. His eyes darted from his boss to Alastair's in frank dismay.

There it is. No reason to deny it. "Yes, I can. He seems easier to discern, unlike some of the others."

"Sir—"

Fisher gestured for silence. "Not yet, Sergeant. I'll get to you presently." Keats' expression clouded.

The chief inspector took a sip of the tea. He set the cup down, pensive. "If one of your kind is able to shift into any form he wishes, our task as keepers of the peace becomes nearly impossible. How can we be assured a physical description is accurate? How would one know that a man is who he claims to be, or even a man for that matter?"

"You can't," Alastair replied. "Though the illusion isn't perfect, the viewer's mind fills in the details." He set his own cup aside. "From your calm reaction, I must assume you've seen one of us *en mirage* before."

"I have." A frown toward Keats. "My subordinate and I spoke on this very matter a few days ago, though he deigned not to reveal many details."

Keats jumped in. "I believe that the Chief Inspector encountered an Unstable, a man burning with fever. He shifted repeatedly, and then died." Before Alastair could pose the question, he received a quick shake of the head. "No, he didn't touch the fellow."

"Thank God," Alastair whispered.

That raised Fisher's eyebrow. "Might I have received this ability even if I did not want it?"

"Yes," Alastair responded, "though it is forbidden to transfer the ability without someone's consent. However, if the man was desperately ill, he might not have known what he was about."

"I see." More judicious thought. "Every society has a governing body. What is yours?"

Keats groaned aloud. "In for a penny..."

"You know them better than I do," Alastair replied tartly. "I haven't had a good history with them."

While Alastair sipped the tea to settle his nerves, Keats patiently explained the nature of The Conclave and the power they wielded, real or imagined. Upon Fisher's urging, he described Alastair's encounters with their superiors, and how their relationship had progressed from bullying to open rancor.

"They're worried one of ours might be the East End murderer," Keats explained.

"A valid concern," Fisher murmured. "Everyone has fears the killer might be one of their own: the Jews, the Irish, the medicos."

"We all want to believe it's someone else," Alastair said.

A sage nod from Fisher. "How many Transitives are there in London?"

Keats answered, "Probably no more than seven hundred."

Alastair caught Keats' eye. He'd not been entirely truthful: he'd failed to mention the Solitaries, those who remained aloof and refused to accept The Conclave's jurisdiction. Exactly how many of them resided in London was a mystery.

The senior cop rubbed his chin with his thumb for a time. The room was noticeably warmer now. Alastair rose, removing his tattered jacket and standing in front of the window. Dawn would be along in an hour or so. The night had eluded him.

"Is the missing woman one of your kind?" Fisher asked, coming full circle.

"No," Alastair said, swinging around. "She is not."

A low, annoyed sigh. "You still have not told me exactly what happened in that alley. Either of you."

"Keats doesn't know," Alastair retorted. "By the time he found me, Jacynda was gone."

"Gone where?" Fisher demanded, rising to his feet. "Good God, man, it's a simple question."

"Which does not have a simple answer," Alastair replied. "One moment, she was there, the next..." He waved a hand to indicate nothingness. "If you wish to book me for murder, then do so. However, it will be deuced difficult to convict me without a body."

The sigh came from Keats this time. "He has a point, Chief Inspector."

Fisher dropped into his chair. "Indeed. I just want to know what happened. In the end, Dr. Montrose, our careers are on the line when we put forward the case that you are not a butchering madman."

"I am not, so you are on safe ground with that assertion."

Alastair turned back to the window. Below, a hansom disgorged a constable. The fellow peered at a note in his hand, and then up at the building.

"Someone is looking for you, Chief Inspector," Alastair said. "There's a bobby downstairs."

"Apparently, the teamster reported where we went to ground," Fisher remarked, shaking his head.

Keats rose. "I'll see what the fellow wants." He hurried out the door and descended the stairs at a rapid clip.

Alastair turned toward the chief inspector. "Why didn't you leave me at Bishopsgate to let the mob sort it out?"

"Keats asked me to intervene."

"Do you usually cater to the whims of your sergeant?"

A wry smile. "Not usually; Keats is a different breed. I always wondered how he knew so much of what went on in Whitechapel. I'd attributed it to a wide net of informants, but now it appears he has a talent other cops would envy."

Alastair mirrored the smile. "You're not the only one with the wrong impression; I thought him a womanizer, a degenerate gambler. I owe him much—my life included, it appears."

"The man is quite remarkable," Fisher said.

The topic of conversation returned, a bit winded, and handed off a sealed envelope to Fisher. As the Chief Inspector ripped it open, Keats took his post by the fire. He had a resigned look on his face.

After scanning the note, Fisher's face turned indignant.

He waved the paper. "This improbable farce continues. The missing woman arrived at the Bishopsgate Police Station just after we departed. She gave a lively account of what occurred in the alley. She states that you, doctor, came to her rescue, fending off an assailant and therefore saving her life. When you went to summon aid for her injuries, minor ones apparently, she staggered off in a dazed state. She remembers entering a

286 | Jana G. Oliver

courtyard and swooning. When she came to her senses, she learned of your arrest and hurried to the police station to put things right. As far as our comrades at Bishopsgate are concerned, the matter is closed, as she is unable to provide a description of her attacker." Fisher raised his eyes. "You're off the scaffold, doctor."

"Thank God," Alastair murmured. *Was it Jacynda? If so, why had she returned? Had she changed her mind?*

"Where is she now?" Keats asked.

"It does not say." The chief inspector stood, tucking the note into his jacket pocket. "I dislike coincidence, gentlemen, and this timely resurrection reeks of it. It reads too much like a Penny Dreadful to be believed. Given what I know of your abilities, that woman at Bishopsgate could be anyone." He strode to the door and secured his coat. "Good morning to you, Doctor. I don't doubt we will be meeting again in the near future." His eyes moved to Keats. "Sergeant, if I may speak to you privately."

Keats trailed behind his superior like a man who sees his future turning to dust.

31

Chief Inspector Fisher halted at the kerb and rounded on Keats, seething. "I can hardly credit your behavior this last week. I have always granted you considerable leeway in your work, infinitely more than any other sergeant at the Yard, and yet you abuse my trust with your half-truths. What has gotten into you?" Before Keats could speak, Fisher continued, "Why didn't you tell me you were one of them? Do you trust me so little?"

Keats dropped his gaze. "It wasn't a matter of trust, sir."

"Then what was it?"

"The knowledge of our existence puts you in particular danger."

"In what way?" Fisher shot back.

"I was concerned you might be harmed, perhaps suffer some setback in your career."

"Fretting about my career is not your job, Sergeant."

"Your career is not the only thing in danger, sir. In the past, *they* have orchestrated the downfall of those they deem a threat, either by character assassination or through outright physical violence. Some unfortunates found themselves committed to an asylum as a means to secure their silence. Those of higher rank are often harder to dissuade, and so may fall prey to a mishap."

"Mishap?"

"A slip in front of a coach, a tumble off a train, something of that nature. Given our leaders' recent behavior toward Alastair, I didn't dare take the risk. That is why I was so reticent to tell you the truth."

Fisher stepped onto the kerb and peered down the street. "You could easily have led me into early retirement to deal with the problem. Why didn't you?"

"Because you are one of the finest police officers I have ever met, sir. If you were to retire, London would be the worse for it."

"And your career, as well."

288 | Jana G. Oliver

Keats sighed. "I prayed I might walk a line between you and *them*."

"No man can serve two masters, Sergeant. You must choose."

"I know that now, sir."

There was a small silence. Fisher's voice, considerably softened, asked, "How did you acquire your...ability?"

"My mother."

A coach clattered by, the horses' breath a billow of steam in the cold air.

A brusque nod. "Is there a cab stand near here?" Fisher asked.

Keats started at the abrupt change of subject. "There's one at Russell Square. Though it is early, you also might secure a hansom in front of the museum."

"Excellent. I wish to go home and freshen up before I begin the day."

"Sir?" Keats asked, on tenterhooks. *Do I still have a job?*

Fisher turned toward him. "Is there a peer of the realm in your midst?"

"Yes."

"Does he have a lick of intelligence?"

"He does indeed, sir."

"I would like to meet with him."

"Yes, sir."

Fisher adjusted his hat. "There is much more at stake than my sudden distrust of your motives, Sergeant." Keats' hope melted. His superior placed a hand on his shoulder. "We will work through this. You're too good of a man to lose. In the future, by God, you tell me everything. Do you understand?"

"Yes, sir."

"Then good morning, Detective-Sergeant." Fisher swung around him and marched away at a brisk clip, coat tails flapping.

As Keats watched the chief inspector turn the corner and head toward Russell Square, a shudder coursed through him.

"A man cannot serve two masters," he whispered. As fate would have it, that was precisely what he was required to do.

‡

2057 A.D.
South Horizons Complex

The reassuring stillness of Ralph's apartment wrapped around her, drawing her in. Other than the occasional whir of his

DomoBot gliding through to check on her, Cynda was left to her own thoughts. Nestled in the retro purple beanbag chair, cradling Ferret Fred to her chest, she'd listened to Chris' Vid messages in chronological order, laughing at his jokes and savoring what made him so unique. Then she wept until there were no more tears.

By now, the report she'd filed would be bouncing around Morrisey's organization. Parts of the journey she didn't bother to mention—Alastair and Jonathon's supposedly being shape-shifters, for example. Other than Alastair's little sleepwalking trick, she'd never seen either of them change. If their kind no longer existed in 2057, she'd sound crazy. If they did, well, it was best not to stir things up.

"Should I work for Mr. Genius?" she mused. She couldn't crash at Ralph's apartment forever. On the other hand, Morrisey's job offer smelt like a Faustian bargain. "Whatcha think, Fred?" she murmured, tightening her grip on the stuffed critter.

The front door beeped, followed by the glide of the DomoBot across the faux-wood floor. "Good afternoon, Master Ralph," it announced in an accent of a proper British butler. Leave it to her friend to program himself a manservant on wheels.

"Good afternoon, Sigmund. Is our guest up?"

"Yes, sir. She is currently in the central room communing with a transference item."

Transference item? Cynda glanced down. *Must mean you, Fred.*

"Thank you, Sigmund. That will be all." The Bot glided away to do whatever Bots did when they weren't under your nose. They probably talked behind their masters' backs, just like their nineteenth-century counterparts.

Ralph appeared in the doorway, studying her for a moment. "Hey."

"Hey."

Dropping his pack, he crowded into the double beanbag with her. It was the kind of closeness she'd never experienced with her own brother.

"How goes it?" he asked. He sounded upbeat, but his eyes reflected concern.

"Just fabulous. How about you?" she replied, cuddling Fred closer. If he'd been alive, his eyes would be bulging.

"I've been better, but then again, I'm not the one who's committing ferret abuse."

She loosened her grip and set her chin on top of Fred's head.

An emphatic sigh. "Talk to me, Cyn."

"How much do you trust Morrisey?"

290 | Jana G. Oliver

Ralph's glasses descended for a cleaning as he thought through the question. "On a scale of one to ten, about an eight."

She blinked. "That high?"

A nod as the glasses returned to his nose. "He brought home four TIC Rovers on his own dime, and made sure you got top-of-the-line medical care. He didn't have to do any of that."

"Yeah, I know. I just don't understand why he's being so...nice. What's in it for him?"

"Good Karma?" Ralph offered.

She shook her head in disbelief.

"I don't know, Cyn. He's a complicated guy." He plucked Fred out of her hands and petted him, then playfully set the ferret on top of her head. It teetered for a moment and fell to the floor, flopping onto its side.

She pulled her knees up, wrapping her arms around them. "I want to go back to '88 and get the tourist."

Ralph eyed her. "You sure that's wise? There's nothing to say the bad dude in the alley won't come after you again."

"I have to do this. Until Samuelson's home, Chris' death will have been in vain."

"Chris would disagree. He knew the dangers involved. Rovers risk their butts so some smug PhD can go whenever the hell they want and then play the big shot back home. It's the job."

Cynda opened her mouth to protest and then abandoned the effort. "I want Chris to rest in peace."

Ralph shook his head. "You're still fudging it. You want to bring Samuelson back so *you* can rest in peace."

He had her on that one. She plucked Fred from the floor, snuggling him close. Ralph snaked an arm around her and pulled her into an embrace as tight as the one she had on the ferret.

"You never told me who helped you deliver Chris' ashes to his family."

"It was Morrisey."

She swiveled in his arms and stared at him. "Why him?"

Ralph pulled her close again. "Because Chris was his nephew."

"Oh, whoa," she murmured. "He told me he had a rich uncle, but he'd never let on who it was."

"I only found out when we delivered the urn."

"Tell Morrisey I'm on his payroll," she said.

A muffled chuckle near her ear. "You already are. He said you'd be going back to '88, that it would be your way of honoring Chris."

She shivered involuntarily. "Who is this guy?"

Ralph shrugged. "He's like a bead of mercury. You can't put your finger on him."

Poisonous and hard to pin down. Not a reassuring combination.

✜

Monday, 1 October, 1888

Alastair paced the room, his anger mounting with each passing moment. Was Keats friend or foe? Why had he helped Alastair escape the mob only to accuse him of harming Jacynda?

When he heard the sound of footsteps behind him, he turned, ready to do battle. The dejected expression on Keats' face made him blurt, "What has happened?"

"He is furious at me. We've always worked so well together and now..."

"He didn't give you the sack, did he?"

"No, but I swear it was close."

Keats slumped into his chair. "You're angry with me, aren't you?" he asked.

Alastair sat in the chair recently vacated by the chief inspector. "I would say that's a fair estimation. I've known you for over a year and now I find you're not what you claim to be. I feel...ill used."

Keats' eyes snapped open. "I didn't claim anything. You decided I was a fop. I just played to your expectations."

Alastair delivered a curt nod. "You could have set me straight."

"I should have, but the longer it went, the harder it became."

"I don't know if I shall ever fully trust you in future."

A sad nod from Keats. "That is fair, though I hope we can come to some reconciliation."

Alastair abruptly changed subjects. "Is there somewhere I can wash my hands?"

Keats waved toward the hallway and closed his eyes.

Alastair peered into the first room he encountered. It wasn't what he expected: a nook of no more than eight-by-eight in size, with one small window for illumination. Maps adorned the walls, festooned with tiny colored pins. Curiosity urged him to step into the alcove, but he held himself in check, marveling at the contents from the doorway.

When he heard the sound of footsteps behind him, he turned,

readying the apology.

Keats peered over Alastair's shoulder into the niche. "I see you found it."

"You weren't particularly clear with your directions."

Keats pushed past him and then lit a gas lamp. The glow made the maps come alive. "No doubt you think I'm quite obsessed with all this," he said giving a sweep of his hand.

"Perhaps I might if I knew what it all meant."

Chagrin crossed Keats' face. "Ah, yes, I suppose it wouldn't make much sense to you." He pointed to the nearest map. "Each of these pins indicates an event, such as a burglary or an assault. I scour the papers and post the pins so that I might discern a pattern."

Alastair maneuvered his way into the room and studied the map. "Given the staggering number of pins, I'd say we're drowning in crime," he observed.

"That encompasses the last few months. The Chief Inspector taught me the technique. He believes that a series of smaller crimes often lead to bigger ones. I'm watching for unusual events that might somehow tie into my investigations."

Alastair eyed his host. "And what are you investigating, Keats?"

A slight hesitation and then, "Anarchists, those who see fit to create mayhem or otherwise attempt to overthrow the established order." It sounded as if he were citing a manual.

"I see. Are there many seeking to overthrow Queen and country?"

Keats' face sobered. "More than you may wish to know."

"Oh..." Alastair gazed around at the various maps and the newspaper stack on the desk. "I am impressed."

Keats frowned. "If you are mocking me..."

"No, just the opposite." The two men studied each other soberly. "Your intervention saved me tonight, and I shall never forget that."

"Perhaps someday you'll be able to repay the favor," Keats replied.

Alastair gave a conciliatory nod.

"Come on, I'll show you where you can clean up," his host replied. "We'll see if one of my coats might replace what's left of yours. Most likely it will be too short in the arms, but at least you'll have something to wear for the time being."

"That's kind of you."

"I think it best you stay here until midday, at least until the furor dies down. You can have my bed if you wish. This cot is comfortable and I sleep here often," he said gesturing toward the bed in the corner of the small room. Keats took a few steps away and then turned, his expression thoughtful. "Do you believe it was Jacynda at Bishopsgate Station?"

"No, I don't. I suspect it was one of our people attempting to deflect scrutiny away from the Transitives."

"I thought of that. If it wasn't her, do you believe that she is still alive?"

"Yes, I do."

"God, I hope you're right." Keats swung away abruptly. "Come along, let's get you tidy."

Alastair held back for a moment, gazing over his shoulder at the maps. Keats was as fixated about police work as he was about medicine. They were nothing more than two lonely men, each in search of a legacy.

What would have happened if Jacynda had remained?

32

To his extreme relief, neither of Alastair's landladies believed him to be a cold-blooded killer. Instead, they'd fussed over him like maiden aunts. Mildred pressed his spare coat so that he would look presentable, while Annabelle insisted he have a piece of fresh apple pie she'd just pulled from the oven.

"Nothing that can't be put to rights by hot pie," she said pushing a plate in his direction. It held a substantial portion of the dessert, and after he'd finished it, the plate was refilled.

The pie worked as a sedative, and after lying on his bed, he fell into a dream-filled sleep. This time, he hadn't ventured—Jacynda was gone. Or at the least, she wasn't in the room next to him, and that was the key.

Five hours later, groggy from the deep sleep, he donned his coat and headed down the stairs. He was met at the bottom by Hix. His fellow lodger clutched something to his chest—a book, it appeared. His free hand adjusted his spectacles.

"Mr. Hix," Alastair politely.

"Montrose," was the reply. The fellow wove around him, trudging up the stairs as one gloved hand skimmed along the railing.

Keen to resume work at the clinic, Alastair hurried along the street. Every noise startled him. He constantly looked over his shoulder, fully expecting a mob on his heels. He paused and purchased a newspaper. There was only a brief article about the events in the alley. Reading it through twice, Alastair couldn't help but chuckle. Instead of being painted as a fiend who preys on unsuspecting women, he was the hero, a man who had thwarted another horrific killing. The cops were denying it was the butcher's work, more likely that of a mimic. In the end, Alastair Montrose was a cleared man.

"Thank God," he said, folding the paper and stashing it under his arm. "Perhaps my life will return to some semblance of normalcy."

The shattered clinic door offered mute testimony to the mob's fury, putting to rest any hope that his troubles had ended.

"Good lord," he whispered.

Threading his way into the room over broken glass and shattered benches, he shook his head in dismay. All the bandages he'd painstakingly wrapped were flung about, as if by a windstorm. Alastair kicked at what had once served as an examining table, now in splintered pieces.

"All our work…"

The crack of broken glass made him turn toward the door. It was Daniel. His partner's mouth dropped open in horror.

"Oh, dear God." He edged his way inside and then halted, staring.

"I'm sorry about this," Alastair said. "If I hadn't been questioned by the police last evening, this wouldn't have happened."

"Police?"

While Daniel slowly circumnavigated the room, taking measure of the damage, Alastair related his tale. The reaction he received was altogether different than he expected.

Daniel flailed his arms in increasing agitation. "It's certainly not your fault; it's theirs! If these people are so ungrateful, then why are we here? Maybe it is true they deserve their lot. God, I'd hoped I'd never say that, but…damn and blast the lot of them."

"Daniel, we can rebuild. I have come into some money, and—"

"No! It doesn't matter if you've received a king's ransom, Alastair. I am through, do you understand? Leah is not happy in London, and her parents write her weekly, begging for us to emigrate to Chicago." He gestured around at their ravaged surroundings. "Perhaps this is just God's way of telling me I'm not wanted here."

Alastair had never seen his friend so angry, so insistent. The ransacking of the clinic had struck a nerve, one not likely to heal quickly. The clinic was Alastair's dream, not Daniel's.

"I wish you would stay."

A quick shake of the head.

"Then, if you feel your calling is elsewhere, I will gladly give you a portion of the sum I have received so that you may begin anew," Alastair offered, his heart heavy.

"No, I leave the money and the clinic to you. I know you will not squander a penny of it."

"You are sure?"

A nod. They solemnly shook hands, and then embraced.

"How soon will you leave?" Alastair inquired.

"Within the week. Leah's parents have already sent us money for the journey. Until now, I have always had a reason to stay."

"You must write when you get settled," Alastair said.

"Of course I shall." Daniel paused, his eyes sweeping the room. "Don't let this place destroy you. It strangles its own. You are too excellent a physician to be lost in this pit of unending despair."

"I shall remember that."

✢

Once cleared by medical for the leap, Jacynda's transfer from 2057 to the nineteenth century went smoothly; apparently, it helped to have the latest time software at your disposal and a computer genius handling the chronsole settings. One thing Morrisey couldn't affect was her nose. Much to her annoyance, the brief respite in '057 reactivated her sense of smell. Handkerchief pressed firmly to her face, she waited for the next train at King's Cross Station.

London felt different, the change evident the instant she stepped out of the alley. More like a shabby old friend rather than an antagonist. She welcomed the dissonant chorus of squeaking carriage wheels, the clamoring vendors and newspaper lads, all rending the air with their particular music.

Tucking her handkerchief into a pocket, she shifted the valise into her free hand. At least this time, she was prepared for the worst London had to offer. Morrisey had insisted she be armed with a personal security version of a neuro-blocker. Masquerading as a silver matchbox, it sat tucked into a hidden pocket in her skirt. Her new time interface was the latest version, the fancy one that allowed you to do forward-momentum time hops utilizing pre-set coordinates. Ralph had even slipped her a mini medical kit should matters really go south. The truncheon she'd collected on Dorset Street had been shortened in length and was nestled in a deep skirt pocket. Then, there were the forged papers that would spring Dr. Samuelson from his cell at Colney Hatch, and a spare time band lest his had gone missing.

"All I need is a pair of boots that fit," she grumbled, wiggling her foot inside the right one in a futile attempt to keep it from gnawing on her toes. Technology could flip her halfway across time, but couldn't make a proper set of footwear. *How wrong was that?*

Now that she stood waiting for the train, her nerves grew taut. She could have easily had Morrisey send her directly to Colney Hatch. Instead, Cynda had requested a site near the train station.

"'Do the thing you fear most, and the death of fear is certain,'" she whispered. "I hope Twain knew what he was talking about."

The roaring behemoth pulled into the station, spewing smoke clouds. She pressed through the crowd toward the closest carriage, the conductor's shouts lost in the babble around her. With heart thudding, she climbed aboard the train, accepting the hand of a gentleman in the process.

"Thank you, sir," she said reflexively.

"My pleasure, madam," was the prompt reply. He doffed his hat in respect. The gesture still caught her off-guard.

Cynda found herself a seat next to a middle-aged couple and waited for the terror to encompass her. When the carriage gave a lurch forward, she forced herself to remain rooted to the seat, offering up a prayer to whatever deity was in charge of steam trains. Across from her sat a nanny in charge of two impeccably dressed children. The little girl's eyes blossomed wide with apprehension under her bonnet. Her brother's glistened with excitement.

"Isn't this grand fun?" the boy asked in a glee-filled voice. An Alastair in the making. The sister gave a tentative nod, as if still assessing the chances of surviving this so-called *fun*.

Cynda winked at her. The child responded in kind. Kids were always the same, no matter the century. As the journey progressed, the little girl relaxed, and in a short time called out the stops with her brother. That proved fortunate, or Cynda would have missed Colney Hatch altogether.

Flagging a hansom, she put in her request for the asylum.

"Are you sure, miss?" the jarvey asked.

"Oh, yes, miss is quite sure this time."

No matter how much she'd hoped, Dr. Walter Samuelson was not the man in the alley; his eyes were a matched set, staring at her without a flicker of recognition.

So who was the crazy?

"It's time to go home, Dr. Samuelson," she announced, mindful of the attendant loitering in the doorway behind them. "MaryBeth is waiting for you."

"MaryBeth?" He looked around with a hunted expression. "Is

she here?" he asked in a henpecked whisper.

"No, but she's worried about you."

The man moaned. "Of course. No one to heckle." That generated a snigger from the attendant.

Cynda pressed on. "That may be the case, Dr. Samuelson, but it is time you went home."

The man issued a resigned groan and dug under his mattress like a dog for a bone. Out came disorderly piles of foolscap. He clutched them to his breast, not unlike the linguist in Pompeii.

"Damn," he murmured, and shuffling forward. "If I'd only had a few more days."

Cynda proffered the valise. He peered inside as if judging the capacity, and then dropped the papers inside with a rustle. Cynda shut the case with a click. When she handed it to him, he clutched it tightly. "I suppose I can't—"

"No!" cutting him off before he revealed something they'd regret. "Besides, with the money you'll make off the...monographs," she said, mindful of their escort, "perhaps you can return someday."

The man brightened instantly. "I hadn't thought of that." He progressed from brightened to beaming in a heartbeat. "Precisely what I shall do."

"Good, then," she replied, linking arms with him. They hiked along the endless corridor toward the main entrance, the attendant trailing behind.

By the time Cynda found an appropriately secluded spot to forward the shrink, she'd acquired a headache of Biblical proportions. It was all Samuelson's doing. He'd been chattering away like a hyped-up chipmunk ever since she'd liberated him from his cell. Weeks of having no one to talk to, at least no one sane, had shoved him into overdrive and she'd not been able to ask a single question. Instead, she'd heard chapter and verse, as if she really wanted to know the inner workings of a nineteenth-century loony bin. He'd even cleared up one minor mystery: His strange scribblings were some sort of cryptic code he used to prevent others from copying his work.

"One can never be too careful," he explained.

Or too paranoid. Things weren't adding up. Samuelson claimed he'd been at the asylum for almost a month, but his landlady said he'd left three weeks ago.

"Time band?"

He shook his head. That didn't surprise her. Apparently, the band had gone AWOL when he had. She put the replacement on his wrist and asked as nonchalantly as possible, "So what happened to your ESR Chip?"

He acted as if he hadn't heard her, making a show of straightening his clothes as if the transfer wasn't going to undo all his work.

"Doctor?"

"Humm?"

"Your ESR Chip. What happened to it?"

"Oh, Geoffrey saw to it and the time band thing, as well. I'm a bit absentminded, you see."

"Geoffrey?"

"My brother."

"Saw to them...how?"

"He took the band first thing, said he'd keep it safe." Samuelson plopped the valise on the ground and rolled up his right pants leg, revealing a reddened area on his calf the size of a quarter. "Then he took the chip out a while back, during one of his visits. Said it would allow me to stay longer, and we could always replace it back when we got home." He rolled down the fabric and straightened up. "It worked. I paid for a week's stay, and it's been—"

"Too long," Cynda said, not caring about the numbers. "Your brother came with you?"

"Yes. He was the one who talked me into the adventure. I'm glad I listened to his advice."

"TIC only showed one transfer on your account."

"Oh, it was some special deal," he said, waving an arm dismissively. "MaryBeth arranged it."

"Is your brother at the asylum?" *If I have to go back to that place...*

"No, he's somewhere in London. He said he had research to do, and that he'd collect me when it was time to leave. When you appeared without him, I figured he'd already gone home."

"Did your brother remove his chip?"

A shrug.

"Does he look like you?"

"Somewhat. He's a bit taller."

A chill vaulted up her spine, lodging at the base of her neck. "One eye a different color than the other?"

"Yes! You must have seen one of his holo-book covers," Samuelson said with a hint of pride.

No, I've seen the murdering creep in person.

"He can't stay here," she said. "Any idea where I can find him?"

"Dalton could be anywhere."

"You said his name was Geoffrey."

"Oh, right, but he usually goes by his pseudonym."

"Pseudonym?" This guy was as clear as a London fog.

"He's a writer. Pens those gruesome murder mysteries under the name of Dalton Mimes."

That rang a bell. "Did he write a book about a deranged killer at a daycare center?"

"That's him. I don't enjoy his work. Far too violent. Very antisocial. Always has been," he said in a professional tone. "Makes him a good writer, though."

"How did you become an inmate at Colney Hatch?" she pressed.

"It was Geoffrey's idea. He said it would be the best way to learn what it was like on the inside. It worked quite well, though I've a lost a bit of weight from the god-awful food."

"How did you get admitted?"

"He forged the committal papers and played the part of my doctor. He's clever with disguises."

Disguises? "What is he researching?"

"Something for his next book, I think. He said he needed to 'up his numbers', whatever that means. He's a collector of all sorts of crime-related paraphernalia. I don't visit his apartment, it's too..." he wiggled his fingers in disgust, "unpleasant." He snatched up the valise and regarded her expectantly, like a child off to camp.

Cynda reworked the interface, excluding herself from the transfer. After another quick scan around them, she sent Dr. Walter Samuelson into the arms of his badgering wife. A reassuring beep told her all was well.

Turning toward the brick wall, she tucked the watch away in the special pouch at the bottom of her onesie. She realigned her skirts, stood upright and took a deep breath. "Two down, one to go," she said, recalling the face of the man who'd knifed her in the alley. "And that one's going home in a box, if I have any say."

The rogue tourist required a drastic change in plans. In many ways, that didn't annoy Cynda in the least. She found herself a nice hotel outside of Whitechapel and settled in for the duration. Tempting as it was to contact her favorite Victorian gentlemen, she held herself in check. She was here only long enough to find the rogue tourist and get him home.

Cynda glanced at the fresh pot of tea and pile of scones on the table near the window. *Duty or food?* She hated choices like that.

Maybe a bit of both. Claiming a scone, she retreated to the bed and activated the interface.

She did have to give her new boss one thing; the guy was state-of-the-art. Her time interface still resembled an antique pocket watch, but the keypad was manageable. Instead of poking at it like a blind monkey with the little stick, a holo-keyboard projected itself on any available surface.

Log On Complete.

Cyn?

Hi Ralph.

Why didn't you transfer with tourist?

She reverted to Rover slang. *There's a bogey here.*

She could almost hear the exclamation of surprise on the other end.

The guy in the alley?

You got it. He's Samuelson's brother, Geoffrey. Some sort of special deal.

There was a pause, during which he was probably accessing the database.

We want this guy, Ralph. He killed Chris.

There was a long pause and then, *SOB.* It wasn't an expression of grief.

The brother is the mastermind behind all this. Debrief the shrink. Will stay here until we work out a plan.

Understood. After another pause, *TEM says to watch your back.*

She stared at the tiny screen. "Mr. Software Genius is worried about me?" *Thank TEM. I'll be careful. Log Off.*

Logged Off.

The rest of the evening was blissfully quiet. After consuming the entire pot of tea and the plate of scones without an answer from the Great Beyond, Cynda called it a day. Snuggling into the wide bed she allowed a heartfelt sigh to escape. She wondered if Morrisey would mind her staying a day or two extra after she'd found the shrink's psycho brother. It would fun to go to the aquarium with Keats and see the Crystal Palace. And maybe she and Alastair could take a train to—

"Get real, Lassiter," muttered, shaking her head. "It doesn't work that way." *But I wish it did.*

Tomorrow she'd do what she did best: hunt for the man in the alley. For the time being, she'd savor the smell of the crisply ironed sheets, the fluffy feather pillow and the crackling fire.

"Almost home," she murmured and then fell fast asleep.

✢

Tuesday, 2 October, 1888

If Chief Inspector Fisher was disconcerted about meeting Lord Wescomb at a pub in Bloomsbury, he didn't act it. As smooth as ever, he followed Keats up the stairs to a private room on the second floor above the Museum Tavern. Wescomb was already in place at a table near the front window, a pint at his elbow.

Keats cleared his throat as the peer rose from his chair. "My Lord, this is Chief Inspector J.R. Fisher of Special Branch." Wescomb gave a nod in response. "Chief Inspector, Lord Wescomb."

"My Lord."

Wescomb offered his hand and they shook solemnly. The peer returned to his seat, picking up the pint. "Would you like a drink?" he asked.

"Yes, I would; however we are on duty at this moment," Fisher replied.

"Ah, yes." The pint returned to the table. "Well, then, we might as well get to it. Keats has made me aware of all that has transpired this week, Chief Inspector. It is regrettable that this knowledge has been obtained by someone outside our sphere," Wescomb said, tugging on his plain waistcoat. His jacket and trousers echoed the same theme. Keats wondered if he'd dressed down on purpose.

Fisher placed both elbows on the table. "The week has been regrettable for me, as well. Though I am relieved to know that my mental state is intact, the existence of your kind has made my task infinitely more difficult and strained relations between the sergeant and myself."

Wescomb gave a brusque nod. "How may I help you understand we are not a threat?"

"To be blunt, my lord, you cannot. I am blessed with a copper's suspicious nature; I consider all men, and women for that matter, as potential criminals until they prove otherwise. The very nature of the Transitives makes my job nearly insurmountable."

"Protecting Queen and Country?" Wescomb asked, tugging on the waistcoat again. Keats chalked it up as a nervous gesture; everyone had them. He looked at Fisher. Almost everyone.

"Indeed. Let us start with the mathematics. How many Transitives are among the aristocracy?"

Wescomb pondered along with another tug. "5 or 6 score I believe. Eighteen in the House of Lords that I know of."

"Are any of them inclined toward Republican sentiment?"

"A few, myself for one."

"Do any pose a threat to our government?"

Wescomb's face turned pensive and for a moment Keats regretted placing him in this situation. If the answer was affirmative, names would have to be put forth. If he replied in the negative and some crazed duke took a potshot at the prime minister, there would be hell to pay.

"Some are more Republican than others and believe the monarchy should be abolished. Others can tolerate the Queen, but would prefer she no longer suck money out of the country's purse."

"And you stand on which side?" Fisher pressed, allowing no ambiguity.

"Time is the ultimate leveler, Chief Inspector. Britain will eventually realize the monarchy is an archaic vestige of our glorious past. Until then, I shout 'hoorah' at Her Majesty when she passes by and don't make too much fuss when she wants more money for whatever her whim fancies." Fisher shifted uncomfortably at his candor. Wescomb grinned wryly. "I judge from your reaction you are a Monarchist."

"Yes. It's family tradition. One of my ancestors served in the court of Charles the Second."

"As did one of mine, but then she was just a mistress, quickly put aside once old Charlie got a leg over."

A chuckle from Fisher. "My progenitor served as a page. He lost his job when he was caught romancing one of the ladies-in-waiting."

"Who knows, we might be related," Wescomb said, grinning like a Cheshire cat.

"Perhaps," Fisher replied, leaning back in his chair. It gave a dry creak. "It appears we're both pragmatic men. You wish your kind to remain hidden from view, and I wish to keep England safe from all threats, foreign and domestic. I propose we could work together toward that end, with my sergeant acting as our intermediary."

Wescomb swiveled toward Keats. "What do you think about that proposal?"

"I think it a sound strategy," Keats replied. "We can't be sure that all of us are on the straight and narrow. One incident will bring ruin to our kind. To be honest, working with the Chief Inspector will offer some degree of protection for him as well, should The Conclave decide to act rashly."

"That's not particularly reassuring," Fisher replied in a less-convivial tone. "I will raise the stakes, your lordship. I keep my more sensitive records in a private cipher. I have already made notes on this situation, and have left instructions that those be decrypted and presented as evidence at an inquest should something untoward happen to me."

Keats let out a long sigh. A classic Fisher counter maneuver. The fellow always had a strategy.

Wescomb nodded. "Well done, Chief Inspector. No wonder Keats holds you in such high regard." A slight incline of Fisher's head acknowledged the compliment. "I will do everything in my power to insure those notes aren't needed. Nevertheless, at present, it is best that only the five of us know of this alliance."

"Five?" Fisher asked, puzzled.

"In addition to Dr. Montrose, I wish to include my good wife, Sephora. I share all matters with her as she has one of the sharpest minds I've ever encountered and has frequently kept me from making a complete ass of myself."

Fisher shifted his eyes toward Keats, seeking an opinion.

"Lady Wescomb is one of a kind, sir," he replied.

"Then we shall leave it at that, Lord Wescomb," Fisher said, offering his hand across the table. Wescomb shook it heartily.

"Come to supper this Saturday. My wife will want to meet you, Chief Inspector."

"I shall look forward to it." Fisher rose. "I am satisfied with the groundwork we've laid; however, I will wish to know more about your ability."

"I agree," Wescomb replied. "Keats can be your tutor. Restraint is the key. Neither of us needs an Inquisition."

"Only the innocent suffer when man deigns to play God," Fisher replied.

Wescomb rose, offering his hand again. "Then we have a bargain."

"For the time being," Fisher hedged. He shook the outstretched palm again, nodded at Keats and trudged downstairs.

Wescomb sighed and picked up his pint. "No fool, he."

"Not in the least."

After a sip of the brew, Wescomb said, "There are worse men to emulate. I believe you have chosen wisely. I just hope that time bears that out."

"If not," Keats murmured, "we all lose."

33

"What is it we're looking for?" Alastair asked, scanning the row of newsprint. He was seated near the fireplace in Keats' rooms, a half-drained cup of wine close at hand.

"Any sort of criminal activity. Anything that sounds unusual," Keats replied, struggling to keep his enthusiasm at bay. After their recent confrontation, to have the doctor accept his dinner invitation had proved a pleasant surprise. When Alastair agreed to return to his rooms and help him scan the papers, Keats was stunned. When he'd asked why Alastair would offer such a thing, the reply had been very succinct. "I can't learn to trust you if I don't know you."

Alastair turned another page. "I see they now have a name for this monster—'Jack the Ripper.' Good lord."

"They received a letter from him. They think it might be the genuine article," Keats replied, "Oh, if you need more wine, let me know."

"No, thank you. I've plenty as it is. My landladies have been splendid about all this mess. No need to ruin my welcome by staggering home drunk." More page-turning.

"There is one tidbit I haven't shared with you yet," Keats began. "I asked a few questions of those who live near the clinic. It appears that a pair of ruffians incited the crowd into destroying the place."

Alastair's face sobered. "Perhaps one fellow who limps and another who talks barely above a whisper?"

"Precisely."

Alastair glared at his host. "Damn The Conclave; why can't they leave me be?"

"Perhaps it's time you took the battle to them."

"I honestly thought I had."

306 | Jana G. Oliver

"No, you need to shake them up even more."

Alastair returned the paper to reading height. "Any suggestions how I do that?"

"None whatsoever." Keats returned to his paper, reading the headlines aloud. "'Child Safely Rescued From Burning Building.'" His eyes skipped over the page. "'Citizens Urge Stronger Police Action Against Ripper.'" Keats snorted. "Don't panic folks, we'll find the bugger eventually."

"Perhaps some things are not meant to be known," Alastair said from behind his paper screen. "Here's one of interest—a team of greys and a wagon stolen from a stable in Rotherhithe."

"That's promising," Keats replied after a long sip of his tea. "I've got paint over here."

"Pardon?"

"Someone stole green paint. It's amazing what people will filch."

Alastair lowered his paper. "Well, you can bet it won't be used in Whitechapel."

Keats chuckled. "Ah, that's more like it. Fifteen casks of rum pilfered from a warehouse in Canary Wharf two days ago."

"Perhaps the painters needed a tot."

Keats chuckled again. "A blasting firm's office was ransacked, but nothing stolen. That seems rather odd. Why break in and not take anything?"

"Does that warrant a pin on your map?" Alastair asked.

"Not likely." Keats folded the paper and set it aside. "Enough of this." A glance up at the clock. "I've got to rub elbows with the revolutionaries. How about I give you a ride to Whitechapel and spare your feet?"

Alastair set aside his paper. "No, I'll walk. I need to think."

"Your feet, not mine."

Alastair handed over his host's coat at the door. "Thank you for supper. Next time I shall buy," he said.

Keats grinned. "Allow me to hazard a guess—in repayment, I will be required to construct new benches for your clinic. Tit for tat."

Alastair smiled broadly. "You can never fool a cop."

"Not unless you're a pretty lady with a nicely turned ankle," Keats said.

They parted at the street, Alastair's long legs setting off toward the East End at a brisk pace. Keats knew he'd swing toward the bridge, just like a homing pigeon.

"What a curious fellow," he murmured. Their friendship had

definitely turned a corner. "At least some good has come of this imbroglio."

Once he'd secured a hansom, Keats made a point of waving jauntily as it passed his friend on the street. In response, Alastair's laughter soared above the sound of the carriage wheels on the cobblestones.

‡

2057 A.D.
TEM *Enterprises*

Morrisey drummed his fingers on the desk, awaiting the verdict. "Is what Samuelson told us correct, Mr. Hamilton?" he asked, uncharacteristically edgy.

Ralph dragged his eyes from the holo-screen. "Yes, it is. His wife negotiated a special deal that allowed him to take along a companion at less than full price. It was valid if both parties were going to the same time period and returning together."

"Understandable. TIC needed cash flow, and the additional weight wouldn't have upped the transfer costs that much."

"After that, it stops making sense," Ralph added. "The Passenger Log shows Walter Samuelson as the only tourist. The Chron Log says the same. His brother's ESR Chip unit didn't register for the transfer."

"Could he have already removed it before the trip?" Morrisey asked.

"I doubt it. The first thing the customer reps do is scan the chip to ensure they have the right person going to the destination and time. After that screw-up last year with—"

Morrisey waved him off. "Never trust the backup logs, Mr. Hamilton. Check the master files and see if there's been any alteration."

"I've already requisitioned them from TIC. The only guy left in Records says he's up to his keister because of the bankruptcy, but he owes me one."

"Good. What about this so-called bogie?"

Ralph consulted the holo-screen. "Geoffrey Samuelson, a.k.a. Dalton Mimes, has a doctorate in history, taught college for a number of years, and then became an author. Until recently, his graphic murder mysteries sold rather well."

"How violent are they?" Morrisey asked, hands tented in his usual pose.

"9.8 out of 10 on the Graphic Violence Scale. They make you sign a waiver before you buy one to ensure you don't sue the publisher for mental distress."

"What would this man want so desperately that he would risk being stranded in the nineteenth century? What is so important that he would kill to obtain it?"

"Fame. Everything in Mimes' profile screams ego."

"Explain," Morrisey challenged.

"When he debuted *Blood-Crossed Nuns,* he held a press conference in front of a convent and handed out sharpened crosses, inviting the onlookers to try them out on the good sisters like a scene in his book. The Vatican had a fit."

"Which in turn sold more product," Morrisey noted. "That makes him a shrewd marketer, albeit a sacrilegious one."

"Mimes pulled a similar publicity stunt in front of a daycare center to plug his latest book. He substituted pruning shears for the crosses and caused another uproar. He craves publicity, and is fascinated with murder and mayhem. What better symbolizes that than the Whitechapel killings?"

"To what end?" Morrisey asked, frowning.

"I think it's the old 'find the Ripper' ploy."

Morrisey's frown deepened. "If he chooses to play that game, it comes with its own set of rules."

"What if he gathers evidence from one of the crime scenes and brings it back to '057 to make his case?" Ralph suggested. Before Morrisey could answer, he shook his head. "Nah, that wouldn't work. His credibility is zip if it's learned he went back to '88."

"Which might be why he's running under the radar. We had no idea he was there, after all. Apparently, he obtained a good deal of information from Mr. Stone before he killed him. I would suspect Mimes knows how to use the interface and plans to return at a time of his own choosing."

"He might have gotten away with TIC showing only one transfer out, but when he and his brother go Inbound together, the ruse is up."

"You're assuming he intended to collect his sibling from Colney Hatch."

"You mean, leave him there?" Ralph asked, incredulous.

"Why not? He doesn't have an ESR Chip. As far as TIC is concerned, there was only one tourist in '88. If Miss Lassiter hadn't been such a good tracker, we wouldn't have found Dr. Samuelson."

"But he'd have to implant his brother's ESR Chip for it to

work," Ralph argued.

"Actually, no. It's not common knowledge, but all you need is for the ESR Chip to come in contact with the skin. He could have easily stuck it on his person with a bandage. The Rover's interfaces wouldn't have known the difference."

"Is that why Mimes attacked her? Did he realize she was getting close?"

"I'm not sure. However, none of this reveals what he's up to." Morrisey addressed his holo-keyboard, fingers moving with the speed of a man who once made his living as a programmer. Figures and diagrams swirled in the air.

"Request?" the computer voice asked.

"Run speculative analysis based on premise that Dalton Mimes, a.k.a. Geoffrey Samuelson, returns to 2057 bearing evidence from the 1888 Whitechapel killings. Factor in psychological profile of subject, personal reading list for the past decade and scan published body of work for potential scenarios."

As the computer worked, an exquisite graphic of Van Gogh's *Starry Night* formed in the air, comprised of colorful binary code. "Analysis complete."

"Hypothesize scenario," Morrisey ordered.

"Subject obtains evidence that will support his claim in 2057. Evidence may be secreted in 1888 to be discovered in present day. As materials will date from appropriate time period, evidence will receive serious investigation."

"If all these events occur, will Mimes be able to pinpoint the murderer?"

"Negative. Evidence sufficiently contaminated to prevent identification of murderer or murderers from suspect pool."

"Bother," Ralph muttered, shaking his head. "This just isn't working. We're missing something."

Morrisey rubbed the side of his nose. "Speculate Mimes' purpose in 1888."

"Personal history indicates Mimes may attempt to implicate an innocent in the crimes."

"Whoa," Ralph said, abruptly shifting forward in his chair.

The computer continued, "Mimes has falsely accused four academics of plagiarizing his work and filed suit against three. All cases were subsequently dismissed. Two of the author's novels, *Forever in Blood* and *Damned Bloody Days,* utilize 'framing-of-innocent' as major plot thread."

"Speculate type of person Mimes would try to frame," Morrisey posed.

A few seconds and then, "Subject would follow generally accepted description of Whitechapel killer as per contemporary police reports; male, single, thirty to forty years of age, with possible working knowledge in the medical field or in the slaughterhouse industry. Current or previous residence in Whitechapel."

"Access Miss Lassiter's Run Report. Review her contacts in '88 and compare against generally accepted description of killer," Morrisey ordered.

"Comparing." The completion beep came nearly instantly, almost like an audible period. "Doctor Alastair Stephen Montrose, probability match 97.8%. Sergeant Jonathon Davis Keats, 58.4%. Mr. Clyde Owens, mortician—"

"Cancel," Morrisey said, pensive. "Speculate why Mimes gave Miss Lassiter the time interface after his attack."

"If premise accepted, the discovery of Miss Lassiter's body in 1888 presented a threat as she was out of time sync. Ergo, her death would be noted by professional researchers, a.k.a. Ripperologists, bringing scrutiny upon Montrose before Mimes could reveal him as the Whitechapel killer."

Ralph murmured, "He figured she'd die in transit. Still, he took a big risk. He admitted he killed Chris, bragged about it."

A sober nod. "Remember his bloated ego? This is a game to him," Morrisey said. "'*Catch me if you can,*' just like the Ripper."

"There's one problem with all this: TIC's bankruptcy. Mimes doesn't know his return ticket is invalid."

Morrisey eyed him. "Insure the chron equipment is calibrated to initiate the transfer from Mr. Stone's interface. When Mimes returns, I want him here."

Ralph turned to the holo-screen and began his work. A minute later, there was a series of three beeps. "Done."

"Thank you. Computer, calculate probability Mimes' plan will come to fruition if evidence obtained and subject's trip to 1888 is concealed."

"94.3%."

"Mitigating factors?"

"Presence of remaining Time Rover in 1888."

"Our ace in the hole," Ralph said.

"Indeed." Morrisey pondered for a time. "Go and pressure your contact at TIC to give you that file. We need to know exactly what happened during that transfer. If you must offer him a bribe, do it. We need that information as quickly a possible."

Once the door closed, Morrisey extricated a nano-drive from his pants' pocket, plugged it into the terminal and tapped in his security code. After the required biometric scans, the computer announced, "Input request."

"Run random security question."

"What was Dante's name before it was shortened?"

"Durante degli Alighieri."

"Cleared."

Morrisey straightened in his chair. "Run history and profile for Geoffrey Samuelson. Query—is he Transitive?"

A brief interlude and then, "Negative. Samuelson does not have Transitive capability."

"Run history and profile for Alastair Stephen Montrose, nineteenth-century physician, London. Same query."

A minute pause, and then a beep. "Montrose's history indicates Transitive status."

"Source?"

"Private memoirs of Hastings, George Arthur, member of London Conclave from 1887 to—"

"Any other citations?" Morrisey broke in.

"Personal biography of Wescomb, Lord John Sagamor Archibald, member of Parliament from—"

Morrisey cut in again, not wishing the minutiae. "Consult previous analysis of Dalton Mimes, a.k.a. Geoffrey Samuelson. Is Mimes aware Doctor Montrose is Transitive?"

"Access records indicate extensive research into Montrose biography over the course of ninety days prior to Mimes transfer to 1888, including memoirs of Hastings and Wescomb."

"Who authorized access to those classified biographies?"

"Joseph Godby of Edgewater, Harper and Godby Publishing Company International."

"Identify linkage to Mimes."

"EHG Publishing Co., Inc. is subject's publisher."

"Probability that subject will tie Ripper murders with the Transitive community in a book issued through EHG Publishing?"

"100%."

"Why would Godby...?" Morrisey murmured. Addressing the computer, he asked, "Speculate reason for publisher's breech of security."

"EHG Publishing Co, Inc. is experiencing financial difficulties secondary to founder's terminal illness. Previous four quarters show losses in excess of three point nine million—"

"Cancel." Morrisey wearily rubbed his face and then placed his head in his hands. "How ironic—sold out by one of our own." He had no need to ask the computer the outcome of Mimes' book—the

Transitives would be unmasked, equated with one of the most disturbing serial killers in history, the illusion of personal security shredded.

Their future now rested on the thin shoulders of Jacynda Lassiter.

"God help us if she fails."

✝

Wednesday, 3 October, 1888

"Good morning, Doctor," the steward said, accepting Alastair's coat and hat. "I trust you have recovered from your adventures."

The doctor gave Ronald a sidelong glance. The man seemed to know everything. "I've quite recovered, thank you for asking."

"It will be no surprise for you to learn that certain members of The Conclave are quite upset about your time at the police station."

Alastair smiled wolfishly. "Excellent. Perhaps that might play to my advantage."

"Precisely my thought, Doctor," the man replied, deftly opening the door and announcing him.

Alastair steeled himself for whatever the quartet might choose to emulate. Instead of some garish display, they were dressed appropriately, drinking brandy and smoking cigars as if this was any other gentlemen's club in London. His eyes bounced along the row of faces from right to left: Hastings, Stinton, Cartwright, Livingston. *War, Famine, Pestilence and Death.* They were far more impressive as purveyors of the Apocalypse than in their current forms. One of them was *en mirage*: Livingston, he thought.

"Doctor!" Hastings called, waving him in. "Come, come, we must talk." Alastair sat in the proffered chair, and this time he took advantage of their fine brandy and a cigar. As Ronald lit the cheroot for him, Alastair noted a faint smile of approval on Livingston's lips.

Hastings jumped in with both feet. "We are pleased you have come to us. No doubt, the loss of your clinic has been quite a shock; however, we are willing to make good on our offer."

Alastair gave a lazy shake of his head, followed by a long puff on his cigar. The smoke curled toward the embossed tinplate ceiling. He wondered if he could still execute a smoke ring. "I'm not here to take your offer, Hastings. I'm here to collect."

"Collect?" the fellow asked, face coloring.

"I have learned that the two men who assaulted me also pressed the mob to sack my clinic. They are your bullies, and so I hold you accountable. I will be submitting a bill for damages—"

"That's unacceptable!" Cartwright spouted, right on cue.

"I note you do not deny it was your thugs who did the damage." Alastair shook his head. "Certainly you do not wish me to go the police and swear out a complaint against them. What a spectacle that will be when the public learns you ordered a clinic to be destroyed in the very heart of Whitechapel. Extremely bad publicity—especially now, when the slightest bit of calumny might ignite a revolt."

Hastings' face darkened, and his fingers tightened on his brandy snifter. Stinton's expression told Alastair he'd rather be anywhere else than in the middle of this debacle. *Perhaps that might be the wedge.*

"I believe recompense is appropriate, Hastings," Livingston interjected. "As it was your decision to send these fools after the doctor without our consent, the money should come out of your pocket."

"No, no, this is not acceptable!" Hastings snarled. He pointed at Alastair. "You will be leaving London today. You have proved too much of a disturbance to our community. What with your arrest the other evening—"

Alastair rose, sending an elongated smoke ring in Hastings' direction. The brandy had hit home, augmenting his courage. After all, they'd started this war.

"On the contrary, I was not under arrest at any time and have been completely cleared. In fact, I have been touted as a hero by some of the news reports." He took another lengthy puff, playing out the moment like an actor. "However, I shall be reasonable. I will not submit a bill for the damage to the clinic, file a report with the police nor relate my story to the newspapers if you grant me one concession."

Hastings' eyes narrowed. "Which is?"

"A seat on The Conclave. Any of you may step aside, I am not particular—though to be honest..." He shifted his eyes toward Livingston at this point, "I would rather you stayed on."

"Is that a compliment?" Livingston teased.

"More caution on my part. Better to keep an eye on you."

"This is nonsense!" Hastings shouted. "You cannot barge in here and demand to be placed on this august body. That would

314 | Jana G. Oliver

require a vacancy, and none of us are inclined to resign."

There was a moment of silence. Alastair bided his time, concerned that his bluff might not work. He blew another smoke ring to calm his nerves. *Come on, take the bait.*

As Alastair began to despair that he'd overreached, Stinton cleared his throat.

"Ah, actually, now that you mention it, I don't wish to do this anymore," he said, glancing at his fellows. "It's been hard on my nerves. I'd sooner tend to my collection."

"What is it you collect?" Alastair asked politely.

"Satsuma tea bowls from Japan. They are quite exquisite."

"I am impressed, sir."

A nod. Stinton rose from his chair. "I hereby resign my position on The Conclave." He reached into a pocket and extracted a palm-sized theatrical mask cast in copper, handing it to Alastair. "I designate Dr. Montrose as my successor, as is my right." He leaned close. "They're your problem now."

"You can't resign!" Hastings growled, but the former member paid no attention. As Stinton exited into the antechamber and Ronald's care, Livingston clapped as if he'd just enjoyed a magnificent opera.

"Well done, Stinton. Well done," he called. He gestured toward the empty chair. "Welcome to The Conclave, Doctor. I hope it's all you believe it to be."

Alastair moved his drink and his person into Stinton's still-warm seat. He'd barely sat down when Hastings hefted himself upright and marched out of the room, swearing under his breath. Cartwright stared first at the newcomer and then at Livingston in what amounted to abject panic.

"I...I must go," he said, bolting for the door.

After another sip of brandy, Livingston pointed toward an ivory chess set on a nearby gaming table.

"Do you play?" he asked, voice honey-smooth again.

"Yes, I do." Alastair finished off the last of the brandy, his ears burning from the strength of the liquor and his heart pounding from the exhilaration of conquest.

Livingston drew out a chair and indicated the board, "Let's start a game, then, Doctor."

Alastair joined him. Staring directly into his adversary's eyes, he replied, "I thought we already had."

34

Cynda's sigh caused waves to ripple across the bath water. When she was a child, she'd play crocodile, hunkering down as far as she could until the water was right under her nose. She'd wait in that position until the little yellow duck would float by, and then surge out and drag the thing under, just like a croc. It was great fun, at least when she was a kid. Though in many ways it seemed silly now, there was a lesson to be learned; crocodiles patiently waited for their prey to come within range and then devoured them.

"Mimes is no duck," she muttered, shaking her head. "More like another croc."

Leaning back, she closed her eyes, savoring the heated luxury that enveloped her, the pure heaven of the hotel's ceramic bathtub. Soaking reduced the ache in her feet and chest, something a Thera-Bed seemed unable to accomplish. The only negative was that the hotel maid had to haul the water up however many flights of stairs to fill the tub, bucketful by steaming bucketful. Cynda made sure to be generous with the tip.

The characteristic sound of an Outbound, a hollow whooshing noise followed by an equally hollow thud, reverberated throughout the room. Staring out into the small space that served as the bathing chamber, Cynda spied a figure wavering on its feet as a post-transfer glow dissipated around it. It was male, clad in period garb. Fortunately, her face was above water when her mouth fell open.

"Morrisey?" When he didn't assume the post-transfer position, she snapped, "On your knees." An experienced Rover automatically went into the pose, knowing that to remain upright increased the chance of cerebral degeneration. He still didn't move. "Do it now! Place the top of your head on the floor and stay there."

Morrisey nearly doubled over, his body quaking. With a low murmur, he clutched his stomach.

"Deep breaths, that's it," she advised, peering over the edge of the tub at the newcomer. His shaking lessened. A quick glance at the bath towel told her it was out of range. She had no choice but to stay put or flash her new boss.

Eventually he raised his head, staring at her with bloodshot eyeballs surrounded by unusually pale skin.

"First time?" A nod. She smirked. "Outbound's a piece of cake. Wait until you go Inbound. That's a real kick in the butt."

A disgruntled frown. He was getting better.

She pointed toward the door. "Sitting room's that way. Give me a moment to get dressed or you'll know why I don't need a corset."

She pointed again. He leveraged himself upright and staggered out the door, closing it in his wake.

By the time she'd donned enough clothes to pass for decent, Morrisey had made himself at home. His boots were off, feet crossed in a Lotus position on the couch, eyes closed in deep meditation with palms resting on his knees. "Thank you for your assistance," he said, eyes fluttering open as she entered the room. He'd recovered faster than any veteran Rover she knew. He got extra points for that.

"What brings you to '88?" she asked.

"We've concluded our research on the two Samuelsons."

"You couldn't have sent the information over the interface?" she asked, curling up in a chair near the fire. Tugging her hair from the pins, she finger-combed it, a section at a time. "Or were you just trying to catch me naked?"

He ignored the jibe. "I had no choice but to make the journey. You left a rather significant detail out of your report, one that is not of common knowledge."

"Which was?" she hedged.

"That the physician you encountered was Transitive."

She stopped mid-comb, dropping her hands into her lap. "I wasn't sure if you'd believe me. Since I'd not heard of them in '057, I assumed that it was best to keep quiet."

"Few are aware of their existence."

"But you are, obviously."

He nodded guardedly. "I am privy to their secret."

"I...I just don't understand how they do it. The Victorians have no idea of what's involved, at least according to Alastair."

"A particular cranial alteration allows Transitive behavior to flourish. The change is shared at death, though precisely how the recipient's brain is altered is unknown. Studies have been conducted, but the vector eludes us still."

"And when they shift, how does that work?" she asked.

"Going *en mirage* affects the neural synapses of those who view them, causing them to see whatever the Transitive chooses."

"No magic?" Cynda asked, disappointed.

Morrisey shook his head. "None."

He stood, stretched, and then returned to his seat. She opened her mouth to ask the question, and then changed her mind. Some things were better left alone. "So what is Mimes up to?"

"He's methodically working toward a Major Time Disruption," Morrisey replied with an incredible amount of nonchalance, given the subject matter. "Once home, Mimes intends to reveal the Transitives' existence, moving their discovery date considerably forward."

"*Considerably forward?* The only way you'd know that is if someone's traveled into the future."

Morrisey's eyes held hers, but he didn't reply.

"I know, it's highly illegal and all that," Cynda said. She leaned forward, intrigued. "Was it Defoe?"

Still no response.

"Great, now you clam up. Okay, we'll just say you're clairvoyant and we'll leave it at that, okay?"

"That suits me," was the terse reply.

A thought grabbed her. "He isn't one, is he?"

"Who?"

"Mimes?"

"No, he is not Transitive."

"Whew. That helps." It was bad enough the guy liked to wear disguises. Hunting a shifter would be like taking on a tiger with a flyswatter. Leaning back, she bumped her head repeatedly against the padded chair like a bored child. It helped her think. "What does this nonsense buy Mimes, other than his fifteen minutes in the limelight and a lot of pissed-off shifters after his head?"

"It's the second portion of his plan that is the payoff. Mimes will implicate an innocent man in the Whitechapel killings and then reveal that person's identity to tout his new book."

A domino fell. "The scapegoat's a Transitive?" A nod. "Which means that all Transitives are very scary people who creep up on you and cut your throat, PSI units or not." Warming to the subject, she continued, "Security will be revealed as impotent, the ultimate opiate for the masses." She snickered. "Now I sound like my brother."

Morrisey didn't reply, as if there were one more conclusion she needed to make.

"A Transitive in '88 will be crowned with the Ripper's legacy, his name tainted forever," she said. "Poor bastard. Probably some clueless schmuck who—"

The brutal truth shot through her. Her eyes swept up to Morrisey's. "Alastair?"

A brusque nod. "It is our belief Mimes has collected evidence from each of the crimes and tied it to Dr. Montrose. Once back in '057, he will 'discover' that evidence and unveil the Whitechapel killer. No doubt he has determined a way that will insure the revelation appears completely legitimate."

"All of Alastair's good work, his personal sacrifice, all lost. He will be remembered for the Ripper's butchery, not his own humanity."

"Precisely. And he will brand his kind in the process."

She studied her companion. "What will happen to the shifters?"

He stared into the fire and didn't reply. An answer unto itself.

"That bad," she murmured. "Are you here to help me catch him?"

"No, I cannot stay." *Was that regret she heard?*

"How did Mimes get here without TIC knowing?"

"He bribed an employee to skip the Outbound ESR scan. Our guess is that he removed his chip before the journey so there would be no record of his passage through time."

"He's a right devil, as they say here."

"Yes, he is. Quite clever. One other thing—Mimes had an accomplice, his brother's wife. They were having an affair. It was their plan to leave Walter in the asylum. Your excellent tracking skills no doubt saved the man's life."

"How'd you find that out?"

Morrisey rose and pulled on his boots, balancing first on one foot and then other. "I find people's flaws and exploit them, Miss Lassiter. It is not a trait I enjoy, but often it works better than force."

He pried open his time interface, his hands betraying a faint tremor. He wound the watch stem, counting each turn under his breath.

Cynda rose. "How do I stop a madman?"

Still winding, he answered, "Madness has its own momentum. You must think like him, anticipate what he will do next." His eyes met hers. "Catch this bastard, Miss Lassiter. Nothing is more important to me." Morrisey shimmered and then vanished in a whirl of light.

She blew a shot of air through pursed lips. "Easier said than done, boss."

‡

"I assure you, sir, I have already given a statement to the police," the office manager protested. "I have no desire to do it again." Keats kept his temper under control, a serious feat of engineering given he'd had only an hour's worth of sleep. He pointed to the article in the Times, the reason he was not still in his bed.

"It says your office was broken into but nothing taken. How can you be sure?"

"Because I know. Papers were strewn around, but they left the cash box intact."

"Was it out in plain sight?"

"It was under a desk, but not hard to find if they looked," the man replied.

"How about spare keys, those to the buildings in which you store your explosives?"

The office manager dropped into his chair, shaking his head. "Those keys are not kept in a drawer, sir. They are on the person of our senior manager at all times." The fellow puffed up. "I am a busy man, sir. Orders cannot be filled nor supplies obtained unless I complete the proper paperwork. Either you depart now, or I will file a complaint with your superior."

Keats tapped the folded newspaper on the edge of the desk. Something wasn't right, but no matter how hard he picked at it, nothing of substance appeared. "I am sorry to have wasted your time," he replied.

The manager waved him off. "Then good day to you." He buried his nose in a ledger, running his ink-stained digits along a column of figures, oblivious to the rest of the world.

In the outer office, Keats paused near a junior clerk's desk. The young man looked up at him expectantly. "May I help, sir?" he asked, his accent placing him from the north.

"When you need supplies, how do you order them?"

"Well, sir, we write out the order on our stationary. Mr. Trimble, the office manager, reviews it, stamps it 'approved', and we send it off."

"That works for everything?"

"Yes, we follow the same procedure."

"Explosives included?"

"Yes, sir."

"Where is the stationary and the official stamp kept?"

"In Mr. Trimble's office," the clerk said, pointing toward the room Keats had just left.

"Are they secured in any way?"

"Oh no, sir. What would be the point? It's just paper and a seal."

"If I were to present one of these approved orders to a firm with which you've had a previous business relationship, would they accept it?"

"Of course, sir. We have excellent credit," the young fellow reported.

"Have you any disputed orders at this point, ones that don't seem proper?"

The man thought, and then shook his head. "No, sir."

Keats' hope withered. He was so close; he could feel it. "If you should discover such an order, please let me know immediately." He handed over his card. Perhaps this was all just his imagination. Fisher was right; he was trying too hard.

Keats took his leave, dejected, hiking toward the main road in hopes of finding transport. He was stopped short by a shout. The young clerk ran up, his face flushed.

"Sir, sir! I'm sorry, I didn't think. I'm a junior clerk, I don't handle the larger orders. Those are Senior Clerk Lowery's responsibility. He overheard us and mentioned it just as you left."

"Mentioned what?"

"A disputed order, sir. A rather large one with an established client."

"Involving explosives?"

The man's eyes widened. "Yes, you are quite right. How did you know that?"

Keats silently thanked Dame Fortune for her boon. "Let's have a look at the paperwork, young man. I suspect you have done the Crown an immense service today."

The clerk beamed and took off at a trot, eager to earn his place in history.

‡

Keats barely acknowledged any of the greetings he received

from his fellow detectives as he steamed toward Fisher's office, his mind ablaze. He tapped on his superior's door but didn't wait for an answer as per custom, entering the room at a trot. He halted mid-step. Fisher wasn't alone.

"Oh, sorry, sir, I..."

"Sergeant?" Fisher rose from his desk. "What brings you to my office in such a state?"

Keats glanced at Fisher's visitor. It was Littlechild, the head of Special Branch. *Who better to hear the news?*

Keats shut the door behind him for privacy. He took a deep breath and launched into his startling declaration. "At present, there are three wagonloads of explosives unaccounted for in the London area. Flaherty is in possession of them."

His superiors traded looks.

Littlechild took up the questioning, "Your report stated that none of the manufacturers had experienced a theft, Sergeant. Now you indicate the opposite. How is this so?"

"The explosives weren't stolen, sir—not in the usual sense. They were taken by clever use of a false instrument."

Fisher gestured toward a chair. "You look as if you could topple over."

"Thank you, sir. It has been a long night." Keats sat and consulted his notes, flipping a couple of pages to refresh his memory. "I noted an article in the paper about a blasting firm whose office had been ransacked. They claimed that nothing of value had been taken. I found that singular. I questioned their office manager about the burglary in detail."

"Go on," Fisher urged.

"I learned that they are in dispute with a gunpowder manufacturer who claims the blasting firm ordered and collected a load of explosives two days ago. However, the blasting firm insists the order is false. With some study of the matter, I realized that what had been taken from their office were sheets of their stationary stamped with the company seal, which are the equivalent of ready money to any of their suppliers. By presenting such a forged order, anyone may collect a load of explosives with few questions asked."

"Good heavens," Littlechild said, shaking his head. "This isn't possibly a minor paperwork squabble, is it?"

"No, sir, it is not. I have spoken with both firms on the matter. The order was forged."

"That accounts for one wagonload," Fisher observed. "What of the others?"

"Flaherty repeated the process with two other manufacturers, submitting orders and collecting goods."

"You are sure it's him?" Fisher asked guardedly.

"He matches the description of one of the teamsters."

"Any notion of where they've gone to ground?" Littlechild asked.

"No, sir," Keats replied. "However, it cannot be that far away, as he used the same team and wagon to pick up all three orders within a two-day span. It was as if the first one was a test, and once it worked, he sped up the process."

"What did he get?" Fisher asked.

"Two wagonloads of gunpowder and one of dynamite."

"Oh, lord." Littlechild groaned.

"I took the liberty of notifying the other manufacturers of the scheme so that no more may be purchased," Keats reported.

Littlechild rose with a troubled expression. "Well done, Sergeant."

"Thank you, sir."

"I'll notify the proper folks. This will have to go all the way to the top," their superior added. "It is not going to be met with shouts of joy, I can tell you."

"I don't envy you that, sir," Fisher remarked.

"Comes with the rank and the pay, unfortunately."

Keats' energy evaporated the second Littlechild left the room. He leaned heavily into the chair, his eyes blinking in an effort to remain awake.

"No sleep again?" Fisher asked.

"Little. The article kept plaguing me."

"Write up a description of the drivers, wagon and team, and have it sent out."

Keats rose in slow motion. The yawn came, despite his effort to stifle it. "Sorry, sir."

As he opened the door, Fisher called out to him. "Keats?"

He turned. "Sir?"

"Extraordinary work, Sergeant. Now get some sleep."

Keats couldn't stop the smile. "Thank you, sir." Shuffling along the hall to find an empty desk to complete his paperwork, he kept the smile in place. It was a moment of personal triumph, and he knew it to be fleeting.

35

"Will there be a promotion for this coup?" Alastair asked, entranced by Keats' report of how he'd uncovered the explosives theft.

"No promotion. It's not a coup unless I catch them," Keats replied, currently *en mirage* as the plain girl Alastair had encountered after his visit to the Wescombs. Keats had caught up with him as he made his way toward the clinic and the task of vigorous bench construction. The cop offered to walk with him if they went the long way around, meandering through the back streets so Keats could perform his duties. They would appear a couple, and attract less notice that way, he'd said. Alastair had readily agreed, fascinated by this side of his friend's life.

"It's amazing how you took that little scrap of information and nurtured it until it bore fruit. I am in awe," Alastair remarked.

Keats studied him for a moment, and then nodded at the compliment. "It helps that things are going well in that regard. In other matters..." His voice trailed off.

"You miss her, don't you?" Alastair asked.

"As do you, I suspect."

"Yes, indeed." Alastair sighed heavily.

Keats mercifully changed the subject. "We shall go a bit more east and then cut north so you can get to your own work. I want to see how the Angel and Crown is tonight."

The pub was full, as were the two just down the street. Alastair followed his friend inside and waited as Keats took inventory of the faces.

"Any luck?" he asked after they'd exited the last one.

"No," was the solemn reply. "Let's cut through Green Dragon Place."

The narrow entrance eventually widened to reveal a street

lined with rundown buildings.

"I've never been here before," Alastair remarked.

"Poor area, like most of Whitechapel. Quite a few Irish, though not as many as over in George Yard or on Wentworth."

"You've really immersed yourself in this, haven't you?"

Keats regarded him with a wry grin. "And your stack of medical books in your room is a mere diversion?"

"You have a point there."

A fully-laden wagon trundled toward them, stacked high with barrels. One of the rear wheels wobbled as a pair of sweaty horses strained in their traces to move the load. Besides the driver, there was another man up on top, his hat pulled low and a muffler slung around his neck. The load gave off the distinctive odor of rum. Two trouncers sat in the back of the dray, each armed with a truncheon. One of them leered at Keats, making kissing noises.

"You're a right plum one, girlie," he called. "How 'bout you come and sit on my lap?" he said, tapping his beefy thigh.

Before Keats could reply, a muffled voice cut through the air from the front of the wagon. "Keep your mind on the job, not your knob, got it?"

The man in the back scowled, but stopped making the noises.

"Come on, let's cross the street," Keats whispered. "The rum's giving me a headache."

Further on, they passed the chocolate factory. Alastair inhaled deeply. Before he thought, he said, "Jacynda loved chocolate."

A look from his companion. "Indeed."

Keats seemed preoccupied. Before Alastair could ask what was troubling him, he spouted, "That wagon. Why are they on that street? There's a stable at George Yard where they could have the wheel fixed. Wouldn't it make sense to have taken the dray there in the first place?"

Joking, Alastair retorted, "It's probably the missing load from Canary Wharf and they're flogging the stolen rum to the pubs near there."

"Maybe."

They walked on. "How was your confrontation with the Powers That Be?"

Alastair rewarded him with a full recitation of the encounter. Keats let out a war whoop and slapped him on the back, actions totally at odds with his feminine illusion.

"I am in awe of *you*, my friend. You didn't merely take the fight to them, you redefined the war. Well done!"

"I imagine it will be a difficult post. Livingston is far too sharp, and Hastings detests me on an elemental level."

"Excellent. It'll keep all of you on your toes."

"At least they'll not plague me any further. I have plenty of other issues as it is." Alastair peered into the Frying Pan's window. "Busy night. Who knows, maybe your fellow is here."

Keats turned and stared back the way they'd come, like a bloodhound catching a scent.

"What is going on in that mind of yours?" Alastair asked.

"The man on the front of the wagon next to the driver. Did you get a look at him?"

"No, he was covered up."

"Those horses were bays, weren't they?"

"Yes, but surely you're not thinking that an Irish anarchist would be so bold as to drive a stolen wagonload of gunpowder into the middle of Whitechapel."

Keats raised an eyebrow. It seemed an odd gesture on a young girl's face. "The man knows no limits to his boldness. What better way to conceal the smell of explosives than under the scent of rum?"

Alastair shrugged. "The wagon's the wrong color, my friend."

A pause and then, "The paint," Keats murmured. "The dray was green. Perfect for an Irishman."

Alastair rolled his eyes. "I see this is going to plague you until it is solved. I'll gladly accompany you. I'm in no hurry to build new benches. This is far more exciting."

Keats gave him a long look. "It could be a lot more than exciting. This could end badly for both of us if Flaherty's involved."

"I owe you from the other night."

"You may regret that debt," Keats remarked, linking arms with him. They walked back the way they'd come at a brisk pace. "As long as I hold my illusion, Flaherty will not recognize me. That is our edge. If it is him, I will send you for a constable while I keep watch. They will have to unload the wagon to fix the wheel. That buys us time."

"And if we are mistaken?"

"Then we laugh and continue on our merry way."

‡

The worn skirt and jacket, ratty shawl and smidgen of dirt on Cynda's cheek dropped her street worth precipitously. Though the clothes were second- or third-hand, they were free of creatures, courtesy of the hotel maid. She'd scrubbed the garments clean with a cheerfulness in direct proportion to the liberal tip Cynda had pressed into her hand. Fortunately, the girl hadn't asked why a lady would want such garments in the first place.

In fact, the clothes were too clean, and Cynda's first task was to grubby them up a bit. Standing outside a beer shop on Commercial Street, she admitted the disguise was perfect. Five offers had already come her way, but no sign of Mimes. That was aggravating. Fortunately, she'd not seen either Alastair or Jonathon, though given the latter's propensity to shift at whim, she could fall over him and not notice.

At the urging of a stocky constable, she moved on. Keen to avoid potential contact with the doctor, she skirted the Ten Bells and headed north to the Golden Heart and then to the Weaver's Arms. No Mimes. He could do many things to alter his appearance, but disguising those eyes would prove difficult. Unfortunately, to recognize him would require that she be within range of his blade.

Dragging her skirts and tired feet to the Black Swan yielded no results besides an offer from a Salvation Army lass to come to their shelter for the night.

"You'll find warmth and safety there," the girl insisted.

"I know, luv, but that's not what I need right now," Cynda replied, falling into the patter. The young girl shook her head and moved on.

While the other women chatted amongst themselves, trading stories of life on the streets, Cynda's eyes wandered over the passersby. Just another night in Whitechapel. In the distance, she heard the clock at the Black Eagle Brewery chime the hour. Nine...maybe she was too early to find her man.

The naphtha lights of a street market attracted her like a lonely moth. Customers rummaged through goods displayed on carts, haggling with the sellers. Most of it was used clothing, but one cart had boots, pots and hair combs. People pawed through the goods, holding them up for inspection.

After another hour, disgruntled and footsore, she rested on a doorstep while keeping an eye out for the constable who would inevitably roust her, just like a CopBot in '057. The longer she spent with the prostitutes, the more she understood them. The drinking made sense now. If you were insensate, the rest of it wouldn't seem so bad.

"Where are you, you creep?" she murmured, fumbling under her skirts to redo the lacing on her boots. "You just couldn't have vanished."

The vibration of the time interface made her jump. Looking around to ensure no one was watching, she turned toward the building and retrieved the mechanism. Once she reached a dark spot in an adjoining passageway, she popped the lid open. The dial lit up. After a few quick turns of the stem, a message appeared.

Go to Green Dragon Place now!

"Why? Is he there?"

As if Ralph knew what she'd asked aloud, the dial read: *No. Major Time Distortion in the offing.* As if anticipating her next objection, the dial displayed a miniature map with a golden dot at the street's location, south of her present position. *Morrisey says 'Go forth and mend!'*

"Great, now I'm a puppy on a short leash," she grumbled, hiding the watch in the onesie. Muttering under her breath, she set off toward Green Dragon Place.

‡

Walking along the street that led to Green Dragon Place, Keats kept his eyes on the ground, as if searching for something. "Cross the street," he whispered. As they made their way across, he knelt as if adjusting a stray bootlace, running a hand through a patch of black on the cobblestones. Rising again, he sniffed his fingers. A knowing smile bloomed.

"What did you find?" Alastair asked.

Keats tipped his head up in a coquettish move. Leaning near Alastair's ear, he whispered, "Fenian fairy dust."

36

While the driver stood nearby holding the team in place, the two guards shifted the load to an awaiting wagon. The horses seemed pleased with the respite. The trouncers had offloaded the top barrels, setting them aside, and then rolled the bottom ones into the replacement wagon first.

"Gunpowder on the bottom, rum on top. Clever," Keats mused. They'd even removed the leather wrapping from the bottom barrels, customary insurance against stray sparks. "Must figure God's on his side to take that kind of risk." He couldn't see the man who'd sat next to the driver, and that troubled him. Where had the fellow gone? With the teamster occupied with the horses, that left two men to handle.

"Still not good odds."

Keats glanced down Old Montague toward the main road. Consulting his watch, he glowered. Alastair had been gone for over a quarter of an hour in his search for a constable. This time of night, they should be three deep in Whitechapel. "Get a move on it, will you?"

There were only a few barrels left in the damaged wagon. If he didn't act soon, he'd have to follow them without any way of notifying Alastair of their intended destination.

Shifting into his real form, Keats took deep breaths to allow the unsteadiness to pass. He had no weapon, only the hope that his friend would fulfill his part of the bargain. Straightening his jacket and his bowler hat, Keats hiked briskly toward his foes.

‡

Alastair was in a foul mood. By the time he'd found a cop, he'd immediately run into difficulty. The fixed-point constable at Flower and Dean wasn't inclined to budge.

"Anarchists, ya say? Now where might they be?" the man asked dubiously.

"Green Dragon Place."

"Not likely. No reason to be there, sir. Can't get a wagon through there."

"I repeat, they are there and they are unloading a wagon full of rum and gunpowder."

"And just who might you be?"

Was it wise to give this copper his name? Had the word truly circulated that he wasn't someone who knifed women for amusement?

"I'm..." Thinking of Keats' precarious position, he went for broke, "Lord Wescomb. I've been working directly with Chief Inspector Fisher of Scotland Yard. Is that suitable enough for you, Constable?"

The fellow blanched, swallowed and nodded all at the same time, a feat in itself.

"Quite, my lord. I apologize. It is just that your clothes are..."

"Suitable for where I am, Constable. Send word to Fisher at the Yard. In addition, we will need at least a half-dozen strong-armed men to subdue these fellows. Can you manage that?"

A brisk nod. "Yes, sir."

"Off you go, Constable."

The fellow hesitated for half a second until Alastair delivered a formidable glower and then took to his heels. Alastair hurried back the way he'd come, praying that Keats had chosen not to play the hero.

‡

Keats' intention to appear unannounced in the Fenians' midst withered on the vine when an old woman stuck her head out of the window across the street from the wagon.

"Oy, you lot, some of us are tryin' to sleep here!" she shouted, unaware her grating voice would wake the dead.

"We're about done, lady," someone called back.

Keats froze. It was Flaherty's voice.

"What ya doin' here in the middle of the night?" the old lady demanded.

"Unloading rum. Why do ya care?"

"Cuz you're keepin' me awake," she called back. "I've a mind to

330 | Jana G. Oliver

call a rozzer on you."

Flaherty crossed the street in a flash, digging in his pocket.

"Here, that should put ya back to sleep," he called and slung a coin heavenward. The old woman deftly caught the disk, examined it in the dim light and then dropped it down her bosom.

"Good night to ya," she said, slamming her window.

Flaherty saw Keats the moment he turned around. There was no retreat. Keats began to whistle; no reason to let them know he was scared witless.

The anarchist intercepted him before he reached the wagon.

"Good evening, Flaherty," Keats said pleasantly. "And what might you gentlemen be up to?" Heads appeared around the side of dray.

"Just unloading a few barrels, *Sergeant Keats,*" Flaherty said, warning the others they had a cop in their midst.

"Pleased to see you're out of Newgate. How'd they treat you?"

Flaherty sneered and spat on the ground. "Like a dog. I have you to thank for that."

Keats gave a disinterested shrug. "As I told you the last time, you find an honest job, and I'll not trouble you." He edged closer, sniffing the air. The two guards traded uneasy looks. "So what's in the barrels?"

"Rum."

"Just rum, eh?"

Flaherty's eyes narrowed as his hand edged behind his coat, no doubt in search of a weapon.

At the back of the wagon, the pair of guards shifted uneasily. "Those two don't know, do they?" Keats bluffed.

"Know what?" one of the trouncers demanded. It was the fellow who'd harassed him earlier.

Keats pointed toward a barrel. "About the gunpowder."

The fellow's eyes grew wide and he backed away. "Hell, you didn't say we were—"

"Shut your gob!" Flaherty ordered. He took another step closer, his hand still behind his coat. "Perhaps we can come to terms, copper. Your kind always wants a bit of brass."

And now for the show, ladies and gentlemen.

Keats slowly put his hand in a pocket, concentrated and then pulled it out. He dare not look down, or it'd ruin the illusion. Flaherty reared back, staring at the gun. It was quite the trick to create an object *en mirage* without it being part of your personal illusion. Keats had to admit he was as surprised as the Irishman. He'd never done it before.

"You'll die 'long with us if you use that," Flaherty hedged.

"Perhaps. Nevertheless, I'm sure God will sort out who deserves the wings and who roasts for eternity. I'm hoping for the former."

"Who told you we were here?" Flaherty asked, glaring.

"No one. It was sheer luck," Keats replied, doing a quick count of the miscreants. Four. If he kept them in sight and they continued to believe he had a gun...

A sound behind them, the crunch of boot on gravel. Somehow, he'd miscounted. He cursed and flung himself sideways as a truncheon descended toward him, aiming true.

The blow clipped his shoulder, driving him to the ground. The sergeant rolled and regained his feet, jamming a fist in the nearest belly. The man who'd leered at him went down in a heap. A body launched at him, slamming him onto the cobblestones.

"Where's the gun?" someone shouted. Keats flailed in a futile attempt to regain his footing. Blows rained down on him. He cried out as a vicious kick caught him in the ribs. *Where were the other cops?*

A strangled cry reached Alastair as he turned the corner. He broke into a run, bowling into the pack of men who encircled a lone figure, knocking one over with his sheer momentum. Punches arced through the air, striking at random. Alastair waded in, knowing that in the middle would be Keats.

His first opponent went to the ground with a solid jab to his chin. Alastair jerked on another's collar, forcibly dragging him off his embattled friend. A knife appeared in the man's hand, swiping through the air. Alastair lunged away, the tip of the blade catching the corner of his coat, rending the fabric.

"Come on, you toff," the man taunted, beckoning with his free hand. Alastair adopted a classic fighting pose, biding time. A vicious thrust came his way—one that would have gutted him if he hadn't moved fast enough. His attacker jabbed again and this time Alastair blocked the assault, deflecting the knife arm and driving a blow hard into the man's ribs. The fellow fell back, the knife clattering to the ground.

Alastair caught sight of Keats. He'd managed to scramble to his feet. Blood coursed down the side of his face and his clothes were in shambles. He stared past Alastair, mouth agape as if a host of angels had descended from Heaven.

A warning cry split the air, and then his friend was mowed down with a vicious swipe of a truncheon, blood spraying. His assailant examined his handiwork and then let fly a kick into Keats' ribs. A low groan came from his friend, but he made no attempt to rise.

Before Alastair could react, a blow drove him to his knees. When he raised his head, his knife-wielding opponent moved in to take his revenge.

‡

"What am I doing here?" Cynda groused, trudging toward her destination. The street traffic was lighter than she'd expected, and as far as she could tell, there was no indication anything was amiss. Nothing that fell under the category of a Major Time Disruption. "If this is a wild goose chase..."

Turning the corner, she halted and stared, trying to sort out the scene. Two wagons sat in the street, one empty, the other loaded with barrels. In front of the full dray a man struggled with a team of bays to prevent them from bolting. They stamped and snorted, disturbed by the brawl raging behind them. Shouts and punches flew in all directions. Along the street, gawkers hung out of open windows surveying the battle below. Above her, someone was laying bets the rozzers would lose.

"Cops?" she said, inching closer. She didn't see any police uniforms. Cynda strained to get a better look at the moving bodies. One stood out from the pack.

"Jonathon." He stared at her, transfixed, oblivious to the danger. She cried out a warning, but it came too late to prevent the truncheon strike. He crumpled to the ground.

Burning with fury, Cynda sprinted forward, dragging her weapon out of her skirt as she ran. Shrieking at the top of her lungs, she wielded the truncheon with uncanny accuracy, cutting down the man closest to her before he even knew she existed.

One of the gang moved toward her, a smirk on his unshaven face. "This ain't no place for the likes of you."

Cynda took a step back, studying the situation. She didn't dare use the neuro-blocker, not with so many witnesses. Adjusting the truncheon in her hand, she impishly stuck her tongue out at the menace. "I can kick your butt any day."

He glared, bouncing the truncheon on his palm.

"Come on," she taunted.

He jammed his weapon into the back of his pants, apparently believing his bare hands would suffice. His next few steps put in him within range. Cynda timed it perfectly, executing a spin kick, planting a booted foot firmly in the man's midsection. She'd aimed a bit higher, but the drag of her skirt and petticoats hurt her form. With a low groan her attacker doubled over, his eyes bugging out.

"Told you," she said, the truncheon kissing him on the head.

A police whistle shrilled nearby. It was immediately followed by another blast and then another from a different direction. It sounded as if all of London's cops were converging on this one street. A member of the gang took to his heels toward the narrow passage at the far end of the road. Someone shouted at him, but was ignored. The sound of boots on cobblestones made Cynda turn. A wave of blue coats rolled toward them, truncheons at the ready. Behind them, more cops poured out of coaches. Derisive shouts came from the onlookers as windows and doors slammed shut.

To her right, a figure rose out of the melee like a bedraggled ghost. It was Alastair. Stunned at the sight of him, she hurried forward. "Are you all right?"

He blinked his eyes in frank surprise. "You're back!"

"Yes, for the time being. Are you hurt?"

"No, but Jonathan..."

Keats was anything but all right. The side of his head bled profusely, blood cascading down his collar and onto the front of his shirt. His lips moved feebly. "She's here," he mumbled. "I saw her."

"Yes, I'm here," Cynda said, cradling him as Alastair examined the wound.

Keats blinked. "I can't see you." She moved a hand in front of his face. No response. She repeated the gesture. Still nothing.

"Oh, God," she whispered. Alastair touched her arm and shook his head to prevent her from saying anything further. She took a quick breath and forced a reassuring tone. "It's pretty dark here, Jonathon. Just stay awake, all right?"

Keats nodded and winced. "I've buggered this up, haven't I?"

"No, you've done well for a damned fool who'd take on a mob by himself." Alastair said, pressing a handkerchief to the scalp wound. It soaked through instantly.

A thick cough. "Flaherty?"

The doctor scanned the area. Bobbies stood guard over the injured Fenians. The tally was two short.

"I think he's escaped," Alastair reported. "I'm sorry."

A weak nod. "At least... he didn't... blow up anyone... important."

"I'll commandeer one of the carriages," Alastair said, rising to his feet. "We need to get him out of here quickly." He headed toward the closest constable, the one he'd accosted on the street. Behind him he heard the sound of ripping fabric as Jacynda shredded one of her petticoats for a bandage. In his heart, he knew it wouldn't make much difference. His friend's days as a cop were over.

37

Jonathon refused to allow her to leave his side—not that she intended to. With Alastair's help, they got him into a carriage and lay his damaged head in her lap for the trip. She tucked a blanket over him, followed by another.

Alastair hovered in the doorway. "I've instructed the driver to take you to the Wescombs'. It's best he be there. We can't guarantee he won't...well...there could be problems with his...You understand?"

"Yes."

"They're sending word ahead so preparations can be made. Keep him warm, and I'll be there as soon as possible."

"You're not coming with us?" she asked, astounded.

Alastair shook his head gruffly. "The accursed constable in charge won't let me leave until Chief Inspector Fisher arrives." The dark frown on his face told her he wasn't happy about that.

"I see. We'll be okay."

"I hope so."

The further they traveled, the more Jonathon's shivering intensified.

"How are you feeling?" Cynda asked, brushing her fingers over his pale cheek.

"Not very well," he said in a weak whisper. "I'm extremely...cold at the moment. Is it still quite dark?"

She had no choice but to lie. "Yes. We're inside a carriage. We're going to the Wescombs."

"Lady...Sephora will be..." He never finished the sentence.

What would he do if he couldn't see? Her heart ached at the thought. Why had Morrisey sent her into that battle? What was she supposed to mend? Was she supposed to prevent Jonathon from being so badly injured, keep him from being blinded for life?

That didn't seem right. If she'd not been at the scene, he might not have sustained such a horrific injury. *What am I supposed to do?*

The wounded man shivered uncontrollably. She bent near his ear. "Jonathon?" No response, other than his irregular breathing. "Jonathon?"

A low moan. He abruptly shifted form, and she started at the change—four decades older in a fraction of a second, a glimpse of what he might resemble at sixty.

Handsome.

He shifted again, this time into a young boy. It was as if he were experiencing every moment of his life, even those he might not live to see.

Fury welled inside her. "Damn you, Morrisey, what are the rules? What am I supposed to mend?" She couldn't reach the interface to ask him; Jonathon's full weight covered her legs. It was up to her. If she chose wrong...

"Then it's my call," she said, digging under her bodice for the medical kit. Removing the top of the Dinky Doc, as the Rovers called them, she fiddled with the settings in the near darkness. Leaning over, she whispered encouragement in the injured man's ear and kissed his cool cheek as she applied the business end of the kit to the back of his neck. He didn't react. Reading the results of the scan made her heart skip a beat. Profound shock. Traumatic head injury. Fractured rib. She turned the kit on auto and let it choose the therapy, returning it to his neck so that it might administer whatever medications were warranted. It beeped. Clasping the kit tightly in her hand, she scrutinized Jonathon's face for any sign of improvement.

A minute went by, then two. He remained himself. Maybe that was a good sign. Her hand shaking, she checked his pulse and sighed in relief. It was stronger now. Cynda recapped the unit and hid it away. It couldn't fix the broken ribs or suture the head wound, but it would keep Keats stable until Alastair arrived at the Wescombs.

Brushing back a stray lock of the injured man's hair, she said, "You'll feel better soon."

To her surprise, he gave a slow nod. "I do. Less cold, and my head doesn't hurt as much. Thank you for the blanket."

"No problem."

He peered at her, frowned and then reached upward. "You have some dirt on your face," he said, brushing it off. "There, now you're perfect."

He can see me. Tears erupted. She made no attempt to stop them.

✝

Emotionally drained by the time they arrived in Marylebone, Cynda was grateful when Lord and Lady Wescomb took charge. In a short time, Jonathon was ferried to a room on the second floor where clean linens, hot water and bandages were in abundance. A warm, crackling fire and a fresh pot of tea awaited them. It was obvious the Wescombs held Sergeant Keats in high regard.

As Cynda began to remove the patient's blood-soaked clothes, he protested, citing the impropriety of her and Lady Sephora's presence.

She bent down to speak into his ear. "Weren't you the one who said you were *experienced*, as you put it?" she chided quietly. "If so, then you should be used to having your clothes removed by a woman...or two."

He glared. "There is a difference."

"Well, I suppose I could seduce you first, but we don't have time. Stop fighting me, or I'll leave."

His eyes widened. "Then have your way with me, madam. I'm hardly in any condition to fight you off." That sounded like classic Keats. Any uncertainty Cynda felt about using twenty-first-century medicine evaporated.

A chortle came from their hostess. "Best to listen to this lady, Sergeant. She's not one to allow much quarter."

A groan from the patient. "So I've noticed." He stared upward at Cynda. "Where have you been?"

"Here and there. We'll talk about that later."

Another groan. With Lady Sephora's assistance, they settled Keats into bed, a cold compress on his rapidly bruising ribcage.

Alastair strode into the room, ignoring pleasantries. "How is he?"

"Better," Cynda said.

That earned a quick frown. After washing his hands in the basin, he began his own examination, ignoring Keats' many questions. Within a short period of time, the scalp laceration was tightly stitched and a proper bandage applied, leaving only the broken rib.

Cynda wavered on her feet. Lady Sephora guided her to a chair.

"You rest. I'll assist Alastair," the lady said.

Cynda acquiesced, her mind tumbling with the events of the evening. As Alastair finished his treatment, Keats' frustration mounted with each passing moment.

"Tell me how it fell out!" he demanded.

"Not yet. How's your pain?" Alastair asked.

"Less than I thought it would be."

"How many of me do you see?"

"One. Am I supposed to see more?" was the snappish reply.

"Ah, yes, you are better."

"What did Fisher say?" Keats asked.

"That it was a shame that Flaherty escaped."

A low sigh. "Blast. I so wanted that bastard." His eyes immediately tracked toward the women in the room as his face turned brilliant red. "I apologize, ladies, that was quite—"

"He *is* a bastard," Cynda said without thinking. To her surprise, Lady Sephora nodded instantly.

"I find no reason to quibble with your opinion of the fellow," she said. "In fact, I think you're being quite generous, Keats."

The moment their hostess left the room, Alastair beckoned Cynda to the washbasin.

"Have you been practicing medicine again?" he whispered, pouring water over his hands and soaping them vigorously.

"Maybe," she whispered back.

Another look at Keats and then a nod. "Thank you. There was little I could have done for him. He would have been devastated if he could not continue his work as a cop." His voice returned to a normal pitch. "Lord Wescomb has offered us rooms for the night."

Cynda shook her head. "No, I need to go back to my hotel."

He eyed her. "Where are you staying?

"Charing Cross Hotel, at the station."

A raised eyebrow. "Then I suppose you'll want your money back."

"No, it's yours. I have enough to keep me going."

He dried his hands with methodical precision. "When did you return?"

"A day or so ago."

"Then it wasn't you at Bishopsgate," he murmured.

That didn't make any sense. She pressed on. "The man at Colney Hatch was the one I was hunting for, after all."

"Really? But how—"

She waved him off. "Doesn't matter. He's home now."

"Then you will be leaving soon?" he asked, laying the towel aside and rolling down his cuffs.

"Not yet," she said. *Not until I find Mimes.* In unison, they studied the patient. Keats was asleep, his color pink and his breathing even. "Thank God," she murmured.

✠

Thursday, 4 October, 1888

Her determination to catch Mimes rose with each clip-clop of
the horse's hooves, overriding the need for sleep. Though Lord
Wescomb had been so thoughtful as to hire a hackney to transport
her to the hotel, once on the way, she diverted it into Whitechapel.
The jarvey thought her insane, and said so.

"I know what I'm doing," she called up to him.

"So did all those other women, miss," he insisted.

"You might be right there."

In deference to history, she made her stand at the Ten Bells,
now that Alastair and Keats knew her to be in London. It was
alleged that a certain mass murderer drank at this pub. If Mimes
was true to form, he'd come here to lay groundwork for the next
killing.

She squinted across the street at the gas-lit clock on the steeple
of Christ Church. Twelve-twenty. The pub would close shortly. A
pair of sailors staggered outside, laughing raucously. The taller
one addressed a working girl, and then nodded at his friend. She
gave her own nod at his proposal and followed the pair down the
street.

Cynda sighed. But for kismet, Kate Eddowes might be
standing next to her, chatting about the weather or how she just
needed a few more coins to get a bed at the doss house. Instead she
was in the City mortuary, awaiting her funeral. By all accounts, it
would be a grand affair. She'd be escorted to her grave by the City
police while riding in an open glass hearse, her coffin of polished
elm adorned with a golden plaque inscribed with her name.
Thousands of mourners would watch the funeral procession as she
made the final journey to the City of London Cemetery in Ilford.
In death, Kate had made the leap from anonymous prostitute to a
permanent footnote in history.

"All because of one man's bloodlust," Cynda whispered.

She turned her attention to the humanity swirling around her.
A young fellow, clearly from the better part of town by the quality
of his clothes, was giving her the once-over. A knowing smile
blossomed, as if the act of commerce he was about to suggest were
a foregone conclusion.

She shook her head, even before he posed the question. He
fished out four pence, rolling the coins in his palm enticingly. "No,

thank you," she said.

More coins. The amount was pathetic, barely enough to buy a couple loaves of stale bread. She ignored him, repulsed.

"Look, woman, I'll not go higher." His accent pegged him as upper crust.

"Double it, and we have a deal." He frowned, and then produced the required coins. The moment he dropped them into her hand, she sailed past him and halted in front of a pinched-face girl further along the sad row. She looked all of sixteen.

"Here," she said, offering the girl the money. "The toff wants a knee-trembler."

"I say, now..." the fellow started, clearly vexed.

Cynda swung toward him and waved a finger under his nose. "Don't start." She returned to her place amongst the street-walkers. A couple of them stared, as if she'd lost her mind. An older one gave a nod of approval.

As the couple walked by, the "john" sent her a sour look.

"Make it worth her time," Cynda said. The expression turned venomous, but he didn't stop to trade words.

A chortle. "That was right nice of you," the older woman said. "Ellie needs money to feed her baby."

"Glad I could help."

"If you're lookin' to make a livin', you can't be handin' off the punters, me girl."

Cynda studied her companion. She had a kindly face, like someone's grandmother. Somebody's grandmother who had to work the streets to eat. "I'm not earning a living; I'm looking for someone."

"Your old man?"

"No, but someone I need to find all the same." She spun out a description of the man in the alley.

"No, haven't seen him."

"Sometimes he wears disguises." On a whim, she described Alastair.

The older woman nodded instantly. "Oh, right, I've seen him about. He acts real odd, talkin' to hisself all the time."

"Does he come here every night?"

"Sometimes. He likes to chat with Marie."

"Marie?"

The older woman angled her head toward a ginger-haired figure near the pub's entrance. She was in her mid-twenties, a red shawl wrapped tight against the cold. Unlike most of the woman, she wasn't wearing a hat. "He fancies her, but she says she won't go with him. Says he's not right in the head."

Cynda studied the girl. *Could it be?* "Is Marie her real name?"

"Oh, no, luv. She just likes bein' called that. Her name is Mary. She puts on airs, you see."

Mary Jane Kelly. In a few weeks the woman would be dead, disassembled in a frenzied attack that would stun London and give historians the shivers centuries later.

The woman continued on, "Mind you, I was surprised he was about at all. I heard he was in the klink."

Maybe Mimes was being too clever. If he built the doctor up as the perfect monster, someone would find out about him before '057 and the author's grand plan would go up in smoke. Screwing with history was a lot like fishing the nuts out of a jar of chunky peanut butter. It could be done, but it was really messy.

"Have you seen him tonight?" Cynda asked.

A nod. "He picked up Rosie. I told her not to go with him, but she wouldn't listen to me."

Cynda's heart sank. "How long ago?"

"Right before you came."

"Where would she take him?" she pushed.

"Brick Lane. She likes one of the side yards down that way. Nice and dark, so the rozzers don't bother with it." She screwed up her face and asked, "Why you want this fellow?"

"He's been impersonating another man, a doctor who has a clinic just down the street," Cynda said, indicating the direction with a tilt of her head.

"Oh, that's not right."

"No, it's not. The doctor is a decent man. This other fellow's been stirring up trouble for him. He needs to learn a lesson."

The woman scrutinized her. "I'm thinkin' you'd be the one to teach him, ducks. You got that look in your eye."

Cynda winked and slipped the woman a sovereign. "Have a pint or two on me."

The woman studied the coin. "No, I won't waste it on drink. I'm off to get a bed. Waitin' for Springheel Jack to cut me throat isn't what's good for me."

Cynda hurried along Church Street in the direction the woman had indicated, sticking to the shadows. *Why had Mimes hired a girl? Was he doing research the old-fashioned way?* He wouldn't dare add another victim to Jack's list just to tighten the frame around the doctor.

Madness has its own momentum.

"The hell he wouldn't," she said, breaking into a run.

38

Cynda hesitated at the entrance to the gated yard. Once she'd spied a couple leisurely walking along the street, she'd followed them for three blocks. Unfortunately, she'd never gotten close enough to know if she'd chosen the right pair. *Why hadn't she asked what this Rosie looked like?*

A shiver overtook her as her eyes swept the streets. Nothing unusual: a costermonger and his cart, and a couple of Grenadier Guardsman.

Another shiver. She knew she was being watched.

After a deep breath, she pushed on the heavy wooden gate, praying it wouldn't announce her presence. Once inside, she gingerly levered it closed.

In the murky twilight, she made out two shadowy figures near the brick wall of an adjoining house. A single, boarded-up window overlooked the yard. It was the ideal place to commit murder.

Cynda inched forward, one tenuous step after another. *What if this wasn't Mimes? What if he was playing Ripper with some other poor girl?* Biting her lip, she edged nearer. The man's hands rested on the girl's shoulders. He asked a question and she shook her head, eyes glinting in the dim light. *Did she realize she'd made a mistake, one that might cost her everything?*

"Your kind always says that," he replied, sliding his hands up until they took position on either side of her neck. She quaked at his touch, as if divining his intention. Adjusting her chin so her eyes were level with his, he said, "I thank you for this. You will make us both famous."

It was Mimes' voice, that nauseating mixture of mockery and arrogance. The girl shrank back, eyes darting around in increasing panic. She knew.

Cynda moved into the only patch of light. "Fame is a fickle

mistress," she announced.

Mimes whirled and stared, his concentration broken.

"Time for you to go, Rosie," Cynda said. "I'll take it from here."

The girl took to her heels, too frightened to shout for help. The gate at the far end of the yard emitted a thump a few seconds after she passed through it. Mimes cursed.

Cynda took a few steps closer to study her prey. He was about Alastair's height, and he'd adapted a similar look to the doctor's, but it wasn't exact if you knew the original. He didn't resemble the photo on the back of his book, but then what author did?

There was little fear inside her, only scalding anger. This man had killed Chris. This man had tried to kill her. This bastard was trying to destroy Alastair Montrose.

As if on cue, a sadistic smile curved onto her quarry's face. "So, you're alive."

"Some of us are hard to kill. Though I have to admit, slinging me in front of the beer wagon was a bit dramatic."

A puzzled frown. "Not my style. You must have more enemies than you realize."

Then who...?

Cynda pushed on, shelving the Shire incident away for later. "Was it you playing Professor Turner that night in the alley?"

A nod. "I'd intended to kill you before you got too nosey, but you didn't come all the way into the alley."

"Something stopped me," she said. *Something with eight legs.* "It's time to go home, Mimes. This isn't your personal playground."

He oozed closer. She fingered the neuro-blocker in her pocket, skittish, her side aching where he'd sheathed his knife the last time.

"Ah, so now you know who I am."

"Your brother was surprised to find out you've been screwing his wife and that you intended to orphan him in an asylum."

A wolfish smirk. "Walter was always a bit slow on the uptake. MaryBeth was the key. Without her, I wouldn't have been able to convince him to make the trip."

"Didn't you think someone might miss him down the line?"

"Probably not."

"You removed your ESR Chip before you went Outbound. Then you used Chris' interface to find your brother's chip." She pressed on. "You removed it so we couldn't find him."

His right eyelid twitched rhythmically. "You've been doing your homework."

"I have the time. Something you don't."

"I can go back whenever I want," Mimes said. "The Rover was oh-so-helpful in setting the interface before I put him out of his misery."

"While you've been here, TIC went bankrupt. You can trigger the watch all you want, and nothing will happen."

Mimes blinked in frank surprise, then frowned. The twitching eyelid grew more prominent. "It appears I shall have to find another resource."

"Why did you kill Chris?"

The change of topic caught him off-guard; he hesitated for a fraction of a second. "I wanted his knowledge...and his interface. I found he had a phobia for water. In the end, fear conquers all."

"Why did you have to kill him if you got what you wanted?"

"Because I could."

No hint of remorse. The rules didn't apply. Her left fist bunched as her right tightened on the neuro-blocker. Her mind conjured up Chris pleading for his life. It took all her control not to flip the blocker level to maximum and make this fiend beg for his next breath. It would be so easy to send him back as a corpse. She doubted Morrisey would complain.

Her fingernails dug into her left palm. "How did he die?"

"Why do you care?"

"How did he die?" she demanded.

"An overdose of chloral hydrate. I'm not a monster."

She resisted the bait, even as her stomach began a slow churn. "We intend to keep Doctor Montrose's history unaltered. He will die with his reputation intact, no matter how hard you try to change it."

A noticeable jerk this time, followed by more twitching. She'd hit home. "You do him a disservice. Like you, I've studied his life. It is nothing, just a pathetic attempt to heal the ills of this cesspool," he said, waving his hand. "All of us crave to leave something behind—something more than a trail of insignificant bread crumbs that is our miserable existence. With my help, Dr. Montrose will achieve a legacy that will endure for centuries. I will grant him immortality."

Grant him? "And make yourself rich in the process."

A laconic shrug. "The price is negligible."

"Not from his perspective."

"He has little choice in the matter. Montrose is an ideal suspect—the perfect blank canvas upon which to paint my masterpiece. He'll outshine all the Druitts, the Sickerts, the

Klosowskis. He'll be the one they remember."

Time to play with your head. "We will ensure that the doctor has an ironclad alibi the night a certain Irish girl is killed in Miller's Court." More twitching. She upped the ante with a lie. "We're willing to falsify documents to show he was otherwise engaged during the times of the other murders. He'll be another dead end, like so many."

Mimes glared. "I've gathered too much evidence. The diary will—"

Cynda launched a cunning smile. "Thank you. Now I know what to look for after you're gone."

He shook his head. "London is a big place to play hide-and-seek."

"You forget, I have time on my side. I'll keep hunting until I find it."

"Who would spend that kind of money just to stop me?" Mimes demanded.

"T.E. Morrisey. You know, the software guy. He's got a few bob, as they say, and he's willing to spend every single one of them on you."

"Why does he care?" Mimes fumed.

"The Rover you killed was his nephew...and my lover. Kiss that lucrative book contract goodbye."

He opened his coat, as if intending to pay a bill at a fine restaurant. Instead, he effortlessly drew forth a knife, angling it so the meager light played along the blade.

"It's precisely the kind *he* uses," Mimes announced.

Cynda began to withdraw the neuro-blocker from her pocket. "Put it down. We're not going there again."

Before she could level her own weapon, he catapulted at her with hell-born fury, the knife slicing through the air. The blade whizzed by an ear, catching on her shawl. As she struggled to pull the neuro-blocker free from the pocket, Mimes slammed her to the ground, her head impacting the hard dirt. The blocker forgotten, she struggled for control of the knife as it quivered in the air above her. A burning cramp rippled through her chest. The knife descended perilously close.

"This time...you die here," he hissed, eyes glowing in the night. "I won't be denied."

A wave of solid black obscured her vision as Mimes cried out and fell away, the knife tumbling to the ground. Dazed, he scrabbled for it. As his fingers reached it, he flew backward as if physically struck.

They both regained their feet at the same moment. Digging inside his coat, Mimes produced another knife, a match to the one at her feet.

With a frantic tug, Cynda freed the neuro-blocker and fired into his chest. He continued to advance. She fumbled with the setting, readying another discharge. His last step faltered, and Mimes folded to the ground.

"About time," she murmured. While she scooped up the closest blade, her quarry's face contorted as he struggled to breathe.

"Not easy, is it?" she asked. "Not as bad as having a hole in your lung." Pulling the second weapon out of his reach, she knelt next to him.

A square of white stuck out of his coat pocket, catching her notice. As she pulled it out, she dislodged a pair of glasses, which fell to the ground. Ignoring them for the moment, she squinted at the embroidery on the handkerchief.

ASM. It was one of Alastair's.

"But how..." She snatched up the glasses, and it all fell into place.

"Hix."

The strange man at the boarding house who shared a room on the second floor with her and Alastair. The man who always wore gloves and smoke-colored glasses. The fellow who had crept about at all hours.

"You stole Alastair's handkerchiefs so you could tie him to the crimes," she said. The madman's eyes only glared harder.

A prickle of unease rippled across Cynda's neck. Rising, she scanned the yard. A few feet away, a patch of uneven light wavered in the darkness. It solidified into a man dressed in Victorian garments, with top hat and full opera cape. His hands were gloved in gray, and one rested on an ornate cane. A distinguished gentleman, with a thin moustache and silver at the temples.

Rover? That didn't feel right. Only one other option. *A shifter.*

She hid the neuro-blocker behind her skirt as she rose.

"Good evening, Miss Lassiter," the new arrival said in a deep, smooth voice.

"How do you know who I am?"

He ignored the question and swung his eyes toward Mimes, who had somehow managed to stand.

Now what? She couldn't use a twenty-first century weapon in this guy's presence.

The stranger shook his head and tut-tutted. "If I were you, I'd up the amount of neuro-blocker and give him a hit before this lunatic obtains another weapon."

She blinked in frank surprise. *How did he know...*

Mimes had indeed produced another knife: a short-bladed one with a hook on the end. The lunatic was a walking hardware store.

"See?" the dark observer remarked. "He is of single mind."

"Enough," Cynda replied. The beam shot through the night air and Mimes' motions slowed, his hands dropping to his side, the spare knife careening into the debris at his feet.

Cynda eyed the stranger, keeping the blocker leveled.

He looked at the weapon and shook his head. "That would be most unladylike. As I see it, you owe me twice over. I am the sole reason this fool didn't kill you a few nights ago."

She puzzled on that. Something had jostled Mimes right before he'd tried to cut her throat. "You did the same tonight, did you?"

A patient nod. "To whom do I address the thank-you note?"

A rich laugh, accompanied by a theatrical flourish of his black cape, but no name.

"How do you know about the blocker?" she asked.

"I am a man of many talents, Miss Lassiter," he said lightly.

Frowning, she gave Mimes a quick glance. He was laboring to breathe, the usual response to a second dose of blocker. One more hit, and he'd no longer have to worry about that. Tempting as it was, she returned the weapon to her pocket. Kneeling beside him again, she placed a time band on his flaccid wrist and tilted his head upward, staring into those disturbing eyes.

"Where's the diary?" she asked him.

A lethargic shake of his head.

"Where?

"No," he croaked.

Cynda stood, winding the interface to prepare the transfer. Glowering at the pathetic pile at her feet, she said, "'*Fear conquers all.*' You called the tune. I think I'll put that theory to the test."

She set the time coordinates, mentally thanking her boss for the new interface. Her old one wouldn't have allowed her this luxury. Mimes opened his mouth to protest as the holo-field generated around him. "Bon voyage." The killer vanished into the transfer effect.

The stranger moved closer. She took a step backward.

"You don't trust me," he said. "I am disappointed."

"I don't trust someone who hasn't bothered to introduce himself."

Another rich laugh. "Where did you send him?"

"To Italy, the Jewel of Campania."

The man furrowed a brow, and then smiled like a shark. "Pompeii?" She nodded. "How close to the eruption?"

Cynda studied the watch. "Ten minutes. I wanted him to savor the experience."

Another one of those rich laughs. "Ah yes: the splintering roof tiles, the dogs' unearthly howls, the incessant earthquakes." He gave a nod of approval.

Cynda stared. Only someone who had actually been there would know those minute details. *Who the hell was this guy?*

Unnerved, she checked the watch as it counted down each second. At the appointed moment, Mimes reappeared in front of them, his face covered in ash, two terrified eyes streaming tears. His mouth opened and closed like a beached fish, clothes venting rotten eggs into the night air.

Ignoring the smell, she leaned close. "Where's the diary?"

Another shake of his head. "So be it," she said, setting the interface anew.

"Where?"

"Spain, 1485. The Spanish Inquisition is just getting a good head of steam. I figured you might like to meet Grand Inquisitor Torquemada. Quite a fascinating fellow. You share a lot in common. Maybe you can trade torture tips, get a firsthand experience on what that's like."

She took her time fiddling with the interface while the stranger watched in benign silence.

"No..." Mimes grunted.

"Yes?" she said, looking up.

A shake of the head. She initiated the transfer.

"You surprise me, Miss Lassiter," her observer remarked. "I would not think you capable of such cold-heartedness." She slid her gaze toward him but didn't reply, remembering Chris' funeral portrait.

Mimes returned, and this time his fear was tenfold. Whatever he'd seen courtesy of the Grand Inquisitor had eclipsed the hell fires of Pompeii.

My God. Banishing the pity, she demanded, "Where's the diary?"

"Key...pocket...New High...Street Bank...vault."

Cynda rummaged through his pockets, extracting the safe-deposit box key. More digging unearthed the skeleton key to his room. In an inner pocket, she found Chris' piece of turquoise. She kissed it for luck and tucked it away.

Something was noticeably absent. "Where's Chris' watch?"

Mimes tried to spit at her, but failed. "Rot...in hell."

"Not on a Rover's itinerary." She rose. "Is it in your room?"

Mimes tried to spit at her again. "Come on, tell me or I'll send you back into Torquemada's loving arms."

"Bank..." Mimes whispered.

"Thank you." She triggered the watch and called a cheery, "Bon voyage." Her quarry departed in a flash.

"Home?" the onlooker inquired.

"Eventually. I thought he ought to do the Grand Tour first."

"How grand?"

"He's got six time periods, and all of them are heart-stoppers."

"As unpleasant as Pompeii?"

"Every one of them."

He tucked the cane under his arm. "I sense something beyond petty revenge. You're generating crippling time lag."

"Really?" Cynda said, eyes wide and hand at her mouth, as if totally shocked. "Oh, dear, I hadn't thought of that. Gee, I wonder how that will affect his sanity hearing?"

She started at the sound of gloved hands clapping. "I am impressed," the stranger said. "Very impressed."

"Who the hell are you?" she demanded. He shook his head. "Why not tell me? It's clear you're from..." She waved a hand to indicate the future.

"Because it is possible that you and I will *not* be on the same side when we meet again."

Same side? "But you saved my life...twice."

A shrug. "I'm that kind of guy." He executed a sweeping bow and turned on his heels, cape flowing like a black waterfall as he strode toward the far gate.

Only one response would do. Cynda dropped the interface into a pocket, raised her hands and applauded. "Bravo!" she called out.

There was a slight hesitation in his step, and then he swept out of the yard.

Cynda lowered her hands, tilting her head in thought. "There are sides to this game? Morrisey didn't mention that."

She tidied up the area, tying Mimes' knife collection together with Alastair's handkerchief. Attaching a one-way transfer disk to the makeshift parcel, it winked out of sight. She could imagine Ralph's astonishment when it arrived in '057. Dusting her hands, she gave a satisfied sigh.

She'd just started to open the gate toward the street when the pocket watch vibrated. Extricating it from under her petticoats, she leaned against the fence, out of sight of the road.

The dial lit up. *Mimes here, worse for wear. TEM sends his thanks.*

"No problem. It was my pleasure," she said, snapping the watch shut. Humming to herself, she set off on a quest for a cab. Hopefully the hotel maid would forgive her, but she just had to have another bath.

✝

"You're sure she hasn't left?" Keats asked. "You're not sparing me the news just to keep me from flinging myself out of the window, are you?"

"No, Jacynda went to the hotel to rest," Alastair said, tying off the fresh bandage. It'd been this way since the moment his friend opened his eyes. "Now stop fussing."

"Which hotel?" Keats demanded, not letting the subject drop.

A tap on the door saved Alastair from replying. A moment later, the maid entered and announced, "Chief Inspector Fisher, sirs."

A low groan from the patient.

"Chief Inspector," Alastair said as the familiar figure strode into the room.

"Doctor. Ah, Sergeant, you are awake. How are you feeling?"

"Rather well, sir, considering."

Fisher shot the doctor a questioning look.

"He is doing quite remarkably," Alastair reported.

A relieved sigh. "I had my concerns. From what I heard at the scene, I had thought the injuries more serious."

"I have an excellent physician," Keats replied. "Sir, were you able to apprehend Flaherty?"

Another sigh. "Alas, no. He vanished into thin air, as is his style. Three of the men were Fenians; the others were hired to help with the load. We've learned little from any of them. They fear Flaherty too much."

Keats' face fell. "I'm sorry, sir. I thought there were only four of them. I have no notion where the other fellow came from. He proved my undoing. We lost Flaherty because of it."

"Your undoing, as you call him, lived on Green Dragon Place. Flaherty took the wagon there so the fellow could provide another set of eyes while they moved the load to the new dray," Fisher explained.

"Ah...that's why," Keats said. "Still, I made a mess of it."

"On the contrary, you've done splendidly. You secured a load of gunpowder and affected the arrest of known anarchists. Through your diligent investigation, you've denied Flaherty the resources to obtain further incendiary devices, and put a crimp in his plans. That's a fine bit of work, Sergeant, and I'll give a good tongue-lashing to anyone who says otherwise. "

Keats stared in astonishment.

"I told you," Alastair said. "You just wouldn't listen."

"But—"

"Enough, Sergeant," Fisher retorted. "You've done a grand bit of work. Leave it at that!"

"I see, sir. Well, if you're satisfied—"

"I'm *very* pleased, Keats. So is Home Office."

Keats blinked. "Really?"

"There is word of a monetary reward for your valor."

The patient beamed. "Alastair was of great assistance, as well as Miss Lassiter."

"Ah, the elusive Miss Lassiter," Fisher said, shifting his eyes toward the doctor. "I had wondered when she would show up. Both of you will be duly noted in the official report."

"I suspect that Jacynda would prefer she not be mentioned by name," Alastair intervened. "She craves…anonymity."

Fisher shot him an intense look, and then nodded. "I'll have her recorded as a helpful citizen, if you wish."

"That would suit her."

"Home Office," Keats murmured, shaking his head.

"Don't report to duty until you are well, Sergeant. Do you understand?"

"Yes, sir. Still, we must follow up on the other explosives—"

Fisher raised a hand for silence. "I will handle that. You recuperate. If Dr. Montrose informs me you are not following his dictums, you will have me to answer to. Is that clear?" A contrite nod. "Excellent. Then good day to you both. I must pay my respects to Lady Sephora." He swung out of the room.

The moment the door closed, Keats yawned, clearly exhausted by the encounter.

"I'll come back this afternoon to check on you," Alastair said, rising.

Keats caught his arm. "Thank you for coming to my aid so dramatically last evening. Given the hell I'd put you through at the police station, you could have easily let me swing in the wind."

Alastair smiled. "You did what you felt was right. It was a difficult position. I deeply appreciate that you did not mention Mr.

Stone's death to Fisher."

"He's still not happy about it all, but I think the Fenian situation will pull his mind away from the issue."

"Nevertheless, we're even now."

Keats smirked. "Well, then, do not expect any latitude when it comes to Jacynda."

"Ah, so perhaps that proposal of yours wasn't entirely based on salvaging her honor?" Alastair chided.

Keats screwed his face up in thought. "Let us say that after her intervention last evening, I have a newfound interest in the lady."

Alastair's eyes glowed. "I see. Gloves off, eh?"

"Indeed."

"Then may the best man win her affections."

A sigh. "She looked remarkably healthy for someone so recently injured. Would you care to explain that?"

"She has an excellent physician."

Keats waved him away. "If you're going to be obtuse, then go somewhere else. I need a nap."

"You need more than that, my friend," Alastair retorted.

‡

As Cynda descended the hotel stairway, she felt like a queen. In contrast to her clothes of the evening before, she wore a bright blue gown overlaid with an etched velvet mantelet. The outfit had the desired effect on the doctor: his mouth fell open. She smiled as he took her hand at the bottom step. "Good morning."

"You look...radiant."

Cynda blinked at the word and then smiled wider than she had in a very long time. "Thank you. I got tired of wearing black and navy."

"The vibrant blue suits you."

She nodded her appreciation. "How is Keats?"

"Annoying as ever. He's quite sure you've absconded again without saying goodbye and he insists on asking awkward questions about your...injuries, or the lack thereof."

"That's a copper for you."

"Why am I here? Your message was cryptic, at best."

Her smile disappeared. "I'll tell you in the coach."

Instead of explaining herself instantly, she asked about the night she'd disappeared. He told it all, from the moment she'd disappeared to his shifting within the carriage.

"Thank God Jonathon intervened," she said, shaking her head. "I had no notion it would fall out like that." Time travel was a basket of snakes. You disturbed one thing, and everything started crawling.

He nodded, clearing his throat. "It complicates matters with the chief inspector knowing of our existence, but it couldn't be helped." He looked out the carriage window. "Why have you come back? Are you still seeking your paramour's murderer?"

"No. I found him. He is no longer a problem."

"When?"

"Last evening, after the brawl in Green Dragon Place."

"You didn't go back to the hotel?" he asked, infuriated. "Do you realize how—"

She waved a hand in front of him. "I know, it's dangerous. It's what I do."

He glowered and then sighed. "Is he dead?"

"No. He's in '057 and not too well glued, from what I hear."

"I see. Well, at least that's settled."

"There is another matter. I need to save a man's reputation."

He gave a quizzical look. "Whose?"

There was a long pause before she said, "Yours."

✝

The stop at the boarding house had taken longer than he'd wished. As expected, the landladies rejoiced in Jacynda's return, pulling her into the kitchen to ply her with scones so that she might tell them of her adventures. Alastair used the diversion to his advantage, making his way upstairs. Employing Hix's skeleton key, he rummaged through the schemer's room. He found little of interest, other than a spare set of glasses and one of his own handkerchiefs. Pocketing it, he swore under his breath. "It is damned fortunate that you are not within my reach, sir." He still could not fathom that a man would dare to ruin the reputation of another solely for profit. The grey fog that had engulfed him after Jacynda spoke of the scheme had faded to righteous indignation. Unfortunately, the malefactor was out of his reach.

And all along, her lover's murderer had a room right across the hall from them.

The second stop proved more difficult. As they waited at the bank counter, Jacynda leaned close and whispered, "Be yourself."

Alastair gave her a disgruntled look. "Are you sure he would

354 | Jana G. Oliver

come here disguised as me?" he whispered. A nod.

The clerk shuffled up, peered at him through thick glasses and delivered an officious, "Good day, sir, madam."

"Good day," Alastair said, playing along. "I'm Dr. Montrose. I would like to retrieve articles from my safe-deposit box."

"Ah, certainly, sir." While they waited, his companion flashed him a wink. Running on little sleep and a bad case of nerves, he desperately wanted this moment to be over. *What if they couldn't find the diary?*

The clerk returned with the speed of a man who had all day to do his job. He shuttled a card across the counter and moved the pen and ink within reach. As Alastair prepared to sign, he noted there were three other entries in what approximated his flowing hand. Jacynda had warned him that Hix/Mimes was skilled at deceit, that he'd gone to extraordinary effort to imitate the doctor. Alastair repressed a shudder.

As he signed his name, trying to match Mimes' mimicry of his own handwriting, he felt absurd. He pushed the card back across the counter with increasing irritation.

"Key?" the clerk inquired after a cursory study of the signature. Alastair produced it from his pocket and handed it over. "This way, please."

Ushered into a private room, the clerk placed the oversized deposit box on the table in front of them, gesturing toward a pair of chairs.

"Let me know when you are through so I may return the box to the vault."

"Thank you," Alastair said, keen to have the fellow gone. When the door closed, he let out a relieved sigh.

"I told you it would go well," Jacynda said, setting her valise on the floor.

"It is extremely disconcerting to know that someone else has been here in my name."

"Disconcerting? No, it's downright creepy. Oh, don't touch anything." She adjusted her gloves.

"Pardon?" he asked, staring at the metal box as if it had teeth and would spring at his throat at any moment.

"Just trust me."

He mulled on that as she opened the lid. Instead of bending close to inspect the contents, he shied back. *What horrors sat inside that metal tomb?*

The first find was a leather bound book—the diary. It looked familiar.

"Your warning was not needed—I have touched that already."

"When?" she demanded.

"One morning, on the way to my room. Hix dropped the book in the hallway. I retrieved it for him."

"Was he wearing gloves?"

"Yes. I thought it odd at the time."

"Clever man."

"Why?"

She hesitated and then explained, "Fingerprints." Before he could ask, she added, "Soon, they'll be accepted in a court of law as a means of identification."

"How extraordinary."

Jacynda set the book aside. Her next find was a wooden container about twelve inches long and an inch and a half thick. Flipping open the lid revealed a knife nearly nine inches in length.

Alastair recognized it immediately. "It's a catling knife, used for amputations. They're wickedly sharp."

His companion removed it from the box, examining the blade. "Double-edged. Perfect," she said. "He had a couple of them with him last night."

Alastair pointed at the white object tied to the handle. "That's probably one of my handkerchiefs," he said. "They seem to be all over London."

Jacynda displayed the incriminating monogram. "At least now you know where they got to," she said lightly. Digging further, she retrieved a piece of paper. "It's a receipt for three knives from Allen & Hanbury's, Ltd."

He peered at the sheet. "Purchased by Doctor Alastair Montrose," he murmured. Curiosity got the better of him, and he peered into the deposit box. It was empty. He'd feared worse.

As if his companion knew his thoughts, she whispered, "No body parts." She frowned. "Ah, damn. He lied..."

Alastair ignored her profanity. "What is wrong?"

"Chris' watch isn't here. That is not good."

"I might have missed it during my search of his room."

Jacynda shook her head. "Not likely. I should have known he'd lie to me. Well, they'll pry it out of him in...well..." He nodded his understanding.

She flipped open the diary, and several sheets of paper cascaded to the table. They all had one thing in common: rows upon rows of Alastair Montrose's signature.

"Good lord," Alastair muttered.

"Practice makes perfect."

Jacynda studied one of the diary pages and when he tried to look over her shoulder, she slammed it shut.

"No, not here. We'll take it back to the hotel. That way, you can..." her voice faltered.

"I can what?" he asked, frowning.

"Get drunk after you read it."

39

"Ready?" Jacynda asked, eyeing him intently from the couch.

Would he ever be ready? That he doubted. *How does one confront something so unimaginable, so heinous?* "Yes," he said in a hoarse whisper. He scooted his chair closer to her.

Adjusting her gloves, Jacynda carefully opened the book, setting it on her lap. She flipped to the first page, then the next. His handwriting danced across the paper, sometimes even and at other times cramped, as if he were agitated.

"He's fabricated your personal diary," she reported. "*'Monday, the 24th of September, 1888. A full day of labor at the hospital and the clinic. Too many to treat properly. One little girl will always remain in my memory, her life waning even as I attempted to aid her. In the evening, I saw to my landlady, who has twisted her ankle. It will heal without complication.'*"

Alastair paled. "My God, I wrote that. He must have copied it from my own diary." He worked through the idea. "I always felt someone had been in my room, but dismissed it as...well...nonsense."

Jacynda shook her head in amazement. "This guy is good."

"But that makes no sense. What if *both* diaries had been found sometime in the future? Would that not have mitigated his scheme?" Alastair queried.

"I bet your real diary would have gone missing when Mimes went home. You'd have no idea where it went—just like your handkerchiefs." She flipped a few more pages. "You clever son of a..."

"Pardon?" Alastair asked, frowning.

Oblivious to his displeasure, she pointed a thin finger at an entry. "When there's a killing, he attaches a piece of evidence on the page opposite to the corresponding diary entry. Somehow, he's gotten close enough to the victims to remove something that would prove you had contact with them." She flipped back a few pages, tracking entries. "Mary Ann Nichols—he has a lock of her graying hair." A few pages forward. "Annie Chapman—one of her rings," she said, indicating a brass circlet on the corresponding page. She turned to the entry dated 30th September. He stared at a small, green piece of fabric decorated with lilies and Michaelmas daisies.

"You might remember that from Kate Eddowes," she said in a hushed voice. "It's a piece of her skirt."

Alastair wiped a hand across his mouth. "He's like a buzzard circling in the killer's wake."

"Most likely he got the evidence before they died. It really doesn't matter, as long as it matches the police reports."

"What of the Stride murder? Surely he didn't miss that one."

Cynda turned a page and shook her head. A half-beat pause, and then a long exhalation. "Of course. Not everyone considers Stride one of Jack's victims. Apparently, Mimes thought the same, and didn't bother to gather any evidence to implicate you in the murder." *Which means he wasn't the man in the passageway.*

Alastair rocked back in his seat. "Implicate me…"

She watched him wrestle with his limitless anger. A stranger had ever so carefully framed him, seeking to destroy the good he'd hoped to accomplish in his life. A century and a half later, the name Montrose wouldn't be known for the care of the unfortunate. Rather, the surname would be sullied for eternity with the blood of the unfortunates of Whitechapel.

"Read me one of the entries that corresponds to a murder," he ordered.

"I don't think—"

"Read it to me! I have to understand this man." Their eyes locked. "Do it," he commanded.

Cynda began at the top of the next page, the entry for Kate Eddowes. "*Sunday, 30 September, 1888. Eternal riddles. One sliced, the other assayed. Centuries hence, they shall puzzle on my night's work. Frustration abounds. My quest bears no fruit. Can it be so deeply hidden, or am I blind to it? Still, such was the joy I felt as her life ebbed under my fingers. Kings and gods have less power than I. I have usurped Death. I choose whether to save life or extinguish it. Will the Grim Reaper be angered that I have claimed some of his own? I think not. No doubt he grows weary of his work, so far behind that he is.*" She halted, praying that would be enough to satisfy him.

"Go on."

"Alastair, I don't think you—"

"Go on!" he shouted. "I have to hear this, don't you understand? I can't put it to rest until I do."

Cynda sighed. "Exactly as it's written?" she hedged, staring at the next paragraph. This wasn't something he should hear.

"Exactly."

She swallowed the lump in her throat. *"'Scalding heat rises from the body into the chill night air. I scent the blood, the offal, it arouses me. I pull myself to the fore, anointing my loins with their sacred essence, savoring the feel. I am more than a mere god. I have become the Eternal Judge.'"*

A cry jarred her from the words. Alastair's chair toppled to the carpet as he flung himself away. Retching with dry heaves, he clung white-fingered to the washbasin, his head bent over in agony. Cynda closed the book and set it aside. Where Mimes' writing had disturbed her, to Alastair it was poison. As he attempted to purge it from his system, the difference between their two centuries couldn't be more stark. 2057 deplored such madmen. 1888 could not begin to fathom them.

Innocence lost is never regained.

Water plunged into the basin from the pitcher.

"Are you all right?" she asked. A quick nod, followed by vigorous washing. Perhaps it was his way of cleansing away the blasphemous prose.

She opened the book again, searching for the last entry. Mimes had already begun his work for Mary Kelly. After only a few words, she slammed the book shut, her stomach churning.

What a sick bastard...

To calm her mind, she popped open the time interface and logged on. Ralph answered instantly.

Hi Cyn. Did you get the stuff?

Yes, but no interface.

Uh-oh.

Have Mimes tell you where it is.

Understood. TEM says to send the evidence here. He'll see that Mimes is prosecuted.

When she looked up, Alastair was righting the chair, his face ashen.

Will do, she typed. *The diary entries will prove he's insane. Or one helluva of a writer.*

Alastair studied the screen suspended in the air. Far from fascination, it caused a furious frown. "Absolutely not," he said. "I shall not permit you to send that venomous tome into the future."

Hold on. We have a problem here, she typed.

"I cannot hazard such a chance. If I am blessed with children, then I would cause their progeny countless harm," Alastair explained.

Cynda typed the doctor's objection.

TEM gives his word that the diary will be returned to '88 for destruction.

Alastair read the reply. "Do you trust this *TEM* person?" he asked in a dubious tone.

She thought on that. "Morrisey was the one who brought me home when I was wounded. He didn't have to. He could have let me die here."

The doctor's eyes widened. "Why does he care about this?"

She told him. His anger melted. "I see. His loss is greater than even I can imagine." The doctor sought refuge at the fireplace, resting against the mantel as if he needed the physical support.

Cyn? the interface typed.

Hold on. Decision being made.

Alastair turned toward her. "Send the diary where it needs to go. I hold you responsible." He turned away abruptly.

Exhaling, Cynda typed, *Doc agrees. We both hold TEM at his word.*

Understood, Miss Lassiter. That had to be Morrisey.

A minute later, the knife case and the diary took the one-hundred and sixty-nine year journey into the future. Alastair returned to his seat and stared at the holographic screen.

Items received, Cyn. Holy crap...you were right about this stuff.

Make sure he's out of circulation. Next time, I leave him in Pompeii.

Understood.

Log Off.

"How soon will we know?" Alastair asked, rubbing his hands together as if trying to warm himself.

"Well, they have the time advantage on us, but still—"

The flash of light blinded both of them as an object appeared on the carpet. Alastair immediately rose to retrieve it.

"Hold on, give it a moment to stabilize. Once it stops glowing, you can pick it up."

He slapped a hand against his thigh impatiently until she gave a nod, and then snatched the cloth-wrapped parcel off the floor. Extracting the book, he studied a page as if to reassure himself that it was the genuine item. Stepping to the fireplace, he asked,

"Care to join me as I consign my alter ego to the fire?"

"I'll get the marshmallows," she said, rising.

"The what?"

"Never mind."

He dropped the wrapping fabric into the flames, fanned open the book and began ripping pages one by one, consigning them to the blaze. His shoulders seem to rise with every sheet, a weight exorcized.

Cynda caught his hand at the last moment. She pulled the square of green fabric off the paper before he slung it into the flames.

"I want to keep a bit of Kate with me," she whispered. *That way, I'll never forget.*

His eyes softened. Leaning over, he placed a kiss on her cheek, and then returned to his task with single-minded determination.

‡

Cynda sank further into the tub, her hair tendriling into waves where it had escaped the loose bun. A sense of supreme satisfaction filled her. Despite her concerns, Alastair had buoyed once the diary was reduced to cinders. He'd kissed her tenderly and thanked her for saving his reputation.

"Isn't it usually the other way around?" she joked.

"Don't make light of what you've done. It means the world to me," he said, kissing her again.

Once he'd departed, she'd checked in with Ralph. The news was mixed: Sending Mimes on his "Grand Tour" had backfired in an unintended way. As she predicted, the time lag had scrambled his brain. It also made it nearly impossible to determine where he'd hidden Chris' time interface. According to Ralph, lots of people weren't amused, her new boss included.

"I shouldn't have underestimated the creep."

On the plus side, Mimes would remain under lock and key until he turned to dust. It seemed fitting. The crazy's scheme to implicate Alastair was the talk of the town. When the publishers' complicity in the matter came to light, the company's stock took a steep dive. One of the publishers committed suicide. Fiddling with history came with a hefty price tag.

The Transitives' secret remained hidden. Apparently, Morrisey had buried that part of Mimes' plan. Given the murderer's diminished mental state, no one would believe him anyway. Walter Samuelson had filed for divorce, citing his wife's infidelity and the lovers' plan to maroon him in a nineteenth-century asylum. In a final stab at his deceitful sibling, Walter signed a multi-million-dollar contract to pen a tell-all book about his experience. It was already predicted to be a chart-topper.

"Hell hath no fury like a wimp scorned," she murmured.

Oddly enough, no comment had been made about her use of the Dinky Doc on Sergeant Keats, and no time-mending guidelines had been forthcoming.

Not fair. How can I break the rules when I don't know what they are?

Cynda found the brown valise she'd used to send Mimes' evidence to '057 waiting for her in the sitting room. The tag stated: To Miss Jacynda Lassiter from R. Hamilton, Esq.

"You nut," she chuckled. She toted it to the bed, plopping herself and the case on top of the feather mattress. Opening the strap, she peered inside the dark interior. The first find was a book entitled *Etiquette for Young Ladies* dated 1887. Ralph's idea of a joke. She thumbed through and found a section on how to refuse a proposal of marriage. *"I have the greatest esteem and regard for you, but I cannot feel the affection which a wife should possess for her husband towards yourself.'"*

"I might need that for future reference."

The next find was a top hat. It was perfect in every detail, though designed for a very tiny head. Stuck inside the hat was a drawing of a pocket watch and the words: *Find me!*

Cynda rolled her eyes. "Real subtle, Ralph." Digging into the bottom of the valise, she discovered a miniature cane. Then her fingers touched something soft—something she knew like her own skin.

Ferret Fred was clad in a black morning coat, gray vest, apricot ascot and black trousers, a tiny pair of gray gloves tucked just inside his coat. She popped the top hat on, laughing at the improbable sight of a stuffed Victorian *Mustela Nigripes*. A piece of paper stuck out of his vest pocket. Unfolding it, she read the message. *Figured you might need some help.*

She tucked the ferret under her chin and cradled him close, knocking the hat off in the process.

A blue blur shambled across the bed.

"Fred, meet Mr. Spider." As usual, Fred didn't reply.

"Taciturn fellow, isn't he?" the spider observed.

"Very."

The arachnid donned the top hat. It was entirely too large.

"What does it say about a woman who talks to an imaginary spider and a stuffed ferret?" Cynda mused.

"Friends are where you find them, stuffed or otherwise," the spider replied. He twirled the top hat and put it back on. "Quite outsized," he said, removing it.

After a wave in her direction, he wandered off the side of the bed. She swore he was whistling *Rule Britannia*.

‡

Lady Sephora met her at the door, as if she were an honored guest. Her blue-gray gown accented her silver hair. Cynda guessed her to be in her late fifties, early sixties, that time of life when beauty came from within. "Miss Lassiter. I was hoping you'd return."

"Good afternoon to you, Lady Wescomb. How is our patient?"

"Quite well. Constitution of a horse, it appears. If he remains much longer, we shall have to sell our property in Kent to pay his feed bill."

Cynda chortled. "Is Alastair here?"

A nod. "They're playing chess, of all things."

"Ah, good. Keep them occupied. I brought them the paper. I thought they'd want to read of their escapades."

"Most certainly." Lady Sephora did a visual sweep of Cynda's clothing. "That dress suits you much better than your disguise ever did."

Disguise? "Thank you."

"Keats told me how you helped them capture the anarchists last night. Quite a brave thing to do."

"Or a rather stupid one, depending on how you view it."

"I've always believed that women are as brave as any man. They are just blissfully ignorant of the fact." An awkward pause. "If I may be so bold, I would like to invite you to a discussion. It is for ladies only, and should be quite lively."

Lively? Probably how to make treacle tarts and blood sausage. "I'm not particularly good with social banter, Lady Wescomb."

The matron shook her head. "Oh, none of that. We intend to discuss how to obtain our emancipation. It's past time women had the vote."

Vote?

Cynda's silence was met by a look of mortal chagrin. "Ah, I must apologize. I had thought you to be of a more...modern mind, and if I've offended—"

Why not go? It might be entertaining. "Oh, I am quite modern, Lady Wescomb." *More than you can imagine.* "I would love to go to a suffragette meeting. I can think of a number of reasons why women should be allowed to vote." *Open door, sling fox into henhouse.*

The lady's face brightened. "Wonderful. We shall dine before the meeting. I know an excellent restaurant that I'm sure you'll enjoy. Alastair says you have a very healthy appetite."

It dawned on Cynda that all of this was genuine; the woman sincerely wanted to spend time with her. "I would be honored, Lady Wescomb."

"Sephora, please."

"Jacynda." Then to Cynda's complete surprise, the woman embraced her.

"I am so pleased. I grow weary of talking about crinolines and the price of apples and how hard it is to find quality silk. Good heavens, there is more to life than all that! Your adventures last night told me you were a kindred spirit."

Cynda didn't know what to say. Lady Sephora didn't seem to notice. "When you've finished with the fellows," she continued, "I'll be in my study. We can plan our excursion from there." Another hug, and then she swept down the hall in a rustle of skirts.

"A force of nature," Cynda whispered, mounting the stairs.

Pausing outside of the sick room, she heard Alastair's voice and then Keats'. They were jesting with each other. It sounded wonderful.

She knocked and pushed the door open. Keats' face exploded into a smile the moment he saw her. Pointing to the chessboard, he crowed, "Excellent timing! I am just about to take Alastair's queen." He waggled an eyebrow mischievously. It gave him an exotic look what with the large bandage on his head.

"Oh no, you're not!" Alastair said, studying the pieces. He moved one. "Check."

"What?" Keats demanded, glaring at the board, his exultant glow fading.

"You were too busy boasting and not paying attention to the game, old man. The *queen* is *mine* in the next move," Alastair retorted, and then gave Cynda a smug smile.

I can't believe this. They're acting like teenagers.

"Queens are notoriously slippery," she advised.

"Speaking of slippery, I do have a few questions, Jacynda, none of which Alastair seems willing to answer. Could you explain why you appear quite healthy, though the doctor claimed you were viciously attacked?"

"He...ah...overreacted?"

"On the contrary, I saw a great deal of blood in the alley."

"I heal quickly."

Keats shook his head. "What about your assailant? Is he not still a danger? Shouldn't you be in New York with your family?"

"No, the evil-doer is gone."

A growing frown. "Don't put me off. You owe me the truth. I was the sailor on Dorset Street that night who saved your skin."

"You?" she asked, astonished.

A proud nod.

"Well, then..." Cynda gave Alastair a look and surreptitious wink before returning her gaze to Keats. *You asked for it.* "All right, if you insist. I am a time traveler from the future. When I got hurt, I went back home to 2057, where they fixed me up. That's why you couldn't find me."

Keats blinked a few times. "You're having me on."

"No. I'm absolutely serious. I travel through time just as easily as taking the train to Oxford." *Well, not quite; the train is worse.*

"Nonsense."

"Every word of it is God's truth, Keats," Alastair added.

Keats' brows furrowed. "Oh, right. Now *both* of you are playing silly buggers with me."

"Jonathon," Cynda replied, "I'm not lying."

"Go on, pull the other one, it's got bells on," he muttered. "Well, I guess I shall just have to come up with my own outrageous explanation, though it'll take some work to top that one."

"Good idea," Cynda replied. "It'll make more sense than anything I can tell you." She dropped the newspaper on the bed next to Keats' knee to distract him. "Top of page 5. Both of you gentlemen are being lauded as heroes. Fortunately, my name wasn't mentioned."

Alastair gave a knowing nod. He opened the paper and read the article aloud.

'Despite grave danger to his person, Detective-sergeant Jonathon Keats, Scotland-yard, did attempt to arrest the anarchists though outnumbered six to one...' Alastair looked up. "They count as badly as you do." Keats ignored him, gazing at Cynda. Alastair nosily cleared his throat. "I'm reading this just once," he announced.

"Go on, if you must. I already know I'm a hero," Keats replied.

"One minor coup and he's insufferable," Alastair grumbled.

Cynda stood at the window with her back to them in an effort not to burst out laughing. Their banter flowed over her like a warm spring breeze. Both had come a very long way. Once Alastair concluded the article, their conversation grew quieter, and then evolved into frank whispering.

"You ask her," Keats suggested in a voice a bit louder than he might have wanted.

Silence—the kind that said something was up. She turned to find both men watching her, each with a question in their eyes. Their intense interest unsettled her.

Alastair cleared his throat again. "Now that certain matters are settled, Keats and I hope you'll stay in London a bit longer this time."

Keats nodded enthusiastically. "You will, won't you?"

Her lack of response ratcheted their apprehension. There was more earnest whispering.

"Jacynda?" Keats prompted. The anxiety in his voice was palpable, endearing.

She presented the pair a brilliant smile. They traded nervous glances.

Always keep 'em guessing.

Cynda turned toward the window, pushing aside the lace curtain to observe the scene below. A figure gazed up at her from across the street. It was the man who had saved her from Mimes' knife...twice.

How did you know I was here?

Making no effort to conceal himself, he tipped his top hat in her direction. She responded with a cautious wave. Pleased by the gesture, he marched off at a jaunty pace, swinging his cane. She could almost hear him whistling.

Cynda let the curtain fall back in place. *Too many unanswered questions.*

She turned toward the two gentlemen. Their anxious expressions melted her heart. "Lady Sephora and I are off to dinner, and then we're going to a suffragette meeting. Should be quite interesting," she announced.

Keats sighed in relief. "Then you're staying."

"For the time being." *Until I find that blasted interface, or Morrisey says otherwise.*

Alastair gave an amused nod of approval. Adjusting her hat, she crossed to the door in a rustle of fabric. "I will see you both tomorrow." She winked at Keats. "I'll bring you more papers."

He beamed.

As she waited for Lady Sephora at the bottom of the stairs, the grandfather clock began to chime in deep, sonorous tones. She touched the solid mahogany case, savoring the vibrations through the wood as each hour pealed forth. Time had always been immaterial to her—insubstantial, like a light fog that chilled her momentarily as she passed through it. Now it felt real, and she sensed its passage.

"Time and tide wait for no Rover," she murmured.

A blue leg waved at her from the clock pendulum. She grinned and then winked at the spider.

Hearing the rush of skirts, Cynda turned to find the lady of the house approaching her, a pleased smile on her face.

"Ready for an adventure?" Sephora asked, pulling on her mantelet.

"Always."

About the Author

Jana Oliver admits a fascination with all things mysterious, usually laced with a touch of the supernatural. An eclectic person who has traveled the world, she loves to pour over old maps and dusty tomes, rummaging in history's closet for plot lines. When not writing, she enjoys Irish music, Cornish fudge and good whiskey.

Jana lives in Atlanta, Georgia with her husband and two cats: Midnight and OddsBobkin.

Visit her website at: www.janaoliver.com

Photograph by Jennifer Berry, Studio 16

VIRTUAL EVIL

Time Rovers ~ Book 2

JANA G. OLIVER

Available Now

Thursday, 11 October, 1888
London

Firearms always add that certain something to a party.

Tonight had been no exception. Head spinning, Jacynda Lassiter pulled herself upright and hastily reassembled the last few seconds of memory. She'd heard a woman cry out, turned to see a man wielding a pistol, and reflexively leapt upon the gun's owner. They'd then tumbled to the floor in a tangled heap. She had always been that way—moving on split-second decisions that came back to bite her on the butt.

From the look of things, this one wouldn't be any different.

A few yards ahead of her, red-faced men in full evening dress wrestled with the assailant, their coattails fluttering like agitated gulls. It took five of them to hold him in place as they bound his arms with a drapery cord hastily snatched from one of the windows.

"My God, look at the Queen!" a voice cried.

Cynda stared up at the royal portrait above the marble mantelpiece. Queen Victoria's ample bosom sprouted a bullet hole where her left nipple should be.

"Oh, great," she muttered. Her time interface vibrated furiously inside a pocket, signaling that someone else from the twenty-first century was in the room. She gave it a surreptitious tap. It promptly started up again. A second tap silenced it.

A solicitous young fellow bent down to offer Cynda his hand.

"By heavens, miss," he exclaimed, eyes wide, "you could have been badly injured!"

He was cute...for a Victorian. A bit too much macassar oil, but handsome nonetheless. Cynda forced a polite smile. That always seemed to reassure these folks. Using his hand as leverage, she rose from the floor with difficulty, attempting to straighten her gown in the process. Fortunately, nothing had torn—a miracle in itself.

"I just need to sit down," she replied as smoothly as she could under the circumstances. Adjusting her bustle as delicately as possible, she settled into a chair. "Thank you, sir."

The young man nodded and moved away, his task complete.

Lady Sephora Wescomb knelt next to her now, her face alabaster. "My God, are you all right? Should I call for a doctor?"

Cynda gingerly maneuvered her left shoulder. She chose to fib: to do otherwise would invite too much fuss. "I'll be fine."

With a quaking hand, the silver-haired matron brushed back a strand of hair that had fallen free from Cynda's bun. "I've never seen such a thing," she exclaimed. "He...he could have killed the prince!"

Or anyone else, for that matter.

Though Cynda was the first to admit her job as a Senior Time Rover was anything but boring, keeping history on track did not usually involve tackling a murderously inclined guest in the middle of a posh Victorian dinner party.

But who was he after? That was hard to say; it was a target-rich environment. He could have chosen from the future king of England, the prime minister, his nephew Balfour, a slew of members of Parliament, a couple judges, and some very rich merchants.

The failed assassin was hauled roughly to his feet. As he turned to face her, Cynda gasped. She blinked in case her eyes were tricking her. The face didn't change. Every Time Rover knew this man like he was family. They called him the *Father of Time.*

"Fool!" he shouted at her. "Do you realize what you've done?"

It was *his* voice. She'd never met him before, but she'd heard him dozens of times in the Vid-Net interviews.

"You fool!" he shouted again.

With that, Harter Defoe, greatest of all time travelers, was frog-marched out of the room, his glower deepening with each step.

A chill crept through her. What had she just done?

"Miss?" a timid voice inquired. A maid offered her a dampened cloth.

"Thank you," Cynda murmured, pressing the linen to her throbbing forehead. Foreheads had a way of doing that after they'd impacted the floor. *I'm getting too old for this.*

"On your way, girl!"

The sharp command sent the domestic scurrying. Cynda raised her eyes to meet the irate face of Hugo Effington. Her host's jaw was set, eyes narrowed, spoiling for a fight. Given his sizeable build, he wasn't a man to cross.

Why are you pissed at me?

"Excuse me, sir," the butler interjected, "I've sent for a constable."

"What?" Then Effington was gone, dressing down the unfortunate person who'd made the report.

Oh, this is just peachy.

She surveyed the scene. It'd been pretty pleasant until the gun appeared. There'd been ample food and delectable gossip. The main topics had swirled around Sir Charles Warren's bloodhound tracking experiments in Hyde Park and the inquests of the latest Whitechapel victims. To hear the upper crust talk, you'd think that the West End was next on Jack the Ripper's itinerary.

Unaware that Cynda was not a contemporary, Lady Sephora had patiently coached her in the niceties of London society as a courtesy to someone supposedly from New York. Although she'd done her best, Cynda found Victorian high society too stilted for her comfort. Despite the bluebloods, the promise of a multi-course meal, and the sumptuous surroundings, she'd been truly bored. At least until she'd nailed Defoe.

Subtle, Lassiter. Really subtle.

She took in the scene again, taking mental notes for the report she'd inevitably file with her boss in 2057. T.E. Morrisey would want all the gory details, along with an explanation as to why she felt the need to be so "bold," as the Victorians would put it.

How do I explain this? Gee boss, your business partner, your best friend, just tried to kill someone and bugger history in the process.

She groaned at the thought. This was off the rails.

At the far end of the long room, near the fireplace and below the now-flawed portrait of his dour and sizeable mother, was the Prince of Wales, the future Edward the Seventh. He was surrounded by a group of grave men in evening garb. Known for his appreciation of the fairer sex, the prince's thickly lidded eyes were situated not on the men around him, but on a cluster of ladies nearby, each resplendent in a gown of unimaginable opulence. Then his gaze moved in her direction, followed by a faint nod. She returned it out of courtesy.

He thinks I saved his life.

Which didn't make sense. According to the Victorian timeline, there had never been an attempted assassination of His Royal Highness at a dinner party in Mayfair.

On the other side of the room, a pair of women busily fanned an elderly woman of immense girth who had sunk onto a couch, lolling back in a faint. She was clad in a rather unfortunate shade of orange, like a prize Halloween pumpkin.

Sephora held out a glass of sherry. Cynda shook her head. "Can I have some tea?" She noted that no one but her friend came close, as if her behavior were somehow communicable.

"Certainly. I'll see what I can do." Sephora downed the liquor and went for another, evidence the event had rattled even her usually unshakable composure.

At the door was a queue of couples keen to depart after the *entertainment*. As they waited, they shot nervous glances in her direction. One young woman was weeping on her escort's shoulder. Others just stared.

"Miss?"

She looked up into the eyes of a young man with a pinched face and small wire-rimmed glasses.

"Yes?"

"The prime minister offers his gratitude."

"I appreciate that. Thank you." *First the Prince, now the PM. Next it'll be the Pope.*

A curt nod and the fellow retreated.

By the time the tea appeared, the prince had departed, as had the prime minister and his entourage. The remaining gentlemen were joking nervously and tugging at their collars. Every once in a while they would look over at her, shake their heads disapprovingly and return to their conversation. The only one to genuinely acknowledge her was Lord Wescomb, Lady Sephora's husband. He gave her a quick wink. That made her smile.

"Miss?" A nondescript gentleman in a black suit approached, his face intense with concentration. He looked like a cop.

Cynda's nerves ignited as she prepared to bluff her way through this mess.

"Good evening," she said through a fake smile. "Great party, isn't it?"

He crooked a brown eyebrow. "I'm Inspector Hulme. I need to ask you some questions, miss."

"I thought the little sandwiches were too salty."

The eyebrow rose a little higher. "Miss?"

"The punch was really nice, though."

"Miss..."

Best get it over with. "I'm sorry. Go on, Inspector."

"Please tell me what happened, from your point of view."

Somebody just tried to rewrite history? "We were about to go in for supper."

"What happened then?" he asked, penciling lines into a notebook. The sight made her wince. Rovers were not supposed to be part of history, and yet Home, or Holm, or whatever he was called, was busily putting her words on that piece of paper. Paper that might end up in a file for eternity.

The boss is going to blow a gasket over this.

She took a deep breath. "I saw a gent with a gun."

"Then what happened?"

"I threw myself at him."

Hulme frowned. "Why didn't you just raise the alarm?"

"I did," Cynda replied, irritated. "There was no...male nearby, so I thought I could slow him down until someone could...ah...secure him."

"I see. Do you usually act in such a rash manner?"

You betcha. "I'm an American. We're...forthright," she replied, hoping that would serve as a suitable explanation. Behind the inspector, she saw Sephora's anxious face. It had more color now. Apparently, the sherry had helped.

Inspector Hulme issued a quick nod. Cynda felt sorry for the poor sod. He'd been brought into the middle of a dicey situation, as the Brits would say—one that could easily make or break his career.

"The assassin spoke to you. What did he say?"

"He called me a fool."

"Do you know him?"

No choice but to lie. "No, I don't." Defoe had pioneered time travel; he knew the dangers of messing with history, and laid the ground rules for all Rovers. The man who'd pulled the gun was not the Defoe she knew.

Suddenly, another hideous thought reared its head. "I would prefer my name not be in the newspapers, Inspector," she added.

His eyebrow crooked up again. "You don't wish to take credit for saving the prince's life?"

She shook her head emphatically. "No, I don't. I *really* don't."

"I think it's only prudent, Inspector," Sephora chimed in. "It is possible that the assassin was not alone in his plot. If Miss Lassiter's name becomes emblazoned in the headlines, that might endanger her."

Cynda mentally thanked her friend, though it was entirely unlikely that Defoe had any accomplices. Rovers were loners by nature.

The inspector nodded thoughtfully. "I shall do what I can to see you are left unnamed."

"Thank you, Inspector," Cynda replied, and meant it. That might cut Morrisey's displeasure a notch or two.

Just a Visitor, Never a Participant. Or at least that's what they taught you in Rover School. In her experience, that was pure bull.

As the cop headed toward the group of men to hear their version of the incident, Sephora sat next to Cynda. "Don't worry, dear. It'll get straightened out."

"Hope so. How's our hostess?"

"Taken to her bed, from what I hear. They've called for a doctor."

Cynda let out a stream of air through pursed lips. "So much for a quiet evening."

It took some time before Inspector Hulme was satisfied. Once that moment had been reached, Cynda was allowed to leave with the admonition that she shouldn't travel beyond London until the investigation was concluded.

"We will need you for the trial," Hulme said, handing over one of his cards.

"Trial?" Cynda managed to squeak out.

"Of course. We will need your testimony to convict this anarchist."

Harter Defoe in the dock?

It couldn't happen.

There were hushed murmurs as she exited the house with the Wescombs. Near the front door she encountered the stone-faced butler, the fellow who'd taken the brunt of their host's displeasure.

"Good evening, Miss," he said. The dull sadness in his eyes told her that there was going to be hell to pay once the guests cleared out.

"Good evening," she returned.

"Thank you for what you did," he added in a lowered voice.

Behind them, Effington's voice rose in angry protest, followed by the inspector's equally vehement response.

Lord Wescomb glanced over his shoulder at the arguing pair and chuffed. "Quite a dramatic scene. It'll be the talk of the town by morning."

"I suspect we will be *persona non grata* for a time," Sephora remarked once they were seated inside the Wescombs' coach. She turned toward Cynda. "Is that how things are done in New York, then?"

Cynda groaned. "Not usually. I am so sorry. I just saw the gun and reacted."

"I must caution you against such rash behavior in future," Lord Wescomb said with a deep frown. "You could have been mortally injured. You should have left it to the men."

Wescomb was right, though not for the reason he believed. If she'd been mortally injured, her interface would have triggered the *Dead Man Switch*, as they called it, and she would have transferred to 2057 in front of forty-plus highbrow Victorians.

That would require a "fix" of epic proportions.

Sephora's next question brought her back to the present. "How did he get into the party in the first place? Is he a friend of the Effingtons?"

Her husband shook his head. "Our host didn't know him, and he wasn't on the guest list. The butler had no notion how he got inside."

Not a problem for a Rover. Transfer in, give yourself a few minutes to adjust and you're at the party. All you need is an empty room.

"Do you really think he was after the prince?" Sephora asked, smoothing her gown and then tucking her hands under the mantelet for warmth.

"Don't know," Lord Wescomb replied. "There was a fine selection of notables there, any one of them worth a bullet."

"John!"

"I'm serious, Sephora. However, I did find it amusing where the missile lodged," he added with a grin. "I bet HRH thought the same. Probably wanted to do that for years. Can you imagine waiting around for your mum to die so you have a job?"

"John!"

For a hereditary peer, Lord Wescomb was remarkably republican in sentiment. Cynda sniggered, appreciating the comic relief.

Wescomb adjusted his waistcoat over a slight paunch. "I suspect that keeping *your* name out of the papers won't prove too difficult."

Sephora turned toward him. "I would have thought it would have been just the opposite."

Wescomb huffed and tugged on the waistcoat again, frowning in his wife's direction. "What man wants to admit that a young slip of a girl prevented an assassination while he was busy eyeing the ladies and snorting his host's liquor? It does nothing for our reputation as gentlemen."

Sephora adopted a quizzical look. "Where were you when it happened, then?"

He cleared his throat. "A call of nature," he muttered. Lady Wescomb tittered, causing her husband to glower at her.

Cynda looked out the window. *Pity I wasn't off powdering my nose.*